An Tir Gallósek: The Mighty Land
Book Three

Treya Meynack in the Western Air

 ## by Maria Kay Anthony

An Tir Gallósek: The Mighty Land
Book Three

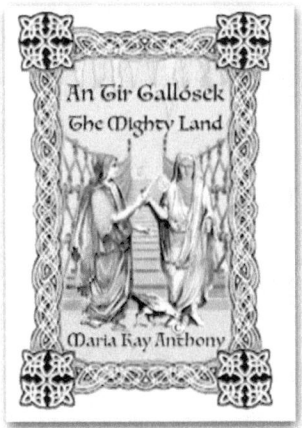

Treya Meynack in the Western Air

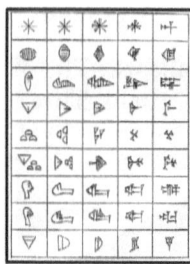

An Tir Gallósek
The Three Volumes:

Pippa Agrippa in Britannia Prima

Marcus Constantinides in Albion Sub Terra

Treya Meynack in the Western Air

Borlowan

Books

Treya Meynack in the Western Air
© Maria Kay Anthony
copyright 2024
text and artwork

ISBN: 979-8-9920376-2-3

borlowanbooks@gmail.com
Borlowan Books/POB 1554/Lawrence/Ks/66044/USA

INTRODUCTION

These stories arose from some questions that I had been considering:

How can we tell whether something is done by magic, or by some complex science that we don't understand?
What is the difference between a god and a person with highly advanced technical powers and tremendous longevity?
What is needed for hope to conquer despair?
And, what might have happened when the Romans left Britannia?

Now and then, new scientific evidence shows up that changes the human story. It seems that technically advanced cultures have been on earth much longer than previously supposed. For people who are threatened by shifting paradigms, it's a problem. For many of us, though, it's a relief to be reminded that we don't know the whole story, we never did, and chances are we never will. Fire, water, earth and air have seen to that by repeatedly rearranging our world.

Much of the history of the known ancient world is well documented, and we have an idea of what was happening, and when. Then there are places and times where we just have to speculate. One of those is Britannia in the late 300s and early 400s. Many details have been discovered, but the overall picture is still dark.

It was a time when the Romans had finally retreated from the wild western isles that were never really theirs. They left behind a scattered population that included Brythonic, Celtic, Roman, Greek, Iberian, Frisian, and Germanic people. After Rome departed, the land and its inhabitants were vulnerable, and invasions and wars were inevitable. But for a brief time in history, the period in which these adventures occur, the British Isles were still fairly peaceful and prosperous. New trade routes were established to fill the void left by the Empire, soldiers took civilian jobs, and life went on.

The early 'dark ages' weren't really as dark as people used to imagine. It was a time of refined cultures, with stories of great heroes and epic adventures. The myths and legends were passed down in the oral tradition. By the time that the stories were scribed, centuries later, they had been fractured and redacted by the culture-blind single-mindedness of institutional religion. But they are still there, manifested in the land and in the people, resonating throughout the mysterious western islands of Great Britain and Ireland.

These books are inspired by the old tales. They are really one story, told across the three volumes, each with a different person's point of view. The stories present the archetypal hero's quest, which involves overcoming obstacles, finding one's place in the world, and connecting with others. These tales are about duty, tolerance, inclusion, kindness, redemption, restoration, accountability, bravery, and self-awareness.

We begin on the ground in book one. In book two we go deep down to get to the bottom of things. We transcend in book three, up into the atmosphere.

The Mighty Land features weaponry, clothing, footwear, jewelry, gemstones, ships, boats, rafts, maps, rivers, seas, hot tubs, cold pools, gardens, orchards, forests, fortresses, farms, castles, libraries, ice caves, crystal caverns, glowing rocks, an impossibly high tower, and a great deal of food. Also, there are festivals, betrothals, weddings, babies, fashion shows, good songs, bad jokes, spectral resonance, music, augury, and geomancy. There are animals too: cats, dogs, sheep, goats, mules, oxen, bears, dolphins, porpoises, and many kinds of birds. Also some creatures not encountered before; some are friendly, others are threatening.

These stories include some non-English words and phrases. Latin, of course, was the language of the soldiers of Rome. Spread over the vast empire, the usages varied, and there were regional dialects.

Brythonic was the common tongue. It includes Cymraeg, Welsh, which once was used throughout what is now England as well as Wales.

Kernowek is also Brythonic. It is the venerable language of the Cornish peninsula. It's related to Welsh, and to Breton, spoken in present day Brittany.

Gaelic and other Celtic languages were spoken in Eire and Scotia, and by many of the tribes throughout Britain.

These languages influenced one another, and became part of common speech, along with words and terms from all the other peoples who had moved to Britain. I have tried to represent this complex and shifting situation by introducing these words in context. I hope that the reader will find it as rewarding as I did to realize the inherent connections in the various languages.

Hail and fare well,
Maria Anthony 2024

Here are my answers to the questions:
We can't.
Nothing obvious.
Love.
Read on...

ACKNOWLEDGEMENTS

These stories came from me. Not artificial intelligence.

When I have used quotes and verses by other authors, I have credited them in the text or annotations, except for 'Conditions for Feasting', and 'In Complaint of Women', which are by King Cormac of Ireland. I also used part of Fionn Mac Cumhail's poem 'A Joyous Peace is Summer' as the refrain for a new song, and I've included an old nursery rhyme about a mill. Otherwise, the textual content is original to me, including the songs.

I relied upon Google translate throughout this project. For the Kernowek language, I used OnlineCornishDictionary.org. They both have audio options to demonstrate pronunciations.

I create my own images using Adobe Photoshop, and its many layers of possibilities. When I've used historical images, such as the Roman paintings and mosaics, they are in the public domain. So are some of the background details. I repurpose bits and pieces, and I draw, paint, and photograph images that I then process digitally.

I appreciate and support Wikipedia and Wikipedia Commons. I get some of the images that I incorporate into my work from them.

My thanks to the ARX Mercatura workshop and online store, for allowing me to use a photo of their beautifully carved lituus in my publishing logo.

I have been influenced by the things I've seen and heard in my lifetime. Stories, songs, books, films, and scenes of far-away places. The portrait of Lord Gwydion as a youth is based on a photo of the late Welsh actor Stewart John Llewellyn Bevan (1948 - 2022), famous for his role as Dr. Clifford Jones in the Dr. Who serial "The Green Death".

I am eternally grateful to my husband Monty Schneck for his continued love, support, and enlightened conversation. Special thanks to Megan Hurt for the encouragement and literary feedback. I also appreciate everyone who wrote the books and created the images that have provided me with information and inspiration for all these years.

Maria Anthony, November, 2024

Contents

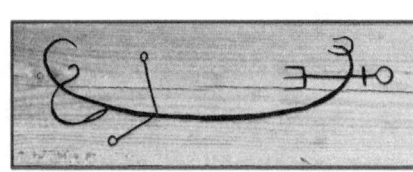

Chapter One - A Scribe in the King's Archive

The library at Trevena was a popular place, attracting locals and visitors alike. It was located near the main dining hall of the castle. Beyond an arch inscribed 'Lyverva Trevena', there was a large high-ceilinged room that was filled with shelves, and lined with tables and chairs. The walls were covered with maps, portraits, and images of ships and sea creatures.

The shelves held collections of scrolls, texts, tablets, and codexes, all sorted into categories: history, mythology, geography, poetry, languages, architecture, agriculture, visual arts, healing arts, domestic arts, handcraft, statecraft, dance, and music. Visitors were constantly amazed at the size of the library in this remote western outpost.

There were two wings off of the main room. One of them was devoted to maritime studies. It had two large round portal windows, made of spun glass, overlooking the ships in the Eastern Bay. There were racks of nautical maps. On the shelves were texts about navigation and shipbuilding. There were sun-wheels, star-charts, wind-charts and tide-tables. The walls were covered with diagrams of vessels, shown in cross-section and rendered in detail. On the table were wax tablets, parchments, chalks, inks, calipers, and magnifying lenses.

The other wing was the children's library, which connected to the nearby school. The central area of the room was for the children to enjoy. It was covered in thick carpets, and surrounded by low bookcases which were filled with texts, toys, puzzles and pictures. Beyond the bookcases, there was a gallery. Visitors came to this outer gallery to purchase mementos. The walls were lined with narrow shelves, and on them were brightly colored scenes of Trevena, painted by the children on tiles, shingles, and whiteboards.

Pippa Agrippa had donated the pigments. She had told the Trevena children about the young people back in Vindavia Nova making pictures that visitors would buy, and they had been inspired. They liked the idea of having a new pastime that could earn them a little coin, and it fired their imaginations to think that their artwork might be displayed in some far away land: a tropical island, an ancient city, or a desert kingdom.

It was a plausible thing to imagine, because visitors came to Trevena from all over, wherever there was a route by water. The first to arrive had been the Pobel Mór, the Sea People. That was long ago, even before the Greeks. The Pobel Mór began to trade their oil, wine, and sheep for tin, copper, and grain. Ever since, there had been a steady stream of maritime commerce.

The deep western veins of precious tin ore were what put Trevena on the map and kept it there. Mining was a grim and dangerous business, but the Kernow miners were incredibly strong and resilient. The raw material was dug up and processed throughout the region, and then transported for shipping. Some of it went further east, but most of it came to Trevena.

Trevena was the most prominent seaport in all of Albion, although the majority of the island's inhabitants were unaware of its importance, or even its existence. Not many ships came to Trevena from the rest of Britannia. It was much easier to cross the channel to the continent for trade. There was no established land route either, between Trevena in the far west and the settled lands of the south and east. There were trails in some places, and some good Roman roads, but much of the land was impassible. The coastal paths were rocky and dangerous, full of washouts that were caused by shifting tides and floods.
Much of the inland region was made up of dense ancient forests and wide stretches of treacherous bog-lands. The Celtic inhabitants of these remote areas had been pushed there by the Roman invasion. Some of the tribes were so isolated, they were still planning their next attack on the Roman Army, not even realizing that it was long gone.

The librarian of the Lyverva was a kind, stout, middle-aged woman named Lady Kaya. She was originally from a place called Dell Beag, Little Dell, on the southeast coast of Eire. She had long reddish-grey braids and wore a flowing lavender gown, covered with a white lace apron. Lady Kaya circulated throughout the Lyverva, informing and assisting the visitors in a charming fashion. She was happy to relate the history of the library to all who would hear it.

The Lyverva was begun by King Gelvin, a distant ancestor of King Arthek. It was because of its remoteness, and the travelers who had visited there, that the library had grown. Generations of traders had come to Trevena from all over the sea-world, especially from Greece and Iberia. Scholars had also come, bringing texts and manuscripts.

King Gelvin was very interested in learning. He had the foreign texts copied in the original languages, and then had them translated. Visiting scholars and scribes were welcome in return to copy whatever they wished from the Lyverva collections. The visitors appreciated that, and they liked the idea that the copies of their own precious texts and manuscripts would be kept safe, housed in this stone fortress by the sea. So the tradition grew, of the royal family as promotors and patrons of the Lyverva Trevena.

But there was another library at Trevena, one that Lady Kaya did not talk about, called Kovskrifva, the Archive. Most people did not know about it. It was a private and secure space, only used by order of the King, or with his permission. High up on the stone flats, near the heavily guarded wells and grain stores, there was a large broch: a double-walled stone tower, like the type that the northern Scotti build, to keep out intruders and the weather. It had a stout wooden door and high barred windows all around the top, with panels fashioned from clear slabs of glass and mica.

Within the outer ring was a narrow circular passage, bordered by the inner wall. The outside of the inner wall was lined with shelves, which were full of book-making tools and supplies. A door on the inner wall opened onto a round room, filled with shelves, desks, chairs and carts. Most of the surfaces were covered with tablets, documents, and boxes piled high with scrolls and codexes. A spiral staircase went up to a second level.

The stairs led through an arched doorway. The upper room was spacious, tidy, and bright. There were two large tables and two small ones, four chairs, and a short step-ladder. There was only one shelf. It was up high, out of reach. The only thing on the shelf was a wooden container, the size of a breadbox.
On one side of the arched doorway was a small alcove with a long narrow window that overlooked the western harbor. In the small alcove was a little table and chair, and a washstand.

On the opposite side of the room there was a large alcove, topped with the blue and silver crest of Trevena. In it was the Archive librarian's desk. Behind it, a vault had been set into the stone wall. Inside the vault were the most rare texts of Trevena, including the Scroll-box of Florian the Red, a copy of the Iliad scribed in ancient Anatolian, Agrippa's History of Cassius Ambrosius, and an old Kernowek translation of the teachings of the Christ.

The rare texts had been copied, and the copies were in the Lyverva. The originals were kept in the vault, along with royal family documents, important contracts, trade agreements, and household records.

The Archive librarian was Master Skell. He had only been in Trevena since the late spring. The previous Archivist had retired, and Master Skell had been summoned to replace him. Master Skell had worked in many different locations. He had recently been the Archivist in a remote monastic settlement somewhere in the north. He was an elderly man, tall and slightly stooped, with lank white hair thinning at the crown. His skin was freckled and spotted with age.

He wore a brown leather headband that held a pair of framed rectangular magnifying lenses before his eyes, to help him see. He dressed in a long-sleeved tunic of white linen. His leggings were also white, and he wore brown sandals. Over the tunic was a blue and silver sash, which indicated a position in the Royal Court.

Master Skell always wore white gloves and long sleeves. Something had happened to his hands and arms. It was rumored that they were burned in a fire, while trying to rescue some texts. He relied upon an assistant named Lugarn, a slender and fair young man, to do most of the physical work.

The Archivist stayed at his desk, and he rarely spoke, except to give orders to Lugarn. Master Skell hardly ever looked up; even when King Arthek was there, he stayed hunched over documents, peering through his lenses, which made his milky blue eyes appear large and distorted. It seemed that he preferred texts to most people. Treya Meynack had been friendly and polite when they were introduced, but he had been abrupt and terse. He was like that with everyone, apparently, so she tried to not let it bother her.

It had been two weeks since she and the others had arrived in the Awel Glor. The ship journey had only taken three days, but Treya had needed a week to recover. The sea had been choppy, and she had gotten sick right away. The others were sympathetic, but it was embarrassing, as she thought that she would be a natural sailor, based on her origins and experience.

By the time they'd arrived at Trevena, Treya was weak and faint. She didn't seem to be getting better, so Pippa and Arghan had installed her in their quarters, under medical supervision.

She had slept for two days straight, after which they made her get up to eat, drink, wash up, and walk around a bit. Then she went back to bed for three more days.

It wasn't just the sea voyage. The transition from underground to surface was more challenging than she had imagined. She had been overwhelmed and exhausted by the heat of the sun, the force of the wind, the harshness of the light, and the confusing movements of the shadows.

She hadn't met many new people in Trevena yet, but so far she was content with the company of Augustus Nett and Del Frankus, who had been to visit her during her recovery. Augustus was tall and pale, with thick grey hair, and bushy side whiskers. Del was shorter, dark-skinned, bald, and clean shaven. She had gotten to know them on the overland journey from Vindavia Nova to meet the ship at Portus Adurni. They had stopped to eat lunch in a little village, and she had gone with them to look at some houses. The houses were all old and crumbling, but the visitors were mostly there to see the tiled mosaic floors, which depicted tropical gardens and strange creatures.

She was comfortable talking to Del and Augustus. They were very much like the An Dhew, thoughtful and good-natured. They mostly talked about their work, which consisted of construction projects involving complicated tools and numerical formulas. Treya didn't understand much of what they said, but she was fond of them, and they treated her like a little sister.

It was in dealing with her that their differences became apparent. Augustus was inclined to advise and instruct her on every little detail of her life. Del, on the other hand, would try to get Augustus to back off, claiming that Treya should be given a chance to figure some things out for herself. Treya appreciated them both.

Which was good, because now she was working with them on the bridge project. The all-consuming bridge project, which seemed to engulf anyone who came into contact with it. During the trip to the crumbling houses, the ex-soldiers had asked her about her former life. She had already agreed with Pippa and Arghan that it would be best to not speak specifically about the Two Kingdoms, even to Del and Augustus, who had heard the tales back in Vindavia Nova. To anyone who asked, she was simply from the 'south', where she had grown up as part of a 'service collective'. That was the description that Master Dmitri had come up with to describe the An Dhew, and it had stuck; the An Dhew were now officially known as the 'Caer Hudol Service Collective'.

So Treya told Del and Augustus all about her previous life, leaving out the details concerning the underground world, and the 'Cult of the Non-Gendered', which had been the original official description of the An Dhew.

The Service Collective wasn't only about service, she had explained. Members were encouraged to cultivate a variety of interests and talents, which might be related to service, or might just be for personal development. All of them had basic instruction in weapons-training, and in tactical, rescue, and survival skills. After all, the main focus of the Collective was to act as a security force. They were all expected to be highly capable. Even though most of them lived comfortably indoors, they all knew how to fish, forage, build shelters, and grow food. Beyond that, members were encouraged to develop at least one individual 'inside' interest, such as painting, scribing, map-making, cooking, or sewing, and one group 'outside' interest, such as team-rowing, climbing with ropes, games involving balls, or competitive swimming.

The 'inside' part had been easy. Treya was a natural scribe. She had a precise neat hand that could copy pages of text without fatigue. She absorbed some of the information, but in truth she was not really interested in most of the subjects. She just excelled at copying.

Finding the outside interest had taken more exploration. She was good at rowing, but she didn't care for racing. Treya was also a decent swimmer, but as with the rowing, she wasn't very competitive. She'd tried the ball games, but they went too fast, and she didn't understand or care about points and scores.

Some of her bunkmates were climbers, and on their days off, they would either be up on some high jagged peak or deep down in a crevasse. She had no desire to go down further into the earth, so she agreed to try the peak climbing. She didn't think that she would like it. She was afraid of heights. But there was something about the facing of that fear that was attractive. She was nervous, but everyone was very supportive. Treya learned about ropes, anchors, and safety lines. She knew how to choose a route, and how to inspect the equipment. She understood that there were protocols, and as long as she followed them, she would be alright.

Treya turned out to be a naturally skilled climber. She had soon realized that she enjoyed the process of gradually leaving the ground behind. The people looking up at her grew tiny. Her hands and feet instinctively knew what to do, searching out even the narrowest cracks and shallowest indentations to gain hand and foot holds. She climbed slowly but relentlessly. Reaching the ragged summit, her legs aching, she would secure herself to an anchor, and relax.

She would gaze at the birds, wheeling in and out of the sunlit clouds of dust and vapor. They were large and colorful, with shiny feathers. Treya had tried to picture their point of view. *I'm seeing their world. Except, they're even higher than I am.*
She pushed her imagination upwards, attempting to see what they saw: the entire underground realm; the Two Kingdoms, the Red Sands, the mountains, woods, rivers and wastelands. *Beyond that,* she supposed, *there would be only darkness, or perhaps the deep fires of the earth.*

She liked watching the birds as they went gliding along on the invisible currents of air. These colorful creatures seemed far more interesting and substantial than the little birds that flitted around the underground streams, eating the tiny pale fish. Treya had wondered if these birds had always been up here, since before the underworld closed, or if they came and went through the roof.

The spider-cracked ceiling of the world was closer here, standing between her and the real sky, a bright blue dome that she vaguely remembered. The real sky would be full of all kinds of birds, flying over land and sea. The salt-sea would be vast, and it would sparkle brightly in the sunshine.

Far below her stony perch, the boughs of hazy evergreen trees moving in the light breeze had looked the way that she imagined ocean waves would appear from the topmast of a ship at sea.

It was while she was resting on the pinnacle, gazing down at the dark shining river and the distant red sands, that she had begun to wonder if she could ever actually leave this world, and go back to wherever she came from. The idea was terrifying, but so was the thought of climbing the jagged peaks, and she did it anyway.

On their journey, when she had told Del and Augustus about her climbing experience, Del had said,

"The Gods must have sent you to us, Treya. We need experienced climbers. How would you like to help build the Trevena bridge?"

Before she could respond, Augustus had exclaimed,

"Del Frankus, you can't ask her to do that! This nice young person, she doesn't need to risk her life just so a king can have a bridge."

"It's as Counselor Agrippa says," Del had retorted. "We're going to do it with maximum regard for safety, or not at all. And Treya can decide for herself."

While Treya had been recovering, Del and Augustus had visited the bridge site. First they surveyed the scene from the Trevena side. Then they had made the long journey down one cliff and up the other one to examine the Tintagel side. They came to visit Treya afterwards.

"So," she asked expectantly, "how does it look?"

"It's challenging," said Del, "but it should be fine. We've built longer spans."

"But none so high," said Augustus.

"The height doesn't affect the construction," Del responded.

"Yes it does," said Augustus. "It's a mental thing."

"You're a mental thing," Del muttered. Treya giggled. Augustus snorted with laughter.

"Counselor Pen Avalen is negotiating with the masons, miners, and sailors who are going to help build the bridge," Augustus said. "I've taken his notes, and written a proposal to present to the Royal Council." He reached into his tunic and brought out a folded document.

He unfolded it. It was one large sheet of parchment, entirely covered top to bottom in really tiny lettering. Treya squinted.

"Why is the writing so small?" she asked.

Before Augustus could respond, Del said to him, "See, I told you, no one can read that!" He turned to Treya and said, "He's been doing technical scribing for so long, he doesn't know how to write like a normal person."

"I can copy it for you," said Treya. "It's what I do, remember? Scribing and climbing. I'm not ready to climb yet, but I can scribe."

She had to confer with Augustus several times, and make some revisions, but four days later the document had been completed. It was six pages long, and copied in her precise measured hand. It was before them now, spread out on the library table. She was with Del and Augustus in the Kovskrifva, waiting for the others to show up. Master Skell was at his desk. Lugarn was at a small table near him, scribing a page of text.

Pippa arrived first. She was wearing her official Councilor medal, attached to a blue and silver sash. She greeted Master Skell and Lugarn, then joined the group at the table.

"Arghan and the Twins are coming," she said, smiling. "They're trying to get away from the King and his last minute advice. They have diplomatically persuaded King Arthek to skip this first meeting, so that we might proceed without worrying about pleasing or offending the Crown."

Pippa greeted Del and Augustus, and hugged Treya.

"We've been so busy," Pippa said to her, "I've hardly seen you this past week."

She touched Treya's head and said, "Your hair is getting longer."

Treya was trying to grow it out. It had always been kept closely cropped under the skullcap. She was finding the process to be awkward.

"It doesn't seem longer," said Treya. "Just... bigger. And why do I have dark skin and light hair anyway? The other dark skinned people have dark hair. It makes more sense. If I keep letting this grow out, it's going to look like there's a sheep curled up on my head."

"Treya," said Del, "you should be happy to have dark skin and light hair." He grinned, rubbing his hand over his bald pate. "It's better than having dark skin and no hair!" The others laughed.

"This is an interesting place," said Augustus, looking around. "Quite a secure location."

"Yes," said Pippa. "I'd never been here before, but when we got back, Arghan and I came here. While Treya was sleeping." She smiled at her friend. "We were trying to find out about Thule, and the Spiral Castle. Master Skell and Lugarn helped us look. But there was nothing."

They heard the others come in down below. Arghan arrived upstairs first, carrying a document bag. He was followed by two men, both wearing the chains of a High Councilor. They were tall, with noble-looking features, shaggy dark hair, and big brown eyes. They were identical twins, but one had a long scar down his cheek. Treya had been introduced to them earlier. They were Bruno and Brutus Marianis. Bruno was the one with the scar. They were both very charming and handsome.

The meeting commenced. At first Treya tried to follow the conversation, but it was complicated and tiresome. At this point, the actual designs and plans had been nearly completed, and the discussions were all about labor, supplies, charters, and compensations. Her attention wandered.

She gazed out the window. Through the clear panes she could see birds wheeling around over the harbor. She looked at the far-away sky and wondered if it would rain. Treya had seen it happen six times already. It was such a novelty to have water pouring from the sky, she was still counting the occurrences. But the sky was clear.

Her gaze wandered around the room. She stared at the wooden box on the shelf and wondered what was in it, and why it was so high up. It seemed very mysterious. She glanced at Master Skell. He never moved. *Maybe he's asleep,* she thought. *Who would know the difference?*
She was going to watch to see if he would ever turn the page of his document, but she was distracted by Lugarn, who had clearly just made a scribing error and had grunted in frustration.
Master Skell turned his gaze to Lugarn. Treya quickly looked away, focusing back on the meeting just in time to hear Augustus say, "Those are both good ideas. We should get them written down." He took out a parchment and pen.

"Treya," he asked, "if I tell you what to scribe, would you be willing to take some more notes?"
She nodded, and he handed her the writing materials.

By the time the meeting was done, she had neatly filled three pages. She didn't understand much of what she'd written, especially all the numbers, but Augustus was pleased. So were the others; they thanked her for scribing, which apparently was something they all were capable of, but considered it a chore to be avoided. She was cleaning the pen, and the others were talking. Suddenly Treya realized that Master Skell was standing right next to her. The others seemed surprised too.

"A good day to you, Master Skell," said Arghan politely.

Master Skell was staring through his lenses at the documents on the table. He turned his uncanny gaze to Treya.

"That is very fine work. My assistant is good at many things," he said, pointing to Lugarn, "but copying is not one of them. How are you called, scribe?"

"Treya Meynack," she replied.

"Will you copy texts for the Kovskrifva, Treya Meynack?" he asked.

"Yes," she replied without hesitation. "I would be very happy to." She smiled at the prospect.

"Come when you can," said Master Skell. He turned to his assistant and said, "Lugarn, you are hereby relieved of scribe duty."

"Yes, Master Skell," he said, looking gratefully at Treya. Master Skell returned to his seat.

Pippa leaned in close to Treya.

"Well! A scribe in the King's archive," Pippa said. "Not bad for a girl from... the south."

The next day it rained all morning. Storm number seven. Treya stood on Pippa and Arghan's terrace and watched the water falling down and swirling across the sea. She felt sorry for whoever was out there in boats today.

After breakfast, Pippa took Treya to meet Bootchie. He sometimes stayed with Pippa and Arghan, and sometimes with Arghan's brother Auryn, his wife Princess Merryn, and their pony, Hobba. But Bootchie's main home was with Bruno and Brutus, who still lived in the old quarters where they and Pippa had bunked with Cassius Ambrosius and Brian Magnus.

Treya was delighted to meet the fluffy orange cat. Bootchie had grown into his role as a royal pet. He was gracious, if a bit aloof. He warmed up more when Treya offered him some of the stinky fish treats that Pippa had brought from Vindavia Nova. He sat with her, purred, and allowed her to pet his cheek. Then he jumped down, and he and Pippa led Treya on a tour of the quarters.

The rooms that Cassius and Brian had occupied were left unchanged, except for the occasional dusting and sweeping. Brian's room contained several outfits inside the wardrobe, and a collection of rocks, feathers and crystals on the mantel.

Over the mantel, there was a large rendering that Pippa had made of him, standing at the prow of a ship with dolphins swimming alongside.

"That's Brian Magnus," said Pippa. "Aboard the Awel Glor, on the journey here."

"That's really good," Treya said, admiring the image. "He looks like a lovely person."

"He was," said Pippa. "He brightened our world."

They went into Cassius's room, where there were stacks of texts, maps, and pictures. His wardrobe was still full of clothing and gear, and his cuirass, helmet and sword-belt hung on the side. The walls of his room were covered with portraits that Pippa had made: of herself, Cassius, Brian Magnus, Arghan, Bruno, Brutus, and Bootchie.

"You did all these?" asked Treya.

"Yes," Pippa replied. "Except for this one." She pointed to a skillfully done little sketch of herself playing the harp.

"Arghan drew that. Cassius claimed it right away. I thought that was so sweet."

She sat down on the bed and Bootchie jumped into her lap. She sighed and looked around the room.

"Cassius Ambrosius. We miss him, don't we kitty?" said Pippa, touching noses with the cat. "Bootchie was Cassius's baby. He used to ride around on his shoulders, holding onto his hair." Bootchie reached out and touched Pippa's hair, as if he remembered too.

They moved on. Pippa still kept her old room. Her shield and trunks were in there, along with boxes of texts, pictures, maps, and cabinets full of art supplies. Her walls were also covered with pictures of her friends. On the mantle was the little old statue of Jove that she had found at Mount Temple, on his tin tray, and surrounded by stones, coins, tokens, shells and feathers.

"I like your collection," said Treya. "Are these things from all the places you've been?"

"Yes," said Pippa, pointing. "I found this little Jupiter when I was a child, at Mount Temple. I've managed to keep him with me all this time." She touched the statue fondly.

"This was my enlistment coin, and my ID tag," she continued. "Here are some pebbles, from when Cassius and I went to the High Falls. And Brian Magnus gave me this." She gently stroked a tiny striped seabird feather.

"And here are a few new things from our recent tour of the underground. See this little white stone? That was a gift from Fishy the Lagaloor. And look at these." Pippa pointed out two coins.

"There's an elegant lady standing on the back of a sea serpent, cutting through the waves. And a man with what we thought were fishtails, but could be some kind of boots. He's in a sort of tube or portal." She turned them over. "Here's a pretty tree with eight stars arcing over it. And this- I think it's some kind of... air ship."

"An air-ship!" Treya exclaimed.

"Well," Pippa replied, "it's clearly a vessel of some sort, but it's not on the water, and the sail looks like a huge bolster that's full of air." She pointed to the bottom of the coins. "There are five dots on each coin. Arghan's never seen anything like them, and he knows his coins. There's a whole bag of them. They were given to us by King Arawn himself. He claims that he has always had them, and doesn't remember anything about them. I think that he is ancient, so ancient that his origins are lost, even to him."

"He said something so mysterious," said Pippa. She closed her eyes and recited from memory.
"He said, 'Long ago, I came from high above the surface. I was trying to reach the salt-sea, but I was blown into the deep woods. I was stranded in the forest. I searched for a way out. There were only trees and vines, in every direction, a brutal woodland that wanted to crush me.' Then the Kowr-Broa, a huge old elk, led him to the realm of Queen Sidhi."

"So she's been around even longer than he has," said Treya.
"Apparently," Pippa replied. "I don't suppose you know anything about them."
"No," said Treya. "There were undercover An Dhew in Annuvin, of course, but that had nothing to do with me. We didn't talk about them. They were the enemy, and the incident with Prince Amatheon had brought shame to Caer Hudol. I'm still getting used to the idea that the Two Kingdoms are allied again. It felt strange to be a Walker in front of King Arawn. Good, but strange. So, where do you think he's from?"

"Arghan and I have discussed the possibility that he came from one of the nearby lost lands, maybe even Lys itself. They supposedly had very advanced technology."

They went out of Pippa's room and back into the hallway.
"These two rooms belong to the twins," Pippa said.
"Whose rooms are those?" asked Treya, pointing to the two doors at the far end of the hall.
"No one's," said Pippa. "They're empty. There's also an empty study room, at the end of the common area. It has good natural light, and its own entrance to the terrace."
They went into the common room, which also displayed Pippa's artwork: portraits of herself, her friends, the Awel Glor, and a large painting of Princess Merryn leading Hobba the pony with Bootchie riding on his back.
"This one is my favorite," Pippa said, indicating a large picture she had made of Cassius while he was stretched out on the floor with Bootchie lying on his chest.

The rain had been increasing. Suddenly the sky thundered, and lightning cracked. Treya jumped and shrieked.

Then she said, "I'm sorry, I'm not at all used to the sky exploding!"

Pippa got out her telyn harp and bowed a rainy day tune while Treya played with Bootchie and the sky continued to pour down.

That afternoon, the sun came out. The sky was a brilliant blue and the water was turquoise green.

Treya was starting to get used to the big brightness of it all. She went with Pippa to the southern gate to meet with Arghan, Bruno, Brutus, Del and Augustus. Also in attendance were the fore-man of the miners enclave, the King's chief bow-man, and the masters of the mason and stonecutter guilds. They took two carts up the steep switchback road to the top of the cliff behind the castle, to view the area where construction would soon begin on the bridge. They got off of the carts and walked to the spot, which was marked with little blue and silver flags.

Treya went to the edge with Del and Augustus. Bruno and Brutus came too. They looked down. It was a dizzying drop into the hazy ravine between the cliffs. Treya gazed across the split. She could see the little flags on the other side sparkling in the sunshine. Just below this level, she could make out the faint remains of the old bridge abutments. If she hadn't known to look for them, she wouldn't have noticed them, they were that eroded.

Arghan had explained that the two cliffs, and the split between them, had changed over the years. The ancient remains of the bridge-span dated back to the early days of sea-trade. Around that time, the land had shifted, and the once widely separated cliffs had come close together. The split filled in with boulders, slate and scree. There was still a chasm, but it was short, and very shallow, and could be crossed by a simple road bridge.

For several generations, it was relatively easy to get from the harbor to the mainland. That's when the settlement of Tintagel grew. Trevena's influence grew also, and so did the sea-trade. With the help of the nearby merchants, settlers, and farmers, the castle was built, and a king was installed.

But one day the ground shook with an earthquake. The village and the castle only received minor damage, but the two cliffs had split apart again under the pressure. The rocks and scree had tumbled out of the newly opened ravine, taking the bridge and part of the road with them, dumping hills of rubble on both sides. Since then, communications and trade between Trevena and the mainland had been challenging.

Del pounded in two wooden measuring stakes near the edge. Augustus peered at them through a metal arc on a tripod, and wrote down tiny numbers on a tablet. The bow-man was examining the ground, and others were making measurements. The plan was to install a mechanical cross-bow in a frame, a seth-ros, or arrow-wheel. The device was similar to the Archimedean Scorpio, but smaller. They would shoot lines across which were attached to bolts, and tied to anchor ropes, which could then be pulled over and secured. Treya wondered how many anchor ropes would be needed. She imagined being suspended over the drop. With the right gear and support, she would be fine with it. She leaned over and looked down.

"Treya," said Pippa, in small voice. "Are you sure?"
Treya turned around. Pippa was hanging way back. Arghan too. They were both pale. Treya and the others went back to them.
"It's terrifying!" said Pippa.

Bruno said, "Pippa, I'm surprised. I thought you were a mountaineer."
Brutus added, "Yes, didn't you and Cassius climb to the top of the High Falls?"
"We didn't really climb. It was just a... steep walk," said Pippa. "And we very much avoided going near the edge."

Arghan asked, "Treya, are you really all right with this?"
"Yes," Treya replied, "it's all good."
Pippa and Arghan looked at one another in bemusement.
"It's challenging work," said Augustus. "But someone has to do it. Del and I have spent most of our careers hanging in the air. We'll be watching over her every step of the process."
"Thank you," said Pippa, hugging him. "That's what I needed to hear."

That evening, the Royal Family were ready to meet their new guest. It wasn't a formal occasion, as when Pippa and the men from Vindavia Nova had first arrived. There was a small reception in one of the private chambers. The Royal Family warmly welcomed Treya Meynack back to her western home. Immediately afterwards, King Arthek began talking about the bridge project with Arghan and Pippa.

Princess Merryn and Queen Elowen, both heavy with child, sat on cushioned seats, surrounded by their attendant ladies. The ladies were all pretty, Treya noticed. Especially one of them, who was petite, with wavy blondish red hair, big blue eyes, and a round freckled face. She was wearing a sparkling pink gown with a wide gathered skirt.

The young woman noticed Treya watching her. She approached and said,
"Hello, Treya Meynack. I hope you like it here. I'm called Lowi. It's short for
Borlowan. I'm the Morning Star." She spun around in a circle. Her skirt
expanded as she twirled.

"What's the morning star?" asked Treya.
Lowi stared. Her big blue eyes grew even wider.
"Don't they have a sky where you come from?" she asked.
Treya was speechless. Then Lowi giggled, and Treya realized that she was
jesting.

"The second planet is the Morning Star," said Lowi. "You can see her before
sunrise in the east, just over the horizon. The foreigners say that she's a love
deity, called Venus." Lowi leaned in closer and whispered, "That makes me the
goddess of love." Then she laughed.

When they returned to their quarters, Treya asked Pippa, "Will you teach me
about the stars and planets?"

Chapter Two - Lesson Learned

It was late July. The surface world had grown much warmer. Treya had gotten used to getting up early to greet the Morning Star. It was nice and cool at daybreak. By mid-morning, she thought it was actually too hot to go outdoors, but no one else felt that way, so she was learning to deal with it. Her pale, dense hair had grown out just long enough to coax into two thick tails. They were clumpy, but they kept the hair out of her face. And Lowi liked them.

She had been spending more and more time with the charming Lady Borlowan. Treya had never met anyone like her. Lowi loved to laugh. She was graceful and free-spirited, and would often spontaneously burst into song or dance.

At first they just met in the afternoons, on the tavern terrace. The tavern was a hall that served wine and spirits. Half of it was terraced, and covered with grapevines. It was on the north side of the castle, and it stayed cool and shady nearly all day. Neither of them drank spirits, but they liked the atmosphere. The servers brought them chilled apple juice, a delicious treat on a warm day.

Pippa had encouraged Treya to invite Lowi to their quarters, so after a couple of weeks of meeting at the tavern, she did. On her first visit, Pippa made a fine sketch of Treya and Lowi sitting together on the balcony, with the sea in the background. Lowi brightened up the place, and Pippa and Arghan seemed to appreciate her presence. She would sing in a high sweet voice while Philippa played the Telyn, and Arghan would prepare a meal that they would all share afterwards. Then they would talk until late in the night.
When they said goodnight, Lowi would hold Treya tight. Treya hugged her back. She liked being close to her.

One day, Pippa brought them both to meet the Pol Pri family of musicians. Govenek, Gorwel, Growen, and Gras all took a liking to Treya and Lowi. Lowi danced around energetically, clapping two sticks together in time while the musicians played. It was delightful to watch. Treya loved being there, but she felt as though she needed to apologize that she didn't sing, or dance, or play any instruments. Govenek had said, "No need to be sorry. We are grateful for your presence. We have enough performers here. We need audience members." Treya and Lowi were invited to come and sing and dance and visit with them again. They had been back several times, with Pippa, and on their own.

The days were busy. Treya liked her scribe work at the Archive. She went three or four times a week. The temperature stayed nice and cool inside of the stone Kovskrifva. Her copying task would be laid out and ready for her. She faced away from Master Skell. He barely acknowledged her arrivals and departures, although he did praise her work on a regular basis. Lugarn was very quiet too. He spent most of his time on the lower level, sorting and studying texts, doing restorations and bindings, and occasionally bringing documents up or down the stairs. When she finished a project, he would collect it, and give her the next one. The Archive didn't get many visitors, but Master Skell and Lugarn always seemed to be busy.

The copying was therapeutic. It didn't matter if the subject was incomprehensible or dull. Copying was something that Treya could do without really being engaged. It was as if the information went right from her eyes to her hand, without really needing to bother her brain. So her mind wandered while she scribed. She would find herself thinking about Caer Hudol. She had to admit that she missed it. She liked her new friends, her new jobs, and her new home, but she missed the An Dhew more than she had thought she would. Before she left, they had all pitched in and given her a bag of coins to start her new life with. She treasured this gift from her comrades, even though she hadn't had any cause to spend it yet.

As a parting gift, Lord Gwydion himself had presented her with some of his famous footwear. He sang the well-worn song, 'take care of your shoes, and your shoes take care of you,' and he gave her a luxurious pair of sturdy boots. They were a soft blue with silver buckles, ready to blend in with the official colors of her new home. She loved them, not only because they were beautiful and comfortable, but also because in them she could feel the care that he had for his people.

She missed the Conn-Danu Royal Family. Lord Gwydion especially. He had such a comforting presence and a kind demeanor. The An Dhew served him equally out of duty and love. Treya had heard about him all of her life. Then he'd suddenly returned. She barely had a chance to get to know him before she left. She sometimes wished that she would have stayed longer at Caer Hudol, but the opportunity had been there, she had gone for it, and now here she was, a surface-dweller.

The bridge project was progressing slowly but steadily. Work took place in the early morning, before the heat and glare of the sun made it too uncomfortable. The anchor ropes had been put in place. According to Del's formulas, eight anchor ropes would be plenty sufficient for support and safety. They had put in sixteen. Advisor Agrippa had declared that any safety measures should be doubled, whenever possible. She was nervous about the whole thing, and was terrified at the thought of anyone being hurt or killed while working on the bridge.

Treya and a miner named Lug were the first to begin the work, amidst the web of suspension and safety ropes. They were harnessed, and hung over the edge in slings. She gaffed for him, moving the ropes and handing him tools while he drove in the spikes that would hold the wooden scaffold in place. Once the scaffolding was set, the masons could begin their work. There was talk of some of the workers setting up camp on the other side, or even staying in the village, rather than making the trip up and down every day.

It was a rainy afternoon. Treya had stopped counting the frequent rainstorms. She hadn't seen Lady Borlowan for a couple of days. The Princess and the Queen were both due to give birth within the next month or so, and had been moved to their confinement quarters. Lowi had been assisting with the transition.

Treya had important news that she wanted to share with Lowi. She held a document in her hand that had arrived for her that morning. She had been invited to be an officer of the Royal Council of the Bridge, the Pons-Cons. There was a meeting scheduled for tomorrow afternoon. She was honored and excited. She decided to go to the tavern and see if Lowi showed up.

Treya sat alone at their table. A server brought her some apple juice. She drank it slowly. Lady Borlowan didn't show up. Treya was disappointed but not surprised. Lowi had warned her that this move of the royal ladies' chambers would take some time.

Treya noticed someone standing nearby, in her left periphery. The figure was backlit, but she could see that they were dressed in a suit of black and silver. The suit reminded her of Lord Gwydion's clothing that he wore at court. The stranger approached Treya. Now she could see that it was a woman. She was older than herself, but Treya couldn't guess her age. Older than Pippa, but younger than Queen Elowen.

The woman was stockily built, but elegant looking. Her dark hair was streaked with white and shorn closely in the back, with a swoop in the front. She was attractive, more handsome than pretty, with smooth clear pale skin. Her large brown eyes were outlined with kohl. She had a compelling presence that Treya immediately responded to.

"Treya Meynack," said the woman, reaching out a graceful hand. Treya took it without thinking. The woman's grip was warm and firm.
"I'm Mimi Ryea," she said. "Perhaps you've heard of me?"
"No, I'm sorry," said Treya. The woman was still holding her hand. It felt comforting.
"That's probably for the best," said Mimi Ryea. "I wouldn't want you to be intimidated. My family is very prominent and powerful."
Based on what she was observing, Treya could believe it.

"How do you know me?" Treya asked.
"Oh," said Mimi, "I've been watching you for some time now." Treya didn't know whether to be flattered or concerned by that. The woman still hadn't let go of her hand. Then Mimi said,
"We need to talk. We should go someplace quieter. Come over here with me." She began to pull Treya in the direction of the stairs.
"I can't," said Treya. "I'm waiting for someone."
"Lady Borlowan isn't coming," said Mimi.
"How did you-" Treya began. Mimi cut her off, saying,
"She doesn't like you, you know. In fact, she thinks you're a dull fool. Little Lowi has been playing you."
Treya felt a thumping pain across her chest, like she'd been hit.
"But why?" she squeaked out.

"To get back at me," said Mimi. "She's in love with me, but I broke it off. Even though she claims that it was her idea. She was using you to punish me. I couldn't just stand by and watch her manipulate you any longer."

Treya felt despair, confusion, resentment, hurt and anger all at once. It felt like a toxic stew boiling up in her insides. She could hardly believe that Lowi would have treated her so badly. But it must be true. Mimi Ryea was a respectable person from a prominent family. She had no reason to lie to Treya. Treya allowed herself to be pulled along. Mimi took her to a little bench in an alcove, tucked away in the corner of the terrace, underneath the stairs. Treya was sobbing. She couldn't help herself.

A server brought Mimi a cup of red wine. Mimi drank some, and then said, "Here, Treya, drink some wine. You'll feel better."

"I don't drink wine," Treya sniffled.

"You've had a shock," said Mimi soothingly. "Wine is medicinal at times like these." She held the cup to Treya lips. Treya hesitated, then took a sip and swallowed it. It didn't taste good, and it burned her throat, but Mimi wouldn't stop until she had taken several sips.

"What is this?" Mimi asked, noticing the document clutched in Treya's hand. She took it from her and read it.

"Well," Mimi said, with a charming smile, "this is really special. The Royal Council wants you to be an officer. You must have done something impressive." That made Treya think about Lowi again. She had brought the letter to show her. She burst into tears. Mimi stroked her hair. It felt so soothing. "Surely you feel honored by this invitation?" She murmured. "Hmm?"

"Yes," Treya said, wiping her face. "I've done some good work for them."

"That's better," said Mimi. She held the cup to Treya's lips and said, "Now drink some more."

The rest of the day and night passed in confusion. Treya had felt dizzy and disoriented after drinking the wine. She told Mimi that she was going back to her quarters to lie down. Mimi offered to escort her. They got up and began walking together up the stairs. But on the way up, Mimi had begun to talk about Pippa and Arghan, insisting that they were only using Treya, and that it was only a matter of time until they turned against her.

"You need to come stay with me," Mimi said earnestly. "I have your best interests in mind. They do not. You mustn't speak to them any more. They're only interested in getting ahead. Getting more titles. You are just conveniently helping them. You should hear them criticize you when you're not around. They're jealous of you. But not as jealous as they are of me. They would try to destroy me if they could."

"No! Thas not true," Treya slurred. "None ofis true." She sobbed.

"It is true," said Mimi. "And if you value your own life at all, you'll listen to me."

She stopped and took Treya by the shoulders. She looked deep into her eyes. Then she said, "Thank goodness I'm here. I'm the only one who can save you. From those wretched so-called friends of yours. And from yourself. You poor thing. It's not your fault. It's the way you were brought up."

She grabbed Treya and held her very close. Mimi's body was warm and solid feeling.

They had continued to Pippa and Arghan's floor. Mimi had waited in the stairwell, saying, "The blacksmith and his bride are in the dining hall. Quickly now, get your clothes, and your coin."

"But-" Treya started to object.

Mimi suddenly kissed Treya, passionately, on the lips. Then she kissed her on the neck, and stroked her hair. "Treya, my only love," Mimi said, "no more arguing. You have to trust me. This is what's best for you. Now quickly, don't keep me waiting."

A little while later, Treya found herself in Mimi's rooms. Treya wasn't exactly sure how events had unfolded the way they had, but there she was. She had done what she'd been told to do. She had entered Pippa and Arghan's quarters, gone into her room, taken her coin and a change of clothes, and gone back to Mimi. Mimi had led her down the stairs and along a hall to her own quarters, on the level above the tavern.

"Sit down," said Mimi. Treya sat on the couch and looked around blearily. Mimi's quarters consisted of a small main room with a hearth, a bedroom, a privy, a closet, and a terrace. The curtains were drawn and the rooms were darkened. Silver cups, wine bottles, crystal bowls and goblets gleamed in the semi-darkness. Treya could see the bedroom through the open door. There was a large canopied bed, covered in black velvet.

Mimi took Treya's bag of coins from her and disappeared into the bedroom. Then she came back out and said, "Bring your things."

Treya obediently grabbed her bundle and followed. Mimi opened the closet. It was dark, only illuminated by the light from the main room. There were some shelves and hampers, some broken crockery, a slop-pot, and a grubby old cot on the floor covered with a threadbare blanket.

"Here you go," said Mimi.

Treya stared at the dumpy little space. "Is this where my clothes go?"

"This is where you go," said Mimi, indicating the cot.

"What?" Treya was so confused. "Why? Why can't I sleep on the couch? Or with you?"

"I would love to take you to my comfortable bed," said Mimi, "but you are not quite ready yet. I would enjoy it," she said as she stroked Treya's hair, "but it wouldn't be fair to you. Even the couch would be more than you deserve right now. You need to learn. You need to understand how deeply flawed you are. You are just like your so-called friends. Only focused on yourself. Your selfishness is holding you back, and keeping you from reaching your full potential. I can help you, but this work needs to be your priority. I need to be your priority. I require your utmost loyalty, and I need to be the sole focus of your respect."

She kissed Treya's neck. "Only when you break yourself down, can you start regrowing. This is the first step. You can thank me later."
"But-"
"Goodnight," said Mimi, closing the door to the closet. Treya stood in the darkness for a long time. Then she dropped her bundle and groped her way across the floor. She found the cot and crawled into it.

She woke up with her head pounding, and a terrible thirst. And she had to pee. There was no light. Treya had no way of knowing if it was day or night. The closet was hot and airless. She groped along the floor until she found the door. She half-expected it to be locked, but it opened.

It was just before dawn. Treya slipped into the privy. When she was done, she found a jug of water and drank half of it. She was in a daze, still feeling the effects of the alcohol. She went out on the terrace. The cool morning air felt good.

She looked out across the water. The sight of Venus in the Eastern sky brought everything back. Her friends had betrayed her. Lowi had used her, and so had Pippa and Arghan. This was what she deserved, for being so flawed, and self-centered. She was lost, cut adrift, far away from her real home. Mimi was all she had. She was grateful that Mimi was willing to help her to become a better person.

She leaned over the rails and vomited. She stood back up, gasping and shuddering. Then she vomited again. And again. There was nothing left, but she was still heaving. Finally she collapsed onto the terrace. After a while, she got up. She crept into the main room and drank some more water. She cautiously peeked through the bedroom door, which was open a crack. Mimi was asleep.

Beside her was an open wardrobe, filled with black and silver outfits. There was a metal box on a low shelf in the wardrobe. The top was open, and Treya could see her coin bag in it, alongside some pieces of jewelry.

Treya stared at Mimi, sleeping peacefully on her back. Her flawless skin glowed in the morning light. Treya was simultaneously attracted and repelled. She didn't understand what was happening.

Get away! cried a voice in her head. *No,* she answered. *I will never grow and be a better person if I don't work on my flaws. Besides, my friends have betrayed me. Mimi is all I have now.*

Treya went back into the dingy closet and climbed into the cot. When she awoke again, it was mid-day. Mimi was up and dressed, sitting at the table, and eating a bowl of strawberries. There were parchments and a pen in front of her. "I wrote to the Royal Council of the Bridge and offered my services as well," Mimi said. "They can make me an officer too, then we can work together."

Treya was confused. "But why would they want you to work on the bridge?"

Mimi shook her head sadly and said, "Do you think that you're better than me? You need to focus your respect, remember? And why wouldn't they want me? They want you, and I have much more to offer than you do. My father is Councilor Banok Ryea. The most famous and prestigious advisor to ever serve the Royal Family. Who is your father?"

Treya was silent.

"Whoever he is, your father is nothing," said Mimi. "Mine is everything. Don't you think that counts for something? Mmm? If you understand that, you may have one strawberry."

Treya didn't know what she understood or didn't understand, but it felt like her stomach was eating itself. She took a strawberry. She was getting ready to bite into it, but Mimi said, "Ah-ah-ah, not in here. Take it to your room." Treya obeyed. She took the strawberry into the dark dirty room and ate it.

She sat there for hours, dozing occasionally. She was startled awake by a knock at the front door. She heard Mimi open it, then close it. There was silence, and then there was a mighty crash, and the sound of glass breaking. Treya ran out into the main room. Mimi was sitting at the table with a document in front of her. Pieces of a broken wineglass were scattered across the hearth.

"What happened?" cried Treya.

Mimi looked at her with what appeared to be cold hatred.

"The blacksmith's wife has poisoned the Council against me."

She handed Treya the document. Treya read it out loud.

"To Lady Mimi Ryea. Thank you for your interest in the bridge project. As of now, we are only meeting with contributors who have technical knowledge and practical skills. Perhaps in the future, when the bridge is completed, there will be a place for a diplomatic functionary. Best regards, Counselor Bruno Marianis."

Treya said hesitantly, "But... that only makes sense, doesn't it? Maybe you can be on the Council later."

Mimi looked at Treya with disdain, but before she could say anything, there was another knock at the door. Treya jumped at the sound. Mimi just stared at her grimly. There was silence, then another knock, more insistent this time.

"Go to your room," Mimi said, pointing. Treya crept silently back into the closet. The knocking continued. She peeked into the main room. Mimi continued to ignore the sound.

Then Del's voice called out, "Treya? Treya Meynack, are you in there?" She heard Augustus call out, "We just want to talk to you, Treya. We're worried about you. Pippa said you didn't come home last night."

Mimi scowled, then she shuffled slowly over to the door. She looked menacingly back towards Treya's closet. Treya ducked down out of sight. Mimi opened the door a crack and said,

"Treya doesn't want to see you."

"I'd like to hear that from her!" cried Del.

"Treya!" called Augustus. "We need you at the meeting. It's getting ready to start." Treya jumped up. Then she cowered back down. Her heart was racing and she was sobbing. She heard Mimi say,

"I find your interest in Treya suspicious. Men of your age fawning over a girl. I'm not turning her over to a couple of old perverts."

"WHAA-" Del was roaring, but Mimi slammed the door. She called through the closed door,

"Don't come back here, or I shall complain to the guards that you are trying to molest my young friend."

It was quiet again. Treya gathered her nerve and went out into the room.

"Mimi," she said tentatively. Mimi glared at her. Treya continued,

"I think I should go to the meeting."

"There you go again," said Mimi. "Wanting to glorify yourself. Forgetting what really matters."

"No!" Treya exclaimed. "I'm not in it for glory. I said I would help. And Del and Augustus are counting on me."

"Those doddering old fools. They don't know what they're doing."

Treya stiffened her resolve. "All the more reason that I should go help them," she said, walking towards the door.

"If you do," said Mimi, in a high shrill voice, "I can't be responsible for what happens."

Mimi pulled a little knife out of her pocket, unsheathed it, and held it against her own wrist.

"What are you doing?" Treya cried in horror.

"What I'm doing is up to you," cried Mimi hysterically. "Go ahead, betray me. Go to your meeting. Just don't expect to find me alive when you come back."

"Mimi!" cried Treya. "You can't be serious!"

Mimi stepped right in front of Treya, holding up her wrist, and pressing the knife blade against the veins.

Treya turned and went back to her closet. She crawled into the cot and covered her head with the ragged blanket.

She woke to the sound of the front door closing. She lay there for a long time. Then there was a sudden and insistent knock. Treya lay still. The knocking continued. Treya cautiously approached the door. She wanted to answer it. But what if it was Mimi, testing her?

"Treya!" It was Pippa's voice. "Please open the door." Treya didn't move. "If you don't open it," said Pippa, "I'm going to break it down." Treya was frozen. "I have an ax," said Pippa. "Stand back."

"Wait!" Treya cried. She didn't know if it was true, but she couldn't let Mimi come home and find the door broken down.

She opened the door, just a crack. Pippa put her face in the opening.

"Treya," she pleaded. "Please come home."

"This is my home now," said Treya, "and Mimi says I can't talk to you anymore."

"Since when is she in control of you?" asked Pippa incredulously.

"I realize now that I'm not capable of making my own decisions, and I cannot allow you to continue taking advantage of me," Treya recited. "It's not my fault, it's the way I was brought up. Mimi is going out of her way to help me."

"I'm guessing she helped you by taking your coin?" said Pippa angrily.

"Yes," replied Treya. "It's for my own good."

Pippa snorted. "You don't believe that nonsense! And what about Lowi?"

"Lowi betrayed me," said Treya firmly. "She was only acting out of pain and jealousy, because Mimi broke up with her."

"No she didn't!" exclaimed Pippa. "It's a lie. Lowi is heartbroken that you've abandoned her. This has to stop! Mimi is a wicked person, Treya. It's not your fault that you fell for her lies. She's extremely manipulative. She may seem to care about you, but she doesn't. She's hurt a lot of people. And Lowi was the one who rejected *her*."

"She warned me that you would say that," said Treya. "She knows that you're jealous of her.

"Jealous of her?" Pippa raised her voice in indignation. "She's a sneaky manipulative opportunist with no real friends. Can you think of one reason why I should be jealous of her?"

Treya hesitated for a moment. Then she drew a breath and recited, "I'm sorry, Pippa. I appreciate all you've done for me, but right now I need to work on prioritizing my loyalties and refining the focus of my respect."

"Listen to yourself!" cried Pippa. "Those aren't words that you thought of, Treya. They are a spell, to poison you and make you a prisoner-"
"I'm sorry," Treya said. She shut the door. She fell to her knees, sobbing. Then she blacked out. She awoke a few minutes later and crawled back to her closet.

The night had gone by in bleak misery. The day arrived with more of the same. Treya stayed in the closet. She was weak, thirsty, hungry, and dizzy. Her head hurt. Consciousness came and went. Then it was nighttime once more. Mimi had gone out again, after giving Treya strict instructions.
"You may come out of your room," she said. "Do not leave, do not answer the door, and do not go into the bedroom. You may sit on the couch and eat the bread I left for you. I have also very generously left you one cup of water."
After Treya had consumed the jug of water without asking, Mimi had to punish her by taking away her water privileges. Treya's mouth and throat were parched, and her lips were chapped.

"Remember," Mimi continued, "I'm the only one who cares about you. And should you betray my trust, I cannot be responsible for my actions." Mimi flashed her bare wrist at Treya and made a slicing motion. Then she left. Treya stood and stared at the crusts of bread. She gulped down the water. Then she turned and walked out onto the terrace.

She had never thought about suicide before. Thanks to Mimi, she couldn't stop thinking about it. *Maybe there was something to it. Perhaps she should consider it herself.* Treya was desperately unhappy, weak and shattered, and absolutely devoid of hope. She was so empty and dehydrated, she felt as though her body was dying anyway. She climbed up on the terrace railing and sat with her feet hanging over the edge. She looked down into the darkness.

The railing jutted out over the cliff. If she jumped, there wouldn't be any one down below to get hurt. She scooted forward and peered down between her legs. At the bottom of the cliff, way below, she could just make out the stony ground.

As far as ways to kill yourself, it would be much more efficient than using a knife. There was no guarantee that a knife cut would be fatal. But once she left the rail, there would be no doubt. She thought about falling all the way down, and the force with which a body would hit the ground.

I wonder how many people change their minds while they're plummeting to their deaths? she mused. *Probably all of them.*

She sighed. Then she flipped her legs around, hopped off of the rail and stood back on the terrace. She was heading back to eat the bread crusts, when there was another knock on the door. This time it sounded urgent.

A voice called out, "Treya, it's Pippa. Listen to me! Mimi needs you. Come downstairs, at once."
Treya threw open the door. Pippa grabbed her arm and pulled her into the hallway.
"Is Mimi in trouble?" Treya asked, with a rising feeling of panic.
"Yes, come on," Pippa said.
They hurried down the stairs until they reached the area just above the alcove bench where she and Mimi had sat. There was somebody crouching on the stair. Pippa also crouched, and pulled Treya down too.

Treya gaped in surprise. The crouching person was Lowi. Before Treya could react, Lowi put her finger on her lips, and pointed. She was pointing to the bench in the alcove. Treya looked. It was Mimi. She was sitting with a very young woman, with long pale hair and a low cut gown. Mimi was holding a cup of wine to the girl's mouth, making her drink, while she caressed her face. The girl wasn't drinking fast enough, and some red wine dribbled down her chin and onto the exposed top of her breast. Mimi leaned over and licked it up.

"Ew, that's enough," whispered Pippa.
"Disgusting," Lowi whispered back.

Treya said nothing. She allowed the other two women to pull her away. They quickly ascended the stairs, and went back down the hallway to Mimi's room.
"But why?" Treya asked suddenly. "Why would she lie to me, and do all those

things to me?" She was suddenly very, very angry. "Mimi hurt me on purpose! She twisted everything. She said she would kill herself if I left. She held a knife to her wrist. She made me hurt my friends. I'm so sorry." She sobbed. "I didn't mean it. Why did she make me do that?"

"Oh, Treya," Lowi said, hugging her. "It's because you're so good and trusting. She preys on the open-hearted and vulnerable for her own sick pleasure. She tried it on me, but I told her to get stuffed. So she decided to get back at me by going after you. Because everyone knows that we're close." She kissed Treya on the cheek. It was a nice, wholesome feeling, to be kissed by Lowi.

They had reached Mimi's room. Treya opened the door and they went in. Pippa went right to the table and began quickly scribing something on a blank piece of parchment. Treya looked at her, and at Lowi. She was so glad to see them. But the great sense of relief was still mingling with a great anger. Treya stamped her foot hard in frustration.
"But why? I don't understand! Why would a person do that?"
"It's just how she is," said Lowi sadly.

"It's just how she *was*," said Pippa grimly, finishing her document with a flourish, and waving it in the air to dry. "She's not doing this here, ever again. I'm evicting her. As a court official, I have the authority. I don't care if she has to take a row-boat, she's leaving on the morning tide. She's been sponging off the Royal Family and using people her whole life. Hanging on to the shreds of her family's legacy, abusing young women, while her famous father lies on his deathbed, over in Brittany. It stops now. Treya, you and Lowi get your things while I find a guard."

Treya and Lowi went into the bedroom, and up to the wardrobe. Treya retrieved her bag of coins. The bag of coins that her true comrades had given her. She hefted the coin bag. It was lighter than it had been.
"Did she take some of the coin?" asked Lowi.
"Yes, she did," said Treya. "To buy herself three more black and silver outfits. These three here." She pointed to the side of the wardrobe where they hung on hooks. "She's got so many already, they wouldn't fit inside. And they're all pretty much the same thing."
Lowi lifted the three outfits off the hooks.
"If these were bought with your money," she said, "then they're yours."
"I don't want them," Treya said in disgust.
"I was thinking more along the lines of a... donation." Lowi giggled and said, "Come on!"

They went into the main room. Pippa was talking to one of the castle guards. Another guard was hammering the document Pippa had scribed onto the outside of the front door.

"What are you doing with those?" asked Pippa, looking at the three outfits.

"I'm not sure," said Treya.
"Come on, Pippa!" cried Lowi, heading for the terrace. "Donation time. There's one for each of us."

Pippa followed them. Lowi took one of the suits and flung it into the air over the balcony. It hovered and flapped in the breeze before it sank out of sight.
The other two women cheered. Then they made their donations too, gleefully watching the clothing disappear from sight.

Treya went to the closet to get her bundle. Pippa and Lowi looked at the grim scene inside.
"Seriously hideous," said Pippa. "If I wasn't evicting her, I'd be tempted to kill her."
"I wouldn't try to stop you," said Lowi.
They left Mimi's room and headed towards Pippa and Arghan's quarters.
When they arrived, Lowi said, "Treya, I have to stay the night with the Princess. But she's just about settled in, so I'll be back tomorrow, hopefully. I love you." She hugged her.
"Thank you, Lowi," she said, hugging her in return. "I love you too."

Pippa also hugged Lowi, and said, "Lady Borlowan, I am grateful to you. If you hadn't sent me that message, this never would have been possible."
Lowi frowned. "I didn't send you a message. You sent me a message! At least I assumed it was you. A messenger came to the royal quarters and said to me, 'Go at once to the tavern stairs and wait quietly'."
"What, really?" exclaimed Pippa. "A messenger came to my room, and said, 'Get Treya, say Mimi needs her, and make haste to the tavern stairs'."
The three women stared at each other in confusion.
"Perhaps it was one of the ladies at court," said Lowi. "They knew how upset I was about this situation."
"And they wouldn't want to get personally involved," said Pippa, "so a message would make sense."
"It's a happy mystery," said Lowi, shrugging. "Goodnight dear ones!" She darted off.
"Goodnight," they called after her.

"First things first," said Pippa. She poured them each a cup of water and they drank. "Now, food. I've got a cold supper all ready. I'm expecting Arghan home sometime in the next hour. Or four. He's working in the shop tonight, trying to catch up on his Angove duties. This bridge project has taken up most of his time lately."

Treya went to the washroom and cleaned up. She was still trembling, and exhausted from all the drama. She was relieved that her friend was acting so normal. She sat at the table and began to devour the bread, cheese, grapes, smoked fish, and cress that Pippa set down. They finished with some honey cakes and lemon-water.

"That was the best meal I've ever had," said Treya.
Pippa laughed and jokingly said, "Please feel free to repeat that when my husband is nearby."

"Pippa," said Treya, suddenly serious. "She's going to be so angry. I'm afraid that she... that Mimi will come here and start trouble."

"That's why she's confined to her room," said Pippa. "I sent some guards to... well, basically, to arrest her, and keep her in her quarters. For her own protection." Pippa smiled grimly. "She's locked in until the morning, when she is to be escorted onto the first vessel leaving the harbor. I also sent a guard to make sure that poor girl got home alright, the one she was forcing wine into."

Pippa shook her head.
"Gods! What a pathetic creature. Not even worthy of being called an opponent. More like a diseased limb that needs to be excised."

She got up and went into the washroom. Treya nibbled at the last few crumbs of cake. She could hear the bathtub being filled. Pippa came back and said, "I'm getting the bath ready for you. The water's nice and hot."

"A bath sounds like paradise," said Treya. "But isn't the hot water for Arghan?"

"Don't worry about that," said Pippa. "There will be time to heat more before he gets home. Besides, he'll be so happy that you're back he won't care." She kissed the top of Treya's fuzzy head. Treya took her bundle and went to her room to get ready for her bath.

She looked around the room as if seeing it for the first time. It was lovely, clean, full of nice comfortable furniture, and lit with softly glowing lamps.

There were pretty pictures on the walls, and a dressing table with a big bright mirror. *It's the most beautiful room I've ever seen,* Treya thought.

Is that the lesson I'm meant to learn from this experience? To really notice and appreciate the goods things in my life? If so, lesson learned!

She put on her robe and went to the washroom, climbed into the tub, and her cares melted away into the glorious warm water.

In the morning, Treya awoke in her lovely bed and greeted the day. She got dressed and went into the common room. She had slept late. It was already mid-morning. Arghan and Pippa were standing on the balcony.

The blacksmith and his bride, Treya thought. *Mimi Ryea had meant that appellation as an insult, but in reality, it was a compliment.*

Treya went out to join them. They each gave her a hug.

Pippa pointed to a sleek little ship that was exiting the southeastern harbor through the sea-gates, and said, "You're just in time."
"Is that her?" asked Treya.
"Yes," said Pippa. "There she goes." They watched in silence as the little ship sailed out of sight.

"Well," said Arghan, "as the harbor-men say, 'delivrans da dhe hager puskes'. Good riddance to bad fish."

Chapter Three - Mutual Support

She had been through a lot in a very short amount of time. Pippa suggested that she might want to take it easy, but Treya was ready to go right back to work. Even though it had only been a couple of days, she was sorry about the time she had spent away, and she didn't want to miss anything else. In truth, she was embarrassed by what had happened with Mimi. Treya knew that she had been a fool, but because of the experience, she had learned to be more circumspect, and when in doubt, to trust her own instincts.

And so, not long after watching the little ship sail away, she returned to her routine with a renewed sense of purpose.

She met with Del and Augustus that morning in their new quarters. Previously, they had been housed in a wing of the old quarters, not far from the rooms where Bruno and Brutus still lived. The two engineers had now been given their own elegant suite, complete with a drafting room and a small workshop. Their rooms were situated on an upper level in the middle of the castle. They were part of the complex of royal administrative chambers, and their long, broad terrace overlooked both the east and west harbors.

Del and Augustus were delighted and relieved to see Treya. She hugged them both tightly.

"I'm really sorry that I worried you," she said. "Thank you for caring about me. I'm lucky to have such good friends."

"We're just happy that you're back with us," Del said, kissing her on the forehead.

"We were so concerned about you," said Augustus, tears in his eyes. He blew his nose loudly into an embroidered linen pocket-cloth. He and Del had both been provided with fine new clothes and gear to go with their status as royal councilors. They looked very well, and seemed to be enjoying their new life at Trevena.

Treya had lunch with Pippa and Lowi in the dining hall. Then she headed to the Kovskrifva, after a stop at the kitchen pantry. She had decided to bring some treats to Master Skell and Lugarn, to let them know that she appreciated them too, even if Master Skell was odd and unresponsive, and Lugarn hardly ever spoke.

They were both at their desks.

"Hello, Lugarn," she said. "Good day, Master Skell." She held up the bundle. "I brought some little plum-cakes. To share."

"Put them in the box," said Master Skell, without looking up. Treya was confused. She looked at Lugarn. He rose, went to the corner, picked up the stepladder, and set it in front of the shelf. Then he sat back down. Treya then realized that Master Skell was referring to the mysterious box on the shelf. She climbed the ladder and opened it. In it were apples, bread, and cheese. It was just a food box! She put the bundle in the box, closed it, and climbed down.

"Why is a food box up on a high shelf?" Treya asked.
"Mice," said Master Skell. "You can't have mice in a library."
Treya laughed.
"There's nothing funny about mice in a library!" said Master Skell.

"No, of course not, sir," said Treya. "I was laughing at myself. This place is so mysterious. So full of hidden knowledge. I thought that the box on the shelf must contain some... special document."
"Such as?" Master Skell looked at her. The light was hitting him at an angle, and she couldn't see his eyes, just the glare off of the lenses.

"I don't know," she shrugged. "A secret map, or something like that." She giggled. "Maybe the map to the Spiral Castle."
"It's a food box," he said, looking back down at his desk. "No eating in the library. Only in the front alcove. Don't leave any crumbs."

She sat down to work. Treya was scribing a long complex document called:

'Applications of Currency in Western Trade, with Conversions from Base Twenty'.

It was eighteen pages long, with passages in Latin, Kernowek, Cymraeg, Breton, and Brythonic. It was mostly full of numbers and charts. It was tricky to copy. Whoever scribed it before her must have found it challenging too, as it was covered in scratched-out errors and cramped inserts. There was one table of gridded numbers that covered four entire pages. It converted weights and measures from the Celtic twenty unit counting system into the common system of tens. It was very exacting.

She'd nearly completed the document during her last session, but the light had faded. The Royal Archive usually closed at dusk. Unlike the Lyverva, there were no lamps allowed in the Kovskrifva, unless there was an urgent need. Fire was an even greater source of concern than mice. To warm the place, heated air was piped in from a nearby furnace.

Treya soon finished the economics document. It had only taken a half hour to complete. She spent another half hour checking it against the original. Lugarn hadn't brought her a new project yet. She looked around. Lugarn had left the room. Maybe he was getting her new assignment. She scanned her work one more time. She was tired of this long, tedious document. Lugarn still hadn't arrived. She turned around.

"Master Skell?"

Master Skell did not look up. She stared at him. He didn't move. There was no indication that he had heard her. *He really must be asleep,* she thought. She turned back around, trying to decide whether she should go look for Lugarn, or take an early break and eat a plum-cake. They had looked and smelled so good, she had wanted to eat one on the way to the Kovskrifva, but she'd just had lunch, so she restrained herself.

"Mystai," said Master Skell.

She turned around again. His distorted blue eyes were looking in her direction. She didn't understand what he'd said.
"What?" she asked.
"When does the day begin?"
"What do you mean?" she replied. She was startled. Did he think that she had been late for work?
He stared at her. The glass windows of the room were reflected in his eye-lenses as grids of light. It was disconcerting.
"Answer the question," he said. "When does the day begin?"
"I think that most people would say at sunrise," she answered.
"I asked you," he responded.
"Well, then," she said, "it may sound strange, but I believe that it begins the night before. I've actually been thinking about this very thing. Since I've been watching the stars."

Master Skell nodded, lenses flashing brightly in unison. Treya continued,
"I feel as though the next day is set in motion when the stars come out at night. It's as if they hold the source of our light until the following day. As the daylight fades, they grow in brightness. As the sunlight rises again in the morning, the stars fade, having done their work for another night. Even if the sky is hidden, I know that the stars have brought forth the light of the day."

She could hear Lugarn coming up the stairs. Master Skell turned his gaze back to his desk.

What was that all about? she wondered. Lugarn handed her the next assignment, then he went back downstairs. She began copying 'Iberian Peninsula Maritime Taxes and Port Tariffs'. It was a short concise document, and she soon completed it. As the western light was fading, she cleaned her scribing materials, straightened up her desk, and checked the alcove to make sure it was tidy.

"Goodnight, Master Skell," she said, heading towards the door. "I wish you a pleasant evening."

"One moment," he said. "I have something for you." He pointed to a small wooden box on his desk. Treya picked it up and opened it. Inside was a silver pendant on a long and slender silver chain.

"It's an apple," said Treya, running her finger along its cheery round surface.

"It's sacred to Pomona," said Master Skell. "She is the goddess of the apple harvest. The pom is the fruit of wisdom."

Treya tried it on. She didn't normally care to wear jewelry, but this felt good.

"I had the chain made extra long, to go over your hair," said the old man. "Keep the apple with you. It's a talisman of protection. If you don't want to wear it as a pendant, just carry it in your pocket."

"I'll try wearing it," she said. "Thank you, Master Skell, for the lovely gift."

"You've earned it," he said.

He must have realized how difficult that currency text had been to scribe, she thought.

That evening, Lowi had come around for dinner, and she also brought Treya something new to wear. The Lady Borlowan was skilled at garment making. Her gowns with the pleated bell-skirts were much in demand among the ladies of the court. Treya had requested a lightweight tunic with pockets, so that she could carry her portable scribe gear without a bag. The tunic was made of moss green flaxen cloth, with forest green brushed velvet trim. It had silver spiral clasps which had been made by Auryn Pen Avalen. There were customized pockets, accommodating two small tablets, a stylus, graphite and chalk sticks, and sheets of vellum and parchment. The fabric in the pockets was waxed, to keep the contents dry.

Treya tried on the tunic. It was very comfortable. She loaded the pockets, then jumped up and down. Her scribing gear stayed put.

"Your work is so fine," said Pippa to Lowi. "And your gowns are so original."

Treya said, "Aren't they? I wish she could show them to more people."

Lowi said, "Treya has told me all about the Dressed in Clothing Walk. It must be glorious to live in a place that hosts such an event."

"Well," said Pippa, "nothing is stopping you from doing it here. The ladies of this court love fine clothing. The men too, for that matter."

"That's a brilliant idea!" Treya exclaimed. "We can make our own Walk!"

"Can we?" Lowi asked breathlessly. "Oh, that would be fun. I'll tell the Princess. It will cheer her." Then Lowi had returned to Princess Merryn, who much desired her company these days.

Arghan went back to the workshops right after dinner. He was in a good mood, having received the demotion that he had so badly wanted. Pippa explained it to Treya:

"We finally got King Arthek to agree that having one person to be both Angove and Trade-master is not a good idea. It's too much, being the Royal Smith and the Master of Trades. The two jobs are very different. It might have made sense back in the day, to have the one person in charge. Back then, there were only a few regular trade partners. That was before they had a proper treasury. Anyway, the new Master of Trades is Edern Pinbren. You met him."

"Arghan's cousin, the tall man," said Treya.

"Yes," Pippa replied. "He's a lovely fellow with a good head for figures. And he knows the trade routes better than anyone else."

"That must be such a relief for Arghan," said Treya.

"It is," Pippa replied. "And as for the Angove position, there's less pressure there too. Auryn has really advanced in his training. He has taken over many of the daily tasks in the shop. Arghan mostly gets to work on projects that he enjoys." She sighed. "He has had so many responsibilities, ever since he was very young. He does so much for so many people. Especially me. He makes me want to be a better person."

She and Pippa took a couple of blankets and went to sit on the balcony. The night had been cloudy, but now a breeze was blowing across the dark shining water, and the stars had come out.

It had been a good day, Treya reflected. *She'd worked hard, and Master Skell had been really appreciative.*

"Oh," said Treya, suddenly recalling the apple pendant. "You'll like this, Pippa. Master Skell gave me a gift, for being such a diligent scribe." She pulled out the necklace, which had been tucked inside her tunic. She had decided soon after putting in on that it would be better inside her clothing, after she had leaned over to pick something up and gotten hit in the forehead with it.

"A silver apple," said Pippa. "That was thoughtful of him."

"He told me it would bring protection, and blessings from the goddess Pomona," said Treya. "And he said that it represents wisdom. I've heard that before. But why does it? Is it because apples are so nutritious that they make our brains work better?"

Pippa laughed. "That may be part of it," she said. "But the story of apple cultivation represents a turning point in the development of civilization. Not just for eating; humans first discovered alcohol by making cider. That importance is why the apple is featured in the Hebrew Testament so heavily. And so heavy-handedly. The Genesis story of the expulsion of the first humans was conceived of by those who still clung to the culture of the nomadic hunters. They had followed the herds for millennia, and were very resistant to change."
"What change?" asked Treya.
"The introduction of agriculture," Pippa replied.
"But that's silly," said Treya. "You can raise crops and still go hunting."

"Yes," said Pippa. "And no. Remember, this was long ago. Before people had metal tools. There were no houses, or settlements. The whole tribal group would migrate with the herds."
"Imagine that you are an early agriculturist, living in this nomadic world. You and a few of your friends have figured out that the seeds of a plant can grow more of that same plant. And that with some nurture and care, the little trees near the river will produce sweet juicy fruit. But it's difficult at first to convince the rest of the tribe to stop moving. You're asking them to change their ancient way of life."

"So you build some huts, plant some crops, and cultivate some fruit trees. You learn by trial and error. A failure would be disastrous, so you invoke the local deities. If there are none, you make some up, and establish some rituals around them that connect to the heavens. Everything depends upon the weather. Too cold, too warm, not enough rain, too much rain, migratory pests... you become obsessed with the sky, and where the sun, moon, stars, and planets are throughout the seasons. You begin to set large stones into the ground, precisely aligned to help keep track of the celestial calendar which now rules the agricultural year."

"Now, imagine that you are one of those old time hunters, and your people are suddenly refusing to migrate, and are going to depend on tiny seeds and little fruit trees to survive, which sounds ludicrous to you. You hunters stick to what you know, and follow the herds. You're not willing to risk survival on some superstitious nonsense, as you see it. So you all go away with the big-game herds as usual, invoking the gods of the hunt, and engaging in its noble and time-honored rituals."

"At the end of the season, you return with meat. The people are appreciative, but not like they used to be. The ruling elders of the tribe are now farmers. The settlement is thriving. The crops have succeeded, and has been plenty of local small game and fish. The settlers have built huts made of stones and reeds. They've begun walling off portions of land and claiming it as their own. What's more, they have begun to keep meat-animals for slaughter. You hunters feel that this is a great affront to the gods. You think that it's a cowardly and immoral thing to do, to skip the hunt, and simply murder captive creatures. You feel as though you don't belong to this tribe anymore."

Pippa took a drink of water, then continued.

"It was the end of the old ways, and the beginning of the new ways. The new ways were about cultivation in more ways than one. They were about learning, and being connected to the elements and the heavens. But they also brought about the human desire to profit from systemized brutality, inflicted on other people and on our fellow creatures. That's what the brother-murder story of Cain and Abel represents. The transition to agriculture and civilization came at a great price. That's why we can never go back to that peaceful paradise, but we can try to make our own world more like it."

Treya was astonished by this eloquent and evocative explanation.
"How do you know so much?" she asked in wonder. Pippa smiled and said,
"That lesson was taught to me by Brian Magnus. Mine was a much shortened version."

They sat in silence. After a moment Treya said, "You have a gift, Pippa. I like listening to you. I like hearing explanations from people who know things."
"Like Master Skell," said Pippa.
"Yes," said Treya, "but his explanations are usually very brief."
"That's a gift in itself," said Pippa with a laugh.
"Master Skell said something to me today that I didn't understand," said Treya, tucking the pendant away.
"What did he say?" asked Pippa.
"Mystai."
"Mystai?" Pippa repeated. "What was he doing when he said it?"
"Looking at me," said Treya.
"Mystai means 'initiate into the mysteries', in Greek," said Pippa. She laughed.

"That's a pretentious thing for a library to call its scribe! But then, the Kovskrifva is rather... lofty. And Master Skell has great wisdom. I suppose that comes with the job." She sighed deeply and said, "Different jobs, different qualifications." She seemed a little distracted tonight.

"Is something wrong?" Treya asked with concern.
"No," Pippa replied quietly. "All is well. It's just..." She looked at Treya and said, "I don't suppose you've ever... killed anyone?"

Treya wasn't expecting that. She shook her head. Pippa smiled grimly. "You've heard the tale, how I slew the traitor Pruntus Dax?" Treya nodded.

"I believe that it was the right thing to do," said Pippa. "It seemed like it back then anyway. But now I wonder. At the time, I didn't really feel anything. I thought *that* was strange. I said some prayers that night for the dead man, but I actually felt bad that I didn't feel worse about what I'd done."
"Surely that's because what you did was right," said Treya.
"Well, that's the idea. Brian Magnus said that I had been guided by righteousness. That helped to ease my mind. That and the fact that being a soldier technically absolved me from any repercussion. That's actually part of the Army's contract with the Emperor: if you kill in service of Rome, the Emperor gets the blame. Glory and blame, all go to him."

The night was growing cool. Pippa and Treya wrapped blankets around their shoulders.
"That was long ago, wasn't it?" asked Treya. "Why are you worrying about it now?"
"I think that it's taken me a while to fully adjust to civilian life," said Pippa. "To develop a different perspective. When we were still in the Army, the incident with Pruntus Dax seemed more normal. I mean, it was extremely dramatic, but it was still something that fell within the context of military service. It just seems so strange now, what I did. I think about my dear sweet Arghan. Married to a killer."

"Arghan is so proud of you, Pippa," said Treya. "You know that. And what you did *was* the right thing to do. If I had been in your position, I would have done the same. I would have slain a brutal enemy of King Gwydion if I'd had the opportunity. And the An Dhew would have taken the collective responsibility for it. That's what service is about. Mutual support."
"Thank you for saying so," Pippa replied.
They both grew quiet. Treya was thinking about something disturbing that had happened in her youth, something she had tried to put out of her mind.

"The truth is," she admitted to Pippa, "I was responsible for a death. It was an animal: a rescued rabbit that had been found in our cart-yard. It had an injured leg and couldn't move around. But it was eating and drinking, and seemed to getting better. Our group of An Dhew were moving quarters from an outpost in the Red Sands back to Caer Hudol castle. I was supposed to take care of the rabbit during the transition. It remained at Red Sands while I helped to move the first supply train. It took all day. I stayed at the castle that night."

"I should have gone back to camp the next morning. But I had met some people near our new quarters that I liked very much, and I didn't want to leave. They were musicians, and jugglers and acrobats. They invited us to join them. I'd never had so much fun before. I stayed for another day and night. When I finally returned to the outpost on the third day, the rabbit was dead. I was horrified. I went back and told the others. Some of the An Dhew were upset with me. Most of them didn't seem to care. One was disappointed that I had buried it instead of cooking it. But I felt terrible. I was sad for days. I still am, I suppose."

"It's sad alright," said Pippa, "but I would have probably wound up doing the same thing in your position. I was so alone growing up. If I had gotten the chance to spend time with fun people like that, I wouldn't have let anything stop me. So, you were negligent, but you learned from it. You figured out what's right."

"I suppose," said Treya. "But sometimes, I don't know if I'm good enough. I love the animal friends that I have now. But I feel like I don't even deserve their company. I remember what happened to the poor rabbit, then I think about a creature like Bootchie. What if I had been meant to be taking care of him and had forgotten? And when I think about Pompi and the Lagaloor, and how well they are taken care of... I'm afraid that if Lord Amatheon and King Gwydion had known what I'd done, they would have hated me."

"Treya," said Pippa, "you wouldn't let anything bad happen to our animal friends *now*, because you learned and grew from what you went through. I would guess that the same thing applies to our royal friends. They both did some cruel things in the past. Things that hurt people and creatures. I believe that they have gone through the very sort of crisis of conscience that you did, only on a much more epic scale. Their relationships with Pompi and Fishy are a way to move on, and to reconnect with their true good nature. Like you did."
"I'm relieved to know that I have a true good nature," said Treya. "At least, I think I must have one."
"Of course you do," Pippa responded. "And sometimes that nature gets tested."

"When I was An Dhew," said Treya, "I don't think my nature was truly tested yet. The An Dhew provided structure and security. Confidence. But also, they kept me insulated from the world. When I came here, I thought that I already knew everything about myself that I needed to. But my insulation was gone, and I didn't realize it. Clearly I was an idiot, falling for the first liar I ran into." Treya felt a tear slip down her cheek. Then another.

"Mimi was no ordinary liar," said Pippa. "She was a master of manipulation. And you were susceptible. Because your heart was open, and undefended." Pippa handed Treya a cloth to wipe her eyes with.

"When I first boarded the Awel Glor to come here," Pippa said, "they made me remove my armor. For safety reasons." She smiled. "It makes sense, not to wear metal clothing at sea. But it was unsettling to go without it. I'd worn that protective breastplate for so long. Without it, in those strange new circumstances, I felt exposed and vulnerable. But I think that has to happen to us sometime. We have to lose our armor, and be vulnerable. Otherwise, we risk getting dragged down into the abyss."

"Thank you, Pippa," said Treya. "I'm so grateful to be here with you."

"Mutual support!" said Pippa, giving her a hug.

The following morning dawned clear and bright. It was going to be a ceremonious day. In the early afternoon, King Arthek and the others would be coming to the Kovskrifva for the inaugural official meeting of the Royal Council of the Bridge, where they would finalize the deal. If all went to plan, Treya and the other Councilors would be signing their names, and signifying them with sealing wax. They had each been given a bronze seal, on a silver and blue ribbon. On the end of the seal was their initials. Backwards of course. Treya liked hers. MT and TM. Like a mirror image.

Treya went to the Kovskrifva early, to get her scribing done before the meeting. Lugarn wasn't there, below or above. Master Skell was at his desk.
She said, "Good day, Master Skell," as usual.
"A good day to you, Treya Meynack," he replied.

He didn't look up, so she continued to her desk and sat.

There was a new assignment waiting for her:

Ornithomancy and Augury, an Illustrated Practical History.
By Occul of Lugdunen, Praefectus Augeres
Contents:

Basic Ornithomancy
Augury and inauguration- auspicious and inauspicious omens
Feathers and flight- wing shape, airflow, group movement
Tracking movement patterns- dexter, sinister, lagomorph, convex, concave, and mirrored
The birds eye view- casting the attention upward and gazing down
Templums and quadrants- using the lituus to apportion and examine the skies
North verses South- a cultural overview of alignments
Left to Right- utilizing instinct to guide reason
Right to Left- employing reason to temper instinct

The Languages of Birds
The calls of the sea birds- gulls, plovers, pipers and terns
The calls of the singing birds- larks, nightingales and moorhens
The calls of the small birds- sparrows, wrens, robins, and blackbirds
The calls of the raptors- hawks, kites, and falcons
The calls of the unearthly birds- owls, cuckoo, flageolets, and mockingbirds
The calls of the growling birds- jays, jackdaws, magpies, crows, and ravens
The exalted realm of the death eaters- buzzards and vultures
The supreme rulers of the sky- eagles and their portents
The birds and the cosmos- the planets, moon, sun, and stars, and the latitudinal shift of the skies
What birds see and hear- beyond the human spectra of light and sound

Principles of Augury
Augury: magical divination, or mere natural observation?
Recognizing patterns- seasonal, annual, and epochal
Messages from the Gods- blessings, prophecies and warnings
'Sort Sol' - The black sun, good or bad omen?
Auguries of the future- portents, divinations and petitions
Wearing the hood- protocols for interacting with officials, and with the public

Treya found herself reading the document. It seemed like a good opportunity to learn to identify the winged creatures of the surface world. It was interesting, too, especially the parts about the bird's eye view. There were eighteen pages of densely packed text and images. She began copying the text, leaving spaces for the pictures, which she would put in afterwards. She didn't really care for rendering images, but she often found herself doing it anyway.

When the noon bell rang in the distance, she cleaned her pen and straightened her area. She rose, took the step ladder from its corner, and set it in front of the shelf. The food box was the only thing that the stepladder was used for, yet the step ladder had to be stored in the far corner. It was all a bit of a nuisance. It made sense to have a food box, but why it had to be so high up, or why it wasn't kept in the small alcove, where the eating actually took place, she didn't understand. Treya opened the box. She was pleased to see that the fellows had been enjoying the plum cakes she had brought. She took one out, along with a chunk of yellow cheese, and wrapped them in a cloth. She closed the box and climbed back down. Holding the bundle carefully in one hand, she moved the stepladder back to its spot. Then she slipped into the little alcove. She set her food on the table, washed and dried her hands, and poured a drink of water.

As she ate, she stared out of the narrow window. Seabirds were flying around over the harbor. She thought of what she'd learned about the way that birds moved: dexter, sinister, lagomorph, concave, convex, and mirrored- that meant right, left, moving shape, curved down, curved up, and symmetrical. She watched the birds. She recognized the gulls, razorbills and terns from their pictures. They were hunting for fish, swooping and diving in and out of view. Their movements were erratic. It wasn't much for an ornithomancer to work with. *Still,* she asked herself, *what can be learned from watching them? Well,* she thought, *if birds are catching fish, that would tell the fishermen where to cast their nets.* It seemed quite obvious, but it was still an example of basic ornithomancy.

Treya finished her food, drank the water, and cleaned the table. She inspected the area for crumbs. Then she went downstairs and out back to the privy, which was connected to the Archive by a covered walkway.
It was a strange environment, this secure industrial area of the castle complex. It was bordered by a high stone wall, made of red granite, and topped with spiky flint shards. There were silver and blue uniformed guards posted at the two gates, and more on patrol in the interior. The wide flat stone plateau was covered with brochs and storage sheds. Red-clay irrigation and plumbing pipes snaked off in all directions. There were cisterns, water-houses and wells, and devices with wheels and gates that straddled canals which had been cut into the stone.

Her first day at work, Treya had brought bread and cheese in her sling bag. She had taken a break in the mid-afternoon and gone outside to eat it. She'd sat on a slab of stone near the Archive. The westering sun had brightly illuminated the buildings, and covered the places in between them with squat dark shadows.

Treya had stared, still amazed at the contrast that existed in the visual world up here. Shadows were never so dark underground. In fact, she didn't remember there even being shadows underground, at least not outdoors. Up here they were everywhere, and they were constantly changing, full of strange surprises and distortions.

Her food was nearly gone when she had noticed that one of the guards was approaching.

Treya had stood up. "Hello."

"Well met," the guard had said. "I'm sorry, but no one is allowed to linger here. Or anywhere in the Kolon. It's a security issue. I'll have to ask you to return to the Kovskrifva."

"I understand," Treya had said. "So, this is called the Kolon, the Heart?" She'd waved her arm, indicating the expanse of the compound.

"Yes," the guard had replied, bowing. "Good day to you."

Since then, Treya had eaten in the alcove. She only went downstairs to use the washroom facilities, as she did now. She cleaned up, then went back into the Kovskrifva. Lugarn had returned. He was pulling a large chair up the spiral staircase.

"Lugarn!" said Treya. "Let me help with that." She got under the chair and lifted. It was made of oakwood, and had silver and blue velvet cushions. It was heavy, and barely fit through the doorway. They wrestled it awkwardly into the room.

"What else needs to be done?" Treya asked.

"We've got to combine the tables to make a big one," Lugarn said. "Then we need to bring up the rest of the chairs." Treya helped him to push the tables together into a long rectangle. The King's chair went in the center. Then they went back down and gathered up most of the remaining library chairs, hoisted them up the stairs, and added them to the others. Treya went to her desk and retrieved the stack of placards she had made the week before, when Master Skell had asked her to create the place assignment cards for the meeting. She helped Lugarn set them into little wooden stands around the table.

His Royal Highness King Arthek Gallósek
Councilor Advisor Bruno Marianis
Councilor Advisor Brutus Marianis
Councilor Advisor Arghan Pen Avalen
Councilor Securitor Philippa Agrippa
Councilor Engineer Del Frankus

Councilor Engineer Augustus Nett
Councilor Scribe Treya Meynack
Councilor Mason Cel-Awal
Councilor Master of Trade Edern Pinbren
Councilor Representative Alun A'Dhintagel

The Councilor from Tintagel would have the place of honor opposite the King. Lugarn wiped the tables and chairs with a cleaning cloth. All was prepared.

"I'm going to wait for the royal party," he said, and he went downstairs.
Treya gazed around the room. The normally spacious Kovskrifva looked cramped and crowded.

"Eleven more people," she said. "That seems like a lot to fit in here."
"Yes, it does," said Master Skell. "Especially with the King's chair taking up so much space."

"They come," Lugarn called from downstairs. Treya could hear the people as they entered the building and climbed the stairs. Pippa and Arghan came in first. They smiled at Treya, found their seats, and stood behind them. Treya took the cue and did the same. Her space was already set up with her scribing materials.

One by one the others filed in and found their places. The representative from Tintagel came towards the end, followed by Bruno and Brutus, who looked very impressive in a combination of regal blue and silver courtly gear and their silvery-white Roman cuirasses. They stood on either side of the door as the King entered. Then they escorted him to his chair, and took their own places.

The King sat, and the others did the same. Everyone was silent. Then the King greeted them individually, looking at each one of them with his piercing blue eyes. Treya had been advised by Arghan to not stare at him too directly. When it was her turn, she focused her gaze on the bright red beard that framed his face.

The King spoke to the group.

"Councilors. For too long, we here at Trevena have been separated from our friends on the mainland. It's been frustrating to be so close to each other and yet so distant. The bridge will change that. I'm grateful to all of you for being here. This project is possible thanks to your skill and commitment. Each one of you is essential to its success. And now I will turn the meeting over to our newly appointed Master of Trades, Councilor Edern Pinbren."

"Thank you, Your Royal Highness," said Edern. He pulled a stack of documents from a messenger bag and set them on the table. "Let's begin with the figures." Edern talked about finances, percentages, contracts and record-keeping. Treya made notes as best she could. When Edern was done, the King introduced Alun of Tintagel, who made a short speech expressing the support and gratitude of the mainland community.

When everyone seemed to be in agreement on all of the issues, the negotiations came to an end. Treya had filled two pages. Edern produced the charter, a large decorative scroll, which laid out the conditions and details. King Arthek signed it. Brutus lit the taper and poured some wax, and the King made his seal. The document and taper were passed around the table, and they all added their names and seals. The King thanked everyone.

Lugarn appeared with the blue and silver Trog-Riel, the royal document case. After assuring that the ink was dry and the wax was set, he put the charter inside it, along with Treya's notes, and took it to the vault.

King Arthek rose. The rest of them stood. Bruno and Brutus escorted him out, and the others followed until only Pippa and Arghan remained.
"I'm going to stay a while and visit with Treya," said Pippa.
"Have fun, ladies," said Arghan. He kissed Pippa and left the room.

"That went much easier than I thought it would," said Pippa.
"I think that's because everyone was so well-prepared," Treya replied.

Lugarn went downstairs and reappeared a moment later with two guards, who removed the King's chair. Lugarn collected the placards and put them away. Pippa and Treya helped move the extra chairs back downstairs, and put the tables back in their places. The Kovskrifva was back to normal. Lugarn surveyed the room. Satisfied, he went back downstairs.

"Come and see," said Treya. She and Pippa went over to Treya's desk.
"I'm working on something fun for a change," she said, showing Pippa the new manuscript. "It's about the augury of birds. I was thinking that you might be interested in that."

"I *am* interested in that," Pippa replied. They both sat. Pippa examined the document.
"I've heard about the Augers," she said. "Before I left Ares Mons Training Camp, my Centurion, Aries Erasmus, claimed the birds had predicted that I

would do great things... that I would walk with giants." She grew silent, momentarily lost in thought. "I suppose they were right. Even though that's probably what was said to every new soldier as they started their career."

Pippa began reading the contents page.
"This is really good," she said. "We should have a copy for ourselves."
"I'd like that," said Treya. "I'm not usually interested in what I'm scribing, but this is different."
"Master Skell," Pippa said, turning around. "Is it alright if we copy this for ourselves too?"
"Of course, Councilor," he replied.
"Pippa, would you be willing to draw the pictures on both copies?" asked Treya. "I can fly through the text, but the images really slow me down."
"That sounds like a perfect arrangement," said Pippa. "You fly through the text and I'll fly through the pictures."
"We'll fly," said Treya, "like the birds."

By the end of the workday they had gotten through two-thirds of Basic Ornithomancy. They bade farewell to Master Skell and Lugarn, and went home, tired but happy.

The next morning, Treya and Pippa would have gone to the bridge, but work was cancelled due to the weather. They were all used to working in the rain, and pavilions had been erected on both sides to shelter the work areas. But today was not only rainy, it was also windy, in that sideways, flattening, coastal way that Treya found both astonishing and alarming.

The bridge construction had been progressing at a rapid pace. Apparently, the men who had formerly been hesitant about doing 'hwel-ebron', sky-work, had been chagrined that Treya, a young woman, and a Southron, was one of the first people on the ropes. It had inspired quite a few of them to try it. So, most of the bridge-site construction was done already. The abutments were finished, and now the parts of the bridge itself were being assembled in workshops. The sailors were making the rope sides that would act as the rails.
Since they were not going to the site that day, Del and Augustus took Treya and Pippa to see the sailors at work on the rail-rigs. The rails were too long to fit in any of the dry-docks, where the net-makers usually worked. Since there were no covered workshop spaces long enough to house them, they were being assembled in a very long hallway near the kitchens. They were laid out side by side, so that they could be made simultaneously, and also symmetrically. Each side consisted of a massive cable and harness that held the netted ropes, which were bound together into long expanses of tightly twisted triangles.

"The trusses are designed so that the force is spread out in an axial pattern," said Augustus.

"So there's not one area that's stressed more than the others," Del added.

The sailors worked quickly with strong hands, the muscles bulging in their tattooed forearms. The ropes had been treated with a solution of distilled pitch to make them more resistant to rot. The hallway had a very strong scent. It was a bit acrid, but not entirely unpleasant, although the kitchen staff had complained, and hung tapestries at each end of the hall to block the odor.

They had an early luncheon together in the dining hall. Then Del and Augustus bade them farewell. Treya and Pippa were heading to the Archive, despite the downpour. The two women put on their oilcloths and ventured forth. They were eager to get back to the bird book.

They stopped under the covered walkway to take off their dripping cloaks and make sure they were dried off before going in. Lugarn was downstairs, seated behind a table stacked with texts.

"Good day, Lugarn," the women said in unison.

"Good day," he replied.

They climbed the stairs and entered the room. Master Skell was at his desk. They greeted him.

"Good day, Master Skell."

"Good day, friends," Master Skell replied. *Friends!* thought Treya. *He must really be warming up to us.*

They took their seats and found their places. They were on the chapter titled 'Templums and quadrants- using the lituus to apportion and examine the skies'. There were several pictures of the lituus, which was a stick that terminated in a graceful loop.

"It's pretty," said Pippa. "How does it work?"

Treya read out loud:

"The lituus is the augur's wand. It is a staff with a spiral crook, used to divide the sky into quadrants and mark out the templum, a ritual space in the air. The passage of birds through this templum indicates divine favor or disfavor for a given undertaking. The lituus is also used as a symbol of office for the college of the augurs to mark them out as a priestly group."

"It's a nice shape," said Pippa. "It looks like the head feather of one of King Arawn's fancy ground-birds."

Treya continued:

"The lituus spiral is a manifestation of the Golden Mean. It is a two-dimensional polar coordinate system, a spiral in which the variable of the angle is... inversely proportional to the square of the radius."

The two women looked at each other and spontaneously burst into giggles.

"Did you understand that?" asked Treya.

"Not at all!" Pippa laughed. "But it sounds impressive. I like the lituus. If we're to be augers we'll each need one."

"Perhaps the smiths could make them," Treya suggested.

"I was just thinking that very thing," Pippa replied, smiling.

They resumed their work. All was quiet. Then from below, there came a knock on the door. Treya heard Lugarn open it, say, "Thank you", then close it. He came up the stairs carrying a scroll-box. He brought it to Master Skell's desk, set it down, and then he went back downstairs.

They continued to work in silence. Treya was enjoying it. The room was cool and the task was pleasant, and she was happy that Philippa was there. She concentrated on her scribing.

"Friends," said Master Skell.

It had been so quiet, the sound of his voice was a bit startling. They turned and looked at him.

"This is for you," he said, gesturing to the scroll box. Treya and Pippa rose and approached his desk.

"Open it," he said. Pippa slid the lid off of the box, and Treya took out the contents.

Together, they unrolled it on Master Skell's desk. Treya was intrigued by the feel of it. It didn't seem like vellum or parchment. It was a strange and unfamiliar material, very thin, supple, and odorless.

As they opened the scroll, it became clear that it wasn't a document, it was a picture. Treya stared at it uncomprehendingly. There were some slate-colored shapes, outlined in gold, against a deep blue background. Several squiggly bright blue lines divided some of the shapes. On one of the shapes, not far from its gold border, there was a silver spiral, marked as 'TT'. Concentric circles in translucent red, orange, yellow, green, blue, indigo and violet emanated from three points in the composition, overlapping to create different colors and effects at the interstices. The spiral was at the center of the three points. In the upper right corner, there was a nautical star, with the East on top. A thin silver edge ran around the border of the scroll.

"What is it?" Treya asked, rubbing her eyes. The thing was difficult to look at.

"It's a map," Pippa said, cocking her head. "But it's tilted. This looks like the western Cymric coast, north of Kernow. I don't understand what all the circles are for." She straightened back up.

"Oh!" she exclaimed. "It's a map of Spiral Castle! Isn't it?"

Suddenly, Treya could see that the slate-colored areas bordered in gold represented land, the dark blue parts were ocean, and the squiggly bright blue lines were rivers. The silver spiral must be the castle.
"I see it!" she said excitedly.

Master Skell said, "We had searched in all the books for information about Spiral Castle, and there was nothing. But Treya Meynack gave me the idea to look for a map instead."
Pippa looked at her friend in surprise.
"I was just making a silly guess about what might be in the mystery box," said Treya. "I never thought Master Skell would take me seriously."
"Where did you find it, sir?" asked Pippa, peering at it closely.

"I sent a message to the Kombrogian Harchif," said Master Skell. "The Western Archive. They have an extensive collection of maps. Old maps. That is, old copies of ancient maps. Most of the originals disintegrated ages ago, but they get periodically re-scribed. This one *is* an original though. The material it's on doesn't seem to disintegrate."

He spread his gloved hands over the map. "Guard this knowledge well. Only share this information with your trusted comrades. Do you understand?" He looked at them each in turn, the light bouncing off his lenses as he moved his head.
"Yes, Master Skell," they replied together.

"Thank you," said Pippa. "This will mean so much to our friends who are searching for their family."
"Yes," said Treya. "It's really very thoughtful of you, sir." She ran her finger along the edge of the scroll. It was smooth and light, despite being deeply saturated with pigment.

"Make a copy for yourself," said Master Skell, "and send this original to your friends, on the next ship making trade that way. Do the scribing in the privacy of your quarters. This will not be copied for the royal archives. It really ought not to even be in here. So... go do that now." He gestured. "Take it away. Work on birds next time."

He settled back and resumed his studies. Treya rolled the scroll back up, put it in the box and tucked it into her sling bag while Pippa went back to their desk and tidied up.

As they were exiting, Pippa said, "Thank you Master Skell. If there's ever anything we can do for you, please just let us know."

"I will," he replied, not looking up.

Chapter Four- A Mid-May Meeting

The fall equinox had just passed when the companions at Trevena received a bundle of messages.
The title page, scribed in neat square text on bleached vellum, read:

Dearest Comrades: Pippa, Arghan, Treya, Bruno, Brutus, and Bootchie,
Salvete from your friends here at Vindavia Nova,
and on behalf of our companions to the South, we bid you greetings.
Enclosed you will find messages from all of us.
Marcus,
2nd September, 406.

In neat square black script on a light blue vellum, the first message said:

Hello dear ones,

Thank you for your correspondence. I miss you all very much, but life here is wonderfully busy, so I try not to dwell on it. Congratulations on completing the bridge project. King Arthek must be very happy, and you all must be very relieved. Please send our best wishes to Del and Augustus. It sounds as though they are enjoying being part of the court. Bruno and Brutus too. I'm glad that the King appreciates them.

We were so pleased to hear that the royal births went well, and that Queen Elowen and Princess Merryn are both doing fine. The Royal couple must be so overjoyed to have a son in Prince Benneth, and your brother Auryn and Princess Merryn are clearly delighted with Princess Grassi. And now you two are Uncle Arghan and Aunt Pippa!

Gwynalli grows big with child, and so does Mear. They seem fine, and are well attended to, but Ajax and I tend to hover around nervously anyway. Going on excursions with the King and working with Prince Amatheon on his projects has helped to get my mind off of it. So has the arrival of the amazing map.

Well done, bold heroes!
Love always,
Dmitri

In curvy purple script on pink parchment, the second message read:

Beloved friends,

I was so happy to hear from you. It sounds as if everyone is doing well and keeping busy. Life here is good, although I miss you all so much, sometimes I have to cry. The women say that's normal for an expectant mother, to be emotional. I am so big! Bigger even than Mear, and she's huge. We are both due sometime next month.
Perhaps by the time you read this, we will already be parents!

My dears, I know that you are far away, and very busy, but please come and see us as soon as you can!

Love always,
Gwynalli

In square script on bleached vellum again, the next message said:

Salvete all,
The flocks are well, and Rosa is teaching the new Agassian hound, Lew, how to manage them. Plans for next spring are coming together. Lord G. will tell you all about it in his message.
I am very much looking forward to our next adventure.
Marcus

Also on the same page, in a somewhat irregular script:

Kosins a'an tir gallósek
Friends of the Mighty Land
I am learning to scribe
But I am still better at pictures
I miss you all the time
Rosa and Lew are in love

Dina-Regna

There was a graphite sketch of the two dogs lying together all curled up, heads resting on each others backs. And there was a separate sheet of vellum, covered with a thin layer of parchment. On it were two brown paw prints, one from Rosa, and a rather larger one from Lew.

The lengthiest document was gracefully scribed in purple ink on pale grey vellum with a silver border:

Pippa, Arghan, and Treya,

Hello, dearest friends. What a wonderful surprise it was to receive the map. It is an epic discovery! To answer your query- Yes, it is possible that it originally came from here. It is indeed an unusual substance, but there are some old maps in our archives that seem similarly made.

We think that it was possibly produced by a stone rolling mill that has been in the scribing workshops for many generations. The mill has one side of soft smooth alabaster. The other is hard polished marble. There are geared wheels which alter the space between them by incremental bits. The engineers don't know what it was that actually got rolled, but they are looking into it.

So, our destination seems to be on the Cymric coast, near the ancient hill-fort of Dinas Dinlle, The Lost City. It also translates as 'no-place city'. It is also called the Fortress of Lugh, so named for the Celtic deity of light, language, and learning. However, it is most commonly referred to simply as Bryngaer, meaning Hill-Fort. Apparently it's a very old site.

Pippa has accurately deciphered the TT as standing for Twr Troellog, which means Spiral Tower. As Arghan has noted, there is no tower reported at that location, just the well-documented ancient earthwork. But it may be as you have suggested, that there is something more, hidden from common view. Theon and I believe that the colored circles depict areas and levels of spectral resonance.

Caer Hudol happily approves the plans for a mid-May meeting. And now we have a possible route to take. Because we have also made an epic discovery! We have found the legendary underground Ffyrdd Gwraidd, the Root Roads. They are a two day ride from the Amal, the Edge of the High Meadow. The trail, such as it is, actually leads away from the place with the shrine that Arghan visited with Amatheon and the Gwithy-Yi.

Dmitri and I went with the An Dhew to follow the path. Pompi came with us. He has gotten much bolder and braver about being outside, and he insisted on accompanying us. It worried me, I admit, taking my vulnerable little friend out in the wild world, but he loved it.

It was all so overgrown, the first time that we tried to follow it, we lost the trail before we'd gone half a mile. So we went back and got Theon to help sound it out for us. He went to the shrine, put his head down, and described the next few stages of our route, warning us to avoid areas with bogs, and trees with sharp and poisonous thorns.

The next day we tried it again. We followed Theon's directions. He had said that we would reach a point where it seemed that we could go no further, and that would be the entrance. Sure enough, the overgrown path ended in a dense and impenetrable wall of trees and vines.

There was a small, dark opening in the copse, above our heads. We suspected that this marked the passageway between the surface and the underworld, but we couldn't be sure. It was brave and bold Pompi who confirmed it, by making his way through to the other side, clucking and squawking the whole time, and coming back to report that it was, you guessed it, INTERESTING!

The entrance was so covered up, it took us four days to get it cleared enough for our group to pass through. When we finally did, it opened onto a wide network of tunnel roads, bound by the ancient petrified roots of giant trees that arch majestically over the roadways. The roots are hard and shiny, and resemble marble, or banded obsidian. The massive trees that once grew from these roots have been gone for many ages, destroyed by ice and fire long ago. But down below, their roots still exist, turned to stone. The Root-Roads run for many miles below these massive, arching, ancient structures.

They are proper roads; once we got our cart through the opening, there was plenty of room. There's very little light in the parts we've explored so far, but there are still lush ferns and mosses beside the road, and streams and pools that are filled with small pale fish. Dendron trees and flowering vines grow along the way, intertwined with the petrified roots. There are little grey birds with bright blue caps and long orange bills. They nest in the thickets and drink nectar from the flowers. It is a strange and marvelous part of the underground world.
It's sad to think that we once knew about these passages and that somehow the knowledge was lost.

We followed the Root-Road for many miles. The ground got rockier, and there were big long slabs of stone here and there, but the main roadway continued to be clear. We camped the first night by a waterfall pool.

We discovered that there were glowing rocks nearby, emitting a much paler green light than we're used to at home. The air was humid, and filled with the sound of crickets and frogs. The pool was steaming. The water was warm! Everyone had a nice bath. Even Pompi. The stones beside the pool were warm too. We stretched out on them after bathing until we were dry.

The next morning, we'd only been traveling for an hour or so when things began to change. The road widened, and the thickets began to thin. The ground on either side of the road turned to marsh. We went over the wetlands on a small stone bridge. Then it became hilly. The road wove in and out of the roots.

Up and down we went. The petrified roots were even larger here, arching far away above our heads, and filled with flocks of chattering birds. Then the vista opened up.

The roots had grown so huge that they were virtually the ceiling of this subterranean part of the world.

The road was now lined with apple orchards, stretching into the distance over gently receding hills, all under the enclosure of these colossal ancient roots. The trees are smaller and scrubbier than ours, but it's extraordinary that fruit trees grow there at all with so little light. Dmitri thinks that they might be assisted by a heat source nearby, perhaps the warm water, or something similar to what was in the As Fod.

There were people picking fruit on the hillsides. We soon overtook some orchard-men along the road, pushing an applecart. They hailed us, and we traveled with them. We wound up in a huge central cavern, where several roads converge.

There we found a prosperous little settlement. Tref Gwraidd, Root Town. The entire village fits under what appears to have once been a truly monumental tree. I wish you could see it. It's all worthy of a song, although none have come to me yet. My mind is on other things.

The people of Root Town resemble the Ek. They were strangely incurious about us, although Pompi drew his share of attention.

You would have liked the town, friends. There were several trading posts that sold produce, dishes and textiles. There was also an apiary, a cider brewery, a cooperage, a wainwright, and a smithy. And a travelers inn, called the Mansio, so there's definitely been some Roman influence there. We slept in beds that night. The next day we explored the area, and discovered from some of the locals which roads led to where. I have tried to make good notes so that we can improve our maps.

There are three roads entering the cavern. One is from the southeast coast; that is the one we came in on. The other two go westward. The northern one is an underground trade-route. It comes out at Caer Liwelyd, Lugh's Castle, which is now within the settlement that the Romans call Luguvalium.

The southern path goes very close to our destination, only it's been abandoned because a collapse has blocked the exit to the surface, and it was never used enough to warrant an excavation. Sounds promising, doesn't it? It's said to come out at a place where Afon Carog, Stony River, meets Afon Foryd, the Estuary, just a few miles east of the hill-fort. There is said to be an old mill. Let's meet up there.

We just returned from our exploratory journey, and I am anxious to get this message to you, so I am going to sign off and hand it to the courier. We will continue to investigate the Root Roads. I don't know if weather will allow any more messages between now and the spring.
I look forward to seeing you all in Mid-May.

 My spirit flies with you,
    Gwydion

And finally, there was a half-sheet of the same grey vellum, inscribed with purple ink in a loose, undulating script:

Well met, my worthy companions,

I didn't go with Gwydion on his search. I did listen, though. It sounds nice there, under the roots, but after Innes Eskern, everything sounds nice. The honeycomb they brought back from Tref Gwraidd is the best I've ever had. I wish I could share it with you.

I have been spending more time in the High Meadow, trying to get used to the surface. It's easier now that Tyronius and Kinta are there, and all the animals. I built a pond for them, with a circulating fountain, like the one I made for the Fishy and friends.

Speaking of which, there was a wedding, of sorts. The Lagaloor had somehow been introduced to the idea of nuptials, and two of them wished to be wed. No doubt they had heard how the King had presided while Arghan had married our companions in the High Meadow. They wanted me to be the royal presider. Fishy was the officiator. Wearing his cape and medal, of course. The wedding was mercifully short. Fishy went squeak squeak squeak, and the bride and groom repeated it. Then everyone gave it a hands up, and it was done.

The happy couple have put up a small curtain and made a domicile in the corner of the adjacent room, so we seem to be expanding our realm. I am hoping that the other humans are all too busy to notice.

> *My heart aches when I think about how much I miss you all.*
> *Your faithful friend,*
> *Amatheon*

At the bottom of Amatheon's message there was a trail of inky Lagaloor footprints.

Chapter Five - Auspicious Portents

It was springtime in Trevena. This winter had been much milder than the last. There were still ice storms and freezing winds, but they had been done by late February. The spring rains were early, and then the warm breezes arrived. The trees came on full green, and flowers blossomed and bloomed. Crops were planted and orchards were tended. New lambs frolicked in the meadows, birds filled the trees, and the fields and hedges came to life again.

As usual, the colder months had been spent in story-telling and pastimes. This year, the events had included a small version of a Dressed in Clothing Walk. It took place during the winter solstice celebrations. It was not a competition, just a display. The clothes had a winter theme.
There were gowns, tunics, and trousers, made of cream-colored woolens, with intricate patterned borders of silver, blue, red and green. The Princess designed some of the outfits herself.
Treya had explained to the others about the use of botanical items, so the Walkers wore evergreen garlands on their heads, and were draped with soft white stoles that were accented with holly. The shiny green leaves and red berries were intertwined with strands of silver ivy. Lady Borlowan organized the show, with help from Treya, Pippa, Arghan, and the royal attendants, who appreciated something to work on besides the usual embroidered pillows.

The Walk was put on mostly for the Royal Court, but it was open to the public, and many people came to see what this new event was all about. The Pol Pri family were there to accompany the Walkers with music. There were not only fashions for women and men, but also for children. Even the royal babies were featured, wearing matching ensembles, much to the delight of the crowd.

The little show was very popular, and there was interest in expanding it into an annual event. Treya had received credit for the idea and its success, even though she did none of the actual work. She was relieved that it had gone well. She had been a bit alarmed back at Caer Hudol, when the pressures of the Walk had seemed to make her designer friends go a bit mad for a day or two. There was none of that sort of stress here, and the event was relaxed and enjoyable for all who were involved.

The month of March was warmer than usual, but also more blustery. The hillside orchards were battered, and some of the smaller trees were broken. The coastal air was filled with flying debris, and occasional articles of clothing which had escaped from drying lines. On some days, it was nearly impossible to stand upright outside. The waves hitting the cliffs were so huge that the sea-spray reached the lower levels of the castle. One wild afternoon, three of the smaller boats in the western harbor broke loose of their tethers. They were rescued by bold mariners in sturdy little crafts.

The wind howled constantly, echoing noisily throughout the castle. At first it had seemed eerie and ghostly to Treya, but after a day or two, it was merely annoying. Along with the winds, there had been wild electrical storms, unusual in that they didn't bring rain.
Sometimes there weren't even clouds; the bolts of lightning had appeared in otherwise clear skies.

On an evening in late March, during one of these storms, a different sort of light had appeared, like a blue fire-ball, flashing over the western harbor. Treya was with Pippa and Arghan. They had seen it from the common room, dazzlingly reflected in the choppy sea. By the time they'd gotten to the balcony for a closer look, the strange blue light was gone.

The new bridge was opened for the season on the Spring Equinox. It had been closed since the Winter Solstice, but by then it had already proven to be very popular.
There had been an inaugural ceremony in October. Arghan's mother and father had come from their home in the distant orchard-lands of Pen Avalen. They wanted to see the new bridge, but mostly they were there to meet their new grand-daughter, and to congratulate the King and Queen on the birth of their son.

Treya, Pippa and Arghan had gone with them to visit the royal babies. Princess Grassi was as sweet and fair as both of her parents, with big bright blues eyes, a tuft of light hair, and a round face. Prince Benneth resembled his father. His eyes were a piercing dark blue, and he already had a full head of red hair.

Arghan's mother, Awel Glor Pen Avalen, was kind and friendly, and showed an interest in everyone. She was warm and welcoming, and treated Lowi and Treya like family. She brought gifts of honeycomb and apple jelly. Arghan's father, Sten Pen Avalen, seemed distant, and mostly kept to himself. They only stayed for two days. They had slept in a spare room in the Angove quarters, and had departed before the day of the bridge ceremony.

The ceremony had been well-attended. Everyone was impressed by the way the bridge had turned out. Treya was proud to have been a part of it. The span was a work of art, as well as an example of fine engineering. It looked very good.

The iron anchors were arranged in a geometrically precise fan-shape. The bridge-slats were of polished cedar, and they shone in the sunlight. Treya and Pippa had gone with Del and Augustus to watch the 'unrolling', as the great bundle of roped-together boards had been unfurled across the chasm and secured into place.

The entrances onto the bridge were bordered with standards of silver and blue, and the walkways leading up to them were lined with rectangular slates, densely stacked together horizontally in the Kernowek fashion.
The surrounding areas had been landscaped and planted, and the roads had been newly graded. Benches had been set up along the route, and food vendors and trade stalls had appeared on both sides.

All the Councilors had been present at the opening. King Arthek made a speech, and so did Alun of Tintagel. After the official ceremony, the Royal party went back to the castle. Del and Augustus had accompanied the King, and Lowi had gone with the Princess. Bruno and Brutus had stayed behind to visit with Pippa, Arghan, and Treya.

"Lady Treya," Brutus had said, bowing, "are you well?"
The first time somebody had asked her this, she had wondered if she looked ill. Now she understood that it was just a polite greeting.
"Yes, quite well, Master Brutus," she'd replied, "and you?"
"Very well, thank you, Lady."
"Shall we step over here and see the view?" Bruno had asked.

They had walked to a scenic lookout and gazed at the sea. Then Brutus said,
"We've been talking to Master Skell. We know you're up to something. Another journey. To the north this time."
"Whatever you're planning," added Bruno, "we want in on it."
"Yes, you *must* take us with you," Brutus had agreed. "We wish that we'd gone with you, back to Vindavia Nova. To explore the underground realms. The tales of your journey filled us with awe, but also with envy. We don't want to be stuck here playing diplomat while you're off having another amazing adventure."

"We thought we were going on a routine trade journey," Pippa had responded. "If we'd known it was going to be so amazing, we certainly would have brought you with us."

"This new adventure into the unknown promises to be truly epic," said Arghan. "We'll have some more tales to tell when we're done. Assuming we survive, that is. We'd love for you to come with us. There are no better traveling companions than the Marianis brothers, in all of Albion. But what about King Arthek? I thought that you were happy with your positions."

The brothers exchanged a glance.
"We are," said Bruno. "That is, we were."
"It's a good life," said Brutus, "but it's also a trap. We went all in at first, but by the end of last summer we were feeling stuck here."
"And now," said Pippa, "are you feeling less stuck?"
"Yes," said Bruno. "We're loosened, anyway. In our minds."
"So there's room for new ideas," said Brutus.

"The King doesn't need us as much now," said Bruno. "He has his new Romans. Del and Augustus have more in common with him than we do. And they love it here."

It was true, the two grizzled veterans had achieved a sort of celebrity status here in the west, which they humbly but sincerely enjoyed. The King regularly praised their skills, knowledge, and experience. They had no desire to return to Vindavia Nova.

Bruno added, "If we thought that our leaving would actually be a detriment we wouldn't go. Don't misunderstand, we've appreciated the opportunity to be part of the Court. And the King is very appreciative of us. We're genuinely quite fond of him. But he wants to make us permanent fixtures. He's even talking about finding us wives."
"Do you not want wives?" Arghan had asked, grinning.
"We wouldn't mind," Brutus replied, "but we'd like to find them for ourselves."

Treya already knew from Lowi that the handsome Marianis brothers were much admired among the ladies of the court, and that there was great speculation about whether they would marry.

"As Bruno says, the King doesn't really need us," Brutus had continued. "And we need to be needed."
He'd turned to Pippa. "Amica Agrippa, you were the first one to make us feel as though our contributions really mattered. Then Cassius and Brian Magnus did too. Now we feel wanted, but not really needed."
"We desire to serve a higher cause," Bruno had said.
"Rightfully so," Arghan had replied. "And not surprising, considering your true natures." Treya looked confused. Pippa said quietly,

"Treya, these two are actually the sons of the rogue Emperor Maximus. They are our secret princes."

"That makes sense," Treya had said. "They look and act like fine noblemen."

She looked at them. *They really are gorgeous,* she thought. *And Brutus is very charming.* She didn't think that she was pre-disposed to like men in a romantic way, but being with them still made her feel a bit giddy.

"I would be very happy if you would come with us, noble sirs," she said sincerely.

"Thank you, Lady," said Bruno and Brutus, both smiling broadly.

It was the second week of May. Their ship was being readied for the journey. They were not taking Arghan's craft, the Awel Glor. It was otherwise engaged in trade, and anyway, it was too large for their needs. This was a smaller and sleeker coastal ship, named The Morhogh, Porpoise.

It belonged to the family of Edern Pinbren. She had a shallower keel, a narrower hold, and a smaller berth-space, compared to the Awel Glor. Unlike that bigger ship, there was no raised helm or a chart-room, just a well-worn wooden pilot's bench at the tiller. The back of the bench was covered in carvings of dolphins and porpoises.

The thick and sturdy mainmast had two different sail options, a short one and a tall one. There was a small lookout platform at the top, surrounded by a low rail. From the platform, there was the option of cranking up a mast extension, which could lift the rigging up to accommodate the taller sail. Behind the mainmast, there was a shorter secondary mast, also with a platform, and there was a small foremast near the bow. The booms were high, with a short radius, which limited wide turns, but presented less of a danger to the passengers than the longer and lower booms on the larger ships. There was an assortment of sails, all furled and lashed to the lower railings. The hull was fully straked: all the wood planks were overlapped for water-tightness and riveted.

The bow and rails of the Morhogh were bedecked with garlands of wilted and wind-blown flowers, left over from the extensive Mayday celebrations of the previous week. The mermaid figurehead still wore a drooping crown of yellow roses and pale green ivy.

The ship was being manned by what Arghan had called a 'skeleton crew', which Treya thought sounded unnecessarily grim. Arghan and Pippa had taken her to meet the three Trevena mariners as they were loading the provisions and gear onto the ship. Their pilot was Santo Pol Sten, a short and sturdy fellow, whom Arghan had known since childhood. Santo's face was freckled and tan, and his thinning hair was bleached white by the sun. His heavily muscled arms were covered in tattoos of ships, anchors, and sea creatures.

Piran Glowbrenn had dark hair, cut very short. He wore a silver hoop earring, and a necklace with silver talismans. He was wiry, quick and agile, and he liked to laugh. Piran's daughter Piri was also called Pixie. Her mother was from the western coast of the Wealas, and she and Piran knew these waters very well. She was slim and lithe like her father, with wispy black hair, also cut very short. At sixteen, she was already a renowned sailor, fearless in the rigging, even in the high winds and rainstorms.

After they had been to see the ship, and Treya had been introduced to Santo, Piran, and Piri, she and Pippa had gone walking. They'd climbed the low rise overlooking the western sea, in order to perform some ornithomancy.
"It's strange to be in the western harbour," Pippa said to Treya. "I haven't been here since Cassius and Brian Magnus went away."

They were wearing the hooded Augur cloaks that Lowi had made for them, which were cream-colored with purple borders. They each carried an elegant lituus. Treya's was made of willow, trained into a spiral and attached to a cast bronze handle. Pippa's spiral was of carved cedar, on a handle of finely wrought tin.
Treya was having trouble focusing. She was thinking about the upcoming ship journey. She was dreading a repeat of her previous illness. Pippa had assured her that she would do much better this time, being more accustomed to the surface world. Lowi, who was going too, was bringing tinctures of mint and chamomile, to sooth any sea-sickness. Still, Arghan reminded them, as the sea churns, so does the gut, and there's nothing anyone can do about it. Treya was relieved that it appeared to be a short sea journey to Dinas Dinlle.

She was overjoyed that Lowi was coming with them. It had been a bit of a struggle for all of the companions to politely excuse themselves from court. The Royal family was loathe to let go of Arghan, Pippa, Treya, Lowi, Bruno and Brutus, but they understood that this was a noble cause, and that there was another royal family who was in need of assistance. Fortunately, Del and Augustus had already taken over most of Brutus and Bruno's duties, and Auryn was well positioned to act as Angove, so Arghan was freed up too. Pippa's official duties had ended with the bridge completion, and the Princess and Queen now lived in the world of mothers and babies, so Lowi wasn't needed as much either.

Augustus was upset that Treya was leaving.

"You haven't even been here that long," he had said. " And you came here with *us*. It doesn't seem right that you're going away without us."

"Let her be, Augustus," said Del. "She's young, and primed for adventure. She'll come back." He took Treya by her shoulders. "You'll come back, won't you?"

"Of course I will," she said, moved by their sincere care for her. "And I'll miss you both, very much."

Treya actually felt a bit guilty about going away, when there was a great deal of scribing that needed to be finished. Very little copying was done over the winter months, so there was a backlog. But Lady Kaya, librarian of the Lyverva, had a visiting nephew, name of Jon, and he was a trusted and competent scribe. Treya had been assured by Lady Kaya that he could do the job in her absence.

She had been nervous about telling Master Skell that she would be leaving. She'd announced it to him on May-day. She had gone with Lowi, who was bedecked with flowers, to bring some May-cakes to the guards patrolling the Kolon, and to the two men in the Kovskrifva. While the rest of the realm was celebrating, Master Skell and Lugarn were working away as usual.

"Glad tidings of the May," Lowi had said as they entered, holding forth the cakes.

"Good day," said Lugarn. Master Skell hadn't acknowledged their arrival. Treya had gotten out the ladder. She had put the cakes into the box, and returned the ladder.

"Master Skell, I'm going away," Treya had said, rather abruptly. He'd looked up at her, lenses glinting, but he had remained silent.

"For maybe a fortnight," she'd continued. "But possibly longer. Depending upon what we find."

Master Skell was still quiet. She went on.

"I'm sorry to leave you. Lady Kaya's nephew Jon will scribe for you while I'm away."

"When do you depart?" he had asked.

"Nine days hence, on the morning tide," she had replied.

Now it was just two days hence. Treya had already packed the small trunk that Pippa had given her, and it was being loaded onto the Morhogh with the other baggage and provisions. She had finished scribing her final document, and she had bidden farewell to Master Skell and Lugarn. Lugarn had shaken her hand, and said, "Safe journey." Master Skell had simply nodded to her, then gone back to his work.

Treya and Pippa were performing this Augury in advance of their upcoming journey. Pippa stood facing the sea, and the open horizon. Treya faced the hills, and the cliffs that bordered the west side of Trevena castle. She had never been to the western harbor before. She looked up at the walls of the castle. It was from one of those high terraces that they had thrown Mimi Ryea's clothing. That whole incident seemed like a dream, almost as though it had happened to someone else.

Staring at the sky now, she was feeling nervous. She remembered her An Dhew training, and steadied her breath. She and Pippa stood in silence, back to back, hoods up, each peering into their own templum in the sky that they had mapped out with their spiral wands. According to Occul of Lugdunen, there were conflicting cultural views over whether an Augur should face north or south, so they had decided that since they were a team, they would do both, and compare their findings.

Treya drew a long slow breath and focused her attention. She could hear distant gulls, crying loudly all of a sudden, but no birds had appeared in her quadrant. As she gazed, her mind wandered back to the time she had spent on the peaks over the Red Sands. She recalled the hazy ceiling of the cavern, and the birds that wheeled around near the sky-cracks. Compared to the pale fish-catchers that populated the underground world, they had looked very large. At the time, with their silver-grey plumage and shiny green heads, they had seemed exotic to her. Now she realized that they were common doves. She still thought that they were beautiful, but she understood that they were not considered very exotic at all by most surface-dwellers.

The cries of the gulls became more insistent. Then Treya realized why. A white-tailed sea-eagle had appeared in her templum, flying diagonally from lower left to upper right.
An eagle! Treya thought. *The most auspicious of all the birds, flying left to right. Beginning in the realm of instinct, and becoming rarified through reason.*

Then another sea-eagle appeared! It came from the lower right, and flew towards the upper left. *Right to left: reason is limited until it embraces instinct.* Then they were gone from view.
Pippa exclaimed, "What glorious eagles!"
Then Treya realized that the two birds were flying around both of the Augers.

They soon reappeared in Treya's templum. Practitioners of Augury were meant to withhold divination until after the observations were complete, but Treya couldn't help thinking that sea-eagles ascending in a spiral pattern was an auspicious sign for a journey by ship to find a Spiral Castle.

The templum was empty again. Treya closed it with her lituus. Behind her, she could feel Pippa closing hers too. They turned to face each other. Then they both looked up, their hoods dropping behind them. The two eagles were still circling, climbing higher and higher, until finally they became little specks and disappeared from view. The two friends grinned at each other. Then they went to find their companions, to tell them of the auspicious portents.

That evening, Treya, Lowi, Pippa, Arghan, Bruno, and Brutus had met together in the tavern to raise a glass to the success of their voyage. Then they all went and said goodbye to the Royal family, and to Bootchie, who would be staying with Prince Auryn and Princess Merryn.

The next morning was foggy. The sunrise had been obscured by dense storm-clouds, although there had been no rain as yet. Now the companions were heading to the ship, carrying the last of their belongings. The western harbor was enveloped in a thick mist.

Treya could feel the mist gathering on her head. She shook it, and the droplets flew off. After some attempts at styling her hair, it had been left to grow into a 'hair-cloud', as Arghan called it. As it had gotten longer, the two gathered clumps of hair had become unmanageable. Lowi had tried to tame the cloud into submission, but it didn't work out. Lowi had admitted she'd no idea what she was doing. Meanwhile Treya's hair grew bigger.

The others had praised it.
"It's like a halo," Pippa had remarked. "The light shines through the outer edges. It's so pretty."
"And so interesting," Lowi had added. "My hair is so flat and boring compared to yours." She'd run her fingers through her own reddish-blonde locks.
Treya wasn't convinced. It felt comfortable to have it grown out, but it got in her eyes and made it hard to see in her periphery. Plus, she thought it looked strange.
She'd been considering cutting it all off again, much to the dismay of her friends.
A solution was found, or so they had thought. Several of the Queen's women were dark-skinned. Their thick black hair was fashioned into beautifully coiled braids. Treya longed for such elegance. It was arranged that she would get her

own hair done by these women. It would take several hours, Lowi reported, but then it would last for many weeks, until the hair had grown out so much that it needed to be redone. The braids could be washed, just like unbraided hair, and the new style wouldn't limit her physical activities. It had sounded like an ideal solution.

On the day that she had met with the ladies, she'd been optimistic. At first it was nice. They had gently combed out her hair, and massaged some scented oil into it. But as they commenced their work, the problem became apparent. As soon as they had begun to plait her locks, Treya shrieked in pain. It felt as though they were trying to pull her hair out of her head. There was no way that she could continue. She was dubbed a 'tender-head', and the project was scrapped. It was through no fault of her own, they assured her. Apparently, if one didn't grow up with having one's hair styled, the scalp couldn't take the abuse.

"I'm the same way," Pippa had said consolingly. "When I wasn't on duty, Cassius used to try to pile my hair up in the Roman ladies' fashion. Bound with long ribbons, and stuck with pins. I wanted to please him, but I just couldn't bear it. I complained so much that he finally stopped trying."
A compromise had been reached. Arghan and Lowi devised a 'hair-band', made of thin springy tin, and covered with sky-blue fabric ("to accentuate your eyes," Lowi had explained). It went over Treya's head and tapered behind each ear, holding the hair back with minimal discomfort. So for now, as they began their adventure, the big damp hair-cloud was at least out of her face.

They were walking along the pier. The mist was so thick, they could only see the front of each ship as they passed. Racks holding ropes, poles, and buoys came into view and then disappeared again.

"There she is," said Bruno, pointing at the ship's bow looming out of the fog. A figure was on the deck. As they got closer, they could tell that it was Piran.

"Salve, Piran!" called Brutus.
"The Morhogh welcomes you," Piran responded. Santo appeared and also hailed them. Piri was there too, sitting in a rope sling, half-way up on the mainmast. She waved at them, and began descending.
"Yow, a'Vorhogh!" said Arghan, properly greeting the ship, using the Celtic vocative form, which may replace the initial M with a V. The three sailors came down the gangplank to meet them. The morning light began to pierce through the gloom, illuminating the scene. Steam rose faintly from the boardwalk as the sun's rays reached it.

Treya was talking with Piri. She seemed interesting, and they both were climbers, so they had something in common.

"I'd like a chance to go up the mast," she said to Piri, "if that's alright."

"Fine," said Piri with a grin. "You can help me on the first watch."

"All on board, friends!" called Santo, as he headed up the gangplank. "The tide's just about right."

He whistled shrilly, and two sailors in silver and blue appeared. They began loosening the ship's lines from the mooring posts. Piran and Piri scurried back aboard the Morhogh to prepare for departure. The others all began to head towards the gangway.

"Master Skell!" Pippa suddenly exclaimed.

Everyone looked. Sure enough, Master Skell had appeared out of the fog. He walked up to the group of companions. He was wearing a grey woolen cloak over his usual linen tunic and trousers. The cloak was beaded with moisture, as were his eye-lenses. He had a small bag slung over his shoulder.

"Master Skell," said Treya, "this is unexpected." She smiled at him. "Have you come to see us off?"

"I'm going with you," he replied. Treya and the others were completely surprised. Master Skell walked up the gangplank and onto the ship before they could even respond. They all followed behind. On board, they gathered around him.

"Sir," said Arghan, "you are most welcome to join our company. But... are you certain that you want to come with us?"

"Yes," Master Skell said. "I won't be a burden. I have my own provisions." He patted the little satchel.

"We are happy to share our provisions," said Pippa. "It's just that, this might be a perilous journey. There's a great deal of uncertainty."

"That's alright." He peered at the others through his wet lenses. "I used to have adventures too, you know. I hope you won't begrudge me one more."

"Your presence is most welcome, Master," added Brutus. "And as the one who provided the map, yours is the place of honor."

"Thank you," said Master Skell. "Carry on as usual. You needn't concern yourself with my safety."

"We are equally concerned with the safety of all our companions, sir," said Bruno.

Master Skell went to the bench up in the bow of the ship and sat, quietly waiting.

I wonder if the King knows that he's leaving? Treya thought. *I suppose that means Lugarn is in charge of the Archive now.* She felt a pang of sympathy for the young man, left alone to run the King's archive.

But she was actually pleased that Master Skell had joined them. He seemed to know all sorts of interesting things that might be useful on the journey.

Besides, she realized, *I've really grown quite fond of the strange old bird.*

Chapter Six - A Little Gem of a World

As soon as the lines had been loosened and the Morhogh began floating free, Treya had felt a bit dizzy. As the sailors on the dock used long poles to push the ship out into the harbor, she swayed back and forth. It didn't help that the fog had suddenly grown heavier. Everything around them had disappeared.

Lowi grabbed her and held her firmly. Treya breathed deeply. After a moment, her head cleared. Her feet were steadier now. It was still strange to feel the ship moving, but it was as if her body was now making many constant tiny adjustments to compensate.

"I'm alright," she said. "Thank you." Lowi released her, and she took a few tentative steps. Then they walked from one end of the ship to the other. By the time they returned, Treya was striding confidently through the mist.

"Well then, Treya," said Piri, "if you're up for it... the lookout awaits."
Piri hopped onto the rope ladder that ran the length of the main mast, and began to climb. Treya scrambled up behind her. The ship was moving very slowly, with only the small front sail, and the climb was easy. Halfway up the mast, she glanced downward. Her friends were staring up into the rigging. Lowi waved. Treya waved back. She looked up. Piri was already on the lookout platform, securing herself with a safety line. Treya reached the platform, climbed over the low rail, and sat down. Piri helped to secure Treya's line.

The ship moved slowly as Santo steered them out of the harbor. Treya looked out, but there was nothing to see except the fog. Even their companions on the ship below were obscured. She peered at the deck. Pippa and the twins were directly under them. Treya could barely make out the figures of Lowi and Master Skell, sitting at the bow. Piran and Arghan were readying a sail. Santo was on the tiller. The ship crept along quietly.

"We'll go slow," said Piri. "Anytime there's fog. No matter how long it takes." She looked out into the dense cloud. "Better a long journey on top of the water than a short one to the bottom." She turned and smiled at Treya. "But the destination is actually not too far. If the weather is good, we can get there in a day."
They were approaching the north end of the western harbor. The fog seemed to be lifting. Piri whistled. Piran returned the whistle. "Kler Lew!" called Piri, letting the navigator know that the starboard direction was clear.

Santo called for the sail to be raised. The mainmast sail was attached to the rigging. Santo leaned hard on the tiller. Arghan began to hoist the sail as Piran wrangled the boom. The ship drifted out of the harbor and slowly began to come about.

"Hold on!" said Piri, grabbing the rail. Treya gripped it too. As the ship turned, the sail fluttered and the lines hummed. Then the sail filled. There was a split second where it seemed as though they'd stopped completely. Then there was a jolt, and they were moving.

As the ship picked up speed, a brisk wind began to blow the mist away, and the sun started poking through. Treya could see that they were following the coastline. There were cliffs on the starboard side. Suddenly the fog was gone completely, and the wide sparkling expanse of the western ocean could be seen. As the ship completed its wide turn to the north, Treya gasped at the sheer immensity of all that water and sky.

"It's glorious," she said. She smiled at Piri. But by the time she looked back out at the water, it had completely clouded over again. It was as though a curtain had opened and then suddenly closed. Santo shouted some curt commands. The main-sail was quickly lowered. The ship moved along very slowly. Piri sighed.

"Oh, well," she said, "it was nice while it lasted. Now it's going to be one of those days."
"One of what days?" Treya asked.
"Creeping along, waiting for the sky to clear," said Piri. "Playing it safe. Even though we know these waters, it's not worth the risk of heading out to open sea in the fog. Not after what happened to Donal and Ruory last year."
"Why," asked Treya worriedly, "what happened to them?"

"They left the western harbor in the morning and never came back," Piri responded grimly. "The weather was like it is today; thick, with occasional clear patches. They were headed out towards Ross Harbor in Eire, by way of Raven's Isle. Hauling a fresh catch, and they didn't want to delay. It's really frustrating to have your fish go bad while you wait for the sky to change. They knew these waters as well as anyone. They thought that they could outwit the fog. But they never reached Raven's Isle or Ross Harbor. We searched for them, and sent messages up and down the coast, but no one has seen them since. So we don't tempt the mist. We don't go further than The Shoe when it's like this."

"What's The Shoe?" asked Treya.

"It's a small island with a snug harbor." Piri replied. "Just a few miles off the mainland. It's easy to reach, even in this soup. That's likely where we'll be going now. The Morhogh will be well-positioned for when the fog lifts. Meanwhile, we can explore the island, and Santo can catch some fish."

As she was speaking, the small mast beside them began to creak. Treya looked over the side. Bruno and Brutus had climbed up, and were sitting on the lower platform. They looked up at the two women.
"We'd like a turn up there," said Brutus.
Treya and Piri scrambled over the edge and climbed down.
"Enjoy the view!" called Piri. "I'm jesting, of course, there is no view!"
The two men laughed as they swung over to the main mast and took their place on the watch.

Pippa and Arghan were sitting in the bow with Lowi and Master Skell. Piri and Treya joined them.
"Piran said that we're going to an island called The Shoe," said Pippa. "What's it like there, Piri?"
"There's a good little harbor," Piri replied. "The island is small, but there are some interesting features. It's easy to get around there, even in the fog. And there's usually good fishing, especially if you follow the birds."
Treya and Pippa exchanged a glance.

"What sorts of birds?" Treya asked.
"Oh, too many to name them all," said Piri, "but there are kittiwakes, razorbills, pipits, cliff-larks, oystercatchers, gulls, robins, blackbirds, linnets, ravens and falcons."
"That sounds very fine indeed," said Pippa. "Perhaps the fog today is a gift, sent so that we might have a chance to visit The Shoe."
"Why is it called The Shoe?" asked Lowi.
"It's actually called Ynys Esgid," said Piri. "Shoe Island. Because it's shaped like a shoe."
"You can tell that from sailing around it?" asked Arghan.
"No," she replied, "but it was mapped, long ago. Supposedly by a Greek mariner."
"Oh, maybe it was... whatsisname," said Arghan. "What *was* his name?" he looked at Pippa.
"Pythias," said Pippa. "Pythias of Massalia. Perhaps he's the one who put the Shoe on the map."
"I don't know about that," said Piri, smiling. "The island has an older name, that has nothing to do with footwear: Inys Wair, Gwair's Island."

"Who is Gwair?" asked Arghan.

"It's a local name for Gwydion Dewin," Piri replied. "The Wizard Gwydion."

There were sounds of surprise from the companions.

"Gwydion!" exclaimed Treya. "*Our* Gwydion?"

"*Your* Gwydion!" Piri replied. "What do you mean?"

Treya didn't know how to answer that. It was Arghan who came to the rescue with an explanation,

"Our quest serves a Lord named Gwydion. There may be some family connection."

"All the more reason to visit the island, then," said Piri.

Piran approached, holding a coastal chart.

"We're here," he said, pointing to a spot on the north side of the Kernow peninsula. "Very soon we cross the open water to Shoe." He indicated a small elongated island that did rather resemble an item of footwear.

"The harbor is in the Sawdl, the Heel." He pointed to an inlet on the southeast edge of the island, then ran his finger along the coastal ridge.

"This is Bone, the Arch. And here on the other end of the island is Bis, the Toe. There's a spring-fed pool, here." He indicated a fan-shaped lake, inland, about a third of the way up.

"That's called Gwäeg, the Buckle."

"What's this?" asked Arghan pointing further south and east. "This sort of round shape, here?" He peered at the map and read, "Gwaed y Cawr. Giants Blood! That's got nothing to do with shoes, does it?"

"Perhaps the poor giant has carbuncles!" Lowi exclaimed merrily. The others laughed.

"Gwaed y Cawr once spewed lava," said Piran. "Hence the reference to Giant's Blood. Now the ground just sends up steam and smoke. You can view it from the rim."

He gave his daughter a stern glance. "No further than the rim, Pixie."

Treya had been thinking about the idea of Shoe Isle. Even though it was named by a Greek, it seemed like another connection to the King of Caer Hudol, the Enchanted Shoemaker.

How old is Lord Gwydion, really? she wondered. She ran her finger along the soft trim on one of her blue boots.

"Why is it called Gwair's Island?" asked Treya. "Did the Wizard Gwydion actually visit there?"

"I don't know," said Piran. "It is said that the island has hidden passageways which lead to realms of great beauty and ancient nobility."

"And others that lead to where the demons dwell," Piri added.

While they were speaking, they had entered open water. The sea became choppier. Piran reached into a pouch around his neck and took out a stone. It was clear and rectangular, with angled parallel sides. He held it up to the cloud-covered eastern sky, making small movements. Then he called back to Santo, "We're good, hold course."

He turned to Arghan and said, "Just an extra precaution. The Morhogh knows the way to Shoe."
"What is that?" asked Treya, looking at the stone.
"It's kanndir, kann-dew, double stone," said Piran, handing it to her. The companions passed it around, gazing through it, and marveling at the double image it made. Then he put it away again.
"There was one of these on the Awel Glor, wasn't there?" asked Pippa.
"Yes, we have several dozen in Trevena," said Piran. "They belong to the King, officially. The mariners share them. They are extremely valuable. Excuse me, we need to confer with Santo." He and Piri walked away.

"Kann means bright white," said Pippa. "Is dir is a variation of dew, double?"
"Yes," said Arghan. "There are several types of menwow, or men-guw, Spear Stone, but this is the only one that creates a double image. From what I understand, part of the light goes straight, and part of it gets redirected. When you find the two brightest spots that line up together, that's where the sun is."

Master Skell had been watching all this with interest.
"The shape relates to a parallelogram," he said, "just as a cube relates to a square. It's called a parallelepiped," Treya and Pippa exchanged a glance, trying not to giggle at the strange-sounding name.
"A parallel Pippa?" joked Arghan.
"Where did the stones come from?" asked Master Skell.
"The grandsire of Edern Pinbren brought them to Trevena, years ago," Arghan replied. "He'd been in the outer Hebrides, trading tin for hazelnuts and spelt. He met an old mariner from the far north, who showed him these stones and how they worked. Master Pinbren was so impressed that he gave him the entire haul of nuts and grain in exchange for them. The old King was upset at first, about getting rocks instead of food. But he soon recovered when he realized the potential. They've made a huge difference in navigation."

"Fascinating," said Master Skell. "And where, do you suppose, is 'far north'?"
"I don't know," said Arghan. "I never really thought about it."
"Oh," said Treya. "Master Skell, are you suggesting that they come from Thule?"

"I'm just asking the question," he replied. "Interestingly, in Cymraeg, Kann Dir could also be interpreted as the Maybe Land."
"Like the As Fod," said Pippa. "We're going to act 'as if' Thule really exists."

From the mast, Bruno and Brutus cried, "Land ahead!"
Piri called, "Shoe!" from the bow. Very gradually, Treya could see land appearing ahead in the mist. There were massive stony cliffs rising from the sea. The tops of them disappeared into the fog. The hazy brightness of their reflection contrasted with the dark blue water. As the ship approached, it became clear that the cliff-faces were covered with birds. The companions could hear the cawing, squawking, and whistling long before they could see the actual birds that were covering the rocky walls and swooping through the air. There were nests all throughout the cliffs, from the shrubby ground along the narrow shore, all the way to the highest aerie. The dark rocks were streaked white with droppings. Treya and Pippa smiled at one another.

"There must be thousands of birds!" said Treya. She was awestruck by the seemingly endless abundance of life on the surface.
"Porpoises!" called Master Skell. Treya looked. He was leaning over the bow. His white hair looked like a wispy crown as it blew around his head-band. She and Lowi went to the bow and looked down.
"Oh!" cried Lowi, "how wonderful!"
There was a small group of the energetic creatures, happily swimming in and out of view, diving under the ship, and occasionally leaping into the air.

The ship had very slowly been picking up speed. The sailors prepared her for another turn. The twins cried, "Kler!" to signal that there were no obstacles.
Santo, Arghan, Piran, and Piri brought the Morhogh about to starboard. It went easily enough. Now she was closely following the shore. The cliffs grew nearer. Birds of many different species were swarming the rock-faces. Some were fishing in the shallows. Others were diving in deep water.
The cliffs receded again, and the ship passed some massive humped rocks, giving them a wide berth. The air was filled with a strange honking sound.
"Morloi!" called Piri, pointing to the biggest rock. It was covered with hundreds of grey seals, all lounging together.
"They're so sweet!" cried Treya.
The seals mostly lay on their backs. Many of them lifted their heads to view the companions with their dark soulful eyes. Their flippers moved gently back and forth.
"They're waving at us!" exclaimed Lowi. The women waved back at them. The ship passed the large rock, and then went by several other sea-boulders, where the sleek creatures were diving and fishing.

"Portha kler," Piri's voice called from above. Treya looked around. Bruno and Brutus were back on deck, and Piri had resumed her post. Arghan and Piran were wrestling with the sail. The wind blew in short swirling gusts, harrying the mariners, but doing nothing to reduce the fog. It took a while to bring the ship around to port. Once they did, though, it was instantly calm, and slightly less foggy. The small front sail filled ever so gently with air. The others were furled, and loose lines were stowed as they made ready to dock.

The ship glided across the calm misty waters of the little harbor, Santo expertly working the tiller. They floated until they came to a stop against a stout wooden pier. Bruno and Brutus jumped off, and Piran and Arghan threw them the ropes. They hauled the ship alongside, and secured the lines. Piran dropped the anchor. The chain made a sharp clicking sound as it unrolled.

Arghan prepared the gangway. Santo grabbed his fishing gear from behind the tiller, and set his line off the stern. He and Piran were staying with the Morhogh. Treya joined the others as they followed Piri off the ship and onto the misty island.

They had spent their day sight-seeing.

By late afternoon, the fog still hadn't cleared, and they'd become resigned to spending the night in the harbor. By the time the companions returned from their journey around the island, two fishing boats had joined the Morhogh at the dock. The Shoe seemed to be a popular spot for ships seeking refuge. Apparently it was a good place for fishing as well. A camp-kitchen had been set up on the beach. As they had entered the misty harbor from their hillside trail, they'd heard the sound of voices. And then there was the wonderful aroma of food cooking.
"Oh, smell that!" Bruno had cried.
"Mmm," Lowi had said, "it smells delicious!"

The group had gravitated to the campfire, where four men were busy cooking. There was a construction of greenwood sticks arranged over the flames. The spits held sizzling packets of fish, which were wrapped in sea vegetables. Two blackened iron pots were set up on the coals. Whatever was in them was bubbling and steaming. There was also a griddle where flatbread was baking.

The fishermen had greeted Piri and her friends.

"Master Santo told us that you'd be a-wanting to eat," one of them had said.

The spits were removed from the fire. A plank was set up, and their contents were emptied onto it. The scorched green skewers were thrown back onto the fire. The blaze burned so bright that for a moment the fog began to hiss and draw back.

They ate white cod, stuffed with leeks and mussels, seasoned with grated dried lemon and salt, all wrapped up in crispy charred kelp. There were also steamed limpets and whelks, hard-boiled bird-eggs of various sizes and colors, sea-cress, spelt-flour flatbread, cheeses, and sauces made with horseradish and dill. Treya especially liked the candied chestnut compote, which was preserved in a sticky old honey jar. To drink, there was beer and apple cider. The apple cider tasted good, but it was very potent, so Treya mostly drank water from her bottle.

The water from the Buckle, where they had all filled their containers, was still cold. The wide dark pool was not far from the little harbor. It had been the first destination on their day-trip. They had followed a narrow trail from the beach, which went up a long flight of natural stone steps before joining a slightly broader path.

The climb had been steep, and the landscape was rugged. Treya had been worried about Master Skell being able to keep up with them. Bruno and Brutus must have had the same concerns, because they flanked the elderly man whenever possible.
But Master Skell was fine. He moved steadily along, with a stride that was short, but resolute. Lowi had been more winded by the climb than he had. Treya had shifted her attention to her friend. They proceeded arm in arm up the hillside.

The companions had passed some green fields, and arrived at a stone circle. The monoliths looked eerie, sticking out of the mist. Nearby were some old tumbled-down stone huts. They seemed to be uninhabited.

"The ground is moving!" Lowi had cried, pointing at a dark patch near the old huts. Treya peered. There were hundreds of little creatures busily running around, their mouths full of vegetation.

"They're mouse-headed voles," Piri had said. "They tunnel under the ground. They come up to gather grass-seeds. That's when the hawks get them." Lowi had shuddered and moved away from the huts.

The group had continued up a narrow path. Soon the ground had become covered with mossy boulders and ferns. When they had reached the Buckle, they rested on the rocky edge of the deep, still water. Piri and Pippa had removed their shoes and gone wading in the ice-cold shallows. Lowi stuck a finger in and shook her head. That was fine with Treya. She had no desire to get in the frigid pool.

Gwair's Isle was only about three miles long and a mile or two across. After stopping at the Buckle, they had hiked through the mist to the north end, where the island narrowed. The wind blew fiercely across the Toe, and the fog was dispersed just enough so that they could see their nearby surroundings. They were on a thin spit of rocky land, covered with patches of stiff grass, and a few bent, scrubby trees. The ground dropped dramatically down to the sea on both sides of the narrow stony point. The east side was filled with large rocks and what looked like a myriad of small coves. On the west side, massive towers of jumbled up stones jutted out of the water.

"It's just like Trevena!" Arghan had shouted over the wind.
Treya looked at her companions. Their hair and clothing were flapping wildly. She could feel the wind flattening the top of her own thick hair.
"Come on!" Piri had cried. "I'll take you to where it's not like Trevena."

They'd followed her as she led them back down the hill. It was a relief to get away from the fierce wind. They had returned to the Buckle, where they drank again and refilled their bottles. Then they took a path that ran in between some big ridges of stone, switching back and forth. They'd climbed for a while, moving eastward and southward. The path had become a jumble of winding stone steps. Before they reached the top, there was a sharp odor.

"Ew!" Lowi had cried, covering her face with her cloak. "What's that smell?"
"Sulphur," said Arghan.
The ground had turned to a dark and porous stone that felt slightly crunchy underfoot. They were climbing up a barren slope.

"Gwaed y Cawr," Piri had announced when they reached the summit. "Here we are. Keep away from the edge, or it'll suck you under. It's like quicksand, but with stones."

They had stood at the rim of a large pit. It was completely filled with pebbles, the large egg-shaped ones that often appear along the southern coasts. Yellow wisps of sulfurous steam rose from under the pebbles and disappeared into the white fog.

"Giant's Blood," Treya had said. "I was expecting something more interesting. These are just ordinary beach pebbles."
"They are *not* ordinary," Master Skell had retorted gruffly.

Goodness, I didn't know he was so sensitive about rocks, Treya had thought.
"I intended no disrespect, Master Skell," she had said. "I just mean that they're commonly found."
"They're mysterious," said Pippa. "Even though they are beach pebbles, the first time I encountered them was near High Falls, which is many miles from the sea."

"Each one is a little gem of a world," Arghan had said. He picked up a shattered stone and held it up in the mist. "The broken ones reveal the light and color within."
As he spoke, a breeze had swirled around them and blown the fog away. The sudden brightness of western sunlight and blue sky was dazzling. The big pile of stones glowed, the muted colors gleaming against the blackness of the pit.

"Oh, they look like pretty jewels!" Lowi had exclaimed. "It almost makes up for the smell."
The others laughed. Treya had picked up a broken chunk of purplish-green stone near her feet and given it to Lowi. Lowi had kissed it and put it in her pocket.

"It's clear now," Brutus had said, gazing out at the wide western sea.
"But look at the fog in the north," said Bruno, pointing. "We've never seen anything like *that*."
The fog had gathered up into a large swath of mist at the north end of the island. It had risen vertically, high up into the air, and was slowly expanding outward.
"It's just having a stretch," Piri had commented. "Give it a moment, it will lay back down."

Sure enough, the pillar of cloud had soon descended, collapsing in on itself, gradually spreading the fog back over them. They had picked their way back down the stone steps, and returned to the harbor.

They slept on the ship that night. Treya, Lowi, Pippa, and Master Skell took the four berths, at the insistence of the others. Treya and Lowi weren't going to argue about it, but Pippa and Master Skell resisted.

"We know you're all capable of sleeping rough," Arghan had said, "but we want the four of you to have the beds. We ask this because of our respect for you." That was hard to argue with. Treya felt a little strange at first about camping with Master Skell in the tiny cabin, but the other women seemed quite comfortable with him. The two double berths were tucked up into the front of the bow-hold. The area was dimly lit by a small hanging lamp. Lowi was bunked over Treya, and Pippa was above Master Skell.

"I know it's late," said Lowi from her berth, "but does anyone want some cheese? I've stuffed it with some of that chestnut jam that we had at dinner. It's pretty good."
Treya put up her hand and Lowi passed her a chunk of the sticky treat. It was too messy to bite, so she stuck it in her mouth all at once. The sweet, cheesy, and nutty flavor combination was delicious.
"Mmm," she murmured, "it's so good!"
"Pippa?" asked Lowi, holding forth another chunk.
"I already cleaned my teeth," said Pippa plaintively. "But that sounds so tempting! Alright, thank you, Lowi." She took the chunk and nibbled on it. "Yum!" she cried, finishing it off.

"Master Skell," said Lowi, "how about you?"
The elderly man's face appeared. For once he wasn't wearing his lenses, and his milky blue eyes looked normal sized.
"Thank you, Lady Borlowan," he said, "but I must decline. At my age, I have to be careful, especially when traveling. My digestive system is very particular. That's why I have these." He reached into his satchel and produced a bar. In the dim light, it looked to be an unappetizing greenish-brown color.
"What is that," asked Lowi, squinting.
"It's made from powdered kelp and ground flax-meal," said Master Skell. "The royal kitchens make them especially for me."
"Oh!" exclaimed Lowi. "That sounds... healthy."
"Would you like one?" The elderly man smiled as he held up the bar in his gloved hand.
"No, not right now, thank you," said Lowi. "Or ever, unless we've quite run out of everything else!" The others laughed.

"Master Skell," said Pippa, "I just want to say that we are grateful for your good company."

"Yes, we're so happy that you came with us," Treya assured him sincerely.
"If we'd known that you were interested, we'd have invited you from the start."

He might be gruff sometimes, Treya thought, *but that's just his way of being helpful.* She felt sorry for him, with his aging eyes, injured hands, and tricky digestion. She lay back in her berth, thinking: *We seem to be all that he has in the world. How sad it must be to grow old alone.*

Treya was roused from her sleep by a clicking sound. It was morning. It took a moment for her to recall where she was. Then she realized that the noise was the chain being wound as the anchor was raised. She sat up. There was a bright little shaft of sunlight on the floor, coming from the open hatch. She looked around. The others were gone. She stretched, dressed, and went up top. She stopped at the privy and the wash-station, then greeted Santo at the helm before joining the others at the bow.

Lowi was standing with Bruno and Brutus. "Hello, sleepy-head," she said, kissing Treya on both cheeks. "Look at this beautiful day!"

Treya gazed out. They were heading north, up the east side of the Shoe. On their left were high cliffs swarming with birds. They passed dark sea-caves and golden beaches. On the starboard side, the morning sun lit up the water, refracting on the bright ocean, and creating a vast sparkling pattern of blue and gold. It was almost too much to take in. Treya shielded her eyes. She noticed that Master Skell was sitting in the shadow below the starboard railing. She went over and sat next to him, taking refuge from the sun. It was an instant relief to be out of the brightness.

Arghan came over to the bow.
"Here," he said, handing her a cup of porridge. "We saved you some breakfast." She sat in the shade and ate a little porridge. She wasn't really hungry, and she still felt sleepy. Perhaps it was from the movement of the ship. She glanced at Master Skell. Behind the thick lenses, his eyes were closed. *He's sleepy too,* Treya thought. She shut her eyes.

After a few minutes, she could hear increased activity on deck. Piri called from the lookout. There was the creaking of a mast, and the sound of a fluttering sail. Treya could feel the ship make a wide sweeping arc that began to take them northeast, but then turned to the northwest. She could tell that they were on the open water. The waves made an insistent chuck-chuck-chuck sound as they slapped the hull.

Treya opened her eyes. Master Skell hadn't stirred. She got to her feet. Most of the others were gathered in the shady area near the mast, looking at the map. She went over and stood with Lowi.

They gazed at the nautical chart. Treya could see that they needed to go past a big peninsula, by way of Inys Hollt, Cleft Island. Then there was a smaller peninsula. Then there was a lot of water to cross.

Pippa yawned. "Nothing to do but wait," she said. "I think I'll take a nap."

"That sounds like a fine idea," said Treya. Lowi nodded.

Treya glanced over at Master Skell. He seemed comfortable where he was. The three women went back below and climbed into their bunks.

Treya woke up once or twice. She could feel it when they entered the channel between Albion and Eire. The sound of the waves changed, and the choppiness became irregular. She groaned quietly.

Lowi heard her. "Sit up, Treya," she said, as she reached in her bag and pulled out a little bottle. She removed the cork stopper and handed it to Treya.

"Chamomile and mint," said Lowi. "Just in case." Treya took a sip. It was light and soothing. She took another, then returned the bottle to Lowi thankfully. She lay back down and went to sleep, as the waves thumped away against the hull.

Someone up top was shouting. Treya opened her eyes. Pippa was gone. Lowi was still sleeping. Treya didn't move. Arghan appeared at the hatch, saying, "We're nearly there."

Treya dragged herself out of bed, and then woke Lowi. The two of them went up topside.

It wasn't nearly as bright out. It was mid-afternoon, and the sun was already beginning its descent in the western sky. The others were standing at the starboard bow, staring at the shore. Piran was standing on the bowsprit. Treya looked up. Pippa was with Piri on the lookout platform. Treya would have waved, but Pippa was also staring at the shore, and Piri was looking straight ahead. The ship was following the coast on the starboard side. The cliffs had transitioned into a rocky hillside, dotted with wildflowers. Great patches of bare stone alternated with dense copses of trees and grass-covered marshy dunes, scattered with red deer.

"There it is!" called Piran. At the same time Piri cried, "Bryngaer ho!" The others were pointing at the hill-fort. Treya stared. On the ridge above the shore there was a low earthwork, upon which the roof of a small stone structure could be seen.

"That's Dinas Dinlle?" Lowi asked. "It just looks like a hill."

"Over there," said Master Skell. "It's beginning to fall into the water." Treya could see that the very front edge of the hill-fort had been eroded away.

Dinas Dinlle receded behind them. Piran came down from the bowsprit and joined them.

"We'll shelter in Caern' Arfon Bay," he said. "It's about five miles north of here. There's a road that runs from the harbor to the hill-fort."

By the time that they were anchored, it was late afternoon. They had sailed along the coast for a few more miles. The ship then turned to starboard. The crew executed several more turns, and they were docked. They had tied up at the far end of the boardwalk. There were four other ships at anchor.

The harbor was a securely run business operation. There was a stall selling food and gear, a washroom, and a fresh water supply. There was even a little watchtower, overlooking the entrance to the port. For a daily fee, a ship could shelter at Caern' Arfon indefinitely.

Treya and Pippa went with Arghan to meet the harbormaster and pay for a week in advance.
"It's two days short of the Ides of May," Arghan said. "So we may be early. Surely this won't take a week, but better safe than sorry."

He also gave coin to the crew of the Morhogh, who would be waiting here while their companions journeyed to the hill fort. Piri was staying behind with her father and Santo. Treya was sorry that she wasn't coming, but she understood that it was for the best. The ship needed its crew, even in port, and besides, it would be difficult to try to explain what they were doing.

Treya didn't really even understand what they were doing. Somehow, they were going to look for a hidden tower near that lump of rock they had passed by, and then climb it to find the long-lost Lady Arianrhod. And then see if she knew how to find the even longer-lost Sira Conn, who was said to be in far-away Thule, a place that might not even be real.

But first, they had to find Lord Gwydion, Marcus and Dina. They were real enough. The thought of seeing them again made her smile. One more night on the ship, and the adventure would really begin.

Chapter Seven - Strength in Silliness

They set out the next day. Treya and Pippa had gotten up early to view the birds from the bow of the Morhogh. Arghan, Master Skell, and Lowi had watched with them. As they held up their augury wands, the first rays of the sun were just beginning to pierce through the morning mist.

They heard the birds before they came into view. A hawk was being confronted by two ravens. The ravens would dive at the hawk, then the hawk would quickly threaten the ravens, one at a time. There was a great deal of loud squawking. Eventually the hawk flew away to the north and the ravens to the east.
"What do you suppose it means?" asked Treya, closing her templum. She pulled down her hood.
"Well," Pippa replied, doing the same. "They had a conflict. It seemed like things would get violent, but they never did. Then they went their separate ways. Is there something to conclude from that?"
The women were silent, staring at the peaceful sky.
"Maybe," said Arghan, "it means that if we run into trouble, we need to not let it escalate into violence. We should temper instinct with reason, like your bird-book says."
"That sounds like good advice," said Master Skell.

After breakfast, the companions prepared for the trek. Cuirasses were retrieved from the hold, where they had spent the sea voyage. Light provisions were packed.
Their copy of the secret map was concealed in an inner pocket of Pippa's tunic.
Brutus and Bruno showed them all the route they would be taking overland to the hill-fort. They used two local maps, which differed slightly, especially along the coastline. Over time, it had become clear to them that having more than one map of a region was useful, as they often had errors, or were incomplete, or features had changed.

They all studied the route. It looked simple enough. Then they hoisted their gear. Bruno and Brutus had brought ropes and hooks, just in case. Everyone carried a light bedroll, a rain cloak, and a portion of the rations. They were ready.

"Meur ras, a'Vorhogh," Arghan said, bowing his head towards the front of the ship. "Meur ras, a'Vorhogh," they all repeated, thanking the Morhogh for the safe journey. They exchanged farewells with the sailors.

"Good luck finding your friends," said Piri.
"In anticipation of your success," said Piran, "I'll be securing some woolens and furs for the northern journey."

Piri gave all the women a hug. Then she climbed up to the high lookout and waved goodbye as the group left the harbor. Treya was excited, but also a little nervous. This was a genuine adventure into the unknown, the sort of thing she had dreamed of. Now that it was real, she had a fluttering feeling in her stomach.

It was a clear, sunny morning. The boatyard was busy. Some farmers had arrived in a mule-cart, and were setting up a produce stand near the entrance. Children and old men were fishing from the pier. Small boats were shuttling back and forth. A big ship was leaving the port. It was nearly out of sight, but Treya could still hear the sailors' cries and the flapping of sailcloth.

The friends marched out of the harbor, after hailing the man on the watchtower. The plan was to head south, following the ridge road, which gradually went down to the coastal route that would take them to Dinas Dinlle. The road was in need of repair, but it was wide. The downhill walk was easy, and they made good time, politely going past a man and a woman who were riding up in the front of a small cart. They were hauling a large millstone, carved with grooves and geometric shapes. It was lashed to the creaking carriage, which was being pulled very slowly by two large oxen. Treya marveled at the size of the huge decorative wheel.

"That's a fine mill-stone, friends," Arghan said to them as they passed.
"Aye, indeed," said the man. "It's bound for Melin Afon Foryd."
"Is that where you're headed too?" asked the woman, eyeing them with friendly interest. Treya looked at her companions. *I suppose we must be a curious-looking mix,* she thought, *with our Roman armor and weapons, Celtic cloaks and trousers, and Kernow court finery.*

"Yes, eventually," Arghan replied. "First we're going to take in some of the sights."
"Take in *all* the sights," said the man. "You'll still get to the mill before us!"

Everyone laughed. They passed the cart. The creaking sound receded behind them.
"Where is the Afon Foryd?" asked Lowi.
"It's not far from the tower," said Arghan.

"Will you show us?" asked Master Skell. They stopped. Bruno unrolled his map.

"This is the river estuary," said Arghan, pointing to a spot east of the hill-fort. "And here is the mill. Somewhere in this area just south of there is where they will have found the entrance to the Root-Roads."

The map was put away, and they continued on their journey. The sun shone with intense brightness overhead. Treya was grateful that her hair-cloud provided such good eye shade.

The companions stopped at a spring. There was a small waterfall, with an old and worn shrine-stone set into the mossy bank. They drank and washed up, and ate some apples and cheese. Then they filled their flasks and continued southward. The coastal brush and salt-marshes on their left soon gave way to scrubby hills, dotted with small pastures, and little squares of cultivated land. Then the road left the ridge. Now they were heading east along the coastal bluff. The sea sparkled on their right side, bright blue, with occasional large patches of dark shadow near the shore.

"Those look like submerged lands," said Arghan, pointing to the dark patches. "Yes! There are rows of trees, and stone walls, drowned long ago."

Treya stared into the deep, clear water. It did look like there might have once been an orchard.

"Tir Coll," said Bruno, consulting his map. "The Lost Land."

"It's true," Brutus said, "the shore was once much wider here. The hill fort would have been further in from the bay."

"And the cliffs have eroded too," said Bruno. "So it wouldn't have been as close to the edge as it is now."

"It's like Trevena," said Pippa. "There used to be much more coastal land." She stared at the map. Then she reached in her pocket, and took out and opened the copied map of Spiral Tower.

Treya smiled to see it. They had done a reasonable job of copying it, colored circles and all. She had enjoyed methodically filling in the gold and blue areas. The had used some of Pippa's excellent but rather smelly pigments. When they were finished, they rubbed wax all over the map, to seal and protect it. The new map had a faintly-sweet yet rather noxious odor that came from the combination of indigo blue, sulfur yellow, and beeswax.

"So," Pippa said, "looking at both of these maps, the tower isn't actually at the hill-fort, is it?" She pointed. "Here, this circle is marked as Bryngaer." She then moved her finger over a bit. "But on the colored map, the spiral is further over here, near the edge, north and east of the hill-fort."

Brutus got his map out. The placement of the hill-fort was the same as on the other chart, although his called it Dinas Dinlle instead of Bryngaer.

"It makes sense," said Arghan. "Bryngaer gets quite a few visitors. It wouldn't do to have the tower right on top of the earth works, even if it is disguised."

Lowi looked at Treya. Then she looked around at the others.

"Was there really an invisible tower on that hill we sailed by?" she asked.

"It's not invisible," said Arghan. "It's... cloaked."

"Cloaked!" said Brutus. "I thought we were looking for something hidden from view. Do you mean that it's hidden in plain sight?"

"Well, yes," said Arghan. "And no. It uses technology like the lenses we told you about."

"Dewdheks," said Bruno, slowly shaking his head. "Colorful toys that make things invisible. Sorry, not invisible. Cloaked."

"Welcome to your amazing adventure, Marianis brothers," said Pippa. She grinned wide enough to show the gap where her tooth had been knocked out years before.

They put the maps away and continued on the coastal cliff-path. The breeze picked up, blowing drifts of white sand along the shore down below, and rattling the seagrass on the dunes. Some men approached from the opposite direction: five red-faced and wind-weathered sailors, heading back towards the port. The two groups hailed one another as they passed. The road grew narrower. On their left were high stone cliffs, but the view to the south opened up onto the sea and shore. Then the road made a wide curve to the left.

As they came out of the curve, the travelers saw another group of men coming their way. These weren't sailors or millers. They were rough-looking fellows, well armed, road hardened, and dressed in dark homespun clothes. Arghan and Brutus were in the front. Arghan hailed the strangers, and then the companions moved over to the side of the road to allow them to pass. But the strange men stopped, blocking the road. Three of them stepped forward; a short bald man, a tall ginger fellow, and a man whose face was streaked with dirt. The other four men held back.

"What's all this?" asked the ginger man, staring at them. "Who are you?" His eyes were bright green. The skin around them was surrounded with fine branching lines, like some sort of tattoo.

"They're soft-bellied Southrons, by the looks of them," the bald man said.

Brutus replied to the first man, "Who are you, pray tell, that wants to know?"

"We are the Watch," said the ginger man. "Making sure that the roads are kept safe."

"We pose no threat, friend," said Brutus, coming to join Arghan and Bruno.

"We'll decide that!" exclaimed the bald man.

"I don't like them," said the one whose face was smeared with dirt. "They're too clean. They smell like a Roman bathhouse."

"They're Romans, all right," said the bald man, spitting. "They think they're too good for Britannic dirt."

"They don't *all* look like Romans, Araf," said the ginger fellow to the short bald man.

"Enough of them do, Hedyn," said Araf grimly.

"And what if they are?" Hedyn asked.

"Then we deal with them," Araf replied. "Rome is the enemy."

Hedyn looked weary. "Even after all this time?" he asked, staring at Araf.

Everyone was watching this exchange. The two men seemed to have momentarily forgotten about the group of strangers in front of them. Treya glanced at the four guardsmen who stood together. They looked bored.

Araf replied,

"Don't you know me by now, Hedyn? Blood is blood. An eternal bond."

The companions had been caught off-guard by this bizarre encounter.

None of them had spoken. Treya was standing closest to Dirt-face. He smelled like rotten eggs. She took a step back. He took a step forward.

Araf was staring at them again. "If they're not Roman, what are they?"

"They're Southrons," exclaimed Dirt-face. "That's the same as Roman."

"Some of them look Iberian," said Araf. He noticed Master Skell. "And what sort of creature is that?" he added incredulously, pointing at him. "Show yourself!"

Master Skell stepped forward, saying, "I am Skell, master archivist."

"You look like a goose," said Dirt-face, approaching Master Skell. "Take that thing off your head, or I will!"

Bruno and Brutus quickly flanked Master Skell, hands on their sword-hilts. Araf and Dirt-face both reached for their blades. So did three of the men in the background, as they stepped forward. The fourth man held a wooden cudgel.

"HOLD!" a thunderous, growling voice cried out. Everyone froze, startled. Treya looked around in surprise, as did the others. After a moment of confusion, Treya realized that the roaring command had come from Pippa! Philippa Agrippa was clearly agitated. Her color was high, and her eyes were flashing. She strode forward and loudly exclaimed,

"Why do you men waste your lives crying over origins and ancestors? Stop complaining and grow up!"

The strangers were clearly shocked by this outburst. Bruno and Brutus relaxed their sword hands and withdrew a few steps, herding Master Skell along with them. There was a moment of awkward silence.
Arghan took the initiative. He stepped forward, smiling, and said,
"It's understandable that the local Watch would want to know about such a large group of visitors. But we too are watchful citizens of this mighty land, like yourselves, and we are friends to all the good folk who live here."
He looked at his companions. "We come from all over." He pointed to Pippa.
"This friend is a Celt from Sud Est. Her father was a Roman soldier. She has achieved as much, and more."
"She's achieved loudness," muttered Araf. Some of the people on both sides laughed, including Pippa, who was still quite red in the face.

Arghan pointed to Treya.
"This friend of ours is from Kernow, although she also grew up in the south. She is a scribe."
He pointed to Lowi.
"This friend is also from Kernow. Her mother was from Eire. She makes fine clothing." Lowi curtsied.
Arghan indicated the twins.
"These two friends of ours are from the western farmlands, but they were raised to be Roman soldiers. And so they were, and many other things besides." The twins bowed.

He pointed to Master Skell.
"And this good friend is an archivist, working in Kernow, keeping alive the legends of the Celtic tribes."
Then Master Skell pointed at Arghan, saying,
"And this friend comes from the ancient kingdom of Trevena, or at least from some apple orchards near there. He's been to more foreign ports and distant lands than any man here."

"If you're from all those different places, why are you here together?" asked Hedyn suspiciously.

"We are all scholars, on a collective journey of discovery," Master Skell replied. "Chroniclers and students of antiquity, myths and legends, come to see the old places, before they are gone. We are here to visit the Fortress of Lugh, to listen to local tales, and search for artifacts." He pointed to Treya.

"Our scribe here carries writing materials, to copy down stories, which we will then share with others, back in our own lands."

"Scholars," said Dirt-face in disgust. "And Romans. It's no wonder they're so clean."

"Being clean is not a crime," said Hedyn. "And they honor the name of Lugh. That's rare, these days." He seemed genuinely moved by the mention of the Celtic god of light and learning.

He looked at the group of companions and said, "You may pass."

The other two men began to protest, but one glance from Hedyn shut them up. The four men in back instantly relaxed, and stepped out of the way.

"Good day to you then," said Arghan. The companions began quickly moving along the road. The men of the back-guard bowed to the friends as they passed, and one of them gave Pippa a Roman salute, which she automatically returned.

Then they heard Hedyn call, "Wait!"

Now what? Treya wondered uneasily.

The friends turned to face the strangers.

"You collect stories," said Hedyn. "Do you know about Pen-Arth?"

The companions all shook their heads.

"Pen-Arth," said Arghan, "that means Bear-Head. What is it?"

"Pen-Arth is a fierce creature," Hedyn replied, "part man and part bear. He was fathered by Hen-Un, Old One, one of the legendary Hanner-Dynion, the Half-Mortals. They have dwelt below the earth since before the great freeze. They know how to speak to animals. Trees and stones too. They look like regular people, but they move more quickly than most people do. Some of them can even seem to fly, by jumping high into the air. They live for thousands of years. If they don't get killed first, that is. Their flesh is as pink and tender as any man's."

Hedyn glared at Treya and said pointedly, "I'm telling a story. Why aren't you scribing?"

"Oh, right!" she said. "Thank you, sir. 'Hanner-Dynion', is that right?"

She pulled out her graphite stick and pad, and began to take notes. Hedyn waited a moment for her to catch up, then he continued.

"Hen-Un was above-ground, wandering in the deep woods of the western Wealas, when he met an attractive she-bear. The two of them mated, but in coupling with the bear the old man's insides were crushed, and he died soon afterwards. The she-bear was with child. Their offspring was Pen-Arth. He lived alone with his mother in a cave, and she provided for him."

"When she grew old and died, he was all alone. He went forth looking for company. No one wanted him. The bears didn't like him because he was part human, and the humans shunned him for being part bear. That was long ago, but like his father, Pen-Arth is also Hir Fyw, the Live-Long, and he still roams these hills at night, attacking people in their sleep. So pleasant dreams, scholars!"

Hedyn turned and strode off, the others following. Treya hurriedly finished the entry.
'Pen-Arth, Hir Fyw, long-lived, spurned by man and beast, attacks sleepers.'

"Stop!" cried a trebly voice. The men stopped. Everyone looked. This time it was Master Skell who had spoken.
"That was well told," he said. "The story-teller should be rewarded for his fine contribution," he said, pointing at Hedyn.

The companions looked at each other. Pippa stepped forward, reached into her pocket, and pulled out a small bag of coins.
"That *was* a worthy story, noble Hedyn," she said, holding out the coin-purse. "And it *should* be rewarded. I'm glad that Master Skell stopped you in time."

Hedyn hesitated a moment, then grabbed the coins. He began to turn away again. Then Lowi stepped up. She took a bag of dried apples from her provisions and held them out, saying,
"These apples too, perhaps? Sweet, from last harvest." He took those as well, and he turned away, sniffing the bag of fruit and jingling the coins as he walked. His comrades followed him down the road.

The companions resumed their journey in the other direction. They hiked for about five minutes, until they were well clear of the men. Then they stopped to recover.
"Oh!" cried Lowi. "That just about startled the pee out of me. Pardon." She disappeared behind a rock. Several of the others had the same idea. Then they rested on the roadside and drank from their water flasks.

"Gods, Pippa," said Brutus. "What a roar that was! For a moment, I thought Cassius was back with us."
"Me too," added Bruno. "You sounded just like him. I wouldn't have thought it possible."

"It surprised me too," Pippa said. "I don't think I've ever made a noise quite that that before. Perhaps I was channeling him."

"That was well-handled, friends," said Master Skell.

"Yes," said Arghan. "We avoided violence. As the birds suggested."

"You saved the day," said Pippa to her husband, "by being your own charming self."

The others concurred, thanking Arghan for his tact and diplomacy.

"At least we got a story out of it," said Treya.

"A useful story," Pippa responded.

"A gruesome story," said Lowi, shuddering. "Who were those men?"

"I think that they may be descendants of the Dumnonii Cornovii," said Brutus.

"Were they Celts?" asked Treya.

"Yes, they were the original inhabitants of this region," said Bruno, "along with some other tribes. But they resisted the Romans longer than most, and they suffered for it."

"Is that why they were so unpleasant to us?" asked Pippa.

"Probably," Bruno replied. "It was a long time ago that the Roman Army slaughtered all the Druids, but the tribes are still resentful. Understandably so."

"I've heard of the Druids," said Pippa. "They were the spiritual leaders of the Celts. What happened to them?"

"They were all gathered on Ynys Pwynt," Brutus replied. "That's Point Isle, the big island that lies just north of here. The Romans under Suetonius slaughtered every one of them. They destroyed the sacred groves and shrines."

"How horrible!" Lowi exclaimed.

"Gruesome," said Pippa, shaking her head. "And sacrilegious. I thought the Army respected the sacred places."

"By the time they got to this end of the world," said Master Skell, "they had lost the plot."

"That's how Rome punished rebellious people," said Bruno. "The destruction was a response to Queen Boudicca's resistance movement in Sud Est. Submission, obliteration or slavery. Those were the only options Rome had to offer. It was brutal, but standard procedure. Rome established a strong presence here, to deal with tribal uprisings, and western invaders."

"Then, what happened to all the Romans?" asked Pippa.

"Their descendants have integrated into the local population," said Bruno. "Roman cultural presence is still strong in this region, especially to the east and south of here, around Castra Deva. But the Army itself is long gone. It diminished over time. First there were the uprisings in the south. Some of the local garrisons were sent to quell them. Many of them didn't return. Then more troops were taken away to build Hadrian's wall. Many of them were eventually re-posted there. After that, the men were shipped out to fight in Gaul, which further depleted the ranks. Then the rest of the remaining troops were taken by the Rogue Emperor Maximus, to fight his war on the continent."

"And die there," Brutus said sadly.

Maximus was their father, Treya remembered. *What a grim yet noble burden these men bear. No wonder they are so dedicated to service.*

"You seem to know a great deal about it," said Pippa.

"We've been doing research," said Bruno. "Master Skell has helped us. We wanted to know more about our origins. It's part of why we were so keen on coming here with you." He smiled at Lowi. "That, and the pleasure of your company."

"I learned about the regiment at Castra Deva when I was at Ares Mons," said Pippa. "It was called... Valeria Victrix. Verum?"

"Yes," Bruno replied. "Valeria Victrix, the Twentieth. It was part of the Reformed Tungrian of the Second, like we were. All of us attached to a legion that long ago disappeared."

"Perhaps it's just cloaked," said Master Skell. The others laughed merrily.

"There was something about the Valeria Victrix insignia," mused Pippa, brow furrowed in thought. "What was their symbol?"

"A razorback boar," Brutus replied.

"Oh!" said Pippa. "Of course. They're the reason Vindavia Nova has a boar on its crest." She put her hand up to her left shield boss. "To acknowledge our connection to the westernmost edge of the Empire."

"Verum," said Bruno.

"Correct," said Brutus.

"It all seemed so impossibly distant and remote at the time," said Pippa. "I never imagined that I'd be there one day." She smiled and kissed her husband.

"The bear insignia comes from here also, you know," said Brutus.

"Not from Pen-Arth, I hope," Treya said.

"No," Brutus replied, grinning. "At least, I don't think so. Agrippa, do you recall hearing about the cult of the Significator?"

"Yes," said Pippa. "The Significator stood out on the field of battle. He wore the bear's head and skin, and displayed the standard, so that the troops could locate their unit."

"When Rome withdrew from the far west, one of the Significators got left behind, with a small group of men, in the deep forest, where they formed a cult.... wait!" She looked at her shield bosses.

"Do you mean that the bear on our insignia is really a soldier in a bear suit?"

"It appears that way," said Bruno.

"So," said Arghan, "Vindavia had the boar and the bear, but the Twentieth had the boar and no bear. Even though the bear legend came from the Twentieth. That makes no sense."

"There were a great many things about the Roman presence in Britannia that made no sense," said Pippa.

"No sense leads to nonsense," Master Skell replied rather cryptically, "and nonsense was anathema to Rome. They were better at breaking than they were at bending."

Treya laughed. "Are you saying that, across this mighty land, there is strength in silliness?"

"Alítheia," said Master Skell, smiling fondly at her.

"That means 'truth' in Greek," said Pippa. "Master Skell, are you fluent in many languages?"

"A few," replied Master Skell.

They were moving again. Treya and Lowi walked hand in hand.

"What a strange adventure we are on," said Lowi.

"Yes," Treya replied. "And we haven't even done anything... unusual yet."

Over the past few weeks, Treya had related her life story to Lady Borlowan. She had told her about her earliest memories of being on the water, about being discovered underground floating on an old piece of a ship, and about the honor of serving the Royal Family as one of the An Dhew.

She spoke of the time spent sailing the shallow waters of the subterranean rivers, and climbing the cliffs of the Red Sands to get a glimpse of the real sky. She explained about her dedication to the hard-working Princess Gwynalli, who had been left alone to run the kingdom after her great-uncle's death, and about the joy and relief everyone had felt at the return of the Lords Gwydion and Amatheon. Treya also spoke of her gratitude to the friendly visitors who had brought her back to the bright and dazzling world of the surface, and given her a new home.

She had found out more about Lowi too, although there didn't seem to be too much to tell. Lowi was born in Trevena. She didn't know who her father was. Her mother was one of the many seamstresses employed by the court.

Lowi was raised to be one too. However, her natural poise and charm had caught the attention of the one of the Queen's attendants, and Lowi had been offered a position as a ladies' maid. Before joining the Queen's court last autumn, she had spent a year training in the Ysgol Merched, the Ladies School, which was located near the vineyard gardens where Pippa and Arghan had been wed.

After finishing her course, she had been given the title of Lady, and assigned to the Princess.

Sadly, her mother had passed away suddenly, from some sort of stroke, while Lady Borlowan was still in training.

"Oh, Lowi, I didn't know," Treya had said, fighting back sympathetic tears. "I'm so sorry."

"I've come to terms with it," Lowi had replied resolutely. "She was so proud of me, and happy that my future seemed secure. At least she had that before she died."

As the time neared, Treya had divulged more about the reason for the journey. They were on an unusual mission, she had explained, which might involve climbing a hidden tower, traveling a secret underground roadway, or sailing to an uncharted land of ice and fire. It was a lot to take in, but Lowi seemed fine with it. Treya had wanted her to know what she was getting into, and that there would be risks, in case she wanted to opt out. But Lady Borlowan was committed to the adventure. Treya had been relieved by that, but also a tiny bit concerned about bringing her into possible danger. She had been nervous when Lowi offered the apples to Hedyn, but also very proud. She knew that had taken courage.

The companions continued along the coastal path. Some dark clouds had moved in, even though much of the sky was still clear. It began to rain. By the time they had put on their rain-gear, it was pouring. They trudged along, single file, against the partially sheltered cliff-face. After a short while, the rain stopped. The dark purple rainclouds headed out over the ocean and dispersed. A few random drops still fell, but the sky was bright blue overhead. Then a huge rainbow appeared, shimmering over the sea from one end of the sky to the other. A flock of gulls wheeled around beneath it, shining brightly in the sunlight.

Treya smiled. The first time she had seen a true rainbow, she was very excited. But like the rain itself, rainbows happened all the time, and she had actually gotten used to them already. Sort of. She gazed at the transparent color spectrum in the sky. It was still quite amazing. She had learned that the colors were always in the same order, as they were on the secret map. Red, orange, yellow, green, blue, indigo, violet.

Even if they couldn't all be detected, they were there. Arghan had explained to her that the angle of light hitting the floating water vapor determined its color, as it does with gemstones. It still seemed very mysterious.

The travelers continued to follow the coastal ridge. It began to rise steeply. The cliffs on their left were receding. The road was rough here. The path was littered with occasional large flat stones, which were surrounded by deep ruts where carts had maneuvered around them. In several places, rubble had been brought in to repair the ruts, and make the road easier to travel.

"There's the hill-fort," said Bruno. Ahead of them, the path could be seen continuing along the ridge. Above that, there was a broad flat expanse, and on it was the earth-work. It was round, like a wheel. The edge of the wheel closest to the sea was beginning to slide down the cliff.
"I wonder why they built such a massive fort right here," said Arghan, staring down at the shore. "What were they defending?"
"Oh!" cried Bruno, who was out in the front with his brother.
"This might be what they were defending," said Brutus. "Food."

Treya hurried ahead with the others to see. They came to an overlook. The cliffs on the left side had completely receded, and the vista was wide open. The scattered farmsteads on that side had been replaced by a long meadow that covered the valley and gently sloped up the opposite hillside. It was filled with bright pastures, fields of flowers, and crops of young grain.

The crops were planted in a patchwork of shades of green. A shining river wound eastward through the valley, growing broader as it joined with smaller streams along the way. Oak, ash, and chestnut trees grew along the river. Herds of sheep and cows were lounging in the shade. On the far side of the river, on slightly higher ground, there was a long row of stone and timber houses, barns, and silos. The meadow was completely surrounded by crumbling drystone walls. Beyond the walls, it was bordered on three sides by dense woodlands. On the ocean side, the ridge created a protective dyke.

The companions stood and took in the view.
"I didn't know there were so many colors of green in the world!" said Treya. She breathed deeply. The air felt wholesome, and everything looked clean and shiny after the rain.

"Is that where you're from?" Pippa asked the twins. "Down there?" She pointed to the fields.

"Possibly," said Bruno. "It was in a big and lush grain field that one of us got whacked in the face."

"And," said Brutus, "it was from a large and secluded grain farm that we were both sent away with the recruiter to join the Army."

"Justinian!" said Pippa. "He came all this way to get you?"

"He and Atticus both," said Bruno. "They were far from their usual route, alright."

"Justinian couldn't find the way back east," said Brutus, laughing. "He had a guide on the way here, but not the way back. We figured it out for him. It wasn't easy."

"He called us 'exploratores'," said Bruno. "That's how our scouting skills were first discovered."

They all stood in silence for a moment, taking in the view.

Then Pippa asked, "Is this a good spot for a break?"

"Yes, let's eat," said Arghan.

Treya was relieved. She was hot under the rain-gear, and she was hungry. And this was a fine spot for a meal-break, with wonderful scenery and nice smooth stones to sit on. She peeled off her oilskin and then helped Lowi out of hers, setting them out to dry the rest of the way.

Lowi sat upon a rock and removed her shoes. They were good, well-made shoes, Treya noted, but perhaps unsuited to the current situation. They were nothing like her own blue beauties, which were not only comfortable and durable, but also seemed to be water and dirt resistant. She sat in front of Lowi and gently massaged her dainty feet.

I hope Lord Gwydion brings that mysterious shoe bag with him, she thought. She had no idea how he made such perfect footwear appear, but it didn't matter. She just wanted the best for Lady Borlowan.

For lunch, they had cheese, grapes, apples, cress, hazelnuts, and honeycomb. Bruno and Brutus had also brought a bag of sailors hardtack and a jug of weak red wine. The bread that had come from Trevena was gone, and the baked-goods vendor at the harbor was between shipments, so they had resorted to trying the hard flat bread that the Celts call 'bara caled', and the Romans call 'bucellatum'. Arghan had brought a crock of smoked whitefish paste. He and the twins dipped fish-paste onto some broken pieces of the dry slabs and began to eat. The crunching was so loud that the women jumped in alarm. Master Skell chuckled as he nibbled on one of his green bars. The three men resorted to scooping out the fish-paste with their fingers, and dunking the hard wafers into the wine to soften them first.

The companions finished up their repast. Pippa rose and stretched, and rapped her fists on her cuirass nine times, in thanks for a good meal. She took a drink out of her water flask and used a little to rinse her hands. Then she brought it over to the men.

"Here's water," she said. "For cleaning. I'll refill it when we reach the stream." She looked at their grimy fingers, crumb covered clothes, and wine-splattered faces, and handed them the flask. Pippa returned to the others, grimacing comically. Treya and Lowi giggled. The men cleaned up and joined them, and they continued on their way.

Just past their lunch spot, the road converged. On the left, it went down, into the farmlands and river meadows. It looked inviting, but they took the right-hand route, which climbed up to the fort. The path made a steep ascent as it snaked around the side of the cliff. Treya was just beginning to get tired when they reached the top.

They stepped out onto the plateau, into the wind, and made their way to the fort. It was oval shaped, and composed of two walls. *Like the Kovskrifva*, thought Treya, *but with earth instead of stone*. There was a low outer barrier, and a higher one within it. In the center, there was an enclosed area that was more sheltered from the persistent wind, containing a sizable but crumbling roundhouse, a fire pit, and the tumbled-down remains of some sort of walled structure.

They walked around the inside of the circle. They stepped into the roundhouse. The floor was made of slate tiles. Plants had grown up through them, thrusting the tiles up at odd but consistent angles, like ocean waves of stone.

They walked between the earthen circles. Then they went around the outside from west to east, until they reached the part that was beginning to slip away.

"There's the river," said Brutus.

"We're close," said Bruno.

From their vantage point, looking north, they could see the glint of water through the distant trees. They turned and gazed at the sea, before going around the other way, until they reached the collapse from the opposite side.

Then they went to the edge of the plateau and followed it around the perimeter. Behind the western end of the fort, there was a flat open space the size of a training pitch. It narrowed as it went around the curve of the fort, then got wide again.

When they reached the eastern side of the earthworks, it appeared as if this open space had once continued, but was now collapsed. The ground had fallen away, and the cliff-side was jagged and unstable. They carefully approached the edge, avoiding the stinging nettles that grew there, and looked out over the steep precipice. Far below, there were some ledges, piled up with dead trees and scree.

"Agrippa," said Bruno, "may I see your map?"

Pippa retrieved it and handed it to him.

Bruno and Brutus compared the colored map to their own.

"This can't be right," said Bruno. "According to the map, Spiral Tower is here." He indicated the collapsed area in front of them. "But even a hidden tower can't just hang in the air. Can it?"

"No," said Arghan, "I don't know how that would work. But then again, I didn't know how spectrum resonance worked until I saw it."

"Could it have fallen?" Brutus asked, cautiously peering further over the side.

"We'd see something, surely," said Arghan, "The thing would be uncloaked if it fell. Wouldn't it?"

"It can't have fallen," said Lowi resolutely, from a safe distance. "It's here somewhere. That pretty map might not be exact anymore since things have shifted around. We just need to keep looking."

"I like your attitude, Lady Borlowan," said Bruno.

"Maybe we can spot something up here from the road," said Brutus, pointing down to the valley below.

They headed back towards the entrance. As they came around the outer wall, they saw a group of children playing on the western field. They looked clean, well-fed and adequately dressed. Several of them were launching a kite into the air. It appeared to be made of silk or linen. It was shaped like a pair of wings, and decorated to look like a sea eagle.

The kite took flight, the line humming as little hands quickly unspooled the length of the kite string. The companions went past the children, praising the kite. The youngsters did not seem at all surprised to meet such a large and diverse group of people behind the hill-fort.

They reached the road. Treya and Pippa both looked back. The kite was soaring over the scene. The fabric was rippling almost too quickly to observe. Treya could still faintly hear the sound of the string vibrating. The eagle bobbed up and down, high above the Fortress of Lugh, looking out over the western sea.

Chapter Eight - A Great Deal of Eating

"Do you smell that?" asked Pippa, sniffing deeply. "I think the mill might also have a bakery."

They were damp, muddy, and tired. They were still following the Afon Foryd, and knew that they must be nearing the Melin. The road had become an avenue, lined with trees on either side. It ran parallel to the river. They could hear rushing water, but the greenery blocked the view.

The journey through the farmlands had been wet but pleasant. It was peaceful walking through the meadow-valley. They had snacked on the dark sweet bramble berries which grew on the side of the road. Treya was picking one when she felt a sharp pain on her wrist. She thought that she'd touched a bramble thorn, but it burned terribly and wouldn't stop. The others saw that she'd been stung by a nettle. Arghan quickly found some dock and squeezed the juice onto her wrist. It had immediately felt better. She took another look at the two plants, the innocent-looking nettle and the curative curly-leafed dock, for future reference.

Distant farm-workers had waved to them as they passed by. The colors of the grain fields shone vividly under the muted grey sky.

When they had reached the spot where the cliff was sheared, they stopped and stared upward. The hillside was piled up with stones and debris. The others had waited while Bruno, Brutus, and Arghan scrambled over boulders and broken trees until they had reached the cliff wall, but they weren't able to find anything that would help to locate the tower.

They had continued eastward. It had begun raining again, not long after they had reached the broken cliff. It wasn't a hard rain, and it was still a nice walk through the rural scenery. They'd passed some farm-hands, heading the other way, sitting on grass-bales in the back of a pony cart.

"A good day to you," Brutus had greeted them.
"And to you, friends," said one of the workers. "So sorry about the weather!"
Treya had smiled bemusedly. She knew they were being polite, but it still seemed odd to her that people would apologize for the weather, as if it were a wayward child that had gotten into trouble.

The road through the farmlands had been clear and was well-maintained.

So was the trail along the river that they were on now. It had been the journey in-between that had caused some difficulties. The short side-path which connected the two roads had been recently flooded, and was covered with silt and debris. It had been slow going. By the time they entered the river road, the rain had stopped, but they were a mess. They had found a shallow area, and gone out onto a gravel bar to wash off the sticky mud as well as they could, before returning to the road.

"It smells like bread, alright," said Lowi. They all sniffed the air. There was the unmistakable scent of baked grains. Arghan's stomach growled loudly.
"I agree with Master Arghan," said Brutus, laughing.

The trees suddenly opened up, and they saw the mill. The path to it ran alongside the diverted stream of rushing water that powered the water wheel. The mill was surrounded by tall oaks and chestnuts. It was housed in a square stone building which straddled the dark and shining canal that turned the paddlewheel. There was a bakehouse, some storage silos, and several sheds and workshops.

"Linum usitatissimum," said Master Skell, pointing to an enclosed field where geometrically arranged bundles of flax were being retted, or left to cure, before getting processed.
"They're making linen," said Pippa.
"Oooh, lovely," said Lowi. Treya agreed. Good linen was soft like silk, only much sturdier.

The travelers were nearly dry by the time they reached the mill. Outside of the entrance, there were washrooms, with gravity-fed water spigots, a fire-pit, and some rudimentary stone tables and benches. They made use of the facilities, and feeling more refreshed, went into the roofed courtyard. There was a wide stall, where a woman sat behind a plank table. A boy was playing with a short-haired grey kitten on the floor by her feet. Nearby were some more tables and benches. Several patrons were sitting and eating. The shelves behind the woman were filled with baskets and trays of baked goods. The smell was intoxicating.

"You are welcome, travelers," the woman said to them. "I do apologize for all the rain. Please try a sample of our Grapes of Corinth bun while you decide on your order."
She held out a woven cane basket, filled with cut up pieces of sweet bread. Treya was tempted to assure the woman that she wasn't to blame for the rain, but she just said, "Thank you," along with everyone else, as she took a piece.

It was delicious. They all walked slowly in a group from one end of the display to the other, staring at the array of breads, cakes and pies.

"What should we get?" Lowi asked Treya.

"I don't know," said Treya. "It all looks so good."

"Apple cake!" exclaimed Brutus and Bruno simultaneously at the head of the group.

"Agrippa," said Bruno, "they pinched your recipe."

They all gathered around. The cake was the size of a small wagon wheel.

Pippa said, "I don't think I'm the first one to ever think of putting apples in a cake." She got closer to it. "It does look like one of mine though, doesn't it? Mmmm, it even has real cinnamon. Smell that!"

"It brings back memories, alright," said Bruno.

"We'd like this, please," said Brutus to the bread-seller.

"How many slices?" asked the woman.

"All of them," said Brutus."

"Is it alright if we buy the whole thing?" asked Bruno, getting out his coin-purse.

The woman laughed. "Of course. If you and your company would care to be seated, I will bring it out to you."

The companions sat down at an open table. The boy got up and brought them a pitcher of water, a jug of milk, some cups, a spatula, and a stack of wooden trenchers. The kitten followed him busily for a while, then it suddenly sat, yawned, and went back to curl up under the table.

The woman picked up the large board that held the apple cake. It must have been heavy, but she handled it expertly. As she approached, Bruno and Brutus began chanting.

"Apple cake. Apple cake. Apple cake." The others joined them. The other customers stared. The woman laughed as she set down the platter. They devoured the cake. It was declared to be nearly as fine as Pippa's.

The companions relaxed. It was good to have full bellies.

Arghan looked out at the sky.

"It's midafternoon," he said. "We've got four to five hours of daylight left."

"Do you think that's enough time to explore the area?" asked Brutus.

Please say no, thought Treya. She was that tired.

"I'm not sure," said Arghan.

Brutus got up and spoke to the bread-seller, petting the kitten, who was now up on the table. Then he returned, saying,

"We can stay here if we want. They have guest rooms. I'm not saying we should, but at least it's an option."

Bruno was seated facing the front entrance. He suddenly leaned forward and said in a low voice, "I don't want to alarm you, but we are being watched. A cloaked figure just appeared outside, and seems to be spying on us."

They all turned to look. There was no one there.

"It's gone," said Brutus. "If they come back--"

Suddenly a man appeared in the doorway. He was of medium build, with a youthful face, fair hair, and blue eyes. On his chin was a small wisp of a beard. He was dressed in Celtic clothes, and wearing pieces of Roman uniform which displayed the same insignias as Pippa's.

"Marcus!" they cried.

"Friends!" he responded. "What good timing!" The companions greeted him heartily. Lowi and Master Skell were quickly introduced. Marcus sat down.

"Dina will be along shortly," he said. "She'll be so happy to see you all."

"Sorry, we didn't save you any apple cake," said Bruno.

"Don't worry," said Marcus, "we've been here for two days already. Doing some exploring. And a great deal of eating."

"Are you bunking here at the Mill?" asked Arghan.

"Oh, no," Marcus replied. "We have a really nice camp set up just inside the entrance to the Root Road. Well provisioned. You'll like it."

"I assume that Lord Gwydion is there, staying out of sight?" Arghan inquired in a low voice.

"You would think that would be the case," Marcus replied, "but actually he's gone with a group of locals to rescue a millstone that got mired on the path to the river road."

"What?" said Arghan, "He went off with a crowd of strangers, to shift a big stone on a muddy road? I thought that he was going to try to not do anything conspicuous."

"You know," said Marcus, "I did remind him of that. Then he pointed out that since he was here, acting like a regular fellow, and all the other regular fellows had gone to help, it would have been more conspicuous if he *didn't* go."

"That kind of makes sense," said Treya. "But also, he probably thought it sounded like fun."

"Yes, Treya," Marcus said with a laugh. "He *is* focused on the mission. But he's also really enjoying the chance to act like an ordinary person."

Dina suddenly burst through the door. She was still wearing her old woven-grass cape, which looked scruffy but elegant. Beneath it was a tight-fitting short tunic of a mossy blue color and matching leggings, which blended in with the soft blue boots she had received from the Shoemaker. Her trident was stuck into her belt, and she was carrying a basket, which appeared to be full of baked goods. Thanks to her time spent on the sunny surface, there was a little sprinkling of freckles across her nose and cheeks. Her long, pale, wavy hair was sun-bleached to almost white, and fell past her belt-line.

Pippa and Treya squealed with delight, jumped up, and hugged her. Dina greeted the others.

The cloaked figure reappeared. "An Dhew!" Treya exclaimed. They were not wearing a skullcap, just a hooded cloak, otherwise they looked the same.
"Well met, Treya Meynack," the An Dhew greeted her.

Suddenly another An Dhew appeared in the doorway, out of breath.
"They're coming!"
"Let's go," said Dina. "Poor An Dhew, they're trying to keep up with him without being too obvious, but he's not making it easy." They left the courtyard and went back out to the road.

A group of nine mud-spattered people and two harnessed mules were pulling and pushing a cart. In the cart was the rescued millstone. Treya recognized the man and woman from this morning, looking much the worse for wear. The cart's harness yoke was broken, and the oxen were nowhere in sight. Some children and a dog were following the scene with great interest.

The group reached the mill entrance. With a great deal of effort, the stone was coaxed out of the cart and onto the ground. The man and woman thanked the group and trudged off towards the courtyard. The cart was hauled away and the crowd dispersed. It was then that Treya realized that one of the mud-spattered men in the group was King Gwydion.

"There he is!" she exclaimed happily.
Lord Gwydion had been conversing with one of the other muddy fellows. He saw them, and ran over at once, shouting, "Friends! You made it!"

He was dressed in dark homespun linen, with no embellishments. His beard was cut short, and his hair was loosely tied back. He had a farmer's bag slung across his shoulder. Despite the fact that he had one blue eye and one brown eye, and was taller than the other men, he blended in with the locals.
He greeted them all enthusiastically.
"Treya Meynack!" he cried, "look at you!" He kissed her on both cheeks.

"Lady Borlowan." He bowed. "Delighted."

"Bruno and Brutus," he said, grabbing them at the same time. "Well met, well met. Dearest Pippa. Noble Arghan."

"Lord," said Treya, "this is Master Skell."

"An honor, Sir," said Master Skell, bowing.

"You seem familiar, Master Skell," said Lord Gwydion, turning his head to one side and peering at the elderly man. "Have we met before?"

"I cannot say for certain, Lord," replied Master Skell. "I am very old, and do not always remember where I've been or who I've met."

"You and me both, brother!" Gwydion replied with a laugh.

"Before we do anything else," said Pippa, "we want to know about Gwynalli and the baby."

"Babies!" exclaimed Dina. "She had twins."

"What?" cried Pippa.

"Two boys," said Marcus. "They're both fair-skinned, like Dmitri, but with Gwynalli's dark eyes and hair."

Lord Gwydion grinned broadly. "My grand-nephews, named after two of the great heroes of An Tir Gallósek. Cassius Ambrosius Conn-Danu, and Nico Constantinides Conn-Danu. Nico being Marcus's real name of course."

"Oh, how sweet!" Pippa exclaimed. "Cassius and Nico. I'm so happy. And relieved. What about Mear?"

"She and Tyronius have a little girl named Lani."

"Wonderful news," said Pippa. Treya could see her relaxing. She knew that it had been bothering her all winter, not knowing how their friends' pregnancies had turned out.

"Marcus," Brutus said, staring at the man's chin, "I have to ask. When did you start growing that beard?"

"When he was fifteen," said Bruno, snickering.

"Well then, it won't be long now!" said Brutus, laughing in delight at his own wit.

Marcus glared at the two men. "At least I don't *act* like I'm fifteen."

"Don't mind them," said Pippa to Marcus. "They're just jealous because they don't have lovely smooth Greek faces."

"It would be a lovely smooth Greek face," said Bruno, "except for this bit of fungus that's stuck to it." Bruno reached for Marcus's beard. Marcus pushed him away.

"Here, Marcus, let me get that for you," Brutus said, joining in the fun.

A moment later, the three of them were on the floor, wrestling like children, and shouting insults. Arghan, Lord Gwydion, and Master Skell seemed highly amused by the display. The women just shook their heads.

The three men finally collapsed, laughing heartily. Arghan went around pulling them back to their feet, disheveled and out of breath.
"Come along, brave heroes," said Gwydion, still smiling. He turned and headed off down the road, past the mill.

The road was empty, except for them. The westering sun shone through the trees, and sent long shadows across the way.
"Are we going to the camp now?" Lowi asked Treya.
"I think so," she replied. "I hope it's not too far." She could tell that Lowi was tired.

"An Dhew," said Lord Gwydion, "would one of you mind running ahead and asking them to bring the wagon? I think some of our friends are footsore."
One of the An Dhew bowed, then ran down the road and out of sight. Gwydion and the others continued.

"Will we have a chance to return to the mill tomorrow?" asked Pippa. "I'd like to get some more baked goods."
"Yes," said Dina. "It's on the way, coming and going." She smiled and patted her slender torso. "That's why our bellies are so nice and fat."

Lord Gwydion reached into his bag and pulled out a harp. It was made of plain dark wood, and was smaller than the one at Caer Hudol. He played and sang as they journeyed.

"Flow, river flow, and go, mill, go
 That the miller might grind the corn
 That the baker might take it
 And into bread make it
 And feed it to us in the morn"

The song made Treya feel better. Her steps seemed lighter. She looked at Lowi. Lowi smiled and took her hand.
"Again?" asked Master Skell from behind them.
Lord Gwydion sang the verse two more times, and they all joined in. Then he stopped walking. The rest of them stopped also. He put the harp away and said, "Quietly, now."

He glanced up and down the road, then he nodded.

The An Dhew stepped off the side and seemed to disappear. Lord Gwydion went next. The others quickly followed, single file. They found themselves on a rough narrow track that went down steeply into a stony ditch.

The track then traversed the ditch diagonally, and came up the other side, into a thicket of hawthorn trees littered with large boulders.

"Watch out, the trees have fierce thorns," said Dina. "Stay on the rocks."

They climbed carefully over the boulders, doing their best to avoid the spiky branches. Some of the thorns were as long as Treya's little finger.

"Oh, it's got me!" The hem of Lowi's kirtle had been snagged. Treya stopped and carefully undid it.

"They're so sharp," said Lowi, examining the thorn. "I wonder if they'd make good sewing needles." Treya took the dagger from her belt, sliced off five of the spikes, and tucked them into the little box that held her graphite and chalk.

They soon came to a cliff, against which a hill of huge stones had been piled up during some natural cataclysm.

The An Dhew and Marcus carefully pulled aside the massive stump of a hawthorn tree.

"Here we go," said Marcus. "The path is as clear as we could get it, but it's still a squeeze. Mind your head."

Marcus and Dina ducked behind a large boulder and disappeared. Lord Gwydion went next, and the others followed. Treya ducked, stepped through, and came out into a narrow corridor between the stones. When they were all there, Marcus and the An Dhew pushed the gnarly stump back from the outside, almost closing the entrance. Then they slipped in and pulled it into place, obstructing the way, and blocking the light.

Treya's eyes were trying to adjust. They were in a dimly-lit cave tunnel, on a trail full of rocks and debris. As they continued downhill, the path became clearer.

The air was cool, and smelled like wet stone. She breathed deep. It was comforting to feel the damp coolness of the underground again.

There was some faint light up ahead. They came out into a small cavern. Two more An Dhew were there, along with a wagon, and two stocky mules. Friends were hailed and introductions were made. Treya hugged the An Dhew. They touched her hair admiringly. These two still wore their grey skullcaps. She glanced at the other An Dhew, who was wearing theirs again too. They had only removed it so as to not appear conspicuous on the surface, Treya realized.

She joined the other women, who were petting the mules.

"These two fellows are Stowt and Siwr," said Dina. "Stout and Sure. They brought us from the High Meadow all the way here. They're very strong." The mules snorted and stamped, as if to agree.

"Lady Borlowan," said Bruno. "Will you ride?" Lowi nodded, relieved. He helped her up. Treya got in with her.

"How exciting," said Lowi to Treya. "I've never traveled by carriage before."

"There's room for two more," said Marcus.

"I'll ride," Pippa said, climbing up.

"Anyone else?" Marcus looked around. "Master Skell?"

"No," he replied, "I'll walk."

"Well, then," said Lord Gwydion, hopping on board, "I'll ride. Wrestling with that millstone just about wore me out." He settled back and stretched out his long muddy legs.

Marcus stood next to the mules and made a clicking sound. They began to pull the cart across the cavern, and the others followed alongside. The cavern was dim, but they had a bit of illumination. Shards of green glowing rock had been lashed with vines to the front and sides of the cart.

"Are these green lights also made by the dewdheks?" asked Brutus.

"No, you'll see," said Marcus, "these glowing stones occur naturally all over the underground realm."

Bruno turned to Brutus with a smile and said, "Hear that brother? We're in the underground realm. It's a real adventure."

"Speaking of adventures," said Treya to the group, "this is actually the first time that Lady Borlowan has ever ridden in a carriage. It was also her first time on a ship, and in fact her first time ever leaving Trevena."

"Really?" Pippa said with surprise. "I wouldn't have known it, Lowi. You're so... calm."

"I've been trained to remain calm," Lowi replied. "But I've been sheltered. I've never even gone over to Tintagel. I had no reason to. Although now I think I'd like to go there. Even without a reason."

"A brave heart and intrepid spirit," said Lord Gwydion. "Lady Borlowan is a welcome addition to our company."

Lowi flushed at this unexpected praise. She smiled at Treya and squeezed her hand.

They had reached the end of the cavern. There was an archway. On the other side, more faint lights could be seen, and the sound of a stream could be heard. The travelers went through. The air grew suddenly warm.

"The water is mineralized," said Marcus. "And hot. We've been bathing in it."
"Oooh," said Pippa. "That sounds lovely."

As her eyes grew accustomed to the strange pale light, Treya could see that they were entering a wide cavern. It was filled with faintly glowing green rocks, ranging in size from tiny pebbles to huge boulders.
Above them was a roof of massive petrified tree-roots. Living trees filled the spaces between the stone arches. They were hung with vines which were covered in sweet-smelling pink blossoms. Small grey birds with blue caps and long orange bills traveled from flower to flower, drinking the nectar. A stream ran through the trees, wrapping around the boulders and creating small pools.

Treya looked up. There was no discernible day-light, no cracks or fissures. No sky-light at all. And yet there were green plants, and birds. They continued along. The ground itself was illuminated by small, round fluorescent pebbles, and glowed with a faint green light.
"Welcome to the western end of the Root Road," said Marcus.
"And to the bright mossy ground," said Dina.

The four passengers stepped off the wagon. The floor of the cavern was an ankle-deep carpet of moss. The greens, blues and grays of the soft covering were lit from underneath by the fine fluorescent pebbles that covered the ground. They crossed the spongy carpet.
"Oh, it's so soft," said Pippa.
"And so sparkly," said Lowi.

They reached the camp. It was tucked in under an archway, and surrounded by steamy pools of water. The mules were unhitched, brushed, and fed.

A big glowing slab of stone was being used as a low table. There were several oil lamps burning on the table, and on the stone shelf beside the pools. The An Dhew who had gone ahead was putting food on the table: spelt bread, crystalized honey, Corinth buns, flaxseed rolls, hard yellow cheese, a great blob of butter, cress, hazelnuts, pickled red onions, and a crock full of stewed greens and grains.

The companions dropped their baggage gratefully, and the ex-soldiers removed their armor and weapons. Most of them removed their shoes and outer wear. Treya took off her cloak and tunic and draped them over a stone, having made sure that her scribing materials were still dry. They all washed their hands and faces in the warm water and dried them on the soft moss.

"That looks good," said Brutus, gazing at the food.
"Yes, it does," Lowi agreed.
"There's these too," said Dina, unloading her basket. ""Sweet-rolls, onion-buns, and cheesy-bread."
"Wo!" Arghan exclaimed. "What a feast!"

"Oh, and this is for Lady Borlowan, the clothing designer," said Dina, pulling out a bolt of fabric. "The linen merchant was open today. They sold out quickly, but I got there early. It's good stuff; 'het-a beste leenen,' as the lady said. They're Frisians, I think. Like Nehalennia and her doggi."
"Oh, Dina, that was so thoughtful," Lowi said. She took the bundle of cloth. "It's so luxurious! I've never felt such fine cloth. Thank you."
Treya touched it. It was soft and cool and pleasant to the touch.

"Alright," said Marcus. "Let's eat."
They sat on the mossy ground around the table.
"Thank you all for being here," said Lord Gwydion. "Good food for the body, and good company for the spirit. Enjoy!"
The companions grew silent as they focused on eating. Little rustling sounds could be heard coming from under the moss.
"Something's moving!" Lowi exclaimed.
"It's just the little mouse creatures," said Dina. Lowi stood up quickly, startled.
"It's alright, they don't bite," Dina added.
Treya grabbed her cloak from off of the stone and made a seat for Lowi. She coaxed her to sit back down. Lowi did so nervously, her feet tucked up under her.

"They're actually voles," said Marcus.
"We saw voles on the island," said Treya. "Mouse-headed voles, on Gwair's Island." She turned to the King and said,
"Lord Gwydion, they claim that it was your island. That you were also called Gwair. Is that true? Are you Gwair?"
He looked at her thoughtfully. "That takes me way back," he said. "Sira Conn called me Gwair. It means grass. Because I was young and green. I went with him several times to Isle Beag. Little Island. Perhaps that is what you mean?"

Brutus pulled out the map, and showed him the island.
"Is this it, sir?" he asked.
Lord Gwydion smiled and said, "It could be. We took an underground road to get there, and then a boat. I'm embarrassed to admit that I know very little about the geography of the surface. Even the places I've visited. And I find the shifting shorelines and islands to be quite baffling."

"That's understandable," said Dina. "The people who sail ships on the sea and know how to get to where they're going are very clever."

"The island is also called the Shoe, Sire" said Treya, "because of the way its shaped. That reminded us of you also." She was hoping that if he had brought his shoe bag, this would be enough of a hint.
"Oh," said Lord Gwydion, "speaking of shoes..." One of the An Dhew went to the wagon and retrieved the shoe bag. Treya smiled hopefully at Lowi.

"Let's see," said Lord Gwydion, "something nice for Lady Borlowan." He put his head in the bag and reached in.
"Take care of your shoes, and your shoes take care of you," they all sang, except Lowi, Bruno and Brutus, who were encouraged to join on the next repetition.
"Take care of your shoes, and your shoes take care of you."

He poked his head back out, and pulled out a pair of soft and sturdy ankle-high boots, pink with silver buckles. There were little blue floral gems set into the toes and heels. He handed them to Lowi.
"Ohh," she exclaimed. "They're the most beautiful shoes, ever!" She slipped them on. "Ahh," she said, "they're as soft as a cloud! As soft as the moss! I'm so happy! Thank you." She hugged Lord Gwydion. Then she did a little dance before sitting back down.

"Let's see what else is in here," he said, smiling at Bruno and Brutus. He went back into the bag.
"Take care of your shoes, and your shoes take care of you,
  Take care of your shoes, and your shoes take care of you."

He reappeared and handed Brutus a pair of mid-calf boots, moss green with silver clasps, and forest green trim. While Brutus was trying them on, he went back in.
"Take care of your shoes, and your shoes take care of you,
  Take care of your shoes, and your shoes take care of you."

Bruno's boots were built the same way, only they were forest green with moss-green trim. He put them on.

The two brothers stood speechless, gazing down at their new footwear. Treya was surprised to see that they were in tears. Lord Gwydion got up and handed the shoe bag to the waiting An Dhew. Then he went to the brothers and put his arms around them, holding them both tightly for a long moment.

They all sat back down. One of the An Dhew brought out a jug of apple wine. They drank one another's health.

"And a health to the Lady Arianrhod," said Pippa.

"Lady Arianrhod," they drank.

"Now we just have to find the tower," said Bruno.

"Oh, we already found it!" said Marcus. "Our first day here. It's right where the map said it would be."

"But... do you mean that it's really on the side of that cliff?" asked Bruno.

"Yes," Marcus replied, "but more like, *in* the cliff. You get there from the road. There's a sort of terrace. The entrance is in there."

"The circles on the map made it easy to find," said Lord Gwydion. "What an excellent map! Good Master Skell, we are in your debt."

"I'm glad to be of service, Lord," Master Skell replied.

"So, were you able to reach the actual tower?" Brutus wanted to know.

"Yes," said Marcus.

"And?" Pippa replied. "What's it like?"

"It's like something from another time and place," said Marcus. "I can see how it became a legend. It's hard to tell what it's even made of."

"Were you able to climb it?" asked Bruno.

"We went up partway," Dina answered. "But it's really, really tall. It will take half a day to climb. Maybe more."

"What?" Pippa was aghast. "It's that tall?"

"We came to find a Spiral Tower, Agrippa," said Brutus. "Surely you had considered that it might involve climbing."

"I didn't know it would be that high up," she replied, worriedly.

"You climbed to the mast lookout," said Arghan. "That was high up."

"Twenty five feet, at the most," Pippa responded. "Not a half day's climb."

"With all due respect, Councilor Agrippa," said Master Skell, "you'd likely be just as dead falling twenty-five feet as you would falling a thousand."

"That doesn't make me feel any better about it!" Pippa exclaimed.

"It's a mental thing," said Treya. "That's what Augustus would say. It's much more difficult to build the same bridge at two-hundred feet than at twenty. Even if the logistics and mechanics are exactly the same, people's perceptions are affected by great heights."

"You'll be fine, Philippa," said Lord Gwydion. "I know you will."

Pippa didn't seem convinced, but she said, "Yes, of course. Thank you, Sire."
Arghan hugged his wife. "I'm also not looking forward to the climb," he said quietly. "We'll get there, together."

Marcus and Lord Gwydion exchanged a glance.
"There's something you all should be aware of," said Marcus, somewhat grimly. "Before we explored the tower, we had to fix the portal. The mechanism wasn't functioning. There was a lens-key stuck in it, on top of another lens key. It seemed to have shorted out the system. Someone must have been in a hurry, or didn't know what they were doing. And to make matters worse, the fail-safe device had come disconnected from its power source."

"What's the fail-safe device?" asked Bruno.
"It's a separate dewdhek configuration that can be used to deactivate the portal," said Lord Gwydion, "even when the lens keys are in place."
"It's connected to a different energy collector than the main system," said Marcus. "We reconnected it, but there's no way of knowing how long it's been disabled."

Treya asked, "Are you saying that whoever is up there has been trapped, with no way out?" It was a dreadful thought.
Lord Gwydion replied, "I'm afraid that's a possibility."
"Couldn't a person just sort of... push through the illusion?" asked Pippa.
"No," said Lord Gwydion, "not without great injury."

The group was silent for a moment. Treya looked at the King. He seemed sad and tired.
Then Lowi said,
"I'm sure the Queen is alright. She must have everything she needs to survive up there with her."
Treya was once again grateful to Lowi for her positive attitude.

"But, you fixed the portal, didn't you?" asked Pippa.
"Yes," said Lord Gwydion. "The lens keys were not only jammed into the device, they had somehow fused together. They wouldn't come out. We had to break them up and extract the pieces. I had to resort to high frequency interference to get them loose. We created a sonic feedback loop using three lens keys."
"I'm surprised the noise didn't attract attention," said Marcus. "It was so loud."

"But it worked," said Dina. "And now we know what happens if you put two lens keys in the same hole."

"That reminds me," said the King, "I have lenses for Lowi, Bruno, Brutus, and Master Skell." He handed out the pendants. "Everyone else still has theirs, right?"

The others answered in the affirmative.

"We're ready for the tower," said Bruno, admiring the shiny pendant.

"I hope we don't run into those awful men again," said Lowi.

"Hail to that," said Bruno. "I don't trust those ruffians."

"Why?" asked Marcus with concern. "What men? What happened?"

"There was a group of seven men, calling themselves the Watch," said Pippa. "We met them on the road, west of the hill-fort. They were rough, but I don't know that they were actually ruffians, just victims of circumstance."

"That's charitable of you, Pip," said Arghan, "but the one with the dirty face was definitely a scoundrel."

"And the bald one too," said Brutus. "Very unpleasant."

"I might be unpleasant too, if my life had been that difficult," Pippa replied.

"How can you be so sympathetic?" asked Lowi. "They were vile."

"Perhaps Philippa is experiencing some Roman guilt?" asked Master Skell.

Pippa laughed. "Well spotted, Master Skell. Very much so, I'm afraid, especially after learning about the slaughter of the Druids."

"Back to the matter at hand, please," said Marcus. "We saw those same men at the mill. They didn't threaten anyone there. What happened? Did they attack you?"

"They challenged us," Pippa replied, "but Arghan was very charming, and they backed off. Master Skell was charming too. He let them know that we were collecting stories, and then the red-haired man told us one. It was a really good story. I gave him a bag of coins, and Lowi gave him some apples, after Master Skell reminded us to reward him for his offering."

"She's leaving out the best part!" Bruno exclaimed. "Before Arghan had a chance to work his charms, there had been some harsh words, and it had almost come to blows. People were going for their weapons, but Agrippa stopped everyone in their tracks."

"How?" asked Dina with interest.

Brutus replied, "She roared, 'HOLD!' so loudly that it scared us all. It was a thunderous cry. We thought Cassius Ambrosius was back with us."

"That was when I just about peed myself," Lowi whispered to Treya.

"Then she scolded the ruffians," said Master Skell. "Most thoroughly. As if they were naughty little boys."

Marcus said, "Now you can see why we were all a bit terrified of our favorite Centurion!" They laughed.

"When we saw the men of the Watch at the mill," said Dina, "they were stuffing their faces. It must have been after you'd given them the coin."
"That's right," said Marcus. "The bread-merchant made the dirty fellow wash up before coming in. He wasn't happy about it."
"Serves him right," said Arghan.
"I spoke briefly to the red-haired man," said Lord Gwydion. "He was a bit rough, but he seemed alright. He told you a good story?"
"A most useful story," said Philippa.

"How is it useful?" asked Lowi. "It was a bunch of nonsense. A man mating with a bear? And the immortal offspring that might kill us in our sleep? He was just trying to frighten us, wasn't he?"
"He may have been trying to intimidate us," Pippa replied. "But that doesn't matter."
"Then what is so great about the bear story?" asked Lowi.
"Nothing, really," said Pippa. "That's not the useful part. Treya, would you please read the notes you made about Hen-Un?"
Treya went over to her tunic and took out the notepad. She opened it and read,

"The character in the story, Hen-Un, Old One, was one of the legendary Hanner-Dynion, the Half-Mortals. They've dwelt below ground since the great freeze. They know how to speak to animals. Trees and stones too. They look like regular people, but they can live for thousands of years, so they are called Hir Fyw, Long Lived. They are powerful and quick, but their flesh is mortal, and they can be killed."

"So," said Pippa, "it gives us new information about the inhabitants of Alba and their origins."
"Lord Gwydion," asked Marcus with interest, "is it true about the Hanner-Dynion? Do you know? Does that explain your family's longevity?" He glanced at Dina. "And that of the Ek?"
"I've never really thought about it before," the King said, "but I suppose it makes sense."

Pippa said, "It seems to address the issue of why those who dwell underground live so much longer than surface dwellers." She looked at Marcus. "Some of us have been bothered by the question more than others."
"How so?" asked Lowi.

"Marcus is worried that since I am Ek," said Dina, "he won't live nearly as long as me."

There was an awkward silence.

"What I think," said Brutus, "is that he's afraid he won't live long enough to finish growing that beard."

They all laughed heartily at that, Marcus included.

"I'm going for the bath, now," said Dina. "I don't know how much longer I'll be able to stay awake." She stood, stripped down to her underclothes, and climbed into one of the tubs, sliding slowly into the warm water.

"Ahhhh." She lay back, her long hair floating all around.

The others did the same, all except Master Skell and the two An Dhew who stood guard. Treya and Lowi joined Dina in her tub. They eased themselves into the steamy pool. Master Skell sat nearby, reclining on a glowing slab. His eyes behind the lenses were obscured by steam.

"Ohhhhh," Lowi sighed. "How is this even possible?"

"Geothermal vents," said Master Skell. "Or possibly a river of lava somewhere far below us."

Just then several voles ran across the stone next to them.

"Oh!" cried Lowi, jumping back with a splash. "This place would be perfect except for those things!"

The bathers gradually left the pools and stretched out on the warm stones. Treya and Lowi lay side by side. After a few minutes, their underclothes were dry.

"Isn't this fine?" said Lord Gwydion, stretching luxuriantly. "We don't have anything like this back at Caer Hudol."

"It's just as well," said Master Skell. "Settlements that are built near this much heat don't usually last very long."

"I've missed being underground," said Pippa. "I was surprised by how much I missed it. Arghan too. We really want to return to the Two Kingdoms. To see everyone of course. But also, just to spend some time there."

"What's the name of the woods we visited that last day?" asked Arghan.

"The Argos Down," said Pippa.

"That was a special place," said Arghan. "I'd like to go back there."

He yawned.

Treya suddenly realized how tired she was.

The food supplies had been secured and covered in the back of the wagon, to avoid attracting any unwanted scavengers. The mules were sleeping nearby. Two of the An Dhew remained on sentry duty.

The others all laid out their bedrolls and settled in for the night. Treya spread her cloak out, and put Lowi's bedding on top of it, but she was having a difficult time convincing her to lay down. She finally did, curling up into a ball.

"Oh, we should warn you recent arrivals," said one of the An Dhew guard. "There are owls down here. Little ones. They come hunting the voles, just before dawn."
"What?" Lowi squeaked.
"Right, thanks for the reminder, friend," said Marcus to the An Dhew. He turned to the others. "They just about scared the life out of us the first night."
"Even though it's warm," said Dina, "keep your blankets handy. You'll want them to hide under when the hunt begins."
"I'll just start now," said Lowi, pulling the cover up over her head. "Goodnight, all," she said in a muffled voice.

Everyone said goodnight. Most of them went to sleep right away. All was quiet, except for the rustlings of the little creatures running through the bright mossy ground.

Chapter Nine - Up, Up and Up

"Aiiiii!"

Treya was awakened by the sound of a female voice crying in alarm, quickly followed by the noise of running feet, and expressions of concern. Then the voice, Pippa's voice, said,

"Oh! Never mind. Sorry, but... holy cats, that is *not* what I was expecting to see!"

Treya sat up and looked around. Lowi was lying next to her. She was wrapped from head to toe in gauzy white. Treya had helped to wind her into this linen cocoon, quietly, while the others slept, after listening to her whimper for nearly an hour. If the wagon hadn't been full of gear, Treya would have tried taking her there to sleep. The Lady Borlowan was clearly not suited to camping on a mossy ground filled with moving rodents who were awaiting an inevitable pre-dawn slaughter.

The others had all gathered around, except for Dina, who had still been asleep, lying on her back. Awakened by the cry, she sat straight up, took one look, and said, "Ugh. Stop making so much noise." Then she just as abruptly lay back down.

"Aww, Pippa," said Lord Gwydion, who was seated at a stone bench, putting on his boots. "Did you think that Lady Borlowan was getting abducted by a giant spider? Because I did, when I first saw her. Only I didn't scream. But I'm still a bit rattled by it."

"Thank you for saying so," said Pippa.

"She *is* alright, isn't she?" asked Bruno, prodding the wrapped figure.

"Come on, Lowi," said Treya. "Time to get up." She began unwinding the linen. Lowi grunted and pulled the other way.

"Another late sleeper!" said Marcus. "It's bad enough that Dina won't wake up in the morning."

Dina raised her head and glared at him.

"Oh, look," he said, smiling. "She's up."

They ate their breakfast as they got dressed and made ready. They were getting a bit of a delayed start. Mostly due to the late sleepers, who had taken some coaxing. Lowi had finally gotten up, and seemed cheery enough. She had actually slept through the owl attack, which had been brief but quite startling. She was mostly concerned about the state of the linen, but it lay flat, just like new, without a crease. She rolled it up with her bedding.

"Why?" asked Dina blearily, as she put on her overclothes. "Why does everyone have to wake up early? Sailors, soldiers, farmers, bakers, shepherds. Everyone but Queen Sidhi. Doesn't anyone else get to sleep late?"

"Musicians do," said Treya.

"That's true," said Pippa. "One day we went calling on the Pol Pri family just before noon, and they were all still asleep."

"Perhaps I should learn to be a musician," said Dina.

"They sleep late because they stay up late," said Marcus, "and you're not very good at that, dear wife."

The companions bade farewell to the two An Dhew who were remaining at camp with the wagon. They said goodbye to Stowt and Siwr, then slipped out through the opening, closed it again, and they were on their way. After climbing through the boulders and thorn trees, they came out onto the road. They soon arrived at the Mill, where they purchased more bread and rolls, hazelnut cakes, a round of cheese and a large bag of dried grapes.

Then they continued along the river road. The side trail had dried out considerably, and was much easier to navigate. They soon were traversing the meadowlands. They passed several farmers near the mill, otherwise the roads were empty.

When they reached the broken down cliff, Marcus and Bruno took the lead, threading their way carefully through the rubble, on what appeared to be a very rudimentary path. The rest of them followed. They went up a steep and strenuous hill for what felt like a long time. Finally it leveled out and began to open up. They entered a small cavern that extended into the hillside.

From the front, Treya suddenly heard Marcus cry, "Others!".

As she stepped into the cavern, she saw why. Hedyn was there, with the four men of the Watch.

They stood, blocking the way.

Bruno exclaimed, "You lot again!"

"What are you doing here?" asked Hedyn.

"As we explained," Master Skell replied, stepping forward, "we are scholars and explorers of historical sites-"

"I mean what are you doing *here*," said Hedyn, indicating the jumbled hillside. "The historical site is up there." He motioned to the top of the cliff. "What are you doing poking around in a rockslide?"

"Master Hedyn, tell us," said Brutus, "what's so special about this particular pile of debris?"

"Nothing," Hedyn replied.

"Then why do you care what we're doing here?" asked Bruno.

"Because we're the Watch," he replied. He looked back at the four men. They nodded in agreement.

"Where are the other two?" asked Brutus, peering around suspiciously.

"Sleeping off drink," the man with the cudgel said. Hedyn grimaced.

"Those two aren't really part of the Watch," he said. "We just let them think that they are."

"Why?" asked Master Skell.

"So we can limit the amount of damage that they do."

"Commendable," said Lord Gwydion. "Protecting the community."

"How many more are coming?" asked one of the swordsmen, looking at him. "Is this an invasion?"

"These five friends have come from Sud Est," said Arghan. "They complete our company."

The An Dhew, Marcus, Dina, and Lord Gwydion all bowed.

There was an awkward silence.

"We haven't all been properly introduced," said Lord Gwydion. "I am known as Crydd, the Shoemaker. This is Marcus, Dina, Philippa, Arghan, Bruno, Brutus, Treya, Lady Borlowan, and Master Skell." He indicated the two An Dhew. "And they are both called An Dhew."

"I am Hedyn," the red-haired man replied. "This is Amser Gwas," he said, indicating the man with the cudgel. "He is scion of the Guardians." Amser Gwas saluted them. He was taller than the others, with blue eyes and black hair.

Hedyn indicated the other three, who were all of medium height, with brown hair and eyes, and freckled faces.

"These are the Porth brothers, Awyr and Seren, and their cousin Glaw." The men bowed. The companions did likewise. Upon closer inspection, Treya noticed that the other men all had the same fine lines around their eyes as Hedyn. Seren's went all the way down his cheeks.

"Amser Gwas means Time Servant," said Lord Gwydion. "And these are the Gate Brothers: Rain, Star and Sky. And Hedyn is Seed. Such noble names."

There was another awkward silence.

"Is anyone else hungry?" asked Dina suddenly.

There were sounds of affirmation on both sides.

The An Dhew unpacked the provisions, while Lowi and Treya laid out a cloth on top of a natural stone table. Cheese-bread, boiled eggs, nut-cakes and sweet rolls were served. The others were engaging in cautious conversation with the men of the Watch.

"Good food for the body, and good company for the spirit," said Dina, smiling at the King.
They sat on the ground around the stone table.
Amser Gwas produced a wine-skin and took a drink. He offered it to Lord Gwydion, who also took a drink before passing it along.

They ate in silence.
"Seed, Time, Rain, Star and Sky," said Lord Gwydion, as they were finishing. "Why are you called the Watch?"

The men were silent. Then Hedyn said,
"Our forbears were the Watch, and theirs before them."
"And what do you watch for?" asked Lord Gwydion.
More silence. Then,
"We watch for the Queen," said Awyr, "but she hasn't been seen by anyone who still lives."
His companions looked at him with surprise and disapproval.
"What?" he said. "We spend all this time and effort. Because of some tale from our grandsire's day."
Amser Gwas seemed angered by that, but he didn't say anything.
"What tale?" asked Master Skell.

Treya didn't wait to be reminded this time. She got out her scribing tablet and graphite. But the men remained silent.

"It is a long story," said Lord Gwydion. "I'll begin it, and then perhaps you can catch us up."
He drew a deep breath.

"Long ago, after the Great Upheaval, the Wise Ones who had survived wanted to prevent another near-extinction. They looked within the cycles of time, and they discovered that over the next few thousand years, several more calamities would be coming to their descendants, from far-off distant space. The Wise Ones used what remained of their advanced technology to build a tower, one that reached high up into the heavens, from which this part of the earth might be protected."

"They built the tower with a shield, so that it couldn't be seen from the earth. Then they installed a powerful deflector system. To run it, they needed someone who was both one of the long-lived, and one of the air-people. Some people are comfortable in the air, and others are not meant for the high places. It takes a compatible disposition. The same goes for the other elements. Not everyone is suited to live under the ground, or on the water, or close to heat."

"The population had been greatly diminished, so there weren't many candidates. But there was one young noblewoman, from a well known and very long-lived house, and she did meet the requirements. So she was sent from her family as a girl to command the Spiral Tower, and protect the descendants. She had some assistants, but they were fully mortal, and needed to be replaced every generation. Otherwise, she was alone in her endeavor." He stopped.
Then he said, "That's really all I know."

After a moment, Master Skell said,
"I'd wager that a calamity has happened as predicted. It was the dangerous blue fire that appeared last spring."
"We saw that!" said Pippa. "It flew across the western sea."
"We saw it too," said Hedyn. "Up close. The blue fire hit the empty sky over the Fortress of Lugh and exploded. For a brief moment, we also saw... it."
"Do you mean the tower?" asked Lord Gwydion.
"Yes," he replied. "It was so high. Impossibly tall. It crackled in a blue blaze. Our hair stood on end, and our steel weapons began floating away. Then the crackling stopped, the tower disappeared, and our blades fell to the ground."
"Our hands and faces were burnt," said Awyr, "and our eyes, as if we'd been staring into the sun."
"We haven't been completely well since," said Glaw. "Seren vomited for days afterward."
"And my hair fell out," said Seren. "Fortunately it's grown back, nicer than ever." He ran his hands through his short thick brown hair.

"Now, Sir," said Master Skell to Hedyn, "will you tell us the story of the Watch?"
"The Watch protects the Queen," said Hedyn. "The Queen in the Tower protects us all. The Watch has existed since ancient times. Long ago, the world was nearly destroyed by cosmic fire."
"Then the great god Lugh built a Fortress of Light, so that we might be protected from the dangers of the great beyond. He brought the Queen from far away, to command the Fortress. And he called upon our ancestors, the settlers in the valley, to serve her."

"The Hedyns come from my family, the Porths provide the Watch, and the Gwas title goes from uncle to nephew in the Amser clan. Or cousin, if there's no nephew. They provide the Tower with a new air-guardian every generation. That takes place during a ceremony. The entrance to the tower is briefly revealed. Then the elder air-guardian comes out, with the Queen, and he receives the gifts of thanks, and returns to the community. There's a ritual, where the secret key is transferred to the new air-guardian. He and the Queen both go through the portal, and then it's closed again."

"It was like a holiday," said Seren. "Our families prepared their entire lives for the ascension ceremony."

"Did the Queen appear regularly to the Watch?" asked Lord Gwydion.

"The Queen would come here to the grotto," said Amser Gwas, "once every twelve years, like a goddess, all in white, with stars in her hair. She would come bearing gifts of gold and silver, to sustain the members of the Watch and their kin. She would praise and honor the elders who served her, and encourage and inspire the next generation."

"Only, it hasn't happened since our grandsires were young," said Seren impatiently. "And the uncle of Amser Gwas didn't return when he was supposed to. That was nearly thirty years ago. He would probably have died of old age by now. So there's no proof that the Queen is still alive. If she ever really existed at all."

"How dare you speak that way about the Queen of Heaven!" said Hedyn to Seren angrily.

"Now then," said Master Skell, "it's reasonable to ask questions. Tell us, according to the story, what did the Queen look like?"

"She had hair like night and day," Hedyn said, looking pointedly at Lord Gwydion. "And one blue eye and one brown eye. Much like Master Crydd, here."

They all looked at the King. Treya was surprised. For some reason, she had pictured the 'Queen of Heaven' as being fair, with golden locks, but this actually made more sense.

"I am her kinfolk, it is true," said Lord Gwydion, "come at last to find out what has befallen her." He looked sad. "I only hope we have not waited too long."

"We'll help you, friends!" said Amser Gwas emphatically. "Finally, something to do."

"Yes," said Hedyn. "We wait to serve our Queen. And to see her, or at least, to know that she is safe."

"Only, don't ask us to climb that invisible tower," said Glaw.

"I couldn't even bear the sight of it again," said Seren.

"We're not all air-people, as much as we would like to be," said Hedyn. "Only Amser Gwas. He was meant to be the next air-guardian. But as you've heard, his uncle never returned when his time of service was over. We don't know what happened."

"I bear the wooden tool of the air-guardians," Amser Gwas said, raising his cudgel. "I've been waiting for many years to take my place. Whatever happens, I am ready."

"Well done, Amser Gwas," said Lord Gwydion. "Well done, all of you Watchmen. You just keep doing what you've been doing. Securing the perimeter. Guarding the tower. We'll go up. You stay near."

"And if the Fates are with us," added Master Skell, "the Queen of Heaven will once again appear before the brave men of the Watch, and noble Amser Gwas will ascend."

"Then we will resume our patrol," said Hedyn, "and leave you to your devices. May fortune favor your efforts."

The Watch swiftly disappeared. The companions stood in silence for moment.

"Crydd," said Dina. "I like that."
"It *is* a sweet name," said Pippa.
"And very well-fitting," added Bruno. "Just like our shoes."

"Now what?" asked Bruno.
"Now we go in," said Lord Gwydion. "Then we go up."
"Up, up and up," added Dina.

"First, does anyone need a break before we start?" asked Marcus. "There are no trees or boulders up there." They dispersed. When everyone had returned, Marcus took out a lens key. Lord Gwydion did the same. They went to the wall, and slowly walked in front of it.

He and Marcus moved their lens keys around, scanning for the sensor. First Marcus's and then the King's lens began to glow, and emit a thin ray of red light. They focused their lenses. There was a humming sound, and the stone surface before them slowly faded away, to reveal an opening the width of a man. A very large gold dewdhek was bolted to a flat stone just inside the opening. It was hooked up to cables that ran up through the roof. The dewdhek was surrounded by a wire cage. Marcus opened the cage, reached in, and set his lens key in the top hole. The device gradually revealed a room on the other side. They could see a white wall through the gap.

The twins grinned at one another in excitement. Lowi gasped in astonishment. "You warned me," she said, "but I still can scarcely believe it!"

"This is it, friends," said the King. "I want you to know that if any of you change your mind about this, at any point, I understand. We can't all be the air-people. I want each and every one of us to return to the ground safe in body and sound in mind. All hail?"

"All hail," they replied.

He went through the opening, and they followed. Then Marcus took out the lens key, and the portal slowly closed behind them.

They were inside a round cylindrical tower, measuring about twenty-five feet across. There were stairs rising up around the edge of the tower wall. The stairway was guarded by a single slender rail of some kind of unusual metal that was tough as tin but shiny as silver. The space was illuminated by slit windows, one every twenty feet or so. The windows appeared to be made of clear glass. The walls and stairs were built of a strange pale substance that showed no sign of being worked with any kind of tool.

They put their heads back and stared. It did indeed go up, up, and up.

"What is it made of?" asked Brutus, tapping on the wall and stomping on the floor. "It's not wood. Or metal."

"Could it be some kind of cast stone concretion?" asked Pippa. "Like the Romans made?"

"It seems too lightweight to be stone," said Arghan.

Lowi was stroking the wall.

"It's tough," she said. "But the surface feels soft. Flaxen almost."

"Perhaps the tower is made of linen," said Dina. The others laughed, but Marcus said,

"That's as good a guess as any so far."

"If not linen," said Arghan, "maybe some other sort of molded fiber."

"I'm going to think of it as solid stone," said Pippa. "I don't much care for the idea of climbing a thousand-foot-high piece of fabric."

"Actually," said Marcus, "we calculated that it's closer to seventeen hundred feet. Maybe more."

"Thanks for clearing that up," said Pippa, grimacing.

"Speaking of up..." said Lord Gwydion. One of the An Dhew went first, with Bruno. The King followed. The rest of them fell in behind. The other An Dhew and Brutus took the rear guard.

"I understand about the Dewdhek," said Arghan. "Well, a little bit. I know that it somehow uses reflections and colored light to make a re-creation of the surrounding texture, and there's a magnetic field to make it resistant to touch. But how does an entire tower stay hidden?"

They had been climbing for awhile. The novelty and excitement had subsided. *So far, it's rather boring,* Treya thought. The windows were placed so that it was difficult to see anything but sky. Round and round, up and up. The conversation was helping them to keep going.

"I'm afraid I don't know," said Lord Gwydion.
"Master Skell," said Pippa, somewhat out of breath, "how do you think it works?"
"I couldn't say for sure," said Master Skell, "but it might be covered in lenticular lenses that redirect light away from the viewer, creating a sort of optical camouflage."
"Asked and answered," said Lord Gwydion with a chuckle.

"A platform," called the forward An Dhew.
"And some sort of room," said Bruno, "off to the side."
"It's mostly empty," said Marcus. "This is as far as we got before, but it was getting dark. It had taken half the day to get the portal fixed. So we decided to go back and wait for you before we tried it again."
The platform was a grated floor, made of the same shiny metal as the rail, covering the width of the tower, with an opening for the stairs. They went up and stood on it. Treya looked down through the metal squares. It was all so homogenous that it was difficult to make out what she was seeing.

"What's in the room?" asked Bruno. They approached it. Over the doorway was a zig-zag shaped line, molded into the frame.
"It looks like an armory," said Pippa, peering inside. They went in cautiously.
"There are some shields," said Marcus. "Regular old bronze. Green with age." The shields were on the floor. He moved closer. "There's no insignia."
There were six white hooks on the wall. One of them held a horse's halter and bridle. Another had a chain-mail skull-cap hanging from it. The rest were empty. The metal and leather items looked incongruous in the smooth white room.
"Look," said Arghan, "there are pictures. Molded into the wall, like the one over the door." They all gathered around. He ran his fingers over the images. "A sword. A helmet. An armored man getting struck by lightning. It doesn't look good for him." Dina laughed. Treya looked. The image did seem slightly comical.

"Then here's an un-armored man," Arghan continued. "He looks happy. Oh, I get it! We're supposed to leave our metal items in this room. Or risk getting struck." He continued to feel along the wall.

"Here's a guide," he said. "Anything longer than this needs to be stowed." He held up a space between his fingers.

"Around three inches long, then," said Marcus.

"Take off your armor and weapons," said Lord Gwydion, "and leave them."

This caused some grumbling.

"We have to do it," said Pippa, peeling off her cuirass and hanging it from a hook. "But I don't like it. It leaves us un-armed."

"Not entirely," said Dina, brandishing her trident.

"If we do this again," said Bruno, "let's *all* bring pointed sticks."

Reluctantly, the companions removed their armor, swords, and knives. Lord Gwydion, Treya and the An Dhew stowed their precious horns.

Bruno and Brutus each carried a rope equipped with a hook.

"We're going to chance keeping the grappling hooks," said Bruno, "even though they're a little over three inches. We might need them."

They exited the room and returned to the platform.

"I'll be honest," said Pippa, looking back. "I don't really feel comfortable about leaving our gear in an invisible room inside an invisible tower."

"Come on," said Arghan, laughing, "let's keep climbing."

Above the platform, the tower width narrowed by about one third, but the configuration was the same: a long spiral of stairs with occasional windows.

"Look," said Arghan, "the rail isn't metal anymore. It's the same stuff as the walls and the stairs." He ran his hand along the rail.

Treya put her hand on the railing. It felt strange; dull and nuetral after the cool surface of the metal. They kept climbing. Outside, a gentle rain had begun. The drops made a faint whispering sound on the exterior. Treya gazed up at the nearest window. It was beaded up with water droplets, which collected until they slid down, to be replaced by more droplets. Then the cycle began again.

Treya shook her head. She was getting sleepy, walking around and around. It had helped to have conversation. But not everyone enjoyed talking about science. Lowi was right beside her, head down. She seemed tired too. *What would Lowi like to talk about?* she wondered. Ahead of them, Pippa and Arghan were also squeezed together on the stairs, holding hands as they plodded upward with matching steps.

"Pippa, Arghan, I was wondering," said Treya. "How did you two meet? And become betrothed?"

Lowi looked up, immediately interested. Treya smiled.

Pippa explained, as they climbed.

"It was because of Cassius Ambrosius and Brian Magnus. They had been summoned to Rome, for a last meeting with the Emperor, before the Army quit Alba altogether. Just before they left, they let me know that while they were abroad, they were going to try and find me a husband, and they wanted to know, what sort would I prefer? I was really surprised. But because I would no longer have a career, or be a Virgin Warrior, they had decided that I should marry. And also, they knew that they would be... going to the west before long, and they wanted to make sure that I was well taken care of."

She smiled at her husband, then continued. "I didn't know what to think, but I trusted them. So I answered their questions as best I could-"

"How?" Lowi interrupted. "What did you tell them to look for?"

"Oh, I know this one," said Arghan, glancing back at Lowi. "My wife described her ideal mate as being strong, resourceful, creative, and kind, possessing the aesthetics of a Celt, and the good hygiene of a Roman."

"That sounds like you, Angove," said Lowi. "But... what about looks? Certainly there was some sort of physical description?"

"Oh, indeed," Arghan replied. "It was very specific. Her true love must have pale skin, wiry limbs, and hair like the tail of a squirrel. And above all, he had to be..." he paused dramatically. Brutus and Bruno both joined in when he continued with, "a draggable man."

The men laughed.

"Angove Arghan Pen Avalen was the most eligible draggable man in all of fair Kernow," said Brutus merrily.

"Whatever do you mean?" asked Lowi, giggling.

"I'll never hear the end of this, will I?" Pippa said, laughing. "I just wanted to know that if I ever had to haul my husband to safety, I would be able to do so." She looked back at them for a moment, before facing forward again. "Cassius was a big fellow. As his aide, I always worried that if there was ever a crisis and he needed to be rescued, I would be unable to save him. So I decided that it would be one less thing to worry about with a husband."

Treya and Lowi both burst out laughing. Then Treya said, "I guess it makes sense."

"But it still sounds funny," said Lowi. They kept climbing.

"So, they went to Rome," said Treya. "But they brought you back a man from Kernow. How did that happen?"

"When they got back from the sea-voyage," said Pippa, "it felt as though they'd been gone forever. I was so happy to see them. And they were bursting with news. That is, Brian Magnus was. He talked for over an hour straight, non-stop, about their adventures in Rome, and how when they were looking for a ship back to Alba they had found the very man I'd described. And that now he was waiting with his ship at the nearest port, and we were all going away very soon, to the west, to Dumnonia. And that's exactly what happened." She looked at Arghan.

"That's right," he concurred. "It was all arranged by Cassius and Brian. I never even had to think about it."
They all laughed.
"I'll always associate Trevena with Brian Magnus," said Pippa, panting a bit. "He was the one who looked at my piece of tin all those years ago and told me that one day I would get to see the shining citadel, perched high on a cliff over the western sea." She grew quiet. The sound of their footsteps and labored breathing blended in with the gentle hiss of the rain.

"Another platform," called the forward An Dhew. "And the tower narrows again after that."
"Look," said Arghan, "now the platform is made of the same stuff." Instead of being metal, the grate was the same white substance as everything else.

"Let's have a short rest," said Lord Gwydion, from behind them.
They piled onto the platform, and most of them collapsed on the grate. Treya lay her cloak down, and she and Lowi stretched out. They drank some water. Some provisions were unpacked, and nut cakes and dried grapes were passed around.

After a few minutes, Marcus said, "Sorry, but we should keep moving."
They hauled themselves to their feet and started up the steps. The rotation was tighter now, and the tower interior felt much closer.
"The tower just keeps getting narrower," said Pippa.
What can this possibly lead to? Treya wondered. They trudged onward. Lowi's head was down again.

"Master Skell," said Treya, "We would love to hear about some of your adventures." Lowi looked up and smiled at Treya.

"Oh, yes," Pippa agreed. "I imagine you've seen some amazing things in your day."

"Will you tell us a tale, friend?" they heard Lord Gwydion ask from behind them. "It would help to ease the climb."

"What sort of tale would you like to hear?" Master Skell responded, also from behind them.

"One about creatures," called Dina, from up front, without hesitation. "Strange creatures from faraway lands."

"Then listen," he said, "and hear the extraordinary story of the mythical firebird."

"Ooh," said Pippa. "A bird tale."

"The firebird is actually a large bird called the Bennu," Master Skell continued. "I had the rare honor of witnessing its death and rebirth. It lives in an ancient temple, deep within the Egyptian desert. The bird looks like a heron, but much, much bigger; bigger than the largest of eagles, and it is bright red, with great curvy plumes of golden feathers on its head and wings. The firebird lives for exactly three-hundred-and-thirteen years. After it reaches that age, it collapses in on itself until the pressure causes it to burst into flames. I was there when it happened. It was very sudden. One moment, it had been preening its tail feathers, and the next moment.... poof!"

"Even though the priest had warned me about what would happen, it was still distressing to watch the destruction of this rare and glorious creature. The smell of burning feathers was dreadful. After it burned up, all that was left was a black smoldering lump they called a corpse-egg. The Bennu's attendant put the corpse-egg into a nest of myrrh, covered it with split aloe leaves, and closed it in the temple, where it was kept in total darkness for three days."

Master Skell's breathing was sounding a bit labored. They climbed in silence for a few moments.

"A corpse-egg," said Lowi. "That's interesting."

"INTERESTING!" Gwydion, Pippa, Arghan, Dina and Marcus all suddenly shouted, out of silly habit. Lowi jumped.

"Oh, I forgot!" said Lowi. "Treya warned me about what might happen if I used the word int-" she paused. "If I used that word."

"I miss Pompi," said Lord Gwydion with a sigh. "I hated to leave him. I hope he understands that I didn't bring him out of concern for his safety. Is that silly?"

"Of course not," said Marcus. "We feel the same way about Rosa. She's happy with Lew, and she loves Azario and Parmaggio, but I know she wishes that we could all be together, all the time."

"I miss Bootchie," said Bruno.

"Me too," said Brutus, "but does Bootchie miss us?"

"I'm sure he does," said Pippa.

"If he remembers that we exist at all," Arghan added.

"Master Skell," said Dina, looking back at him as she climbed. "What about the story? Was there a new firebird born from the corpse-egg?"

"There was," said Master Skell. "After three days of rituals and chanting, they opened the temple to welcome the hatchling, which had already regenerated from the carbonized core. The new baby bird was the size of a hen. It was already out of the nest, and was gobbling down the worms and grain that had been left for it. Its eyes were enormous, black and shiny, and surrounded by curved pinfeathers that looked like luxuriant eyelashes. It had a long neck, and huge feet. The feet were webbed, but they also had big claws with sharp-looking talons. The neck, belly and legs were bare and stubbly. The head and breast and wings were covered in downy plumage, like little puffy pink and gold clouds."

"Amazing!" Lowi exclaimed.

"That would be a sight to see," Treya said.

"Master Skell," Marcus asked, "are you sure that it really happened that way? I know that sometimes priests play tricks. To inspire the temple-goers."

"What, Marcus" said Brutus, "are you suggesting that the legendary firebird was really a chicken in disguise?"

Everyone laughed, including Marcus.

"I saw it with my own eyes," said Master Skell. "And that was long before I had these lenses."

"Thank you, Master Skell," said Dina. "That was a good creature tale."

"Another platform," called the An Dhew.

"Already?" Lowi responded. "That story certainly sped the time along."

"Yes, it did," said Treya. "But also, the segments between platforms are getting shorter. In proportion to the shrinking diameter."

"Treya!" exclaimed Pippa. "You sound like a real engineer."

They gathered closely together on the platform. They looked up into the tower. There was nothing discernible, just more of the same stairs and windows, only narrower.

"What's that sound?" asked Pippa.

They listened. There was a high piercing whistle, that rose and fell in pitch erratically.

"It's the wind," said Arghan. "It's really shrieking out there. I don't know what this tower is made out of, but it seems to block out sound."

Just then a huge bolt of lightning shot across the sky, lighting up the windows, and there was a big crack of thunder. Everyone jumped. The light was so bright it could be briefly seen through the strange walls of the white structure.

The wind howled shrilly. Treya felt the sensation of rocking from side to side, like on a wave-tossed ship.

Lowi cried, "We're moving! What's happening?" Treya grabbed hold of her.

"It's alright," she said. "Really it is. A tower this tall would have to be able to move a little with the wind. They build them that way, so they don't break. Isn't that right, Master Skell?"

"Based on the estimate of seventeen hundred feet," said Master Skell, "it should be able to move around three feet in any direction."

"It stopped," said Lowi. She took a step. "Wait, no it didn't."

"Think of it like being on a ship," said Treya. "You're always in motion, even though you're not consciously aware of it. But your body learns to make little adjustments, and it gets easier."

"Let's keep going," said Marcus.

They continued to climb. There was another lightning strike, but not as big. The thunder sounded further away. The wind outside continued to make a shrill whistling sound. Treya looked up at one of the windows. The raindrops were now going sideways on the glass.

On they climbed. After a while, the rain stopped.

"Here's another platform," called Bruno from up ahead, "and then it ends! There's a corridor. And something else. I think it's a viewing area."

They squeezed onto the platform. Treya looked up. There was just the shallow dome of a ceiling. A passage led down from the platform to a terrace, where a section of the hallway had been extended outward. The walls of the extension were paneled in huge sheets of window-glass. The companions gathered in front of the windows. Besides the scattered raindrops, there was nothing to see on the other side except fog.

"It's so clear!" Pippa exclaimed, gently touching the glass.

"The window is, anyway," said Brutus. "I wish the sky would clear, so we could get some idea of where we are."

"How is it possible," said Marcus, touching the window, "to have such big panes of window glass up here?"

Arghan rubbed the window, then scraped his nail across it slowly, listening.
"This isn't real glass!" he exclaimed.
"How can that be?" asked Bruno.
"If it's not glass, what is it?" asked Brutus.
"It feels... not alive," said Pippa, touching the window. "I don't want to say dead, that sounds too negative. But it's like the white concretion. It seems... unnatural. Again, that sounds worse than I intended."

"Master Skell," said Treya, "what do you think?"
"If I had to guess," he replied, "I'd say that this tower is built from what you might call 'man-made' materials. Harvested from nature, but processed far beyond it."
"Yes," said Lord Gwydion. "I think that the spectral map was made from some similar technology."

The rain abruptly stopped, and the mist began to clear. An immense, inky-purple, anvil-shaped storm cloud filled the sky. Flocks of seabirds wheeled silvery in the distance. Overhead, vultures were calmly floating in a lazy sun-wise spiral.

Against the dramatic backdrop of the sky, the command station appeared from out of the clouds. The structure was almost directly above them. It was wide and low and ovoid-shaped, with slit windows all around the top. It was made from the same pale man-made material as everything else. On the far end of the station there was a walled-off area with a white triangular tower rising from it.

Treya was on the right edge of the group. She could see that the covered hallway they were in was a just a long tube. It looped around to the left. There were no visible supports. Beyond that, the view was obscured, but then the tube could be seen to rise, and come back around to connect to the station above.

"I don't understand," said Arghan. "How can this narrow tower possibly support all these structures?"
"Look!" exclaimed one of the An Dhew, who was peering out of the left-hand side of the window.
"Oh!" Marcus said. "Not good!"
"That must be from the fireball," said Master Skell.
"Oh no!" cried Pippa, staring in horror. "The corridor's been blasted open!"

They all gathered to see. Just before the walkway looped around again to the right, there had obviously been an impact or explosion. A twenty foot long section of the facade had been ripped away, clearly by something big and hot. The gaping edges of the corridor were stained and distorted. The material had melted into clumps and drips, and there were long thin loose strands, fanned out like wing-bones, vibrating in the wind.

"Can we tell if the floor is intact?" Lord Gwydion asked.
"No, Lord," said the An Dhew. "The view is blocked."
"But, either way, we'll be able to get through, won't we?" asked Lowi.
"Yes, of course," said Treya. She was very glad that the twins had insisted on bringing ropes and hooks.

Pippa had been slowly lowering herself down to the floor. Now she knelt in front of the glass, head down.
"Pippa," said Treya with concern. "Are you alright?"
Pippa looked up and smiled. "Yes," she said. "I'm just trying to find the ground. I know it's down there somewhere. Is it too far away to even see?"
Treya and the others looked down. Far below them, the world was a hazy blur of tans, greens and browns.
"It's so indistinct," said Arghan. "It's hard to get a sense of scale."
"Look at the Afon Foryd," said Lord Gwydion.
"Where?" asked Pippa. "I don't see the river."
The King knelt behind her and gently repositioned her head.
"Oh," she said. "That's very tiny."
Treya followed her gaze, and she saw it too, a faint thread of brightness, much smaller than she had imagined.
"We're so high up," she said, "it's barely visible. It looks like a fine crack in porcelain."
"Or one of Marcus's beard hairs," said Bruno.

They continued along the hallway. They were going up a gradual incline.

"It's getting... wobbly," said Lowi. The corridor was becoming distorted. Parts of the wall were puffed out, and others were sunken in. The piercing wind grew louder. The slit windows along here were damaged; not shattered like glass, but partially melted, and covered in a faint green glaze. Air was coming in through these ragged holes in the windows, whistling fiercely. The hall grew more and more misshapen. A slightly acrid smell clung to the walls. Alongside the whistling sound, the wind was now also making a loud roar as it blew through the holes in the corridor.

Bruno and Brutus were out in front. By the time they all caught up, the two men had already installed a rope railing, and Bruno was on the far side. The companions stood before the damaged section. The floor was still there, Treya was relieved to see. It was full of holes, and would take some negotiating, but it seemed mostly intact. The wind was intense.

"Everyone, take great care through here," called Lord Gwydion. "Go easy, and watch out for one another."
"Keep a hand on the line," said Brutus. "But don't use it unless you need to."

One by one they stepped out into the ruined corridor. The howling wind blew in sideways from the opening, and it also came up through the holes in the floor, causing their cloaks to flap wildly. The travelers focused on moving forward, avoiding the gaps, stepping carefully around the great melted blobs, and ducking the strangely delicate wing-shapes.

Treya was almost to the other side. Over the wind, she could hear Pippa's agitated voice behind her, and Arghan speaking in raised but soothing tones.

She looked back. Pippa was standing with one hand on the rope, and the other holding onto Arghan, who was directly in front of her. She seemed frozen, staring at the gaping hole in the floor.

Oh no, Treya thought. *She's panicking. Should I go try to help?*

Then there was a sound. It was a soft sound, but it somehow cut through the wind. It was pleasant. It took Treya a moment to realize that Lord Gwydion was playing his harp. He walked directly behind Pippa, who was moving along now, still clinging to her husband.

The King kept playing after he had reached the other side, until they all had arrived. He put his harp away and they continued on in silence. They were still going up a slight incline. The sound of the wind began to fade. By the time it was just a persistent whistle again, the corridor had leveled out. It widened, then it ended. There was a short flight of steps leading up to an open arched entry-way.

Over the arch, there was a sign, composed of three symbols. They were black against the white background. The first was a circle, bisected horizontally. Then there was a tilted triangle with hatched lines. Then a vertical diamond with evenly spaced horizontal lines.

"What are these symbols?" asked Marcus.

Master Skell replied,

"These are the glyphs of the Pobl Pen Du, the dark-headed people of Sumer. Their writing came to this part of the world with the Phoenicians, whom locals hailed as the Pobl y Môr, the Sea People, but these symbols predate that time. They are called logograms. They're not like letters that make sounds. These represent words and concepts."

"Master Skell, what would we have done without you?" asked Treya.

"Indeed," said Lord Gwydion. "How fortunate we are, to be blessed with your scholarly wisdom and good company."

"But, what do the symbols mean?" asked Pippa.

"What do *you* think they mean, Councilor?" Master Skell replied.

Pippa stared at the symbols. Then she said,

"Stability, Ascendance, and Protection."

"I didn't realize that you knew ancient Sumerian, Pippa," said Treya.

"I don't," said Pippa, "but these look like a bridge, a rising cloud and a shield."

Master Skell said, "Well done. A circle with horizontal line across it is a seat. Either a literal chair, or the center of something, a base. Or a bridge. The triangular shape is an air symbol. It means scent, as in incense, but it often refers to clouds or the atmosphere, and tilted this way, it means something that is highly refined, or rising. As Pippa mentioned, ascendance. The biconic shield refers to home, and to protection, and justice. It is a shape sacred to Vespa, goddess of the hearth, to Nehalennia, of the dogs and apples, and it is used by shipwrights as a protective rove with which they rivet their strakes. The shape also represents actual diamonds and gemstones, and relates to purity, clarity, and light."

"So, altogether it means something like Throne of Heavenly Protection," said Treya.

"Yes," said Master Skell.

"Seat of Highest Justice," Marcus offered.

"Good one," the scholar replied.

"Center of Heavenly Light," said Pippa.

"Very appropriate," he responded.

"Clean Home Smell," said Dina.

"Sure!" he said, laughing merrily. "That's very important too."

With Bruno and Marcus still in the lead, they went up the stairs and through the archway.

They continued down a covered hallway. There was a small domed room just off the hallway to the right, with an asterisk shape molded into the doorframe.

Master Skell, Arghan, Lord Gwydion and one An Dhew squeezed into it. The rest peered in from the entry. The ceiling and walls of the room were composed of large clear octagonal panels. There was a central hub, with a console that was covered with brightly colored icons.

Running across nearly the width of the room, there was a long white tube structure. It had small round holes at regular intervals, and it was centrally mounted on a cranked gimbal, which was located next to the control console.

"It's a celestial observatory of some kind," said Master Skell.
There were five smaller perpendicular tubes coming out each side of the main one, at regular intervals. From them extended little panicled branches of three or five round discs. There were very small tubes, made of shiny metal, sticking out of the discs themselves.
"Look, there are gemstones in the little tubes," said Arghan.
"Perhaps this thing lights up," said Lord Gwydion.

They left the star-room and continued along the corridor. The corridor ended at an arched opening. A circle with a horizontal line was molded into the doorframe. The companions went through. They were in a long interior and window-less room. It was difficult to see. Support pillars ran up to the ceiling at regular intervals, connected by fanned spokes. The pillars stood in serried rows, fading away in the dim light. At the very far end of the dark room, there was a well-lit opening.

The large room appeared to be mostly empty. Near the entrance, there were some tables and seats molded into the floor. On the table there was a tray, filled with growing mushrooms and other fungi. There was a large glowing green slab suspended over them, casting a faint eerie glow in the otherwise dark room. Near the table, there were two broad shelves, also created as part of the room. On one shelf there was a large wooden crate, and on the other, a smaller wooden box.

They began to head towards the bright doorway. As they passed the first pillar, a small light appeared near the top of the post.

"What's that all about?" whispered Bruno.
"Motion activated, I'd guess," Lord Gwydion replied quietly.

As they passed the next pillar, another light came on, and the one behind them went dark again. On they went, from one little island of light to the next.

There was one last patch of darkness before they reached the light of the door. They passed the final pillar, and the little light came on. Everyone gasped and jumped. Lowi began to shriek and then immediately covered her mouth.

Before them was a little girl. She was standing perfectly still, staring at them with big dark eyes. She was thin and a bit hunched, and her skin looked waxy and yellowish. She wore a threadbare blue gown, and her head was covered by a snood of the same faded fabric.

"It's a child!" Pippa exclaimed.
Arghan said, "Hello. What are you doing, standing here alone in the dark?"

The companions drew closer. The child blinked, and looked around.
Suddenly she cried,
"Lights on!"

All the pillar lights turned on at once, illuminating the long room.
"Strangers!" the child exclaimed.
"Its alright, we're fr-" Arghan began to say, but the child shouted in a very loud voice,
"LADY! Strangers in hall!"

A figure rushed in through the doorway, waving a long wooden spoon around defensively at no-one in particular. She was very thin and haggard looking. Her long and disheveled hair was pale with dark streaks, and her grimy white gown was ripped up the left side seam. Her face and limbs were dirty, and her skin looked damaged. The wooden spoon appeared to be coated in algae, and as she had brandished it, she'd covered herself in streamers of green slime.

The most disturbing thing of all was the woman's eyes: she had none, only what appeared to be two indentations of shiny scar tissue.

"Lady," the child cried again, "strangers in hall!"

"Stand back!" the Lady cried, waving the spoon. "I'm warning you!"

Treya and the others all stood in silent shock, staring in astonishment at the Queen of Heaven as she blindly threatened them with a wooden spoon.

Chapter Ten - As Close as We Get to Us

"Who's there?" the woman cried. "Friend or enemy?"

"Friend," said all the companions at once.

"What the-?" The woman lowered the spoon, turning her head from side to side. "Tegan, count number of strangers?"

"Twelve strangers," said the girl.

"Twelve!" the woman exclaimed. "Nobody at all for century after long century, and now they send twelve at once? Idiots!" She threw the spoon to the floor. Her vacant eyes seemed to stare hauntingly.

"Is there a man at least?" she asked impatiently. "A big strong man?"

"Two big strong men," said Tegan, scanning the group and settling on the twins. She took the Lady's sleeve between her thumb and finger, drew her over to Bruno and put her hand on his upper arm. Then she took the lady's other hand and laid it on Brutus.

"Yes!" said Lady Arianrhod. "Let's have both of you. You don't know how I've been waiting for this!" Despite not being able to see, she began pulling them towards the arched opening.

"Wait!" cried the King. "Sister! It's me, your brother Gwydion." He stepped forward and gently put his hands on her shoulders.

The Lady stopped in surprise, although she didn't let go of the two men.

"Brother!" she said. Her sightless eyes looked up at the King, who was half a foot taller than his sister. "I remember you," she said. "You're bigger now." She let go of Brutus for a moment and felt the King's upper arm. "Not quite big enough, though."

She resumed her grip on Brutus and began to lead the twins through the door.

"Tegan," she called. "Bring crate!"

"Tegan bring crate," said Tegan. She went back towards the shelf. Her gait was awkward and her steps were measured and plodding. She picked up the large wooden crate, and returned to follow the Lady and the twins, who had disappeared through the doorway. Everyone else went through also.

Arghan went up to Tegan and said, "That looks heavy. May I carry it?" Tegan stopped, stared, and then extended the crate out to Arghan. When she took her arms away, he suddenly staggered under the weight and almost dropped it.

Marcus came to the rescue and grabbed one end. Together, they hoisted it through the doorway. Tegan shuffled in ahead of them. Marcus and Arghan exchanged a glance of astonishment at the girl's strength, but they kept quiet.

The group passed through a round central courtyard room which was lit by large frosted skylights. It was furnished with a wooden table, covered with white bowls and dishes, and some chairs with tattered blue upholstery. There was a small sink with a ceramic water reservoir. On one side of the room there were several dormitory-style bedchambers and a washroom. The courtyard ceiling was filled with all sorts of hanging plants, including a sprout garden, spilling over with baby cresses and mustards. A recirculating fountain fed a small clear pool, and there was a separate tank filled with algae. On the other side of the room were some large rectangular devices. Treya had no idea what they were, but there was no time to wonder about them. They had gone right through this courtyard room and out another door.

Next, they went through a small round foyer with large windows that looked out over the rooftop. The room had a central console facing the windows. The console was covered with colored panels. The windows and the console all had a bit of the green glimmer that had been left behind by the fireball, and the room had a burnt metallic odor.

They came out onto an open rooftop. The roof platform was protected on all sides by a twelve-foot high wall made of the white building material. There were some large cube-shaped objects on the roof, and rows of covered conduit. Against the wall near the doorway, there was a roofed and screened-in porch with a bench in it. At the far end of the rooftop, there was a streamlined triangular tower, about thirty feet high, which seemed to be composed of the same compound material as everything else.

But it was actually hard to tell what was out there on the platform, because the rooftop was completely inundated with birds. They clustered thickly on the ground, not really caring to move out of the way for the people. They covered the cube shapes, and were lined up on the walls.
There were many species to be seen and heard, mostly sea birds, but there were also quite a few blackbirds and even some crows. The edges of the platform were packed with nests. There were loose eggs here and there. The white walls were streaked with droppings. There was a great deal of chirping and squawking going on, even though most of the birds were resting. Small flocks were flying around, looking for a roost. Hundreds of them were perched diagonally on the cross beams of the tower. The windy top of the tower was the domain of a group of large vultures.

The Queen pushed through, still pulling the twins.
Birds ran around in front of her in excitement, and fluttered around her head and shoulders. Shoving the creatures gently but efficiently aside with her feet, she led the two men to the base of the tower. Despite not being able to see, she seemed to know exactly where she was going.

"Tegan, where crate?" she asked.
"Here crate," said Tegan. Arghan and Marcus set it down carefully before the Lady. She felt around for the clasp, and then heaved the top open, revealing row upon row of slots, all with different symbols.
"Strong men, can you read?" she asked impatiently.
"Yes, Lady," the twins replied together.
"Find the 2160 charge. It's under the nine symbol, that's an upside down triangle. There are some other sizes in there too, but find the one marked 2160."
She grew silent. "Is that right? Arggh, I don't know if I can do this in my head!"
She took a deep breath, then said quickly, but more calmly,

"Number nine can gets a 2160 charge this cycle. Right?" she grimaced to herself, moving her fingers around in the air as she spoke. "Axial cycle complete. Pentang 108 to Arian 108. One season of Axial cycle is the same as the combined vortices of the dewdhek. That's... 6480. Double that is 12960. Reverse the first two digits of the biconic numeral and drop the third."
She clapped her hands together and declared, "Yes, it's the 2160."

Bruno and Brutus had located the nine symbol and extracted the 2160 charge, which appeared to be a metal and glass tube. The metal part had some symbols stamped into it. The number 2160 was written in white pigment on the top.
"Got it," said Bruno, hefting the tube. "It's really heavy."
"What are we doing with it?" asked Brutus.
"Replacing the burned out one," said Lady Arianrhod. "The can won't open for me. The system's been shut down since the explosion. We've been completely vulnerable because I'm not strong enough to replace the blasted charge." She felt around in the crate, then reached into a slot and pulled out a tool. It had a cylinder attached to a handle. She gave it to Brutus and said, "Come on!"

The Lady bolted towards the tower faster than Treya would have thought possible, even from a sighted person. She scurried up the side, scattering birds as she went. There were no steps or ladder, just the angular tapering frame. The Lady's torn garment flapped in the wind, exposing her left butt cheek. Treya averted her eyes. She looked at Bruno instead as he tucked the charge carefully into his pocket. It pulled heavily on his tunic. Then he and Brutus went up too.

All the companions watched nervously. As soon as the climbers rose higher than the protective wall, the wind hit them with full force, buffeting them around. When they reached the top, the vultures begrudgingly flew off. The twins took their remaining rope and quickly secured all three of them to the tower.

At the top of the tower there was a mast, and attached to the mast was a vertical array of ten fan shapes, arranged in an opposing decussate pattern, with five on each side. The fan shapes were set into frames, molded from the white substance. They had a grid-work that was shiny and black, with silvery panels in between. The fans were attached to a tubular central hub that was slid down onto the mast. At the base of each fan shape, on the mast, there was an outward facing dark metal cylinder, surrounded by a shiny metal ring.

The others watched their progress from below. The Lady Arianrhod was giving instructions. Brutus hunched over the Array, holding the wrench. They could hear him grunting with effort. The Lady spoke, and he stopped. Then he repositioned himself and tried again. There was another grunt, then a loud clunking sound, and a cheer rose from the tower.

Brutus removed the old charge from the cylinder and put it in his pocket. Bruno took out the new one and handed it to Brutus, who installed it with another clunking sound. A low hum could suddenly be heard over the wind. It grew in pitch until it went out of range and disappeared. A small violet light appeared at the top of the tower. The Array shifted slightly, then reset itself with a series of clicking noises.

The rope was undone, and the three climbers came back down and returned to the others. The flocks of little birds immediately reclaimed the tower supports, and the vultures settled in at the windy top, looking rather annoyed.

"The used charge goes in the bottom row," said the Queen, feeling her way around the crate. Brutus withdrew it from his pocket. It was scorched, and the glass was shattered. He put it where the Lady had indicated. Bruno put away the wrench. The Lady closed and latched the crate.
"Tegan," said Lady Arianrhod, "transfer crate to shelf. After crate on shelf, transfer spoon to algae pool. Leave spoon in pool. Do *not* put spoon in storage room."
"Spoon on floor, Lady," said Tegan.
"That's why I'm telling you! No spoon in storage room!"
Tegan took the crate and went back inside. Arghan didn't offer to carry it this time.

The Queen returned to the foyer, and the others followed. She groped her way to the central console.

"Lady push red lever," she said. "I mean, I need to push the red lever. Sorry, I haven't spoken to anyone but Tegan in a while."

"Here," said Bruno, guiding her hand. The Lady flipped the lever. The colored panels hummed. They all went white, then black.

"Now the green one," she said. He guided her hand to the green lever. She flipped it. There was a soft humming sound, and the panels lit up white. Gradually they turned back to color. The Queen seemed to relax a little.

"Thank you," she said to no one in particular. "The entire system was down because of that burned out charge."

"Sister," said Lord Gwydion. "Stop and speak to us now. What happened when the fireball hit?"

Lady Arianrhod left the foyer and went into the courtyard. The others followed. She found a bench and sat down.

"Throughout these long years," she said, "the instruments have detected fierce firestorms and huge burning chunks of debris far off in space, but they didn't ever approach us. We tested our devices, and did periodic drills. But nothing ever happened. Until finally it did. The system detected a huge blue fireball, heading right towards us."

"When the moment of impact came, I set the capacity to maximum. It was a gamble, because there's only enough power at maximum for the shields to last for a few minutes before something blows. So it had to be timed just right. The shields held. Before the can was blown, the Array did its job, repelling the blast and sending most of the charge deep into the ground. But when the fireball hit, a giant ring of bright light erupted, and engulfed the console room. I was wearing my eye-shield, but it wasn't strong enough. Now I'm blind."

"You save us all, Lady Arianrhod," said Lowi. "The whole of Alba owes you a great debt."

Dina came over, put her face in front of the Lady's, and looked closely at her scarred up eyes.

She put her hand up suddenly in front of the Queen's face. Then she took it away, and just as quickly put it back, staring all the while.

"You are not blind, Lady," said Dina. "You just can't see."

"What are you," asked the Queen, "some sort of spiritual counselor? I don't need your nonsense."

"No," said Dina. "I mean it. It's not just ruined flesh and old skin. It's almost as if your eyes are covered with some sort of very fine stone. If we could melt it off, you'd be able to see again."

"Melt..." said Lord Gwydion thoughtfully. "I'll melt the axe when the tree is dead. Oh!"
He turned to his sister. "Ari, we might be able to restore your sight. Lie down."

"I don't understand," she said, as she allowed herself to be maneuvered into a supine position.
"We have medicine," he explained. "Made from the petrified sap of the first tree. It might restore your vision."
"Have you tried it before?" the Lady asked.
"Not for this specifically," said Gwydion, "but it's been very effective in some other situations."

"Marcus," said Dina, "do you have a clean hand-cloth?" He reached into his tunic and handed it to her.
"And we'll need a bowl of water," she added. Pippa went to the table and picked up a bowl. She took it to the pool, filled it with fresh water, and set it down in front of Dina.
Lord Gwydion took out his medicine bag and poured a bit of the powder into the bowl. Dina dipped the fabric in it and swirled it around. Then she took the wet cloth and draped it over the eyes of the Queen.
"This might hurt," said Dina. "That will mean it's working."
They all waited.

"Do you feel anything yet?" asked Gwydion.
"No," said Lady Arianrhod. "Or... I don't know. Maybe there's a tingling sensation. Yes, there's a little--- oh, now they're itchy. So itchy!" She sat up and began scrubbing her eyes with the cloth.
"Not so rough," said Dina. She stopped the Lady's hands and removed the cloth, staring at the roughened flesh. "I think it's working."
Lord Gwydion also looked closely. "Yes," he said, "there's an eyelash poking through! Keep going."
They helped her back down, and Dina dipped the fabric again. She gently massaged the Queen's eyes. It was clearly uncomfortable. The Lady grimaced and made little noises. Dina dunked the cloth again. This time she wrung it out, dripping water into each eye, then laid it over both of them. Everyone was hushed. The Lady lay still, breathing deeply. Then she sat back up again, rubbing her eyes with the cloth, but less aggressively this time.

They all looked. Her eyes seemed to be crusted shut, but at least they appeared to be closed eyes now and not gaping scar-holes.

"That's so much better," said Lowi.
"I can see lights and shapes," said the Queen. "But I can't open my eyes."
"Should we do it again?" asked Lord Gwydion.
The Lady sighed deeply. She looked haggard and exhausted.

"Wait," said Pippa. "First have a drink of water. And maybe a bite of food."
"What do you have?" asked the Queen. "Do you have cheese? I really miss cheese."
"We do," said Arghan. "And we have bread that's made with cheese."
"Bread!" she responded. "I forgot about bread."
The Lady drank a cup of water and gobbled down a piece of cheese-bread.
"That was the best thing I've ever eaten," she said. She lay back down, and they repeated the process. By the time she sat back up and wiped her eyes, they seemed quite normal, although they were still shut.

"Oh, they look fine," said Bruno.
"But I still can't open them," said the Queen. She began to try prying her right eye open with both hands.
"Stop!" said Dina. "I think they need to be flushed out from the inside. Lady, I'm sorry, but you need to think of something sad so that you'll cry."
"My entire existence has been sad," said Lady Arianrhod with a grim smile. "Is there something in particular I should dwell on?"

There was silence. Then Lowi said,
"Lady, will you tell us about Amser Gwas?"

"Oh!" said the Lady, waving a hand in Lowi's direction, "that one's clever! Right to the point." She sighed. "Amser Gwas Twenty-five was the nicest one yet. It's a good thing, because we were stuck in here together for a long time. I had to watch him grow old and die, last winter. That's never happened before. I dragged him outside for a sky burial. It was so sad. He should have had a chance to return to his family long ago."

"It was my fault. It was when we were all set to enter the Grotto, was it thirty years ago? I was dressed in my best gown, wearing my star-net, carrying the gifts. He was all prepared to resume his life on the surface, and I was ready to greet the new ascendant. But there was a mixup with the lens keys. I was excited, not paying enough attention. There was already a key in place. I guess I didn't even look, I just stuck the other one in there on top of it."

"I knew as soon as it happened that I'd done something terrible. They wouldn't come loose. We tried for days, weeks, months, and then we finally gave up. Oh, and the supposed fail-safe had apparently failed, because I had neglected to maintain it properly. So it was doubly my fault." She sobbed. "He was so close to getting his life back. I'm sure everyone is terribly disappointed. I wouldn't blame them if they've given up on me---OH!" The Lady's hands flew to her face.

"IT BURNS! OHHHHH!" She jumped to her feet, and then fell to her knees. "MAKE IT STOP!"

Dina pulled her back to the bench and got her to recline again. Then she said, "Now, we need fresh water. And a clean cloth." Pippa went back to the table, grabbed a cup, scooped water out of the pool and brought it back, while Lowi got out her hand-cloth. Dina slowly poured water into each eye, shielding the water with her other hand to keep it from going in the Lady's nose or mouth.

The water was gone. Dina took the cloth and put it into Lady Arianrhod's hand. Still lying flat, she dried her own face. Slowly, squinting, she opened her eyes. Then she sat right up.

"I can see!" she exclaimed in astonishment. She looked at Dina. "Thank you, Healer," she said. "I'm sorry I was rude to you."

Lady Arianrhod stood and looked at the visitors. Her eyelids were red, but otherwise she seemed alright. Her face was clean. Her skin seemed healthier. Treya looked at Lord Gwydion, then at his sister. His left eye was blue, and his right eye was brown. Her left eye was brown, and her right eye was blue.
Everyone gathered around and met Lady Arianrhod. When it was their turn, Bruno and Brutus both bowed simultaneously.
"I'm so grateful for your help," she said to them.
"It is an honor to serve," said Bruno.
"You should know that the Watch awaits your return," said Brutus, "and the next ascendant is ready."
"Really?" She seemed deeply touched to hear this news.

"Lady, I know there's much to discuss," said Master Skell, "but why is there no system for self-calibration? So that the Array doesn't need manual compensation. So that the inhabitants of the tower might have a chance to take shelter in time."
"Master," she said, "I've been asking myself that same question for a while now."

"Can you build one, Lady?" Brutus asked her.

"Unlikely," she replied. "I can barely take care of the gear I have. I'm not particularly clever, you know. I'm afraid that I'm here simply because I'm from the right family, and heights don't make me swoon. I'm not complaining, I just think they could have done better."

"It's not right!" said Dina heatedly.

"What's not right?" asked Pippa.

"It's not right," she replied, "that a child was locked up in this tower, told that the safety of the world depended on her, and then abandoned."

"I'm so sorry, little sister," said Lord Gwydion, getting choked up.

"Stop it, King," said Dina. "It's not your fault. You were a child too. It's the fault of the mother."

"It certainly is," said the Queen. "The fifth-iteration Lady of the Danu was actually supposed to be the first Queen of the Tower. When she brought me here, the Old One realized that she was also elementally suited to the task. He wanted her to do it first. He said that she was perfect for establishing the position, and that would give me a chance to grow up and into it over time. She agreed. I was happy, and felt very relieved. But after we got home she denied that the Old One had ever said that, and told everyone that I was making up the story because I was afraid. After a short time I got sent back to the tower. And I've been here ever since."

"What a selfish monster!" said Marcus.

"Dreadful!" exclaimed Pippa.

"What do you mean, Lady," asked Dina, "by elementally suited to the task?"

"Our family is descended directly from the elementals," she replied. "The elementals are like regular people in many ways, with vocations, and families, only they're stronger and quicker and more clever than regular people, and they can live for thousands of years. They live right alongside regular people, too, because even though the elementals exist in the same space as regular folks, they tend to only manifest in the vibrational realm of their particular element. I don't pretend to understand it. This is just how the Elder explained it to me. He said that there were the Dyn Tân in the realm of fire, the Undines of the water, the Sylfs of the air, and the Gnomens of the earth."

"When humans first arrived in Alba, he told me, many of the elementals expanded their frequencies and manifested physically. Some mated with the humans. The Hanner-Dynion are the offspring of the elementals and early humans. Their first descendants, our ancestors, were long-lived and clever too.

From them, we get much of the technology we have here, including the white building material, which is a composite made of alabaster, marble, seashells, milky sap, and plant fibers."

"After the Great Scattering," she continued, "the connection between humans and elementals became diluted and obscured. But it's always there to some degree. That's why some of us are more suited to particular elements than others."

The Lady drew in a deep breath and let it out. She looked at the companions. "I can still hardly believe that you all are here. It's been such a long time."

Just then Tegan came in the room. She carried the spoon. She went to the algae pool and held out the spoon for a few long moments before setting it down very slowly. Then she came over to the Queen and stopped.
"Lady," she said.
"Yes, Tegan?" said the Queen.
"Rope on floor, Lady," she replied.
"Leave it!" the Queen said impatiently.
"Rope on floor," Tegan insisted.
"It belongs to the visitors," said the Lady, visible annoyed. "Leave it!"
"We did leave our rope on the floor," said Bruno. "Is that a problem?"
"No!" exclaimed the Queen. "The rope on the floor is not the problem."

"Lady Arianrhod," said Lowi. "While we're here, I would be honored if I could make you a new gown. Dina just gifted me some lovely white linen."
"I'd like that," the Lady said, looking down at her stained and tattered garment. "All my other clothes are..." she glared at Tegan and continued, "put away for now."
"Do you have a sewing kit, or even just a needle?" asked Lowi. "We can pull thread from the linen."
"Needle in storage room," said Tegan.
"Wonderful," said Lowi to Tegan. "If you direct me to the storage room, I'll grab it. What is the needle in?"
"Needle in storage room," Tegan repeated.
"Yes, but what is it *in*? Is there a needle safe? Or a sewing box...?" Lowi trailed off. Tegan showed no sign of comprehension.
"Put things in storage room," Tegan said. "Get them off floor."
Poor creature, Treya thought, *she's simple.* She was trying to feel sympathy for the child, but she was having a hard time. Tegan was a little off-putting. And Treya had seen the way she handled the heavy crate. There was something very odd about little Tegan.

"We'll help, Tegan," said Bruno. "Will you show us where to look?"

"Tegan show," Tegan replied, turning around awkwardly, and going back out of the room.

"Let's all go," said Master Skell. "I want to see this storage room."

They all followed behind.

"I'm not sure this is a good idea," said Lady Arianrhod. "I'm afraid you'll be shocked. Tegan doesn't exactly grasp the real purpose of the storage room. Or of housework, or logistics. It's too bad, because that's actually meant to be her function. But she's useless. Worse than useless, as you'll soon see."

"That's so cruel!" said Lowi. "She's trying, isn't she?"

"Do you not understand, Lady Borlowan? Tegan is an automaton," said Lady Arianrhod.

"Oh!" said Treya. "That explains it."

"Yes, it does," Marcus and Arghan both agreed.

"It's rather obvious," said Lord Gwydion.

"The way her lips move," said Dina, "it's not quite right."

"What are you talking about?" Lowi asked, confused.

Lady Arianrhod said, "Tegan is a machine. They were making a housekeeping device for me. And they were trying to be helpful. So I wouldn't be as lonely. They made her humanoid. So instead of looking like a cold creepy machine, she looks like a cold creepy child. The problem is that they didn't understand that since she's just a device, she takes things literally. You have to be very specific. But they weren't specific with her initial control command. She was told to 'keep rooms tidy, and if things began to clutter up the floor, put them in the storage room.' Not very specific."

"Oh!" said Marcus. "So... everything that's put on the floor goes in the storage room?"

"Everything," the Queen replied. "Big and small. Furniture, bookshelves, the wardrobe with all my clothes, leaves that fall from the plants, feathers that drift in from outside, boxes of food, barrels of wine. Important things, too. Spare lenses, reels of cable, toolboxes, the bucket of compound mix that goes in the machine to make new parts... any loose thing that was ever on the floor." She looked around the rooms.

"Why do you think this place is so empty?"

They had reached the storage room.

"I haven't seen the hoard since the fireball," said the Lady. "I suppose it will be even worse now."

Tegan opened the door.

"Oh!" cried Lowi in horror.
"By all the Gods," said Pippa.
"Oh, this won't do," said Bruno.
"Not at all," Brutus agreed.

Treya looked into the doorway. Except for a space of about eighteen inches at the top, the large room was completely filled. The things were packed so tightly that nothing fell out of the door when it was opened. The room was piled from top to bottom with such a wide variety of items that she could barely take it all in. Tables, chairs, dewdheks, cutlery, scribing pads, clothing, potting soil, cups, shoes, tools of all kinds, frames for the Array, rolls of shiny material, books, buckets, bedrolls, cushions, barrels, cans, jars, boxes, and bags. And those were just the things that were immediately visible. The space was very densely packed. Items were stacked in and around other items. Some things appeared to have been jammed together until they were crushed.

"There's no room for anything else," said Pippa.
"Don't be too sure," said Arghan.
"How does she get things so high up?" Treya asked. "Does she climb up on top of the pile?"
"Drop something, and you'll see," Lady Arianrhod replied. "Not anything you'll miss, obviously."

Treya reached in her pocket and took out a stick of chalk. She broke off one end, casually dropped it, and stepped away. Everyone drew back and watched. At first Tegan didn't respond. Then she began moving to the chalk. She reached down, picked it up, and moved back to the door. Then she began to rise. It took a moment to comprehend that her legs were extending, telescoping upward and curving over the pile of stuff until her body disappeared entirely, and all that they were looking at were two long graduated flexible tubes that seemed to be made out of the same white man-made material as everything else.

The companions stared in disbelief. Then Tegan's legs retracted and she returned to normal height.

"Ohhh," said Lowi, looking as though she was going to faint.
Tegan stood before the open door, empty handed.
"So, Tegan," said the Queen, "where needle?"
"Needle in storage room," Tegan replied.

"Alright, never mind," said Lady Arianrhod tiredly. "Thank you for your offer, Lady Borlowan. I'm sorry we weren't able to find a sewing needle."

"Lowi," said Treya. "I have those thorns. They might not make the best needles, but we can try." She reached into her pocket and pulled out her quill box. She opened it, and showed the contents to Arghan.

"Angove," she said, "do you think you can turn a few of these into sewing needles?"

"No problem," said Arghan, examining the thorns.

"Lady, have you ever attempted to re-program her?" asked Master Skell, peering at Tegan's empty countenance.

"I would have tried," she replied, "but I don't know how to use the screen."

"Would you mind if we had a go?" asked Lord Gwydion.

"Not at all," said the Lady.

"Wait," said Treya. "Does that mean you're going to... erase her personality and start over?"

"If it's possible," said the King.

"If you call that a personality," said Lady Arianrhod.

"Is that... the right thing to do?" Treya inquired hesitantly.

"Let's ask her," said Lady Arianrhod. "Tegan."

"Yes, Lady," said Tegan.

"Should we replace your character with that of someone who would actually be useful to have around? Someone who might have used their amazing legs and great strength to replace the number nine charge, instead of refusing to do anything except jam things into the storage room? Someone who I'm not afraid is going to someday shove me in there too and crush me to death?"

Tegan was silent. Then she said,

"Rope on floor."

Everyone was quiet.

Treya said, "Lady, forgive me for questioning you. I don't see how you've managed to put up with this for so long."

"It was a good question, Treya," said Master Skell. "One that raises many ethical concerns."

"There's a panel on her back," said the Queen to her brother. "I pushed the round button once, and a screen came on, with some symbols. I didn't know what any of it meant. I was afraid of making things worse, so I left it alone."

"Let's see," said Lord Gwydion. He went around to Tegan's back and untied her smock. It only came open enough to access the panel. The rest of the garment was built onto the mannequin. He and Master Skell stood before the panel.

"The start button is on the top of the right side," said the Lady. Lord Gwydion ran his finger along the side of the panel.

"Here it is," he said. He pushed the button. They all gathered around to see. Nothing happened for a moment. Then a green dot appeared in the middle. It expanded until the screen was filled with green light. On the screen were the same sort of symbols they had seen earlier, in white against the green.

"Let's see," Lord Gwydion said. "Circle with line again. Home, or bridge."

"This next one looks like a bed... on a sailboat," said Arghan.

"That means mouth," said Master Skell.

"It doesn't look like any mouth I'd want to meet!" said Brutus.

"The third one looks like a sideways triangular skillet," said Pippa.

"That means female," said Master Skell.

Arghan turned his head to the side and looked.

"Oh," he said, smiling, "there it is."

"Home first," the King said. He pressed the icon. A long, dense document appeared, taking up the entire screen. It was written in a much smaller version of the symbols. There were a lot of them, and they were difficult to make out. At the bottom of all the text was a red line. It was flashing.

"I think that we won't be able to continue until you tap on that line," said Master Skell. The King touched it.

"I wonder what I'm agreeing to," he mused.

The symbols disappeared and were replaced by what looked like an ear. Lord Gwydion tapped the ear. A grid appeared.

"Good," said Master Skell. "Language selection. Let's change it."

"Oh, I didn't know that was an option," said the Queen.

Master Skell peered closely at the screen. The grid was reflected in his lenses.

"There's Coptic. And Greek. Here you go, Common Brythonic."

"That's as close as we get to us," said Lord Gwydion. He touched the square. The language screen went away and was replaced by the first screen. "Good," said Lord Gwydion. "Instead of the glyphs, it now says Language, Command, and Vocabulary."

"Vocabulary is represented by the symbol for woman," Marcus noted.

"That's makes sense," said Arghan. "They always know what to say."

"Look at the languages again now," said Master Skell, "and see what the symbol language is called."

The King touched the home icon and peered at the grid. "It's called Iaith y Llys," he said.

"That translates as 'Language of the Court'," Master Skell explained. "Please continue, Sire."

The King touched the command icon and read the screen.

"Tegan has a text command capacity of seventy-seven characters. That's not much. No wonder she's so limited."

"Can you make her smarter?" asked Lowi.

"No, I wouldn't know how to do that," said Lord Gwydion.

"I'm not sure it's a good idea to make machines too clever," said Master Skell.

"I agree," said Lady Arianrhod. "Even the simplest things can go terribly wrong. And that's with *good* intentions. Imagine this technology in the wrong hands."

"If Rome had had this..." Marcus began to say. Then he stopped.

"The human race would have been destroyed," Master Skell finished for him.

"Ouch!" said Brutus. "That's harsh."

"But probably true," added Bruno.

"Lady Arianrhod," said Pippa, "can you tell us, when you say 'they' designed this machine, who do you mean?"

"The Elder," she replied. "The Old One. He came from someplace west of here. He was kind. He said he was going to return and check on me, but he never did. Looking back now, I think he must have been overwhelmed by the circumstances, but at the time he seemed like an all-powerful being."

"What did he look like?" asked Lowi.

"He was very tall," she replied, "with a huge headful of thick hair and bright green eyes." She addressed her brother, "Gwydion, do you recall Lord Arawn of Karrek Du? He looked like him, but with an even bigger forehead."

"Of course," said Gwydion. "King Arawn is our ally. Some of our friends here have met him."

"We think that he came from the lost kingdom of Lys," said Pippa.

"That old story?" said Bruno. "Do you think it's true?"

"Yes," said Arghan. "We've seen plenty of drowned settlements along the coasts. It only stands to reason that some of the island kingdoms wouldn't have survived."

"There's a song about it," Treya added. "Called 'The Last Days of Lys'. The Pol Pri family sang it for us."

"A song?" said Lord Gwydion. "That means that there's something to it. And then there's the symbol language. Llys does mean court, but it might also refer to the ancient kingdom." He returned his gaze to the screen.

"Let's look at vocabulary," said the King, pressing the final icon. A new screen appeared, dense with text. "There's a list of eight-hundred words." He poked at the screen. "Oh, we can change them if we want to. There's a tool that lets you enter new ones and erase the old ones."

"So," said Pippa, "to do this right, you need to come up a concise command that's literal, specific, and won't be misinterpreted." There was silence while they thought about it.

"Right," said the Lady. "Good luck with all that, brother. We have a gown to design." She turned and headed back to the courtyard. The others followed. Lord Gwydion and Master Skell stayed with Tegan.

The next day, Pippa, Arghan, Treya, and Lowi were sitting with Lady Arianrhod on the bench inside the screened-in porch. The others were still in bed. It was mid-morning, and the birds were very active. When they saw the Queen, they had become excited, running around her feet and fluttering around her head. Some even landed on her shoulders. There was much chirping and birdsong. It was all they could do to keep the birds from coming into the porch while they entered.

"The rooftop was meant to be a space to have for myself, maybe to grow a little garden," said Lady Arianrhod, carefully shutting the door. "The Elder didn't realize that this part of the sky was already inhabited. But it's alright, I like the birds, and they like me. I come out here every morning."

"Some people keep birds in a cage on their rooftop," said Arghan.
"But these birds are keeping a cage with humans on theirs," said Pippa, smiling. "Is that what you're saying?"

"Lady Arianrhod, do you have a favorite bird?" asked Treya.
"The buzzards are the most interesting," said the Queen, pointing up at the Array. "See that one with the really crooked neck? She thinks that buzzard there- the one below her, with the spotted white feathers on its back- she thinks he's an embarrassment. Because he flaps too much."
"What?" Lowi laughed.

"Vultures are judgmental," the Lady explained. "Of everything, including other vultures. It's considered bad form to flap unnecessarily. It either implies that you don't know how to properly catch an air current, or that you are trying to draw attention to yourself. Both are things that they disapprove of. Watch."

She got up and left the porch. She went over to the tower and scrambled up the side. Treya was relieved that the night before, some of the Lady's clothing had been rescued from the storage room. The gown she was now wearing was rumpled and creased, but it was fairly clean, and more importantly, it covered her backside.
When the Queen reached the height of the fence, the buzzards slowly began to glide off of the tower, one at a time, catching the wind with their open wings. Crooked-neck still perched on the top of the Array. Sure enough, the spotted vulture was the only one who flapped. Crooked-neck ducked in a rather dramatic and exaggerated fashion as Flappy went by, before spreading her huge wings and gracefully sailing off of the Array.

The companions laughed. The Queen climbed down and came back into the porch.
"It's so funny," said Lowi. "That bird really did look annoyed."
Treya yawned. She was tired out, although not in a bad way. They had stayed up late working on the new gown, but not as late as the men had stayed up working on their projects.

After returning to the courtyard from the storage room the previous evening, the companions had shared a meal of cheese, bread, cress, dried apples and nut-cakes. Then the fellows had decided to take some food to Lord Gwydion and Master Skell, and see what they could do to help. That led to them getting started on dismantling the storage room hoard. They barely noticed when it grew dark outside and the indoor lights gradually came on.
When the ladies were ready to go to bed, they went to say goodnight to the men. The King and Master Skell were still working on Tegan. The others had been bringing items into the hallways. There was stuff everywhere, but looking into the room, the pile had appeared as big as ever.

"My dear friends," the Queen had said. "Beloved brother. Thank you. Please don't wear yourselves out. It took a long time to get this way. Don't expect to fix it overnight. We're going to bed now."
"Wait a moment, Treya," Lord Gwydion had said. "May we have a graphite stick and a pad please?"
"Of course," she'd replied. "Do you need me to scribe?"
"Thank you for offering," Master Skell had said, "but that won't be necessary."

When the women had gotten up that morning, most of the men had still been asleep in the other dorm rooms. Even the two An Dhew lay stretched out on benches in the courtyard. Dina was still in bed too. Arghan was sitting alone, eating some breakfast. He rose.
"Come and see!" he said.

The women had followed him down the hallway and into the long pillared room.
"Look!" Lowi had exclaimed. They had stared in surprise. The room was lit up with a soft warm light. There were couches, carpets, chairs, cushions, tables, lamps, bookshelves, pictures, sculptures, toys, games, art supplies, a wardrobe, and a tool bench.

"I can't believe they managed to do this!" Lady Arianrhod had exclaimed. "No wonder they're exhausted. Let them rest. Let's go visit the birds."

After watching the birds for awhile they came back inside. Arghan excused himself. Treya, Pippa, Lowi, and the Queen were in the courtyard room, quietly working on the gown, when the rest of the men finally got up. Dina appeared also. The women commended the men on the lovely room, and the men complimented them on the graceful garment.

Lord Gwydion embraced Lady Arianrhod and said, "Will you walk with me, sister?"
They strolled off into the pillared room. They stayed in there for a little while, speaking together.
When they returned, Lord Gwydion said, "I'd like the An Dhew to go down and locate the Watch. Let them know that the Queen will appear in the grotto tomorrow at noon."
"The An Dhew are your personal guard, Sire," said Marcus. "They're not supposed to leave you."
"It's alright," said Lord Gwydion. "I have all of you to look out for me."

In the courtyard room, Bruno and Brutus were busy with something over by the pool. Master Skell stood nearby and watched. The women drew closer. Behind the pool, a large rounded obsidian obelisk was standing upright on a shelf, buttressed by some white blocks.
Small silver lamps had been placed on two of the blocks. On another, there was a silver bowl filled with cress and mushrooms. Around the base of the obelisk, there was a delicate ribbon of white linen.
"We found some special items, so we've made a shrine to Vesta," said Brutus.

"Like we did when we were children," said Bruno. "Down there, somewhere, long ago." He waved in the general direction of the farmlands below.
"Who is Vesta?" asked Lowi.
"She's the goddess of hearth and home," said Bruno.
"What's a goddess?" asked Lady Arianrhod.
"A kind and pretty lady," Bruno replied.
"With a great deal of power," added Brutus.

"Goddess is a feminine manifestation of rarified energy that manifests as a personality," said Master Skell. "In this case, the character is nurturing, sheltering, and receptive."
"The lamps represent the hearth," said Brutus. "Vesta is the goddess of the sacred flame."
Bruno pointed to the obelisk, and said, "That's the fascinum. For protection. I used a strip of the white fabric to adorn it. It was on the floor. I hope that's alright."
"Fabric that was on the floor," said the Queen with a big grin. "That's better than alright!"
"The bowl represents Cornucopia," Bruno continued. "It's usually represented by a horn-shaped basket of food, but we used a bowl."
"What is Cornucopia?" asked the Lady.
"It means Horn of Plenty," said Brutus. "It's any large open container, so crammed full of good things that they're spilling over."
"Perhaps the storage room is my Cornucopia," said the Lady. "Good things keep appearing from it."

Dina had been eating breakfast. Now she came over to join them. They all looked at the impromptu altar.
"I think we're sleep deprived, brother," said Bruno.
"Why, does this seem mad?" asked Brutus, with a sheepish grin.
"I like it," said the Lady. "Thank you. Goddess Vesta is welcome to dwell in the sky-tower with me."

Arghan and Lord Gwydion came into the room.
"What have you been up to?" Pippa asked.
"We're working on the sky-viewer," Arghan replied. "The thing with the tubes, in the little room, that's the sky-viewer. Pippa, I was going to use some of our gemstones to replace the ones that are missing. You don't mind, do you?"
"Of course not," she replied. "What an excellent use for them. But will they fit?"
"Some of them will," said Arghan. "The openings have adjustable apertures."
"Perfect," said Pippa.

"Arghan," said Lord Gwydion, "I'm still surprised that you've carried those around with you this whole time."

"The mysterious Lord of an underground kingdom gave me a bag of rare gems," said Arghan, with a grin. "I didn't know what else to do with them. I liked carrying them around. And now they get to be useful. What did you do with yours, Marcus?"

"I passed them along," Marcus replied.

"He put them to a good cause," Lord Gwydion added.

"When Marcus found out how much they were worth," said Dina, "he gave them to Terranes to help run Vindavia Nova. We're expanding the school, repaving the roads, and planting a vineyard."

"Well done, Marcus!" said Pippa.

"Yes indeed," said the King, "I'm very happy about that. And I am grateful that Arghan is willing to restore the sky-viewer so we might use it tonight. I don't know if it will help, but it's worth a try."

Arghan pulled out the bag of gemstones. "I'll need a tray, to sort these." He took a shallow bowl from the table and gently poured the gemstones into it. There were faceted rubies, emeralds, amethysts, peridots, cabochon sapphires in yellow, blue and indigo, and discs of amber, moonstone and rutilated quartz.

"Oh!" Lowi cried. "They're so beautiful. Wait, is that a... button?" she asked, pointing to an abalone disk with four holes in it.

"Oh, yes!" Pippa said. "There are several buttons. We can use them on the gown! And where are the bears? There are two amber bears carved into beads. Or do I mean two amber beads carved into bears?"

"Here they are, Lowi." She held out her hand. "Three large buttons, five small buttons, and two bears."

"I'm so excited for you, Lady Arianrhod," said Lowi. "Tomorrow is going to be a special day." She took the beads and buttons and returned to the dress, which was lying on a bench in the courtyard.

"The Watch are going to be so relieved to see you, Lady," said Pippa.

"And Amser Gwas Twenty-six is going to be very happy," said Dina.

"What else will you need for tomorrow?" asked Treya.

"I wear my diamond hair-net," the Queen replied. "It's up there, in the little blue box." She pointed to a shelf over Pippa's head. Pippa took down the box, set it on the bench, and opened it. Lady Arianrhod picked up the hair-net, a fine white metal web, set with tiny sparkling diamonds. She draped it over her head. The ladies made appreciative sounds.

"I don't want to forget it," the Queen said, taking it off and holding it. "That's happened before. It's embarrassing."

"Maybe put it someplace noticeable, where we won't miss it?" Pippa said.

"Here," said Dina. She took it and draped it over the fascinum. The shiny hair-net gleamed against the dark obelisk.

"Perfect!" the Queen exclaimed, and the women laughed in delight.

"What else?" asked Treya. "You bring gifts, don't you?"

"Yes," said the Queen. "Gold and silver. That's in the vault, hidden under the console."

They followed her into the control room. She reached up behind the console, turned something, and a drawer slid out. In the drawer were what appeared to be full bags of coin. She picked one up and closed the drawer again. The console locked into place and the drawer seemed to disappear. She handed the coin-purse to Treya.

"There's one more thing," said the Lady. "Just this time. I hope just this time."

They followed her into the big room. She went over to the shelf and picked up the square box. It was made of dark brown wood, with a hinged lid. She set the box on a bench and opened the lid. She reached into the box with both hands.

"This is what remains of Amser Gwas Twenty-five," she said, holding up a gleaming skull. "The buzzards did a very good job of cleaning him up. The rest of him was taken by wind and weather. I thought that I should have some remnant of him, in case we were ever able to get out of here again. Something to give his family."

She held up the skull, peering into its empty eyes. "He's been a good friend. He's been my only friend."

"Oh," said Lowi. "That's so sad."

"Now you have many friends, Lady Queen" said Dina.

"Thank you," she said. She set the skull back into the box. The Lady took the bag of coins from Treya and put it in the box too.

"What's that?" asked Treya. In the corner of the box there was a scroll, rolled up and sealed with red wax.

"It is a message from Amser Gwas to his kin-folk," said the Queen. "His health was starting to fail. It seemed clear that he would never see them again. So he wrote them a letter. He sealed it, so I don't know what it says."

She closed the box, and set it back on the shelf.

"Ready," she said.

Pippa, Treya, Lowi and Lady Arianrhod were all back in the courtyard. The gown was finished. The King had re-joined Master Skell. They were still working on Tegan near the storage room. Marcus was helping Arghan with the sky viewer. Bruno and Brutus had gone to assess the damage to the blasted corridor, and to see if there was anything they could do to make it more secure.

They sat. The Queen looked around. Then she said, "I hate to be rude, but I could use a nap."
"I think we all could," said Lowi.

When Treya woke up, it was dark inside the bed chamber. Light was spilling in from the doorway. People were speaking.
The An Dhew are back, thought Treya, climbing out of her bunk. She stretched and went into the courtyard. The Queen and Pippa followed. Dina and Lowi came too, moving slowly.

"They found the Watch," said Lord Gwydion to his sister. "They will be there at noon."
"Thank you, brother," said the Lady. "I am prepared for tomorrow."
"We must all prepare too," said Marcus. "We depart after the ceremony."
"So soon?" cried Lowi. "Must we?"
"It pains me to leave, after such a short reunion," said Lord Gwydion. "But Ari, now that I know you are alright, I need to continue the search for our sire. And we mustn't keep our friends in the harbor waiting for us."
"Of course, you should get on with the journey," she said. "And I need to focus on training the new Amser Gwas."
"Now that we know how to find you, Lady," said Pippa, "we will continue to support you and your work."
"The An Dhew are all at your service," said one of them.
"Thank you," said the Lady.
"Bruno and I have made some temporary repairs to the blasted corridor," said Brutus.
"Well done," she replied. "It can be repaired properly, now that you've rescued the compound. It will give Amser Gwas something to do."
Just then Master Skell appeared, with Tegan following behind.
"We're ready, Lord," said Master Skell.
Lord Gwydion went over to his sister. He reached into his pocket and showed her the tablet.
"Say this, just like it's written," he said. The Lady looked at the script.
"Tegan," she said.

"Yes, Lady."

"Fill blue jar with clear water. Next, bring blue jar with clear water here to me. Next, transfer blue jar into my hand."

They all watched as the automaton carried out the task. Some of the water splashed out as she brought it over, but otherwise the experiment was successful.

"Thank you, Tegan," said the Lady. She drank the water. Tegan stood still.

"Do you want to try a command?" Lord Gwydion asked his sister. She smiled and nodded.

"Tegan," the Lady said.

"Yes, Lady."

"Go to empty bench. Next, pick up small yellow cushion. Next, transfer small yellow cushion to floor in front of Tegan."

Tegan went and picked up the pillow and set it gently on the floor.

"Haha!" exclaimed the Queen. "That shouldn't be so satisfying. But it is! Alright, you can put it back."

Tegan didn't move. The Queen said, "I mean, Tegan."

"Yes, Lady."

"Pick up small yellow cushion. Next, transfer small yellow cushion back to empty bench."

Tegan did just that.

The Queen clapped her hands in delight. "My brilliant big brother can overcome anything," she said. "And clever Master Skell seems to know everything. I'm so fortunate!"

"So the new command is all about... obeying commands?" Pippa asked the King.

"Basically," he replied. "We tried a number of different phrases. What we finally settled on was, 'Allow Lady to instruct Tegan. Do what Lady tells Tegan to do. Follow Lady's directions. Perform tasks as Lady commands'."

"Simple, but brilliant," said Arghan.

"Now that you know how it works, Lady," said Master Skell, "you can change the command if you wish, or the vocabulary. Say, if you need to perform a specific technical task. And then you could go back to this mode if you want. It's saved under the title Tegan Nova."

"Tegan Nova is welcome in the sky tower," said the Lady. "Thank you."

"And thank you, Lady Arianrhod, for being up here," said Lowi, "doing this difficult work to keep us safe. Never getting to spend time on the surface."

"It's alright, Lady Borlowan," said the Queen. "I don't really care for the surface. I prefer it up here."

Later that night, after a relaxed and enjoyable meal, the companions all went to the Sky-Viewer. Arghan, Dina, Treya, Lord Gwydion and Lady Arianrhod went inside. The others crowded around the doorway to watch.

Treya had her pad ready to take notes, and to copy the patterns of the stars. Arghan was also going to be sketching a sky map, and so was Pippa, in the doorway. Arghan sat at the console. He flipped a lever, and a green light appeared. There was a humming sound.

"It takes a moment to warm up," he said.

"What do you know about Thule, sister?" asked the King.

"Only that Thule is a cold northern land," she replied. "The name means 'Sacred Fire'."

"That makes sense," said Dina. "If you lived in a winter world, fire would be very important."

The tubes began to emit red light through the holes. Then green. Then blue. The Queen turned the wheel and the entire assembly shifted upward. She moved it up and down incrementally. The gems began to shine. Suddenly, there were the outlined images of continents, islands, and seas, stretched out over their heads, curving over the northern horizon.

It was in the room, but it was also outside of it. It was overhead, but it was as if they were looking down at it.

The scene was dazzling. Treya was trying to take it all in, and struggling to find the words to briefly describe this spectacle in her notes. The map was made from shapes that were created by contoured outlines of colored light. There were green land masses, and blue oceans, rivers and lakes. A bright field of stars shifted with the images.

At the northern horizon, the scene curved away and disappeared. Outside of the control room, in between the bright areas, there was the vast blackness of space. The actual stars were dimmed and indistinct. Inside the room, the colored lines continued, falling across the companions in shifting bars of spectral light.

Lady Arianrhod turned a dial. The view zoomed in closer, and went to the north. The curve of the earth seemed to be coming right at them. Pippa started to cry out, then stopped herself.

They were looking at a series of white outlines, scattered widely along the same latitude across the northern regions.

Lady Arianrhod pulled a viewing scope out of a hatch in the console. It was attached to the console by a long cord. She held it up to her eyes and looked at the map.

"This is confusing," said the Lady, peering through the scope. "There are a number of places called Thule."

"What do you mean, Lady?" asked Treya.

"Several of these northern lands are labeled Thule," said the Lady. "But they have different names. There are three that I can chart from here: Thule Mawr- the big one, Thule Litrík- the colorful one, and Thule Esta- the eastern one."

"Which is closest to Alba?" asked Dina. "Can you show us?"

The Lady moved her fingers, and the screen slid forward again, traveling north and west. Treya recognized the Kernowek peninsula. She was relieved to have found a reference point.
The map moved past the coastline and out west of Scotia. There were scattered green islands within the large blue-outlined areas. Then the scattered islands turned white. One large and irregularly-shaped white island hove into view.

"This is Thule Litrík. It is the closest one to us," said the Queen. "Thule Mawr is much, much bigger, and it's way further west. Thule Esta is far to the east, above the continent."

"Thule Litrík it is then," said Lord Gwydion.

"I'm pausing the viewer here," the Lady said. "Copy your star charts, scriveners. Quickly please. This thing can't stay on for too long, or the gems start breaking."

Arghan and Pippa were busy sketching. Treya had been so entranced by the images that she had forgotten about charting the stars. Now she focused on them, and tried to represent their locations in reference to Thule Litrík. Everyone was silent while the three of them scribed their star-maps.

"It's getting hot," said the Lady, putting the scope away. "I'm shutting it down."
She turned a knob, then flipped the switch on the panel. The colored lines withdrew inwardly, disappearing as they came towards the viewers. When they were gone, the open holes of the tubes flashed with blue, then green then red.

The room was dark. Treya could still see the brightly-colored lines of the world, even though they were gone. They seemed to be attached to her eyes, jumping across her vision as she looked around. Slowly, they faded.

"How is this technology possible?" asked Marcus. "There would have to be some sort of... signal devices up in space, to get that view of the earth."

"I don't know," said Lady Arianrhod. "And I don't know who does." She put her arm around her brother. "We're just very old children, aren't we? Playing with the toys that the grownups left behind."

They all returned to the courtyard room.

Pippa, Arghan and Treya compared their star-maps. They looked reassuringly similar.
Bruno stared at the charts. He recited, "Big bear, little bear, northern star."
"Yes, of all the quadrants of the sky," said Arghan, "at least this is the one we know best."
"Unless the skies are clouded and we can't see the stars," said Brutus.
"It's true," said Arghan. "We are going to need the stars."

"We should sleep now," said Master Skell.
"I don't know if I can," said the Queen. "I'm nervous about tomorrow."
"I'm a little nervous too," said Lowi. "About tomorrow, and about our upcoming journey to the frozen north that depends upon the stars."

"Lie down, friends," said Lord Gwydion. "Relax and find peace. I will play you to sleep."

The companions went to their beds. The King stayed in the courtyard room. He took out his harp and began to play a tune. First it was major, then minor, then major, then minor. Treya felt the tension leaving her back and shoulders.

Lord Gwydion began to sing:

"Arth fawr, arth fach, seren ogleddol
 Dewch â ni arweiniad ac eddol
 Nid y beddol, nid y beddol"

Big bear, little bear, northern star
Bring us guidance and health
Not the grave, not the grave

The next thing she knew, it was morning.

Chapter Eleven - Morhogh Ho!

It was the big day. There was a gentle rain falling and the sky was filled with mist. Inside the courtyard room, Lowi was in her element. Getting royal ladies ready for big ceremonies was her specialty. The normally soft-spoken Lady Borlowan had taken command of the situation. She made sure that Lady Arianrhod washed her hair first thing in the morning, so that it would have time to dry. She wrapped the Lady's locks in twists and rolls, with scraps of linen. Then she actually forbade the Queen from going outside to visit the birds, which she apparently did every morning, whatever the weather.

"With all due respect, Lady," she had said, "you need to stay clean, and let your hair dry. It's just for one day. The birds will understand."
The Queen had still looked uncertain. "But they're used to me coming out there. I've not missed a morning, ever. Even the day after the fireball. I learned to feel my way around."
"How about if we cover the Lady with a shawl?" Treya had asked.
Lowi had reluctantly agreed. They had used a leftover piece of the white linen. Pippa and Treya had held it over the Lady as they walked about. The birds had been excited to greet the Queen, swarming around her feet and chirping loudly.

After they visited the birds, the women took a light meal together.
"We should leave the rest of our food with Lady Arianrhod," said Treya. "We can get some more, right?"
"What if you can't?" asked the Queen. "Take your food. I'll be fine."

"How?" asked Lowi. "What is it that you eat, Lady?"
"Mushrooms, algae, and cress," she replied. "And sometime I eat eggs. I don't really like them, but they're nutritious, and there's way too many of them to hatch."
"That doesn't sound so bad," said Pippa. "But we should still leave something."
"No, the new ascendant will probably be carrying food," said the Queen. "And I don't want to feel responsible for you going hungry on your journey. You can bring me something to eat when you come back this way with Sira Conn." She walked over and looked at the altar.
"May Vesta protect you and guide you safely home."

When it was time to descend, they gathered in the big room. The companions had all their gear packed, and they were ready to head to the harbor after the ceremony.

Lowi entered with Lady Arianrhod.

The Lady really did look like the Queen of Heaven. The gown that Lowi had created was elegant. It was form fitting at the bodice. The skirt billowed like a gossamer cloud. The shiny buttons had been added at the waist and on the cuffs of the puffy sleeves.

The amber bears were facing one another on either side of the collar, with a delicate drape of linen between them, falling down the back like a cape. The Lady's hair hung in lush curly ringlets beneath her sparkling net.

Treya thought about the way she had appeared when they had first seen her. *Was that really just the day before yesterday?* she thought in amazement. *No wonder we're all so tired.*

Arghan brought over the box and set it in front of the Queen. He opened it. The Queen looked inside.

"Amser Gwas, the letter, and the gold and silver," she said. "All here."

Arghan peered in the box. "Are they gold and silver coins?" he asked.

"No," she replied. "It's just gold and silver."

Lady Arianrhod reached in, took out the coin purse, and handed it to him. He opened the bag and poured a bit into his hand.

"It literally is gold and silver," he said. "Big grains and nuggets of both. And some electrum mixture. It's a lovely treasury." He replaced the precious metal, tied the purse and put it in the box. The Lady closed the box, and he picked it up.

"I'm sorry we're leaving so soon, Lady," said Treya. "It's a pleasure and an honor to be in your company."

"All hail!" said Brutus.

"All hail!" the others agreed.

The descent was uneventful. The twins had re-enforced the damaged area with some cables and planks. Everyone passed through it without incident. Around and down they went. There was a crackling thunderstorm at the same level as there had been on the way up. The walls glowed eerily during the lightning flashes. The friends kept going downward. After a while, the storm ended, and the windows showed blue sky. Treya's thighs were beginning to cramp when they reached the platform with the armory.

"Is it alright if we take a break?" she asked.

"Yes," said Lord Gwydion. "We've made good time. Let's relax for a while."

They all settled down wearily onto the grate, except for the two An Dhew who stood guard at the opening. Lord Gwydion went over to them.

"Please, friends," he said, putting a hand on each of their shoulders, "take a rest. We're safe here, and you two journeyed far yesterday."

The An Dhew came and sat down with the others. They all passed around some dried grapes, and a jug of apple wine that had been found in the storage room.

"I want to know more about my niece and her children," said the Queen. The companions had been filling her in on their adventures, and on the fate of her family members. "I can hardly believe that of all of you, it was Gofannan who managed to find a wife. He was so quiet and shy. Not like you, Gwydion, or bratty little Amatheon. Although it sounds as though Theon got the family he deserves, a bunch of squeaky animals."

"He takes good care of the Lagaloor, and they love him," said Marcus.

"And don't forget," said Pippa, "Fishy is a great hero."

"Right," said the Lady Arianrhod. "He saved Queen Sidhi from the snake-headed monster of the pit." She shuddered. "How did we get talking about this? I want to hear about the babies. Gwynalli's sons. Nico and Cassius."

"They are handsome children, with strong limbs," said Lord Gwydion. "They have pale faces, with dimpled cheeks, like Dmitri. Almond shaped brown eyes and bushy dark hair, like Gwynalli."

"They may look similar," said Marcus, "but their personalities are very different. Cassius is bossy and charming. Nico is sincere and trusting. Cassius plays him like a harp."

"But little Cassius loves his brother," said Dina. "Almost as much as he loves himself. And that's a lot."

"Well," said the Queen, "when those babies grow up, I hope they have more babies. And so on. Eventually, I'll need to be replaced here. We don't live forever; the death of Uncle Math has made that clear."

"On that note," said Lord Gwydion, smiling, "we should probably get going."

Dina, Lowi, Master Skell and the Queen waited on the platform while the others went in to get their gear. The companions put on their armor and replaced their weapons. Treya felt better having her dagger and her horn back in her belt.

"Oh!" she said, feeling her head. "I just realized, I should have removed my headband."

"Gods, Treya!" said Pippa. "You had a big piece of metal, right on your head, this whole time. How did we all miss that?"

"Because it's so nicely disguised," said Arghan, "under the pretty fabric."

They proceeded to descend the stairs. When they reached the bottom they gathered around the portal. Lady Arianrhod was smiling, but her hands were trembling. The women all stood around her supportively.

Arghan and Marcus went to the portal and used their lens keys to activate the system. As soon as the dewdhek appeared, Marcus inserted his key. The space between them slowly dissolved, and they could see light and movement on the other side of the opening. Bruno and Brutus stepped through and flanked the portal. The rest of them came through, and lined up beside the twins on either side. The Queen came last, standing between them.

The terrace of the cavern had been decorated with flowers, and the long flat stone had been laid with a cloth and covered in food and drink. There were twelve people there. Five were the men of the Watch: Amser Gwas, Hedyn, Awyr, Seren, and Glaw. The others were two teenage boys, a middle aged couple, two young women, and a very old man. They all lined up directly before the Queen's entourage and bowed.

The companions did the same, except for the Queen. She nodded. Then she spoke:

"Brave men of the watch. Devoted family members. The powers above thank you for your service. We humbly apologize for not being here sooner. There was a mechanical problem that kept us from being able to exit the tower. But thanks to our friends," she indicated the companions, "the problem is resolved." She took a deep breath, then continued.

"It cannot have been easy, over these past years, to keep the faith. Please accept this token of gold and silver." She reached in the box and took out the purse. One of the boys came forward, took it, bowed, and then gave it to the middle aged woman, who in turn gave it to the old man.

"And now," said the Queen, "this is difficult. It is to my great shame and sadness that Amser Gwas Twenty-five never got to return to his family. He was a kind and noble companion until the end." She lifted up the skull. It stared out at the crowd with empty eyes.
"I've brought you what remains of his mortal body," the Queen said. She set the skull back in the box and withdrew the scroll.

"Amser Gwas Twenty-five wrote a message," she said. "I will read it to you. I don't know what it says." She broke the seal and opened the scroll. Her voice was trembling as she read:

"Dearest family and fellow Watchmen. It has been my great privilege to have lived and died in service of the Queen of Heaven. No one else has had that honor. Her friendship and devotion never wavered, even when my declining health had become a burden. She always treated me with great care and kindness." The Queen paused. She looked as if she might cry. Then she continued.

"The Lady might try to tell you that it was her fault that the portal jammed, but with all due respect, it was my fault and no one else's, she was just too kind to want me to believe that. She is a great Queen and a fine person. I wish success to the next Amser Gwas, and all the Watchers and their families. I, Amser Gwas Twenty-five, leave you now, in my seventy-seventh year of life. My spirit flies with you."

Tears were streaming down the Lady's cheeks. Nearly everyone else was crying too. Lowi pulled out a cloth and dabbed the Queen's eyes. The Lady replaced the scroll and closed the box. The middle-aged man came forward and took it, placing it reverently in the center of the table.

Introductions were made all around. The Queen was escorted by the two boys to a stone seat that had been covered with a sheep skin. She sat. The rest of them sat around the table, on the ground.
The Lady addressed the men of the Watch.
"Before we begin, I want to again thank you, our brave Watchmen. You were all injured by the fireball to some degree. Our Healer is coming around now with a cloth. It has medicinal properties."

Dina unwrapped a parcel from her bag. She withdrew five linen hand cloths which had been soaked in the remaining medicine water and then air-dried.
"Take these. At night, use just enough water to dampen it. Not too much, because there's medicine in there, and you don't want to wash it all away. Apply the cloth gently, on your face, and around your eyes, before you go to sleep. The cloth needs to dry out. Once it dries out, keep it somewhere safe. It can be dampened and reused. Don't wash it. The medicine should last for several applications. The Lady has more powder, if it's needed."

The Watchmen all put the cloths into their pockets, and Dina went to her seat.
The feast began. Several jugs of ale were shared around the table. People were relaxing and engaging in conversation. At one point, the middle-aged lady opened the box, took out the skull, closed the box, and set the skull on top of it. Brutus filled a cup with ale and set it before the skull, to sounds of approval. Everyone toasted the late Amser Gwas Twenty-five.

Treya and Lowi smiled at each other. All this strangeness was beginning to feel quite normal.

They enjoyed each other's company for about an hour. Then the Queen rose. Everyone else did too. Amser Gwas Twenty-six went to stand before the Queen. He bowed, and she put a lens key pendant over his head. He tucked it into his shirt.
The middle-aged man came forward and handed him a large basket, full of food.
"We will leave provisions," said the man. "Every new moon."
"Thank you, friends," said the Queen. "Let us not wait twelve years to do this again. At the next summer solstice, we will appear once more."
The crowd seemed very happy to hear that.

"Next summer solstice," said one of the boys. "I can hardly wait!"

The Queen stood there, her new helper by her side. She looked at her brother and smiled. Lord Gwydion took out his harp, played the strings, and sang:

"O-ro, o-ro, we come and we go
We welcome our friends, to come back again
O-ro, o-ro, o-ro"

They all sang it, two more times. At the end of the third chorus, the Lady Arianrhod and Amser Gwas stepped through the opening. Marcus retrieved the lens-key and closed the portal. The Watch and their families cleared the table in solemn silence, removing every trace of the celebration. They bowed to the companions and left the terrace. It was over.

"Oh," sniffled Lowi. "That happened so fast. This has all happened so fast."
Dina came over and gave Lowi a big hug.
"We come and we go!" said Dina.
"Then, let's go," said Marcus. "To the harbor."

That evening, back on the ship, the events of the past two days had seemed like a strange and wonderful dream. So much had happened. As she recalled the adventure, Treya had been making notes, with Lowi's help. She didn't want to forget the details. She'd sat on the stern rail with her, and scribed until it was getting dark.

By the time that they had returned to the harbor that afternoon, there were four new ships at anchor; two from the distant North, one from the nearby Hebrides, and one from the Iberian peninsula. The companions had walked along the dock, admiring the different vessels.

For some reason, the far end of the pier where the Morhogh had anchored was now busy with activity. The food vendors had even moved to their vicinity. The once quiet spot was bustling. A fire pit had been constructed on the adjacent gravel bank, and racks of fish were slowly roasting high above the flames. Log benches were set up, and there was a table covered with baskets of provisions, platters, cups, and jugs.

"Morhogh ho!" Arghan had called, as they approached the gangplank. Piri had appeared with a yip of delight. Piran hailed them from above, as he climbed down the rigging. Santo stood at the top of the gangway.
"Welcome back, travelers," he had said. "Welcome, friends, old and new. Come aboard."
One by one, the Captain had greeted them as they stepped aboard. They had crowded onto the deck to make introductions.

It was a bit of a squeeze. Treya had looked around, making a mental note. They were a group of twelve: Master Skell, Lord Gwydion, two An Dhew, Pippa, Arghan, Marcus, Dina, Bruno, Brutus, Lowi and herself. That, along with the three crew members, made for a crowded little ship.

"What's going on here?" Arghan had said to the crew. "I thought you were going to keep things quiet. It looks like you're hosting a festival."
"We tried to keep things quiet," Santo had replied. "All we did was ask about procuring some winter gear, which apparently nobody does in summer, unless they are getting up to something of interest. The locals are desperately bored, and extremely inquisitive. And there just happens to be two ships full of north-men docked here, from the continent. They been very helpful, I must say. They've brought us food, and furs, and a map."

"A map to Thule?" Dina had asked.
"No," Santo said, "it's a map of Thule itself."
"That's even better," Arghan had said. "If it's the right Thule."
"There's more than one?" Santo asked with alarm.
"Yes," said Arghan, "but we know which one we're headed for." He put his hand on the skipper's shoulder. "Santo, we found a star chart."
"Oh!" exclaimed Santo. "You don't know how I've been worrying about that."
"Yes I do," Arghan said, laughing. "That's why I'm giving this to you now."

He handed the skipper his neatly scribed copy, which had been declared the clearest and most accurate of the three.

"It looks surprisingly straightforward," Santo had said.

"Surprising, perhaps," Piran had said, making a sign of protection. "Nothing in that part of the world is straightforward."

They looked at the map of the island that the Northmen had given them. The outline of it was wildly irregular. It's branching fingers spread out across the sea. There were some words written with runic symbols on the map, and a paragraph in what appeared to be the Northerner's speech.

"This looks like what we saw in the viewer," Pippa had said. "What a strange shape it is. All those tendrils reaching out into the sea."

"Created by volcanoes, I would imagine," Master Skell had noted.

"Perhaps that is the reason that Thule is the land of sacred fire," Dina had said. "Because of the volcanoes."

"It's much bigger than I thought it would be," Lord Gwydion had sighed. "I've never been to any island except the Shoe, and the Isle of Manannán. I'm afraid I don't know where to even start looking."

"That's where the story comes in," said Santo.

"There's a story?" Lord Gwydion's eyes lit up. "What does it say?"

"I don't know," said Santo, "I can't read it, and the North-Man didn't have enough Brythonic to fully explain it. But I figured Master Skell would be able to translate."

Master Skell looked closely at the square of dense text at the bottom of the map. He pointed to a spot on the east coast.

"This settlement is Höfn, the Port. Nearby is Hornafirði, Horn-Harbor. There's Vatnajǫkull, that's a glacier pool. In there are ice caves, íshellar. We're not looking for the large ice-cavern, but one of the smaller ones, whose entrance is hidden from view. In this ice cave there is a dormant volcano, Eldfjall, where the cave gnomes keep watch over 'kaldr hildingr', the Cold King. Well! That seems like a good place to start."

"It certainly does," Arghan had agreed.

"It looks right," Pippa had said. "But does it actually say that this is Thule?"

"No, it's called Hellisland," said Master Skell. "That means Cave-Land. Or White-Land."

"White-Cave-Land," Arghan had said. "There are supposed to be ice caves where we're going, after all."

Master Skell had been studying the map up close. "It's seems clear that Hellisland is Thule Litrík," he'd said. "Litrík. That means colorful. Look at some of these names. Rauð Laug. Red Pool. Gullsandar. Gold Sands."
"They sound colorful, alright," Arghan had replied. "It must be quite a place."

"What an extraordinary gift this map is," Treya said.
"The Northerners are known for their enthusiastic hospitality," Piran had commented.
"We never asked for any of it," Santo had said. "And we never told them anything, except that we were looking for winter clothes. But they seem to know what we're doing."
"Yes," Piran had added, "and they've come around every night, and told us tales, and sung songs. The Scots and Hispanians too. We don't understand too much of what anybody says, but it's been a jolly time."

While the companions had settled in, Santo had gone to the harbor-master to let him know that they would be departing on the morning tide. It had quickly gotten about the harbor that the large group who had just arrived were the ones going on the mysterious northern journey of the Morhogh, which would be leaving the next day. A celebration was quickly planned for that evening. The news of it had reached the Morhogh before Santo even returned to the ship.

The daylight was fading. Treya finished her notes and put away her scribing materials. She and Lowi walked to the gangplank.
"Have fun, youngsters," said Lord Gwydion.
"Not too much fun," said Master Skell.
The King and the scholar were sitting on the deck with Santo and Piran in the semi-darkness, watching the activity. The An Dhew were close by. Everyone else had gone down already. Bruno and Brutus were waiting for Treya and Lowi on the dock below. The ladies descended the gangway.
"Thank you for waiting," said Lowi.
"Our pleasure, ladies," Bruno and Brutus replied.
They walked towards a large crowd that was queuing up for roasted fish.

Some men passed by. They had long braided beards. Their heads were shaved, except for some spiky strips. They wore trousers with blue and white vertical stripes. They were naked from the waist up, covered in tattoos, and had amulets draped around their necks. The men were well armed with fine-looking weapons. They were speaking a language Treya hadn't heard before. The two men nodded as they passed.
"Who are these people?" Lowi asked, wide-eyed.

"They are from Nordvegr, the North-Way," said Bruno. "From across the cold sea, on the continent. They come here to fish in the nearby waters. The fish haven't shoaled yet, so they are waiting."

"Is it like it is back in Kernow?" asked Lowi. "Where some poor fellow is stuck on the side of a cliff until he finally spots the shoaling and raises the alarm, and everyone goes into action?"

"I think it must be," said Bruno.

"There are northern women here, too," said Brutus. Treya looked where he was indicating. Two tough-looking and well-armed females were carrying a large barrel between them.

"Female warriors," said Treya. "Pippa ought to like that."

They reached the edge of the fish-queue. The four of them waited. Finally, the others appeared, carrying the roasted fish, steaming hot, on long wooden skewers. Piri had a full arm-load.

"That took forever," she said. "I'd better get these back to the ship right away. They'll think that I ran off with their coin."

"Come find us again when you're done, Pixie," said Treya.

They sat down on some driftwood logs. Arghan produced a wineskin, and Marcus brought out a large jug of lemon water. They all had a drink. Then everyone got started on a fish. The rest of the full skewers were stuck point down into the sand.

"My," said Pippa, "they've got quite a business going on there."

"It's no wonder," said Brutus, already reaching for his second one. "These are good."

Piri returned and sat down, helping herself to a fish. Treya was done with hers. She cleaned her hands and took out her pad to make a few more notes about the events of the day. The light was lingering, and she could see well enough.

People came and went. There was still a large crowd around the fish vendor.

"What a good place to people-watch," said Arghan, looking around. "Oh. Hello, sir."

Treya and the others turned to see who he was addressing. A thin elderly man was passing near them, making his way slowly towards the crowd. He wore a brown skull-cap and robe, and carried a crooked staff. He was tattooed with little dots all around his eyes, and there was a thick black line that ran from his lower lip to his throat. He was gazing at their fish as he went by.

"Would you like one of ours, good elder-man?" asked Arghan, indicating the fish. "We've got more than we need."
"And it's a dreadfully long wait," said Pippa. "Will you join us?"

The man came closer. They made room for him on one of the logs, and Lowi brought him a fish. He nodded three times in quick succession, took the fish and began methodically nibbling away at it. When he was done, Bruno offered him the wine-sack, but the man shook his head. He did take a drink of water, and poured a little on his hands, wiping them on his robe.

"Do you want another fish, sir?" asked Lowi.
The man shook his head. Then he pointed at Treya, motioning to himself. Nobody moved. He did it again, gesturing specifically to her scribe pad.

"He wants to scribe something," said Arghan. "Treya, will you let him use your pad?"
She put a fresh sheet on top and handed it to him along with the graphite stick. He began to scribe something that seemed to take most of the page. He handed the page to Arghan, and gave the gear back to Treya.

"Thank you," said Arghan, looking at the sheet. "What does it mean?"
The man crossed his arms over his chest and hugged himself.
"Protection?" Marcus asked.
The man nodded. Then he went back slowly, the way he had come.

Arghan was holding up the sheet, peering at the image.
"This is..." he began. Then he said, "I don't know what this is."
They gathered around, trying to make sense of it.
"It looks like a boat," said Brutus, "with a trident stuck through it, and antennae... or maybe they're oars? Or lamps?"
"Is that a snake?" said Dina.
"Wo," said Pippa. "This is really... different."
"Here, Treya," said Arghan, handing it to her. "We can show it to Master Skell and see if he knows what it's all about." She put it into her pocket.

There were shouts and cheers coming from over by the fire. People were gathered in a big ring around the fire-pit. The fish vendors were gone, and a group of boys were doing handsprings and cartwheels around the ring, causing the crowd to back up and make more space.

A tall man with a red-crested helmet came into the ring and blew a loud note on a long brass horn. Two drummers appeared, playing an upbeat rhythm. A whistle player joined them and began a lively tune. Suddenly a dog came running into the ring. It was an Agassian-type hound, with fur of black, brown and white. It was wearing a fancy ruffled collar. The dog looked happy. Its tail wagged energetically. The crowd cheered.

The show began. A girl came out with a hoop, and the dog jumped through the hoop. Two more girls appeared, each with a hoop, and they proceeded to juggle the hoops as the dog continued to leap through them. The crowd cheered enthusiastically.

"Are you thinking what I'm thinking?" Dina asked Marcus.
He replied, "I can guess that you are thinking about teaching Rosa to jump through a hoop."
Dina grinned. "Wouldn't she love it?"
"Yes, she would," said Marcus with a smile.

The show went on. A woman came out wearing a wide-brimmed hat with dozens of little furry balls hanging from the brim. The balls looked like cat toys. While a dark brooding gentleman played a buzzy little stringed instrument, she led the crowd in an incomprehensibly maudlin and dramatic song. The balls on the hat bounced and swung around comically, in complete juxtaposition to the tragic tone of the performance.

After the singer, two very short men appeared. They leaped over the fire, while a very tall man threw long strands of seaweed at them and they slung them through the air back at him.

Then there was an adorable little girl in a cat suit. She did very impressive front and back handsprings around the fire-pit. After that, there was an acrobat who balanced on the back of a pony, and a juggler on stilts with flaming wands.

The finale was a pantomime bear, performed by two small and very skilled actors inside a bear costume. The creature appeared in the ring amidst oohs and ahhs. It stood on hind legs and sniffed all around, growling. Then it sat down and scratched its ear with its back foot. The crowd laughed. The bear held up an empty fish skewer, and shook its head in comic sadness. The crowd laughed some more. The bear got on all fours and rubbed its butt against some driftwood, as if scratching an itch. The crowd howled with laughter.

Suddenly, the bear was running, charging at various members of the audience.

The crowd screamed in terror and delight. The bear was getting rowdy, and knocking people over. Several of the people it had knocked over had somehow gotten into a brawl, and were wrestling on the ground, or knocking over more people.

It seemed as though things were getting out of hand. Bruno and Brutus stepped in front of Lowi and Treya. But then the tall man with the helmet stepped up and blew the horn again. Everyone stopped and went back to their places. The bear stood in the center of the ring and raised its arms. The drummers played a roll. Then the entire top half of the bear shot up into the air and landed nearby.

Both of the boys in the suit were bowing. The cat-girl and other acrobats were going around with baskets collecting coin, and showing off by doing flips and cartwheels without spilling any.
Arghan, Marcus, Brutus and Bruno all contributed generously.

The show was over. The crowd dispersed.
"That was so fun!" exclaimed Lowi. Everyone's mood had been lightened.
"That bear was so convincing," said Pippa.
"The bouncy dog was the best part," said Dina.

The companions went back to the ship. Santo was standing on the dock, speaking to some of the North-Men. There was one big bald man with huge blond whiskers who seemed very pleased to greet them.

"Vinir! Friends!" Cried the big man, as they boarded the ship. "Vindr ok Vatn. Wind and Water. Heill Óðinns. Good Fortune of Odin."
"Vindur og Vatn. Heill Óðinns," echoed voices throughout the harbor.

The next day, they rose early. The crew were preparing the ship to leave on the morning tide.
The companions were trying to stay out of the way. Four of them were up in the lookouts. Treya and Lady Borlowan were on the lower mast platform. Bruno and Brutus were on the high one. Lowi had overcome her nervousness and managed to climb the rope ladder, with much encouragement from Treya and the twins.

Down below them, Arghan was speaking with Piran. Together, they walked around the Morhogh, stopping occasionally to peer over the sides.
"What are they doing?" asked Lowi. "Is something wrong with the ship?"
"They're inspecting the boats," said Brutus. "We'll probably be using them when we get to where we're going."

"Those little boats?" asked Lowi. "I thought they were just for emergencies."

"Sometimes there's no harbor, apparently," said Bruno, "and you have to row to shore."

"What's also likely," said Brutus, "is that we'll want to go up some waterway where the ship won't fit."

"I've never been in a boat," said Lowi nervously.

"We've never been in one either!" said Brutus.

"I have," said Treya, "I'm skilled at rowing. Well, at least in a flat boat, on a river."

It was time to depart. The four of them came down, and the passengers all gathered on the deck. Piran was with them. Santo and Piri were making the final rounds, inspecting the hold, and making sure that things were secured.

"Good crewman Piran," said Bruno. "It has come to our attention that we might have to use the small-boats, and that most of us are completely inexperienced."

"And at least one of us is nervous about it," said Lowi.

"How many of you *have* been in a boat before?" asked Piran.

"Do river-rafts count?" asked Treya.

"Um... sort of," said Piran.

"How many of you have actually been in a rowboat on the sea?" asked Arghan. Master Skell raised a gloved hand. Lord Gwydion looked uncertain, but he raised his hand. No one else moved.

"Well," said Arghan to Piran, "we had better find a place where we can do a bit of training. We probably need to do a safety drill anyway."

"You're right, Angove," said Piran. "We actually should have done one before we left Trevena. We sometimes stop at Caergybi, before we head onto the open water. There's a small inlet. I'll talk to Santo, once we're under way."

Treya looked down in the hold. It was full of carefully secured supplies and gear. Armor had been stored away. The crew's hammocks had been raised to accommodate the cargo, and were right up against the ceiling.

The ship was ready. The gangplank was pulled, and the anchor was raised. The harbormaster himself came down to cast them off personally. He seemed convinced that their presence had been good for business.

They drifted slowly out of the harbor, coming around to the south as they entered the channel. They were back in the bay. It took some maneuvering to get headed northwards. Finally, the sails filled, the ropes hummed and the wind blew. They were on their way.

Treya and Lowi were on the fore-deck benches, with Arghan, Pippa, Piran, and the twins, looking at the map. Treya had her pad, and was taking notes. Master Skell, Lord Gwydion, and the two An Dhew sat in the bow, watching the playful porpoises that swam with the ship. Marcus and Piri were on the lookout. Dina was sleeping down below.

"Here's where we're going," said Piran. He pointed to a small circular cove. "Treafaddyrd."
"Treafaddyrd, what does that mean?" asked Treya.
"It means treachery, in the old dialect," said Piran. "Probably because of all the rocks. But it could also mean beautiful town."
"In other words," said Arghan, "it would be a beautiful place for a town, except for all the rocks?" They laughed.

"If the wind keeps up, we'll be there soon," said Piran. "It's just a short way up the coast from here."
"Is it near where the Romans attacked the Druids?" asked Pippa.
"I don't think so," Piran said.
"Who *were* the Druids?" asked Lowi. "Where did they come from?" She looked at Pippa.
"I don't really know," said Pippa. "Master Skell?"

The elderly scholar turned his reflective gaze towards them and said,
"The Druids were descended from the devotees of Pythian Apollo and the Sellai priestesses. Their ancient traditions were brought here by the Sea-People. Over time, their ranks grew, and their spiritual way of life flourished. The early Druids worshipped Jupiter, Demeter, Apollo, and many other Greek and Roman deities. They brought with them the tradition of the Oracle of the Dodonean Jupiter, and rituals of the Eleusinian mysteries."

"The Romans knew that and they still destroyed their temples!" exclaimed Pippa.

"The Druids eventually replaced the Roman gods with their own localized ones," Master Skell replied. "They were very well-organized and powerful. And they would not submit to the Empire. Their downfall was having a well-known holy island, Ynys Pwynt, where they all gathered at the same time. Perhaps they thought it was too far west to be in danger."

"When Caesar first came to these isles," said Brutus, "the Romans were met with a unified show of force."
"And they turned around and went back home," Bruno added.

"But when they came back nearly a century later," said Master Skell, "they found a fractured land, with dozens of warring tribes fighting with each other. There was no unified front. The Romans played tribe against tribe. It might even have been the Celts themselves that told the Romans about the Druids gathering on Holy Isle."

"Why would they have done that?" asked Treya.
"They were probably tired of being manipulated," said Master Skell. "The Romans used physical control to subdue people. The Druids were more about mind-control. They alone knew what the Gods wanted. So the people were very dependent upon them, and they had great influence over every single aspect of their society."

"That sort of thing makes me suspicious," said Pippa.
"Yes," said Arghan. "What's to stop folks like that from abusing their power?"
"Indeed," replied Master Skell. "Corruption seems inevitable. Most of the people in those sorts of positions are trying to do what's right. But sadly, there are some who are only in it for the power."

"The Romans and Druids both had a lot to offer," Master Skell continued. "And they both could be cruel and controlling. Druids thought Romans were demons, and Romans thought Druids were barbarians. They didn't understand each other's brutality. After all, which is worse, ritualized human sacrifice, or forcing slaves to fight to the death for entertainment?"

"They're both horrible," said Arghan.
"Yes, they are," Master Skell replied.
The companions were silent.

"Why were they called Druids?" asked Lord Gwydion.
"The priest or instructor was called Gwydd," Master Skell replied. "Gwydd refers to knowledge. Like your own name, Sire," he said, nodding at the King, "which means both Keeper of Wisdom and Old Man."

"I thought that a *goose* was a gwydd," said Piran. "No offense, sir. I've heard it called that."
"That's also appropriate, good Piran," said Lord Gwydion, laughing.

"The head priest became the Dur-Gwydd," Master Skell continued, "or Durwydd. Druid also means men of the oak trees in some of the Celtic regions. In Gaelic, it means sorcerer or wise man. Dru means timber in Sanskrit, and the Greek dryads are spirits of the trees. So you see, Druid is a powerful word."

"And what is the Oracle of Dodonean Jupiter?" asked Pippa.

"The Sellai," said Master Skell, "were the original priestesses of Dodona, in ancient Epirus. Dodona was where Apollo wrestled and defeated the giant pythonic serpent that lived beneath the earth. In doing so, he took the name, Pythias. In that area was the first grove dedicated to Zeus/Jupiter."

"The grove was filled with the oldest of oak trees," he went on. "There was a huge beech tree in the center, which was worshipped as Dodonean Jupiter, and as Jupiter Phegonaeus, 'one who lives in a beech tree'. In the beech tree, a sacred dove spoke with Jupiter's voice."

"The trees were hung with strands of little brass bells. The woods were filled with deer and hare, and many types of birds. There were also elementals, and nature spirits. And there were fauns, satyrs, nymphs, dryads, forest fairies and wood gnomes. It was in the grove that the oracular dove of Dodona would reveal her prophecies."

"But you may have already guessed that the dove wasn't really speaking. It was a woman, the priestess, cleverly concealed. Because the former priestesses had been harassed and molested by evil men, they created the legend of the talking bird, to detract those who prey on women."

"Cowardly scoundrels," said Marcus distastefully.

"And what are Eleusinian mysteries?" asked Treya, scribing away.

"Mystai," Master Skell said to Treya with a grin, "they involve study of the natural world, especially of trees and the heavens, birds and the weather, esoteric lore, cleansing rituals, devotions to Demeter and Apollo, and a dedication to truth and light. Like you, Treya, the devotees counted the day as beginning the night before. They wore white and gold. They revered all plants, especially holly, ivy, laurel, oak, hazel, chestnut, ash and beech. Once a year, there would be an initiation ceremony, where the novices were said to have rowed across the water in the Cwrwg Gwidrin, or cwch gwydr. Which translates as glass boat."

"Where I come from, cwch gwydr means beer glass," said Piran with a laugh.
"There was probably some of that too," said Master Skell, smiling.

"Treafaddyrd!" Piri cried from the lookout. Piran climbed quickly up to the watch platform. Piri came down and joined the companions. The ship entered a small secluded bay. The water was turquoise blue and amazingly clear. It was indeed full of rocks. They were dark red and black, with bands of orange and pale green. Some were big, like islands, and covered with lichen and seaweed. Others were hidden just below the water. The ship moved cautiously around the obstacles.
On one of the islands, a flock of cormorants were sunning their wide-open wings.
"Cormorants," said Pippa. She counted quickly. "Seven of them."

"What say you, Augers?" Master Skell asked. "What sort of omen is it?"
Lowi suddenly went below deck.
"Augers!" said Marcus. "What do you mean, sir?"
"The ladies are reviving the ancient practice of predictive ornithomancy."
"Telling the future with birds?" he asked incredulously.
"It's more of a process of reflecting on observations of the natural world," said Pippa.

Lowi returned. She handed each Augur their lituus and draped them with their robes. Treya and Pippa pulled up their hoods and stood back to back. They each raised their templum and waited. Treya stared. Unlike on land, the scene changed as the boat drifted along. The cormorants receded, and five sleek-looking ducks came into view. They had blue and white bodies and shiny green heads. They were relaxing on the rocks. The largest male quacked loudly as the ship crawled past.

Treya felt Pippa closing her templum, so she did too. She lowered her hood and they both turned toward the others.
"Whatever you're up to, Augers," said Brutus, "it certainly looks impressive."

"Well," said Treya, "aside from the seven cormorants drying their wings, I've got five colorful ducks, resting on an island. The drake was quite vigilant."
"I've got three buzzards, gliding on the air," said Pippa.
"So?" said Marcus. "What does it mean?"
"I don't know," said Treya. "Pippa?"

"Hmmm," Pippa said. "Right then. The seven cormorants drying their wings, that's us, the seven passengers who came from Trevena. We're powerful, but sometimes we're vulnerable, like them. From them we learn that there is time for action and a time to be still. And like them, we draw strength from the light, and it protects us."

"The five ducks are our friends from the south. They're grounded and confident, full of knowledge and gifts to share. And they're very attractive. So attractive, that strangers may sometimes be a little too interested, so they must remain vigilant, but relaxed."

"The three buzzards are the crew of the Morhogh-"
"We're buzzards?" exclaimed Piri indignantly.
"The buzzard is highly respected in many cultures," said Master Skell, "and ranks high in the ornithological hierarchy."
"They ride the wind," said Pippa. "They know the wind. They are skilled navigators, and masters of any situation. We trust them to know what to do."

"Oh, that's alright then," said Piri, grinning.

"Well done, Augers," said Lord Gwydion.
"Very impressive," said Bruno. "You know who would have enjoyed that little display?"
"Brian Magnus," Brutus replied immediately, smiling. Then he looked sad.
Pippa smiled. "I miss him too," she said.

The Morhogh dropped sail and stopped. There was a splash and then a clicking sound as the anchor was lowered.
"It's beautiful," said Lowi. "Look at the beach!" The wide arc of golden sand sparkled in the morning light. A fine mist drifted along the shoreline.
"Is that where we're going?" asked Pippa.
"Yes," said Piri. "It's a good place for a swim, if you like. There's a freshwater spring nearby to wash off the salt."
"Really?" asked Pippa. "Because I want to swim. I just don't want to be sticky with brine afterwards."

Piri organized a drill whereupon hearing the alarm, the passengers were supposed to put on one of the cork vests that hung along the side-rail, and gather by the small boats. They were divided up amongst the three vessels, so everyone knew where they were going. They tried it once. Then Piri had them put the vests away, and disperse. They tried it again. This time it went a little quicker.

They took a break and sat on the sunny deck. They had a light meal of bread, shrimp, pickled red onions, and dried apples. Dina appeared from downstairs, blinking in the brightness.

"Dina," called Lowi, "we're going to the beach!"

Twenty minutes later they had changed clothes, stowed their valuables, and gathered whatever they needed for the trip to shore. They put on the cork vests and met the crew at their muster stations.

Santo and Piri were lowering one of the boats. Bruno and Brutus were lowering another, and Arghan and Marcus were lowering the third. The three ladders were unfurled and Arghan, Piri, and one of the An Dhew all climbed down into a boat and secured the other ends.

"The trickiest part is getting on and off," said Piran. "Keep your weight low and balanced. Find a place to sit and keep still." One by one, they boarded the boats. Bruno, Brutus, Lowi, and Treya went with Piri in the slightly larger craft. Treya was being put to the test, having been invited to take an oar.

Dina and Pippa were being piloted by Marcus and Arghan, and Master Skell and Lord Gwydion were being rowed by the two An Dhew.

They took off. Treya pulled the oar, watching Piri for her cues. It was easy, and fun. They made their way along the water, bumping up and down gently as the choppy little waves hit their hulls. Halfway between the ship and shore, Arghan called, "This looks like a good place. Stop rowing. Circle right."

The three boats practiced going in a circle to the right, then the left, then going forwards, then backwards, always returning to the same spot.

"Come close together," said Piri. "Fishtail your oars to keep in place. Then extend the port-side oar over to the next boat, so they can grab it. This is how we stay together in rough water."

The three boats were locked together, bobbing gently.

"Who is looking forward to swimming?" asked Arghan. "Because we need a volunteer to go in so that we can demonstrate a rescue-"

"I'll do it!" said Dina. She immediately stood up. Dina flailed her arms dramatically, as if she were losing her balance. Then she hurled herself overboard.

"DINA!" hollered Marcus. Lowi shrieked. Lord Gwydion and Master Skell were laughing merrily at the performance.

Everyone looked. Dina was floating face down in the water, drifting towards the shore in front of the boats. She was either very committed to her role, or else she was in real trouble.

"What do we do?" cried Lowi.

Arghan had already tied a rope around his waist and handed it to Marcus, who secured it to the boat. Arghan slipped into the water. Marcus crouched in the bow. Arghan quickly reached Dina and rolled her over. Her eyes were closed, and she wasn't moving. Arghan lay on his back, put his hands under her shoulders, called, "Pull!", and Marcus began pulling the rope. They reached the boat. Pippa helped Marcus haul Dina up into the bow. Arghan climbed up behind. The little boat wobbled in the water.

"The cork vest really makes you float," Dina said, as she sat up and pulled the wet hair out of her face.

"Dina!" cried Lowi. "You were so convincing."

"A bit too convincing," said Marcus, covering his wife with a cloak.

Dina wrung out her hair, shivering.

"That water is a lot colder than I thought it would be," she said, wrapping the cloak tightly around her.

"Yes it is," said Arghan. "That's my swimming for the day."

"It will be warmer in the shallows," said Piri.

It was. Not only was it warmer along the shore, there was a long tide pool that was like a steamy bath. Even Arghan got in it. After awhile, Dina took her basket and began to stroll along the shore, picking up shells and stones. Lowi and Master Skell went with her.

When they had all regrouped, Piri led them to the fresh water spring, just up the hill from the beach. They quickly rinsed off in the frigid water, amid the mosses and ferns. Dina took the opportunity to wash her finds from the shore. She lay them out to dry on the moss.

"Look what Dina found," said Lowi. "Master Skell says it's Roman Glass. The bottom of a bottle."

Arghan picked up the translucent blue object.

"That's Roman glass, alright," he said. "Forged in fire, from Mediterranean sands."

Dina packed her basket. They began to go back down the trail.

"That looks like a cave," said Brutus, pointing up at the rocks.

"It is," said Piri. "A very small one. There are much bigger caves around here."

"May we see it?" asked Pippa.

"I suppose so," said Piri. "Only because Father and I've been there before."

"We'll be careful," said Arghan.

They climbed the short but steep trail to the dark opening.

"Is that... poop?" asked Dina, pointing to a very large pile of dried-up animal droppings, about twenty feet from the cave.

"Bear poop," said Piri.

"What?" squealed Lowi.

"Don't worry," said Piri. "It's old. They're away for the summer, filling up on fish. They won't come back until fall."

They reached the entrance. Piri went in first, and they all squeezed inside. Treya couldn't see very well. The light at the opening was bright, and the inside of the cave was dark. After a while her eyes adjusted, and she looked around. The small cave was littered with sticks and leaves.

"See," said Piri, "just a dirty little cave."

"Someone lives here," said Arghan. "Or at least, visits." He pointed.

There was a natural stone shelf across from the opening. It was covered with debris. Upon closer inspection, the debris turned out to be shells, feathers, stones, leaves, and bits of broken glass and ceramics. There were also some wooden food trenchers, clay jars, a blackened and dented tin cup, and a candle stub inside an abalone shell.

"What's that smell?" asked Lowi. Treya sniffed the air. There was a faint but sharp smell of rotten fish. It seemed to be coming from a long and slender clay jar with a tightly corked lid that was in the middle of the shelf.

"It's garum!" said Marcus.

"No!" said Pippa incredulously.

"What's garum?" asked Treya.

"Fermented fish-sauce," said Brutus.

"Made from old rotting fish guts," said Pippa.

"It's delicious," said Bruno.

"It's disgusting," said Pippa.

"I wouldn't mind trying it," said Arghan.

"It's not ours, though," Lowi pointed out.

"It's real garum, from Rome," said Brutus, looking closer. "What's it doing here?" He reached for it.

"Don't, Brutus!" Pippa exclaimed.

"But when will we ever have another chance--"

"Leave it, good fellows!" said Lord Gwydion. "As Lady Borlowan has pointed out, it clearly belongs to someone else."

"Actually, the way it's set there, it does look like an offering," said Arghan. "Is this some kind of altar?"

"I think that you're right Angove," said Master Skell. "It has that sort of feel to it."

"Look at this," said one of the An Dhew. He pointed to the area over the entrance. "It's a bear. Carved in the stone." They looked at the image. The bear was ferocious, claws up and fangs bared.

"We should get going," said Piri. Everyone agreed. They began to file out.

"Wait," said Dina. "I think this belongs here." She took the piece of Roman glass and placed it on the altar in front of the garum.

They reached the boats and put on their cork vests. It took some shoving and maneuvering to get the heavy vessels back into the water and headed the right way. Treya had enjoyed the landing, pulling on the oars until the boat flew up onto the sand and stopped with a satisfying crunch. The launching was a nuisance.

Piri gave Brutus her oar on the way back, and he and Treya pulled together. They worked well as a team.

By the time they had returned to the ship and secured the gear, everyone was tired. They sat down out of the way while the crew prepared to leave. The anchor was being raised. Piri was up in the low platform, and Dina was taking a turn on the high one.

The anchor was stowed, and the front sail was hoisted. The ship started to creep along. The starboard shoreline began to recede. Arghan and Piran were looking at a chart and conferring about the course.

"We go due west, then north," said Piran. "Then through-"
"BEARS!" cried Dina from the lookout. "Or... yes, one of them is a real bear!"

In the misty haze along the shore there was a strange sight. Five figures were gathered on the shingles, facing the sea, watching the ship go by. There was a boy, a woman, a man, and two others. One of the others was a tall fellow who was wearing the head of a bear and a long furry cape.
He wore Roman-style sandals, and he held a staff in his left hand. Attached to the staff was a bit of tattered red fabric.

The other figure certainly appeared to be an actual bear. It had dark fur and shiny little eyes. It stood upright, sniffing at the air. The little boy held its huge paw in his left hand. In the boy's right hand there was a small wooden sword.

"Is that... the Significator?" asked Pippa. "Bearing what's left of the standard?"

"He's *bearing* it alright," Brutus said. Treya had to laugh, despite the surreal gravity of the situation.

Pippa went over to the side of the ship and saluted, Roman style.
The figure in the bearskin returned the salute. The little boy raised his sword.
The ship continued, and the group on the shore faded from sight. Everyone was quiet.

Then Pippa said, "The last remnants of Valeria Victrix. Thus ends the Roman conquest of Britannia."

"Anyway," said Piran, getting back to business as if something remarkably strange hadn't just occurred. "We go due west, then north." He was pointing as he spoke. "We pass by the west side of the Isle of Manannin. Then through the channel. Eire to the west and Scotia to the east. Then we go north, past the Outer Hebrides."

"That's as far as any of us have ever been. The Morhogh has been to the Faroes before, but with a different crew. Once we reach the Faroes, that's when we'll really need to depend on the star map."

"Thule Island is big, but the water is so much bigger. If we go too far north, we risk getting lost in a frozen sea, even in summer. And if we go too far west, we could just sail off into the wide empty ocean."

Everyone was quiet. The enormity of what they were attempting was beginning to sink in.

Chapter Twelve - Waiting for the Stars

"The Helm of Awe," said Master Skell, "is a protection stave against evil spirits, jealous enemies, and the aggression and anger of rulers. There are nine distinct Helms of Awe stacked within the one symbol. The stave is carved into a lead plate, which is then pressed onto the forehead and into the skin."

"It looks like a flower," said Lowi.
"A stick-tight flower perhaps," said Arghan. "These trident shapes look like barbs."

"The sharp trident shape means defense and protection," said Master Skell. "And when this two-pronged shape has curved open arms, it means oxen. It's based on the rune 'Uruz', the aleph, the ox, which over time morphed into the letter 'alpha'. It stands for strength and vitality, and the primary position."

The companions were sitting close together. Tents had been set up, on the stern deck and over the helm-seat, to keep out the wind and rain. The friends were in the stern, looking at a document. Master Skell was translating it for them. The document had been brought to Santo that morning by the bald man with the blond whiskers who had recited the Odin blessing.

"He said it was from the Vitr Einn," Santo had told them as he handed it over, "whoever that is."
"The Wise One," Arghan had replied. "We met him last night."

They had sailed north from the Druid's Isle in the late morning. Less than two hours later, they had passed the Isle of Manannán, off on the starboard side. Then they'd sailed through the North Channel. By that time it was mid-afternoon. A light rain had been falling. They had passed close to tiny Rathlin Island on the port-side, and now they were winding their way around lovely Islay on the starboard.

Treya had studied the map.
Their journey would take them past this south end of the Inner Hebrides, and around the small islands of Berneray and Minguley, after which they would turn to the north. Then they would be following the great sprawling expanse of the Outer Hebrides, until they came to Grimsay and Stornaway. After that, it was open sea to the Faroes, and then more open sea to Hellisland.

"Please go on, Master Skell," said Treya, who was taking notes.

"Right," he said. "For success in rowing. Carve this stave on leather and color it with your blood. Put it under your oar. No one will row better than you."

"Ew," said Lowi.

"I'm not too keen on the blood-letting either, Lady," said one of the An Dhew, "but the Caer Hudol rowing team might benefit from that symbol."

"Yes," said the other An Dhew, "we've lost to Karrek Du the last two matches."

"There are rowing competitions between the Two Kingdoms now?" exclaimed Treya. "What fun!"

"What other staves are there, Master Skell?" asked Arghan.

"This one is a double sigil," he replied. "Blood oxen and earth oxen. Carve them on the inside of the lid of your treasure chest. The two symbols are for preventing theft: the first works by day and the second by night. Fascinating. Blood by day and earth by night. Hot and cold. Opposing forces."

"Their shape reminds me of the tower Array," said Dina.

"I can see that," said Marcus.

"This is the Lesser Hagall," said Master Skell. "Guards against malevolent forces. Write it on the shoulder blade of a seal in mouse blood."

"No!" exclaimed Lowi. "Master Skell, are you making things up?"

"Certainly not," he said. "Here's another one, for fishing. This stave should be drawn in wren's blood on an amniotic membrane with a pen made of a raven's feather. Then put it in a gimlet hole under the prow of your ship and you will always have a good catch."

The group burst out laughing.

"Or, alternately," said Master Skell, "here's one you can just carve into the prow, and skip the wren's blood bit."

"I like that one," said Arghan.

"This one is Hill Stave," said Master Skell, "to open passage in rock or hill."

"Say, that sounds good," said Lord Gwydion. "Unless there's some grim ritual that goes along with it?"

"Carve this stave deeply into a rowan post," said Master Skell, "and shave it down into a wand."

"So far, so good," said Lowi.

"Then color the grooves with blood from beneath the root of your tongue."

"Ewwww!" Most of the group cried out in disgust.

"Oh, what is wrong with them?" asked Treya. "Who thinks of doing these things?"

"The North-men seemed so nice," said Lowi. "But they're horrible."

"They're both," said Master Skell. "Nice and horrible. Incredibly nice if they like you. But if you have something they want, they'll take it. And if you resist, they'll enslave you, and torture you."
"Like the Romans," said Dina.

"Yes, Dina-Regna," said Master Skell with a chuckle. "Although both Romans and Northmen might take offense at the comparison. But you're right, they both showed no mercy, and they both believed that there was some kind of honor in acts of unspeakable cruelty." The group fell silent.

"But enough of that," said Master Skell. "Let me find something less gruesome. There are several more protection symbols. Here. This one is Angurgapi. Inscribed on a pot lid, or the bottom of a tub. Any sort of container. Keeps the contents safe. Or worn as a medallion to keeper the wearer safe."

"That looks nice," said Lowi.
"It's a face," said Bruno.
"What does Angurgapi mean?" asked Treya.
"Either, 'dreadful look' or 'cucumber face'," said Master Skell.
Lowi giggled. "Cucumber face. I love it."
"It's a fascinum," said Marcus. "Seen straight on. Like the Greek eye talismans that ward off evil."

"Here's one about strength and protection for the feet," Master Skell continued. "Ginfaxi goes under the left toe. It looks like a windmill. Gapaldur goes under the right heel."
"Those are nice," said Arghan.
"Splendid," Lord Gwydion agreed.

"Here's a good one," continued Master Skell. "To win a girl! Carve this stave on bread or cheese and give it to her."
"It's a complicated pattern," said Brutus, squinting at the page. "How would you carve something like that into bread?"
"Or cheese?" Bruno added. "What a mess that would be."

"Here's one for wealth," Master Skell went on. "Draw this stave on a piece of un-tanned goat-hide and keep it it secretly under your left arm. Success in trading is guaranteed."
"Ha," laughed Dina, "that reminds me of the terrible song. About the man whose armpit smelled like a goat."

"Rufus!" exclaimed Lord Gwydion, Pippa, Arghan, Marcus, Bruno and Brutus simultaneously.

Lord Gwydion laughed merrily and said, "Perhaps this explains how Rufus earned his coin."

"And ruined his love-life," Pippa added.

"Here, finally, at the last," said Master Skell. "It's the Otturstafur. The symbol that the Shaman scribed for us. It is the stave of eightfold protection and repulsion. To scare your opponent, carve this stave on a piece of oak and throw it at his feet."

"Really?" said Brutus. "Somehow that just doesn't seem very intimidating. But there must be something to it, right? Or else why would they bother to scribe about it?"

"But," said Lowi, "it's all superstitious nonsense, anyway. Isn't it?"

Nobody said anything.

Then Lord Gwydion said, "Marcus, you're my favorite sceptic. What do you think?"

"I think the rituals are most likely superstitious nonsense," he replied. "But there might be something to the staves. After seeing ancient symbols being used in advanced technology, it makes me wonder if these don't have some scientific function that's gotten lost over time."

"That's very perceptive, Constantinides," said Pippa.

"Verum," Master Skell agreed.

"Marcus," said Bruno. "How'd you get to be such a wise old man?"

"It's the beard, of course," said Brutus.

The afternoon turned to evening. The ship kept moving. The stars were out, the moon was bright, and the winds were being cooperative. The skipper and crew had traveled this route before. After they left the Hebrides, they would be in unfamiliar waters, but for now they were proceeding confidently.

The companions had a meal together on the deck. Then Piri brought out a reed whistle and Piran got out some spoons. They played a lilting little tune. Lord Gwydion took out his harp and began to play along, adding a loping rhythm.

Lowi went up to Bruno and Brutus and spoke to them briefly. They both drew their swords and put them on the ground in a 'X' shape. Lowi proceeded to do a complicated dance which involved leaping high into the air and in and out of the crossed swords. The music grew in intensity, and the companions stomped and clapped along in time as Lowi danced. It all stopped with a flourish. Everyone applauded.

"The sword dance on a ship," said Arghan. "That's a new one for me."

The twins put their swords away as the musicians played a gentle tune to wind things down.

Piran took the helm so Santo could get some rest. The night-watch was in place. Everyone found a spot to sleep.

The next morning, the skies were clear and the sun shone brightly. The Outer Hebrides were still sliding by off of the starboard side. Even though it was sunny, the temperature had dropped.

It seemed like a good time to take stock of the cold-weather gear. The bundles of woolen and fur clothing were hauled up to the deck. The ladies were not very impressed with the way they smelled. The men strung the clothes up on a line, in hopes that it would air them out.

By late afternoon they had left the Hebrides behind and were in open water. It was a bit unnerving to Treya to look all around and find no land anywhere.

Treya stood with Lowi and the Twins, looking out to sea. She was catching up on her notes. She scribed-

The ocean is deep blue-green, and the sky is the color of a robin's egg.

That made her think about birds. Ever since she had come to the surface there had been birds. But there were no birds to be seen out here. That was also a bit unnerving.

Finally, land was spotted off the starboard bow. They had reached the Faroes. They came about to the west and dropped anchor. Santo went below to his hammock. They would be waiting for the stars to come out before they continued. So far the sky was clear. They needed it to stay that way.

The companions went through the winter clothes, choosing pieces, and bundling away the rest. Many of the heavy blankets and skins were put in the bunks with the bedrolls. It wasn't really cold enough for them yet, and they were bulky, but the temperature was dropping, and they were going to be prepared.

Treya and Lowi put on fur jackets and wool hats, and went for a walk around the deck. Piran was at the helm, hunched over the pilot's bench, focused intently on something. Bruno and Brutus were nearby, also focused.

"Gentlemen," Treya asked, "what are you doing?"

"Santo liked the Northerners' fishing stave," Piran replied, "so I'm adding it to his bench, while we're stopped."

"Did you carve this whole bench?" asked Lowi.

"Yes," said Piran. "It's good to have something to do on long sea journeys."

"It's lovely," said Lowi. "And what are you fellows doing?" she asked, turning to the twins.

"We're trying our hand at carving," said Bruno, holding up a wooden disc covered with some rudimentary lines, deep gouge marks, and what appeared to be a smear of blood. "I'm making Cucumber Face."

"It's more like you're making chopped pickle," said Brutus with a laugh.

"Bruno, are you bleeding?" asked Lowi.

"Yes," he replied. "I guess I should have started with something bigger. This thing is hard to hold on to."

"Maybe if it was secured with some sort of clamp," said Treya.

"That would have been smart," Bruno sighed.

"And what are you doing, Brutus?" Treya asked. Brutus held up a short broken plank.

"It's a plank, not a log, but it's oak," he said, displayed his version of the Otturstafur.

"Clever!" said Treya.

"Bruno," said Lowi, "will you leave Cucumber Face for now and come with us? That wound needs to be cleaned and bound. We don't want a little injury to compromise the mission."

"Yes, Lady Borlowan," said Bruno. He set his medallion on the helm bench and went with the women to take care of his finger.

Dusk settled in slowly. The companions ate. Most of them rested. Treya thought about making some more notes, but she was tired, and anyway, not much else had happened today. She cuddled up next to Lowi in one of the bunks and went to sleep.

She was awakened by a sliver of bright starlight that shone through a crack in the deck above. It was dark in the cabin. The ship was moving. Lowi was asleep. The other berths were full of sleepers also, hidden amongst the piles of bedding.

Treya slipped out of the bunk, pulled on her jacket and hat, stepped into her boots, and headed topside. She went to use the privy, then washed up quietly, as there were others sleeping nearby on the stern deck and under the little tent.

She greeted Santo at the helm, then walked silently along the port rail. Except for the swish of the water, the humming of the lines, and the whispering of the sails, all was quiet.
She walked up and stood in the bow. The stars made a stunning display against the dark sky.

"Big bear, little bear, northern star," she sang to herself. She found bright Ursa Major, then little Ursa Minor, and then followed the line to locate faint Polaris, their guide star. She stared out ahead of her. The bright stars were reflected in the dark sea. When she relaxed her vision, it looked like there was one big world full of stars. She stood there for awhile. Then she went back down, shucked off her gear, and crawled into bed.

When Treya awoke again, it was mid-morning. The ship was still moving. The air had grown colder. She was alone below-decks. She put on her warm clothes and went up topside. Pippa and Arghan were on the topmast lookout. The mainmast extension had been cranked up, so the platform seemed lower than it really was. The big sail was in place, pushing the Morhogh along at a brisk pace.

Marcus and Dina were on the lower watch platform. The rest of the friends were in the bow, resting and watching the porpoises.

Treya looked out. There was nothing to see except dark water and pale sky, but at least the sun was visible. The moon was visible too, something she still found unnerving during the day, but it was considered auspicious.

After a while, they ate a light meal on the deck, then changed the watch. Bruno and Piri climbed up the topmast. Brutus went to the lower platform. The afternoon dragged on as the ship plowed ahead. The moon disappeared, but the pale sun remained. The air grew colder. The companions bundled up. They sat down in the bow, mostly silent, their breath steaming in the cold air.

"I don't know how you do it," said Lowi after a while. "It's only been a couple of days, but I feel as though I've been on this ship for a month. Sorry, I don't mean to complain."

"Lady Lowi," said Piran, "you complain all you like. You're a fine passenger. Especially considering you never traveled anywhere at all before this."

"I didn't mind it when there was a shoreline," Lowi replied. "I think I'm just not comfortable on the open sea."
"Sensible," said Piran. "Anyone who is comfortable on the open sea is fooling themselves."

Pippa said, "Perhaps there's something we could do to pass the time-".
"ICE!" screamed Piri from above. "Ice to starboard."
"Ice to port!" cried Brutus.
"DROP MAINSAIL!" bellowed Santo. "RAISE FORESAIL!"

Arghan and Piran scrambled to unhitch the mainsail. Then they very quickly installed the little navigation sail, connected it to the tiller-rig, and raised it. The ship slowed to a crawl. Everyone else clustered around the front of the bow and looked at the sea.

It was a strange site. Long narrow drifts of ice were floating on the water. Some were very tiny, and easy for the ship to push out of the way. Others created obstacles of long frozen slabs, which were covered with tall conical ice formations.
The cone-shapes were blobby, like huge drippy sand castles of frozen water.

The skipper was standing. He navigated very slowly around the long slabs, his eyes on the water ahead. At the base of the slabs, the ice spread out thinly, reaching out in tendrils that were so delicate that some broke off as they were hit by the gentle wake of the slowly moving ship.

"At least they're not burgs," said Arghan. "They're more like flow-drifts. So we don't have to worry so much about how far they go below the water."
"You've seen this sort of thing before?" Marcus asked.
"No," said Arghan. "This is completely new."
"What could be doing this?" asked Pippa.

Treya stared at the network of frozen tendrils. They were like long knotted fingers reaching out to the travelers.
They reminded her of the shape of of Hellisland on the map. Master Skell had said that the island probably looked that way because of its volcanic activity.
"Maybe volcanos?" Treya suggested.
"Volcanos in the ocean?" Marcus said in alarm. "Gods, we *are* a long way from home."
"They're not quite volcanos," said Master Skell, "just hot jets of water." He was looking off to the left. His lenses were bright from the reflected sky.

"Oh!" said Lord Gwydion, shading his eyes. "I see them. Shooting up out of the ice!"

"PORT-SIDE!" cried Piri. "Ice islands!"
The companions gathered at the port rail. The ship was coming about to starboard, to avoid a long bulbous ice flow. As it did, the view opened up. They were passing a massive clump of blobby, cone-covered frozen islands. Hot geysers of water were shooting out of the tops of the ice cones, creating rainbow prisms in the air.
As the water fell onto the mounds, there was a great deal of sizzling and bubbling as the hot liquid spread out, melting its way down into the water where it finally froze, creating the delicate tendrils that crept along the surface.

Pippa took off her gloves and got out her pad. She began to sketch the strange scene, blowing on her hands intermittently to warm them. The sea gradually cleared, and the ice islands receded behind them. The crew struggled with the small sail to turn the ship back around to port so they could get on course again. An extra watch was set on the bow, to help scan for ice chunks that were big enough to be obstacles.

Arghan had been standing tensely at the rail, watching the sky, ever since they had turned to starboard to avoid the obstruction. He relaxed a bit now. Pippa put away her pad and went over to join him.
"Are we back on course?" she asked.
"I hope so," he said.

The water was clear for a while, then more pieces of ice began to appear, floating on the sea. These were chunky and jagged, compared to what they'd just seen. Arghan pointed out that they were likely to have fallen off of frozen cliffs by the sea. It was an indication of land nearby, and as their destination was a glacier pool, it seemed like a good sign.

The ship crawled along now, stalling for time until dark in hopes that it would be a clear night. The companions were quiet. As the sun went down, the misty sky began to clear. A purple twilight hung over the sea. The faintest of stars began to appear. When they finally spotted Polaris, Santo made a slight course adjustment. They moved very slowly across the cold, dark water.

The watched changed, and some of the companions went below to rest.
Treya napped with Lowi, wrapped up in a blanket on the deck. They awoke to the sound of excited voices.

"Treya! Lowi!" called Dina. "Wake up and see this." Treya threw off the heavy blanket and helped Lowi to her feet. A strange greenish light was being reflected on Lowi's skin. They looked up.

"It's the northern lights!" Treya exclaimed.
"Oh!" cried Lowi. "I never imagined that anything could be so beautiful!"

The sky was covered in a rainbow of green, orange and yellow, as if some giant hand had painted a wash of watercolors across the heavens. The bands of color were reflected in the sea. The highlights on the waves sparkled like little gemstones. Treya and Lowi joined the others at the port rail and stared at the spectacle.

"LAND AHEAD!" cried Piran suddenly from the lookout. "HELLISLAND!"

Lit up by the aurora, and silhouetted against the large and newly risen full moon, the rugged and dramatic landscape of Thule Litrík rose before them.

"Drop sail," called Santo. "Drop anchor."

They had made it.

Chapter Thirteen - Fros Tredan

"This has to be Thule Litrík," said Santo. "It's very colorful." His breath came out as a cloud of vapor that dissipated into the bright morning air. It was just after dawn, and the air was frigid. Most of the companions were huddled at the rail, ready to get a look at their destination in the daylight.

It was almost too much to take in. The beaches were striped in gold, white, tan and black, and the shore was littered with snowdrifts and ice mounds. The stony cliffs above were covered with a wall of ice that was continually breaking apart and falling into the sea.
The rugged land was covered in striations of saturated tints that didn't even look natural, like the colors of the rainbow gone to rust. Above the sea cliffs, there were red ochre hills, dotted with acid-green pools. The pools streamed down into the ocean, creating layers of intense orange, burnt umber, and yellow. Dark mounds of volcanic rock covered the middle ground, interspersed with crevasses filled with snow. Above them were great cone-shaped mountains. Several of them appeared to be smoking, but it was hard to tell for sure in the morning haze.

There was a layer of ice on the water's surface all along the shore line, about the width of three ship-lengths. Some of the chunks that fell from the sea-cliffs broke through it, and others just skidded and bounced. A flock of pelicans were floating along, right next to the ice. They didn't seem to mind all the crashing and splashing.

"I suppose that in the winter this is all frozen?" Pippa inquired.
"It might be frozen now," said Santo, "except for all the geothermal activity."
"I could go for some geo-thermal activity," said Dina. "In a hot tub." Her face could barely be seen inside her parka hood.
Treya thought about the warm pools back at the Root Road camp. It just made her feel colder.

They were anchored facing the opening to the glacier pool. The surface water was frozen at both ends of the opening, but the middle appeared passable. It was a very wide entrance, and only partly obscured by ice chunks. Beyond it was the bright blue bay, covered in floating fields of ice.

"Lord Gwydion," said Treya, "how did Sira Conn and his men even get here? Where did they find the ships?"

"Back then," said the King, "Caer Hudol had a small presence on the south coast, at the Port-Mouth. Where it used to be, anyway. The Port-mouth has moved around over the years. But it was way back when the Sea-People were here. Sira Conn got his ships from them. They were really more like big galleys than proper ships. That's all I know."

"They might have taken the same route as we did," said Santo. "It was a good course. The wind and water brought us right to this spot. As it most likely would have brought *them*. So even without the story, this would be the place to begin searching." He shielded his eyes and stared across at the opening.

"I never thought that I'd ever be steering the Morhogh into a glacier pool," said Santo, "but here we go."

The anchor was raised. The clicking of the chain echoed back across the water. The small sail was hoisted. Arghan, Bruno, and Brutus were standing by with punt poles, ready to fend off the ice if necessary. The ship moved slowly along. There was very little wind. They approached the opening.

"It looks as though there's plenty of space to get through," said Marcus.

"Yes," said Arghan. "Let's hope that it's still that way when we're ready to depart."

The Morhogh sailed through the gap, and came out into the glacier pool. The expanse of white ice and blue water was dazzling.

There were frozen chunks of all sizes and shapes, bobbing gently in the calm water, casting rippling and illuminated shadows. Slowly, Santo maneuvered the ship through the larger obstacles, while the punts-men kept the smaller ones away.

Treya looked up. A huge rough-legged hawk was gliding overhead, keeping a keen eye on the ship.

"Ice tunnel ahead!" called Piri from the lookout.

Everyone crowded up front to see. The ship was headed towards a large opening. A bright blue tunnel extended beyond it.

"According to the story," said Pippa, "we're not looking for the large ice-tunnel, but one of the smaller ones, whose entrance is hidden from view."

"According to the story," said Marcus, "there's also a volcano in there. And cave-gnomes."

The Morhogh came slowly around to starboard and began to crawl along near the edge. The companions had a glimpse into the large ice tunnel. It was a brilliant blue, high and wide and shining. The tunnel was reflected in the bay, making the blue water appear even bluer. They continued to skirt the cliff, weaving slowly around the ice chunks and the rocks that lined the edge of the water. They came to a series of big round boulders that were blocking the way.

"Ice tunnel on port side," called Piri from the lookout, "just beyond those rocks."
"Drop sail," Santo called. "Drop anchor. This is as far as she goes."
The small sail was dropped. The anchor chain unreeled. Then it stopped.
"It's shallow," called Piran, looking at the remaining anchor chain. "Eight fathoms at the most."

Treya looked over the rail. The water was brilliantly clear. She forced her gaze past the riot of color and reflection on the surface, and down into the depths. The world below was pale and sparkly. There were groves of sea vegetation rooted to the floor, and tall streamers of kelp waving in the current.
Schools of tiny silver fish darted around fantastically shaped boulders. The boulders resembled otherworldly people or creatures.

The boats were readied. The travelers were prepared. They put on the cork vests as well as they could over the bulky clothing and climbed down. The three crew members were staying with the ship. Treya and Brutus were rowing Lowi and Bruno. Dina and Pippa were being piloted again by Marcus and Arghan, and Master Skell and Lord Gwydion were once more being rowed by the two An Dhew.

"Continued success!" cried Piri from the mast.
"See you soon," called Dina, waving to her. The boats were unhitched and they began to row.

As soon as they had cleared the first big boulder, they saw it. It was smaller than the other one, but still large enough to travel side by side. Together, the little fleet entered the ice tunnel.
They moved slowly and steadily along.
Freezing drips from the ice tunnel roof would occasionally rain down. The cold air smelled good. It was peaceful, if a bit eerie. Graceful skates swam around the bows of the boats, much like the porpoises did on the open sea.

"We're going around a bend," called Arghan. The tunnel looped around to the left. They came out into a pool within a red sandstone cavern. It was a natural harbor.
The cavern was hung with dripping icy stalactites from the fractured ceiling, and large crystalized stalagmites were sticking up out of the water.

They headed the boats toward a narrow gravel bank and landed. They debarked, then pulled the boats way up out of the water and tied them to some rocks. They removed their cork vests and stowed them.

There was a walkway leading in both directions from the gravel bank. "Which way?" asked Bruno. No one responded.

"Back towards the sea first, I think," said Master Skell. They took the path that went back in the direction they'd come. For a while it was open, and ran parallel to the water's edge. Then it veered off to the right and became a closed tunnel. They proceeded in silence. The tunnel entered a small round chamber, before it resumed on the other side.

They stopped in the small chamber. It was empty. There was a short cave opening on one side that appeared to have been filled in with rubble.

"That didn't happen naturally," said Arghan. "People have been here."

Treya went closer to take a look. It was warmer by the closed cave entrance. She was tired, and weary of the cold. She sat down on a rock near the walled up hole. Even the stone seemed warm. She grew very sleepy. Her body became numb.

She was dreaming, even though she wasn't really asleep. The room was dark, and filled with a pool of black water. There was a huge damselfly, silhouetted against the deep darkness. She was flapping close to the surface. As she bobbed up and down, Treya wanted to shout to her 'don't touch the water', but she couldn't move her mouth. The damselfly's foot hit the surface, and the dark liquid began reaching up the poor creature's leg, pulling it down into the darkness...

She heard voices.
"What smells?" asked Pippa.
"There's something not right behind that wall of stones," said Dina.
"Treya, get up," Lowi cried. "TREYA!"
"Get her out of there," said Lord Gwydion. "Everyone move away from here!"

Treya opened her eyes. She was disoriented. The twins picked her up between them and piloted her away from the closed cave entrance.

"Treya, take some deep breaths," said Lowi.

"What's happening?" she asked. She tried to breathe slowly and deeply.

"There are poisonous vapors in there," said Lord Gwydion. "That must be why it's filled in with rubble. I don't know why anyone would bother. It would be much easier and safer to just find another cave. Let's keep well away from that doorway. Be vigilant."

Treya was gradually regaining her mobility. After they had gone down the tunnel about forty feet, sniffing the air suspiciously the whole time, they stopped. The twins helped Treya to sit down on a stone bench. Brutus squatted in front of her and rubbed her hands. Lowi was rubbing her shoulders. Treya's whole body felt on pins and needles, like when a limb wakes up after having the circulation cut off. She drank some water.

"Alright," she said. She got up and forced herself to walk.

By the time they had gone another thirty feet or so, Treya was feeling better. Then the tunnel suddenly ended, and they were in a small cave. The sun filtered through the cracks in the ceiling. There was just enough light to see. The ground had a strange bumpy texture. It was covered in what seemed to be a fine combination of ice and ash.

There was something on the ground. As they got closer, it became clear that it was a man, a tall man wearing a cloak, lying on his side, as if he were asleep. The figure was the same color as the floor, covered in a speckled white ice-dust concretion from head to toe. His body seemed to be completely frozen to the ground. Even the side of his head appeared to be stuck fast.

"Is that him?" Marcus asked.

Lord Gwydion knelt down in front of the man's head.

"It's him," he said sadly. "I'm afraid we're too late."

"Why, is he dead?" asked Marcus. Lord Gwydion didn't answer at first.

Then he said quietly, "I don't think so. But I don't know how to save him. I feel so useless."

"If he's still alive," said Dina, "he's trapped under there. It's like it was with the Lady. We need to get rid of the hard stuff." She rapped on Sira Conn's back percussively with her trident.

"What about the medicine?" asked Pippa, touching the pouch that hung from her neck.

"Good idea!" said Arghan.

"Will there be enough?" asked Marcus. He took out his medicine bag.

"Friends," said Lord Gwydion, coming out of his reverie. "Thank you, but put those away. This goes beyond the healing powers of the tree."
"Why?" asked Pippa.
"Because the tree medicine only works upon contact with flesh," he replied, "and this is some sort of... mineral."

"There must be something we can do!" cried Arghan. "If we can't dissolve it, can we... chisel him out? Dina, what do you think?"

"I don't see how," she said. "What we need is a way to gently break it apart and knock it off of him. Without it becoming dust, in case the stuff still has poison in it. Or maybe poke a small hole and blow medicine into it?"

Arghan pulled out his pocketknife and tried to chip some of the material off of the back of the man's hand.
"The steel doesn't even scratch the surface," he said, shaking his head.

The companions stood and stared at the cold stony figure on the cave-floor. It was hard to not give in to defeat. Lord Gwydion looked crushed. Marcus and Dina were holding one another. Marcus was crying. Pippa was sobbing too. Treya felt helpless. After all they'd been through to get here, it was tragic to have to give up now. Knowing that Sira Conn might yet live, and that they couldn't help him made it feel even worse.

"It's the moment we've been waiting for," said Master Skell suddenly. He stood at the feet of Sira Conn. Master Skell removed the eye-lens contraption from his headband. He held it over the frozen figure, and snapped it in two.
"No!" Pippa exclaimed.
"What are you doing?" Treya cried in alarm.

"Don't worry," said Master Skell. "Just stay back."

He held a lens in each hand. He crushed them both with his fists, then he tossed the contents into the air. They spread out into a sort of net, which then fell and covered Sira Conn entirely. Master Skell had removed his gloves, Treya noticed. She was surprised to see that his hands looked fine. There were no scars or burns. Master Skell raised his arms into the air. Then he drew them down quickly and held them over Sira Conn's still form.

"Shield your eyes," called Master Skell, "from the mighty fros tredan. That's Kernowek for electrical current. Such a colorful old language."

The air began to crackle, and an arc of white electricity covered Sira Conn's body. Everything became too bright to watch, and the companions all looked away, protecting their eyes from the intense light.

There was a whooshing sound, and the bright light was gone. They stared at Sira Conn. His body was covered in what looked like frost flowers. The flowers seemed to be forming from the flux-net which had been created by the crushed and fused lenses. The flowers would grow, and some would fall off, leaving new ones to form underneath. After a couple of moments, the sleeping King could not be seen at all, under the crystalline flakes. Between and beneath the white flakes, little currents of electricity were crackling.

Lord Gwydion took a step closer and tentatively reached out his hand.

"Don't touch him yet!" cried a strange voice. Lowi screamed. Everyone looked. A much younger man stood where Master Skell had just been. He was tall and handsome, with thick golden hair and amber colored eyes. The man smiled radiantly.

"BRIAN MAGNUS!" cried Pippa, Arghan, Marcus, Bruno and Brutus. Marcus began to faint. Dina caught him, and he straightened back up, still swooning.

"Is it... really you?" Marcus asked.
"As much as it ever was," said Brian Magnus. "Hello, little Nico. Look how far you've come! Rescuing kings. Fighting monsters. And married to the Royal Dina-Regna." He bowed in her direction. "Doctor of physic." Dina waved.

"Beloved friend, can we hug you?" asked Brutus. "I don't mind a little charge."
"Better not," he replied. "As much as I would love to, Brutus. I'm not as attenuated as I used to be. I'm afraid I'll hurt you. And my gloves have disincorporated already."

"I should have guessed that it was you!" said Pippa.
"Philippa," he said, "all these adventures happened because as a child you refused to leave the Jupiter Temple. This group of friends is here now because of you. I'm here now because of you."

"But," cried Treya, "where's Master Skell?"
"This *is* Master Skell," said Lord Gwydion. "He appears to be an eternal primal force that takes on the persona of a supernatural being, who has manifested here as a human. Who was pretending for a while to be a different human."

Brian Magnus smiled and bowed. "Lord Gwydion, it's been an honor."
"Likewise, Lord Magnus," said the King.
Brian Magnus bowed to the two An Dhew and they bowed in return.

"I recognize you now, Lord," said Lowi. "You look just like the pictures that Pippa made of you. Except you're even more handsome in real life."
"That's me!" said Brian Magnus. "And this may very well be real life!"

"But... we saw you eat!" Bruno exclaimed.
"And drink, and sleep," Brutus added.

"I had to try and fool you this time," Brian Magnus said. "I'm sorry."

"You mean this whole journey you've just been pretending to eat those seaweed bars?" asked Pippa.
"Yes," he replied. "And there's really only the one bar. I just made it look like more. You know I have to travel light. I have trouble carrying certain things. And wearing certain items. For some reason, the cork life vest was exhausting!"

"Only one bar," said Treya, "Really?" She had looked in his bag, and it had been full of the seaweed bars.

"Yes," Brian Magnus replied. "I had to come up with something that I would appear to be well supplied with. Something I could offer to share, but that nobody would like. I frustrated the Trevena kitchens with my order of one green bar made of kelp and flaxseed. They wanted to try and improve the flavor and texture. But I resisted. It needed to be dreadful, so none of you would want any. The chef tried a small piece. She described it as 'slimy, yet gritty'. So, perfect."

"I'm glad that you had so much fun fooling us!" said Bruno, just about in tears.
"How could you have been so close and not told us?" asked Brutus plaintively.

"Noble lads," he replied, "you know how I love you. My brave and handsome princes. I've learned the hard way that it's not always healthy for my friends to be around me for too long."
"That's sad," Lowi said.

Pippa came up very close to Brian Magnus without touching him.
"Cassius Ambrosius," she said. "He's really gone. Verum?"
"Verum, sister," said Brian Magnus, smiling tenderly.
"Then, what's going on?" she asked. "How are you still here?"

"I was on a long mission," he replied. "I completed the mission, but a large constellate of my energy was still going to be hanging around here for a while, until the rest of the system could catch up. I wanted to take a position where I could help you all, and watch out for you, without drawing any attention. And I wanted to spend time with my new friends, Treya Meynack and Lady Borlowan." He bowed to them.

"Oh!" said Pippa, "it was you that sent the message that exposed Mimi Ryea!"
"Guilty as charged," he said with a charming smile.
"Really?" Lowi responded. "I've often wondered who sent it."
"That was so kind of you, sir," said Treya. "I'm very grateful."

"See," he said, "I've been looking out for you all this whole time. Indirectly. Who do you think got the River Lord to vouch for you, Marcus? And to casually let you all know that Sira Conn was in Thule?"

"Lord Santoni was there because of you?" asked Marcus.
"No," Brian Magnus replied, "he was there checking on Dina-Regna, as he said. I just took advantage of the situation. It required some effort to get him to show up at the right times. Water elementals aren't naturally punctual."

"We've been doubly blessed by your friendship, Brian Magnus," said Arghan. "Triply blessed, now that you're you again."
"Beloved Angove," Brian Magnus bowed towards Arghan.

"I don't understand it all, Lord," said Bruno, "but I know that it's difficult for you to be physically here...and... " He was getting choked up.
"We're grateful for that," said Brutus.
"He sacrifices his own comfort and safety for our benefit," said Pippa.

"It *has* been challenging to maintain these forms for so long," Brian Magnus replied. "But that's how much I wanted to stay with you. I've bent my own rules nearly to the breaking point."

He smiled. "You see, there are systems and procedures for just about everything these days. There didn't used to be, but for the sake of maintaining order, they had to be put in place. I helped put them there. For the systems to continue securely, there are certain guidelines as to how much an entity such as myself may... interact with the world and its inhabitants. If there's a powerful direct interaction, it sets off a sort of alarm, and there's the possibility that some other... forces might decide to get involved."

"Um... wouldn't you say that this qualifies as a powerful direct interaction?" Marcus asked. He indicated the form of Sira Conn, which was still crackling with energy.

"Yes, Marcus," said Brian Magnus. "I knew my time with you was coming to an end, and that you would be needing my help, so... this is my final act. And now, we only have a few minutes, before I am gone."

"What?" Bruno cried. "So soon?"
"No!" cried Treya. "Can't you come back and be Master Skell again? We won't tell anyone! "

"I'm sorry, dearest friends," said Brian Magnus. "Please don't make this any harder. Tell them back in Trevena that I stayed in Cymru, to retire. That's what the ship's crew will think also. Sorry, but they won't recall Master Skell being on the second part of the journey. Anything I might have said or done will be attributed to someone else. They're good folks- Santo, Piran, and Piri. Hard working, salt of the sea. May they receive the blessings of Jove. And all of you. And me too." He laughed charmingly. He turned his radiant gaze to Treya.

"Treya Meynack, the Kovskrifva is yours," he said. "Care for it well. And thank you for being my friend." She put her hand up to her apple pendant, trying hard not to bawl.
"Thank you, Master Skell," she said, sniffling. "Can I still call you that?"
"I am honored by it," Brian Magnus replied. "And now, you must leave here too, dear friends. Get Sira Conn out of this place, as soon as he is able, even if you have to carry him." He pointed. "See, he is nearly free."

They all looked. Sure enough, Sira Conn was beginning to slowly move his arms and legs.

"NO!" cried Bruno. He was looking at Brian Magnus, but Brian Magnus was gone. They stared in shock. The twins, Marcus, Treya and Lowi were all weeping. Pippa picked up his bag. She looked in it.

"Just the one green bar," she said. "And this." She reached in and pulled out Master Skell's lens-key. She kissed it and put it back in the bag.

"We come and we go," she said cheerfully, even though there were tears in her eyes too.
"O-ro," said Lord Gwydion, smiling sadly.

A moan came from the man on the floor. They gathered around him. He was still curled up on his side, but his eyes were open. The white-petaled discs were sliding off of him. The color of his skin looked a little more normal. He moved his head. There was no sign that he had ever been stuck to the ground.

They could now see that he was wearing a fur cloak and leggings, padded boots, and a wool cap over his long dark hair. His body was beginning to rock and shake.

"Help him stretch out on his back," said Dina. It took awhile before the man could relax his muscles, but finally he lay flat. "Give him some water," she said.

Lord Gwydion knelt before him. He held up the man's head and tipped his flask gently so he could drink. He drank for a long time. Then he looked up at Lord Gwydion. He had dark shiny eyes.

"Do I know you?" he asked.
"Sira Conn, I am your first born child," said Lord Gwydion.
"Little Gwair?" Sira Conn said. "Is that really you?"
"Gwair no longer, Sire," he replied. "I am Gwydion."
"Gwydion," Sira Conn echoed. "How can it be? I must have been asleep for a very long time." He seemed to be having trouble keeping his eyes open.

"Sire," said Lord Gwydion, "don't worry. We've come to take you home."

He signaled the two An Dhew. They had been fashioning an impromptu litter out of some fur cloaks. They bundled Sira Conn into it. Bruno and Brutus got on either end and they hoisted him up. They went back quickly through the tunnel the way they'd come, staying as far as possible from the walled up cave entrance as they passed through the chamber. They came out of the closed tunnel into the cave harbor.

Marcus was out in front. "Others!" he cried suddenly.

It was so unexpected. Treya felt a shot of adrenaline rush through her body. She looked ahead. There was a group of six men standing beside their beached vessels. Two were tall and elderly looking. They wore their hair and beard in long white braids. The other four were very small and wiry, with darker hair and wide and pointed dark eyes. They were all armed with blades and cudgels.

The group of men had been having a discussion. When they saw the companions they stopped. They turned to face them, then began advancing in their direction. The men were calling out in a strange language. Several of them used the words 'kaldr hildingr'. Treya thought that she had heard that before somewhere.

The strangers kept advancing. They seemed agitated, but not menacing.
None of them were reaching for weapons. They barely looked at the companions. Their focus was on the recumbent king, lying semi-conscious in the litter. Treya remembered. Kaldr Hildingr was from the story on the map. It was 'cold king'.

"I think these are your people, Sire," Treya said to Lord Gwydion.
"I think you're right, Treya," he replied.
The groups met. The two elder men bowed. The companions who weren't carrying Sira Conn bowed in return.

"We are the Khan-y-Kumus," said one of the tall fellows, going up to the stretcher and looking intently at Sira Conn. "The King's Men. We've been waiting for this day. The day you would wake him and take him home to his children. It's all he ever wanted." The man was beginning to weep.

Sira Conn raised himself up, looking at the elderly man.
"Gryfyn?" he said in confusion. "When did you get so old?"
"I am Gwyan," said the man. "My grandsire was Gryfyn. I've always resembled him."
"Oh! How long have I been out?" cried Sira Conn. The effort seemed to exhaust him. He put his head back down and shut his eyes.

"Come with us," said Gwyan, motioning down the path in the direction from which they'd come. "It isn't far. We have Sira Khan's belongings. And he can greet the last elder. Kew is the only remaining member of the original crew." The companions hesitated.

"Kew?" said Sira Khan. "Please, take me to him."
"Of course," said Marcus. "Lead the way." They began walking down the path.

"Where are *they* going?" asked Brutus. Two of the short fellows had run off.
"They're bringing a cart," said Gwyan.
Less than five minutes later, the two men reappeared, driving a cart that was pulled by a very stout and fluffy pony. Sira Khan was laid inside the cart and made as comfortable as possible. The group followed the red sandstone tunnel for a short distance. Then the tunnel ended, and they came out onto a dirt path

under a bright sky. The path went over a rise. A little settlement appeared before them. There was a small harbor and a tidy village. The cobbled lanes were colorfully landscaped with flowering shrubs. The buildings were set into the ground, and the roofs were covered with turf. There were wide fields of grasses surrounding the settlement, greener than anything Treya had seen yet. Fluffy ponies were running through the grassy meadows, and newly shorn sheep were grazing all over the place, including on the tops of the houses.

"Look at the ships!" cried Arghan. In the harbor were three very unusual vessels. They were long flat single-mast galleys with curved ends. The bows were carved to look like sea serpents. Two of the ship's masts were bare, and one had a faded old red and white striped sail, hanging slack.
The sides of the galleys bristled with oars, out of the water and in the upright position. As the companions drew closer, it became clear how old these boats were. The galley with the sail was the only one with intact rigging and usable oars.

"Those must be really ancient," said Pippa.
"They still look seaworthy," said Bruno.
"Look at the hulls," said Arghan. "What craftsmanship."

They arrived in the village. Around thirty people were gathered to meet them. Some of them were women, also very short in stature. A fire was burning, and a pot of something was bubbling away over it. A bench was brought out, and Sira Conn was helped onto it. Lord Gwydion gave him another drink of water.

Two of the short fellows came out, carrying a chair between them. On the chair there was a man. His hair and beard were long and white. He was shrunken and bony. He was so old that his skin was practically transparent. The chair was set down by Sira Conn's bench.

"This is Kew," said Gwyan. "He's the only one left from the original journey. The only one who knew the Sira Khan from the long years before the dark spirit of the cave took him. Kew has never given up hope of your recovery, Sira."

"Kew, dear companion," said Sira Conn, struggling to rise. "How can this be? You were a little boy!" He sat back in exhaustion. "Just yesterday. How can it be that you're so aged? We've only been here for a short while. We have to return, and regain the Kingdom. I'm so ashamed that I ran away."

"You had no choice, Sire, but to regroup," Kew said in a faint husky voice.

"What happened to me?" asked Sira Conn. "I was... I was in that cave. There was a strange smell. That's all I remember."

"We were exploring the caverns, Sire," said Kew. "We should not have let you go ahead on your own, but you were so quick. There was a burst of poison gas from the small cave. You took it full on. By the time we reached you, you were frozen to the ground, covered with that stuff. We couldn't move you. We were starting to get ill too. We wrapped scarves around our faces and piled stones into the opening until the evil vapors were trapped... " Kew's voice trailed off.

"We tried to uncover you. But it was impossible. Cutting, melting, nothing worked. So we've waited. Me, and these men. They are the descendants of your men and the good-wives of the ice bridge who came to stay with us here. I've lost reckoning, Sire, but it's been at least eight-hundred years. Maybe longer."

Sira Conn sat up and howled in anguish. It was a piercing and uncanny sound, like a wild creature in pain. Everyone was startled.

"Forgive me, friends," he said, after a moment. "I'm grateful for all you've done."

He forced himself up and stretched out his hand. "Kew," said Sira Conn. "Faithful companion. You were always there for me."

Kew stretch out his palsied old hand and took Sira Conn's in his own.
"I've lived to see the day, Lord," said Kew. "That's all I ever wanted."

Some women came around and gave everyone a ladleful of the hot liquid. Treya felt some trepidation when it was her turn. The drink was milky and salty. It didn't taste good, but it was kind of soothing. Sira Conn seemed to feel better after drinking his.

Two of the men brought forward a large bundle, wrapped tightly in oil-cloth.

"The Great Sira Conn's weapon, and his other belongings," said Gwyan. "We take them out once a year, clean them up, and then wrap them away again." He touched the bundle. "Now they are restored to his Highness."

"Thank you, Khan-y-Kumus," said Lord Gwydion. "I wish we could stay, but the ship is waiting for us, and the people of Caer Hudol await our return." He looked at the group of people. "Do none of you wish to come back with us?"

"No, Lord," said Gwyan. "This wild northern country is our home now. We've no desire to return to the south. We will accompany you back to your boats."

Sira Conn was helped back into the wagon. His belongings were set in alongside him. The same company made the short journey to the gravel bar.

He was guided onto the boat, taking Master Skell's place, wearing his cork vest. Marcus handed Gwyan a bag of coins. Somber farewells were exchanged. The vessels were launched.
The men on the shore saluted until they were out of sight.

Treya was exhausted, physically and mentally, and really tired of being cold. Everyone else seemed done in too. They rowed back through the ice tunnel in silence.

It was a huge relief to see the Morhogh anchored right where they'd left her. They paddled swiftly, and pulled up alongside her.
"Morhogh Ho!" Arghan called quietly.
"Ho!" Piri appeared over the port rail. "You're back already! Did you find him?" She noticed the bundled-up figure of Sira Conn reclining in the rowboat. "Oh, you did! I can hardly believe it!"

Piran and Santo helped them on board. In a short time, they were back on deck. Sira Conn was taken down below and installed in a bunk.
He ate a few bites of bread, then he lay down. Lord Gwydion sat on the floor beside his bed. Treya and Lowi climbed into a berth and went right to sleep under the warm covers.

Chapter Fourteen - A Lot Going On

"The lads would like to have a word with the two of you," said Pippa. "But they're shy, so I'm helping to get things going."

It was the morning after the rescue of Sira Conn. He was still resting down below. Lord Gwydion, Dina, and the An Dhew were with him.

Pippa was with Treya, Lowi, Bruno and Brutus. They were sitting under the stern-shelter. The men looked nervous.

"First off," said Pippa, "they have tokens for you."

Bruno and Brutus each held out a small piece of hard tack that had been roughly incised with the Norse stave for winning the heart of a fair lady.
Bruno said, "Will you take mine, Lady Borlowan?"
"Oh," said Lowi. She took the talisman and smiled nervously.

"And will you take mine, Lady Treya?"
Treya took it. "Thank you."
Treya and Lowi exchanged a glance. So did Bruno and Brutus.
"Go on," said Pippa. "Brutus, say something."
"Well... when Lowi first appeared at court," said Brutus, "Bruno fell in love with her right away."
Lowi blushed charmingly. So did Bruno.

"Then when Treya showed up," Bruno said, "Brutus was very interested in getting to know *her*. But then the two of you became a couple. Or seemed to. And our hopes were dashed."
"Are you really a couple?" asked Brutus.
There was silence.

"Well," said Lowi, "we're a couple of close friends, who love each other. That's all it's been."

Brutus and Bruno looked at each other. They seemed tongue-tied.
"Ladies," said Pippa, "the gentlemen don't want to offend you in any way, or intrude upon your relationship, or do anything to ruin the friendship they have with you. Having said that, Lowi, Bruno would like to be your husband, and Treya, Brutus would like to be yours."

Treya was startled, but not completely shocked. She had sort of seen this coming. She just hadn't thought that it would come so soon. Her mind was reeling with the possibilities.

She realized that Pippa was still talking.
"... so we had the idea that you two could move into the old quarters," she said. "There are those two empty rooms, and that lovely study. And plenty of common space."

"I like the old quarters," said Lowi. "All the pictures and mementoes."
"It's been lonely since everyone left," Bruno said.
"Is that what you would like, Brutus?" asked Treya. "For us to move in there?"
"We'd go wherever you wish," said Brutus. "But yes, we'd like that."

Lowi's blue eyes were huge. "What do you think, Treya?"
"I always want to be with you, Lowi," said Treya, "and I don't see why that would ever change. But you're clearly fond of Bruno."

"What about you, Treya?" Lowi asked, glancing at Brutus. Treya gazed at him. He looked so hopeful. And handsome.

"Back when I was An Dhew," she said, "I saw marriage to a man as a trap. Now I see that it doesn't have to be that way."
"Is that a yes?" asked Pippa.

"If Lowi's in," said Treya, "I am too."

"Well," said Pippa, "that's settled then. What a relief. Bruno and Brutus have been on pins and needles since they discovered that you'd all be together on this journey." She got up and left the shelter. They followed.

The five of them went to join the others who were gathered in the bow, putting together a late morning meal. Nobody said anything about the engagements. It was exciting news, but it could wait for the right moment.

Arghan had built a small fire on the deck brazier, down out of the wind. He and Marcus were squatting beside it, cooking a large halibut that Santo had caught in the glacier bay. It smelled delicious. Treya and Lowi found a bag of dried apples and the last of the cheese-bread. Bruno and Brutus brought a wineskin and a jug of lemon water. Lord Gwydion, Dina, and the An Dhew came up topside to join them.

They sat around the fire. Piri brought them a platter. Arghan took it and held it out. Marcus lifted the cooked fish and set it on the platter. As he stood back up, the wind gusted, and the flames leaped up. There was a sizzling sound, and the sudden odor of burnt hair.

"OW!" cried Marcus, grabbing his chin.
"Marcus!" Dina exclaimed. "Are you alright?"
He took his hands away. His wispy little beard was gone. The others stared. Then Bruno and Brutus both stood up and began to applaud.

"It's alright, Marcus," said Dina. "You can try again sometime."
"Or not," said Marcus, rubbing his chin.

Arghan gave everyone a piece of fish. It was really good. Treya felt like it was already giving her new strength. They ate in silence.
Treya noticed that Pippa wasn't eating. She looked pale. Pippa suddenly said, "Pardon me," and walked to the rear of the ship.

After a while, Arghan asked, "Where's Pippa gone?"
"She went astern," said Treya. "But it's been a while."
"I wonder if this sea journey is not agreeing with her," said Arghan.
"We'll check on her," said Lowi.

Dina, Treya and Lowi went to the back of the ship. Pippa was alone in the stern. She was standing, hunched, by the rail, eyes closed. She looked pale and shaken.

"Pippa," said Treya, "are you alright?"
"I got seasick," Pippa replied. "On calm water. It happened yesterday morning too. I thought I was a better sailor than that." She stood to face them, arms crossed under her very full breasts, propping them up as if they were heavy. Lowi looked at her curiously.

"Pippa," said Lowi, "when was the last time you had your moon cycle?"
"Six or seven weeks ago, why?" said Pippa. She suddenly put her hand on her abdomen and began to laugh.
"Holy cats! Am I pregnant?"
"I think you must be," said Lowi, putting her arms around her and kissing her on the cheek.
"Congratulations," said Treya and Dina, hugging her gently.
The men had all come over to see what was going on.

"Pippa," said Arghan, "are you alright?"

"Pippa's pregnant with a baby," said Dina.

"What wonderful news!" cried Lord Gwydion. "Congratulations, Pippa. Congratulations, Arghan."

Arghan was speechless.

"Lowi just figured it out, Arghan," said Pippa. "That's why I've been sick in the morning."

"Oh, Pippa," he said. He held her close.

They went and sat back down in the bow.

"Arghan," said Pippa, "don't be so worried." Arghan did look rather grim.

"Yes, Angove," said Lowi, "you're going to be a wonderful father."

"It's not that," said Pippa, taking a sip of lemon water. "He's worried about me giving birth. Because of the dart that went through me, here." She pointed to her right side.

"What!" exclaimed Lowi. "What do you mean, dart? Like an arrow?"

"When we were in the Army," said Bruno, "Agrippa threw herself into harm's way and saved the life of our General, Cassius Ambrosius. The dart went all the way through her, and barely pierced his skin."

"We were there," said Brutus. "It was the bravest thing we've ever seen."

"We were all terrified that she wouldn't pull through," said Marcus. "But the doctors saved her."

"The doctors did the best that they could," said Pippa, "but actually, it was Brian Magnus that saved me, and let the doctors take the credit."

"Another of his secret good deeds," said Arghan.

"I'm surprised you haven't heard about this before, Lowi," said Bruno. "It's one of King Arthek's favorite stories."

"Hardly the sort of thing that you'd hear in ladies' chambers, though," said Pippa with a laugh.

"So," said Lowi, "you're worried that Pippa might experience... complications in giving birth."

"All women risk that," said Pippa resolutely.

The companions fell silent. Treya could tell that Lowi was concerned. Everyone was.

"Come and have your child at Caer Hudol," said Lord Gwydion. "You've seen what our medicine can do. And the skills of our healers are far more advanced than those of the surface world."

"I can attest to that," said Marcus.

"Oh, and we can come get you by cart, on the Root Road," said Dina, "so you don't have climb through the Red Sands."

"Great idea!" said Pippa. "I like it."

"Oh," exclaimed Arghan. "Me too! What a relief. Let's move to Caer Hudol to have our child."

"Not just yet, though, right?" asked Brutus. "You are coming back home first?"

"Because it's going to be difficult enough to explain the loss of Master Skell to the King," said Bruno. "Please don't make us return without you."

"Of course we'll come back first," said Pippa.

"We'll plan the journey for the fall," said Arghan.

"How about the fall equinox?" asked Marcus.

"That sounds perfect," Pippa replied.

"We'll meet at the Mill," said Lord Gwydion.

"It's a plan!" said Dina enthusiastically.

Marriage and babies, thought Treya. *Life just flows onward, even during the boldest of adventures.*

"Shoals port-side!" cried Piri from the topmast.

Piran quickly went up the small mast to the lookout. They all gazed out. In the middle distance, the ocean was churning. As far north as they could see, there were shoals of fish. They were too far away to see the actual fish, but the undulating movement of the water made it look as if the sea was boiling.

"I've never seen such a shoaling!" Piran shouted. "It goes on for miles, far as the eye can see."

The Morhogh sailed slowly eastward. The shoals disappeared into the northern haze.

Sira Conn was still asleep down below. One of the An Dhew was staying in the bunk near him. Dina was down there also, asleep in one of the berths. Piri was on the topmast lookout, and Piran was on the lower lookout. Everyone else was on deck. Lord Gwydion was in his usual spot, on the port side of the front bow. Pippa was on the other side, in Master Skell's old place. They were watching the porpoises as they wove in and out of the path of the ship.

Treya and Lowi were sitting with Brutus and Bruno on the front deck. The wind had dropped, and the pace of the ship had slowed.

"The porpoises are leaving," said Lord Gwydion suddenly.

Treya and her companions went to the rail to see. The creatures were swimming quickly away from the bow, flipping their tails and chattering excitedly as they went.

"Whale off port-bow!" Piri cried from the topmast lookout. They all looked, but didn't see anything. "No, wait," called Piri. "Not a whale."

"Now there's something off starboard bow!" cried Piran.

Everyone grew very tense. Arghan guided Pippa away from the rail.

"What is that?" Bruno cried, pointing to a shape jutting out of the water. It was sort of triangular, and had a pattern of circles on it.

"Some kind of fin?" Arghan replied.

The shape sank beneath the surface. Then the water around it began to swell.

"ROGUE WAVE STARBOARD!" Piran screamed. A huge plume of water suddenly appeared high in the air above them and came crashing to the deck like a waterfall. The ship lurched up and down. Everyone jumped back.

"Piri, come down here now!" called Piran, as he clambered down the mast. "Everyone stay away from the rails!"

Piri began to scramble down the rigging, still staring at the ocean. Then she stopped and pointed to the front of the ship.

"SEA MONSTER!" she screamed.

In front of the bow, a small island rose from the sea. It was a pale purple color, tall and bulbous, and nearly as wide as the ship. The shape continued to loom. The companions were frozen in shock and terror. Higher and higher the island grew. The bulbous mass began to taper, until it sort of resembled a giant turnip. A pair of yellow eyes came into view. Then another pair below the first, slightly bigger and offset. Below them, there was a bright orange beak. Piri cried out in terror and scrambled the rest of the way down to the deck, where she clung to her father, trembling.

At the same time that the creature's eyes had come into view, three of the triangular shapes had appeared and begun to rise from the water and curl up and around through the air. They were attached to long tubes, also covered with circles. It took a moment for it to sink in that they were the creature's long arms, covered with suckers, and that the arms were attached to this bulbous head. The thing rose higher out of the water. The beak opened and shut. One of the arms went back under water. Then another. The seas began to churn.

"WAVE!" Piran shouted, pointing upward. Two mighty plumes of water hit the deck with such force that they knocked some planks loose and flung them overboard. Arghan grabbed hold of Pippa.
Bruno and Brutus stepped in front of Lowi and Treya to shield them. The creature's arms were retracting back into the water.

Lord Gwydion went up to the railing and raised his hand in greeting. The An Dhew bodyguard went too, staying close. The beast's four eyes moved back and forth, examining them. The creature stopped churning the water for a moment, but then it started coiling back up for another attack.

Just then Dina appeared from below, looking bleary-eyed and irritated.
"What's all the noise-" she began. "Oh! A sea creature." She went to the front of the bow. The creature stopped moving. All its eyes were on Dina.

"Hello." Dina waved. Amazingly, the creature raised a flipper in response. Dina and the sea-monster stared at each other.

Santo appeared from the helm. He carried a small harpoon concealed behind his back. Arghan held up a hand to stop him. Santo stood by, nervously.

Dina looked back at the others and said, "It's just hungry for fish, and it thinks that we might be competition." She turned back to the water.

"Don't worry," said Dina to the creature. "We don't want your fish. We wish you all the fish you can eat. In fact, there's a whole big bunch of fish, was it that way?" She pointed northward. Two of the creature's eyes slid across to follow her hand.

"Actually, it was more that-away," said Arghan, pointing a bit more westward. The creature's other pair of eyes slid to look at him, while the first two stayed on Dina. Dina adjusted her arm so she was pointing in the right direction.

The creature slowly lowered its bizarre limbs. The beak disappeared into the water, and then the eyes. The island sank back out of sight.

It was gone. Santo returned immediately to the helm and took the tiller. He seemed calm enough, but he still kept the harpoon nearby.

"What was that thing?" Pippa asked the question on everyone's mind.
"It's the Krookie!" said Piran. "The Kraken. The legendary giant squid of the cold sea."
"There's a picture of it in the Lyverva," said Treya. "I never thought we'd meet one."

"Dina," said Piri, "you saved us!"
"Maybe," said Dina. "It didn't really want to hurt us. It was just hungry and frustrated."
"Dear wife," said Marcus. "You never cease to amaze. I don't suppose you know how you did that?"

"No," said Dina. "It just happened." She looked out at the water. Then she yawned and said, "I'm going to lay back down."
"I'll come with you," said Marcus. They went down the hatch.
Treya and Lowi were still shaking from the encounter. They climbed into a pile of blankets under the stern covering.
Everyone was exhausted. Except for the pilot and lookouts, they all went to sleep.

Treya was awakened by the calls of the crew. She felt the ship coming around, and heard the sounds of the sails dropping and the anchor being let out. The sun was almost set. She woke Lowi, and they left the stern shelter. The air was warmer than it had been before they went to sleep. In the dim light, they could see land off of the port bow. Santo was securing the helm.

"Santo," asked Treya, "have we reached the Faroes already?"
"You slept through the Faroes," he replied with a grin. "These are the Hebrides, lasses."
Treya and Lowi looked at each other in delight. Then they went with Santo to join the others.

The companions were all sitting on the deck. The sails were furled, and the ship looked neat and tidy. The lanterns had been lit, and the deck glowed with golden light.

Sira Conn was sitting beside Lord Gwydion. He appeared to be completely recovered. Treya looked. This was the first time she had been able to really see him up close. He looked young. Surprisingly young. His hair was black, without a touch of gray, and his skin was smooth. His face was round, with wide-set eyes, and dimples in his cheeks. It was very different from the slender and angular faces of his offspring.

Treya and Lowi must have been staring, because Lord Gwydion said, "It's true, friends. He looks like he should be my son, instead of the other way around." Sira Conn rose and bowed.

"Lady Treya, Lady Borlowan, it's an honor. I thank you for being a part of my rescue." His manner was charming. They sat. Arghan took a drink from a wine skin and passed it around. The women had some lemon water.

Two An Dhew appeared and set down the bundle. "Sira Conn, your belongings," one of them said. He stood.
"Thank you," he replied. "I hope the harp is alright after all this time."

The An Dhew unwrapped the fabric. On the top was a closed sack. Sira Conn opened it and withdrew the contents. It was a harp. It was tall, and curved up on both sides. The harp had a matte black finish and silver pegs. Sira Conn ran a finger along the strings. They rang out tunefully. "That's a relief," he said, slipping the harp back into its sack.

The next item was a mid-length coat. It was black with silver toggle buttons and a wide collar. Strands of ivy were embroidered in silver on the collar and sleeves. The An Dhew held it up for Sira Conn. He pulled off his parka and slipped into the coat. It looked old-fashioned and elegant. He suddenly seemed a lot more royal.

Next, the An Dhew handed him a pair of black gauntlets. He put them on, and then he reached into the bundle and pulled out a huge sword in a heavy leather scabbard. He drew the blade. It was made of layered Damascus steel, with a design that looked like waves. The hilt was yellow bronze and the handle was white bronze. The pommel was silver and carved to look like an eagle, with ruby eyes.

"I remember that!" Lord Gwydion exclaimed. "Aderyn Dur. The Steel Bird. Can you still do the moves, Sire? Oh, wait, I shouldn't ask that, after what you've been through."
"No, I'm alright," Sira Conn said. "And I could use some exercise." Looking behind him, he backed away from the others. "Stay clear," he said. He held out

the sword and turned in a complete circle. He took a deep breath, then he crouched. He jumped high up into the air. As he came down, the sword whirled around him. He seemed to defy gravity. He was leaping, doing flips and aerials, all the while slashing the huge sword through the air. He ended in a double flip, during which he passed the sword from hand to hand several times.

They all cheered and applauded. He replaced the sword and sat back down, breathing heavily.
"That was so impressive!" exclaimed Marcus, wide-eyed.
"I've never seen such a display of skill," said Pippa. "You must be a great warrior indeed!"

Sira Conn laughed. "Not at all. It's all just for show. I was never in a battle. I've never seen any kind of combat, or faced a worthy opponent. My only enemy turned out to be the mother of my children."

"Oh," said Lowi, "but you must have loved her at one time?"
"No, never!" Sira Conn exclaimed. "We found ways to get along, but we never really cared for one another. We were just following custom. It was a strategic marriage, arranged before we were born. I had no desire to wed the Danu. I had a bad feeling about her. Turns out I was right."

Dina was looking at the sky.

"That bird has been following us since we left Hellisland," she said. "Now it's coming closer."
They looked up. There had been so much happening, Treya hadn't even noticed the bird. It did look like the same one that had been gliding around the ship in the glacier pool.

"That's a mighty big bird," said Bruno. "What is it?"
"It's rough legged hawk," said Treya.
"The legendary gwalch coes garw," said Santo. "The great fisher of the northern sea."

The huge raptor came circling closer until they could see its shiny eyes, and the ruffly leg feathers that give the bird its name. It flew over them leisurely. Its wingspan was over four feet wide. The bird glided to the bow, flapped once, and landed on the mermaid's head. It turned back and looked at the companions. It turned around again, threw back its head and let out a mighty squawk. Then it flew off, back to the north and out of sight.

Treya and Pippa smiled at each other. It went without saying that this seemed auspicious.

"You had a bird friend once, didn't you, Sira Conn?" asked Dina.
"Kili," he replied. "She was a falcon. The best in the mews."
He looked at Lord Gwydion.
"Is there still a mews in the High Meadow?" he asked.

"No," the King replied. "We stopped keeping birds a long time ago. Amatheon couldn't bear it. He's very sensitive about animals."

The friends grew silent.

"So," said Pippa. "There's a lot going on. We found Sira Conn. And we found out that I'm pregnant." She looked at Treya, Lowi, and the twins. "But there's one more thing. Two more things, actually. Brutus Marianis and Treya Meynack are betrothed. So are Bruno Marianis and the Lady Borlowan."

The companions cheered.
"It's about time!" shouted Arghan.
"I am honored to be here on this auspicious occasion," said Sira Conn.
"Congratulations, dear friends," said Lord Gwydion.

"We wanted our ladies to have some tokens," Bruno said.
"Something that would last longer than the bread," Brutus added.
Bruno handed Lowi a round wooden pendant. It had been pierced with a loop and strung on a cord.

"It's Cucumber Face!" exclaimed Lowi.
"Piran finished it for me," said Bruno. "I'm a hopeless carver."
"I love it," she said, putting it on. She looked down and admired it. "Thank you, Bruno."

"I'm sorry, Treya," said Brutus. "I should have made you a pendant too. I don't know what I was thinking. Girls like jewelry, not planks."
He held out the oaken board in which he had carved the protection symbol.
"Not this girl, Brutus," she said. "Don't second-guess your instincts. This is perfect."
She hugged the piece of wood.

Brutus and Treya sat side by side next to Lowi and Bruno.

"My," said Lord Gwydion. "What adorable young people. I'm so happy for you." He looked around at the company. "My debts to you all are too great to ever repay, but if there's anything I can do for you, just let me know."
"Same goes for me," said Sira Conn.

"How about some music?" asked Pippa.
"Splendid idea!" said Piran.

The two harps were brought out. A quick test showed them both to be in tune.
"I don't think that most instruments would have survived so well," said Pippa.
"These harps are special," said Brutus.
"Like everything else about the underground world," added Bruno.

The two Conn Danu lords sat side by side.
"What shall we begin with?" asked Gwydion.
"A stately tune," said Lowi. "Something... ceremonial, that the newly betrothed couples may dance in celebration."
"What?" said Treya.
"Oho!" said Sira Conn. He began to play a slow tune in 3/4 time. Lord Gwydion joined in. Piri got out her whistle and followed along. Piran joined in with the spoons.

Lowi pulled Treya to her feet. Brutus took her hands. Lowi and Bruno got in position. They all followed Lowi's lead. The couples stepped in, then out, then side to side. Then they all four put up their hands and walked in a circle. Then they reversed the circle, after which they began the steps again. Treya had felt awkward at first, but by the third round it was second nature. They went through it two more times, then ended with flourish.

Everyone applauded enthusiastically. The dancers sat down. Lowi kissed Bruno on the cheek. Inspired, Treya kissed Brutus on his. He took her hand.

"Now what?" asked Pippa.
"I wish that Tyronius was here," said Lord Gwydion, "to sing the song about Rufus."
"That song by Catullus?" asked Brutus. "Agrippa knows it."
"She used to sing it for General Ambrosius," added Bruno.
"Pippa?" said Lord Gwydion. "Will you share it?"
Pippa shook her head, but she said, "Only because you asked me, Lord. My apologies, Lady Borlowan. This is also not the sort of thing you hear in ladies' chambers."

Pippa took a sip of water and began.

"Do not wonder, o Rufus, why no woman
  wants to place her dainty thigh under you,
not if you should undermine her with a gift of rare clothes
  or with the pleasures of a transparent jewel.
A certain bad story hurts you, by which a wild billy-goat
  is said to dwell under the valley of your upper arms.
All fear this; nor is it strange: for it is a very bad
  beast, nor one with which a pretty girl would lie.
Therefore, either kill the cruel pest of the noses
  or cease to wonder why they flee."

The group exploded with laughter. Santo bellowed so loudly that the deck
vibrated.
"I must get you to scribe that for me, so I can learn it," said Lord Gwydion.
"No need," said Sira Conn. "I'll remember it."
"Really? Just after hearing it once?" said Marcus.
"I remember every song I've ever heard," he replied. He then proceeded to sing
the song about Rufus, word for word and note for note. The companions
applauded.

"Lord Gwydion," said Pippa, "Now that we've accomplished our missions, and
you've had a chance to relax, do you have a song about the Root Road?"
"Hmm, maybe... " he said. Then he sang,

"Down we go to the realm below
 We bring with us a light to show
 Up we rise with the dark in our eyes
 We bring to light a piece of night"

"I think that's the refrain," he said. He continued.

"Once there were trees, too old to believe
 Too big to survive, and at long last they died
 But down below, their roots turned to stone
 And created a road that we call our own."

"Down we go to the realm below
 We bring with us a light to show
 Up we rise with the dark in our eyes
 We bring to light a piece of night"

Some of the others had joined in on the chorus this time. Lord Gwydion sang,

"When the world was new, and time was on our side
 Before the fates conspired to throw us far and wide
 We knew the road, like a dear old friend
 We knew it before, now we know it again"

"Down we go to the realm below
 We bring with us a light to show
 Up we rise with the dark in our eyes
 We bring to light a piece of night"

"The road is our lifeline
 The road is our blood
 Through flowery fields
 Through water and mud
 Under the arches
 Under the ground
 We travel together
 The road we have found"

"Down we go to the realm below
 We bring with us a light to show
 Up we rise with the dark in our eyes
 We bring to light a piece of night"

Everyone was singing by the last chorus. The song ended and the company applauded and cheered.

"Did you just compose that on the spot?" asked Lowi.
"Yes," said the King.
"It's very impressive, Gwydion," said Sira Conn. "As are all your skills. I'm very proud of you. If I may be allowed. I know I wasn't there when you were growing up."

"You were there when it mattered most," said Lord Gwydion. "At the beginning. And you've been with me here all along." He touched this chest. "You've been with all of us."

The two men embraced. There were more than a few tears shed among the friends who had observed this tender moment.

Santo went downstairs, and returned with a jug.

"This is the last night we'll spend all together," he said. "As long as the wind is with us, we should be at our next destination by the afternoon. We'll make anchor near the hill-fort. From there the landing party can take the boats ashore. There's just enough of a beach. A path goes up the hill from the strand and connects with the river road that goes by the Mill. It will mean the least amount of walking."

"Thank you," said Lord Gwydion. "I'm so grateful for your kindness."

"The success of this journey relied on all of us," said Arghan. "But none more so than the captain and crew of the good ship Morhogh."
"All hail the captain and crew and the good ship Morhogh!" cried Dina.
"All hail!" they cheered.

"I love this ship," Pippa exclaimed. "No offense to the very fine Awel Glor, but the Morhogh is the best ship that ever sailed the western sea."
"I'm glad you feel that way, Pip," said Arghan, "because we'll be with her again in September. Santo has agreed to pilot us to our meeting point."
"Assuming Edern Pinbren approves," said Santo. "And I'm sure he will. Even though this journey wasn't sponsored by the King, we made many potential trade connections at Caern' Arfon. The Master of Trades will be happy to send us back."

Lord Gwydion struck up the harp and sang,
"A health to the Morhogh and her gallant crew
 And all our brave companions too!"

They all sang it two more times.

"Sira Conn," said Pippa. "Will you sing something?"

"I can't think of anything fit for such a celebration," he said. "Forgive me."
"Sing something that's not fit, then," said Dina. "We'd like to hear you."

He plucked a diminished minor chord.

"Inside the stony shroud
 In the cold water room
 I am there
 I am there"

"The harp unstrung
 Plays a song of doom
 I am there
 I am there"

"Spring returns
 The stone melts away
 I am here
 I am here"

"Wo," said Arghan, wiping away a tear. "That was powerful."
"Beautiful," said Pippa.
Lord Gwydion's eyes were shining.

"Pippa," he said, "do you have a song?"
"There's a song I made up long ago," she replied. "When I was a child in the temple, working on the mosaic. I used to sing it for Cassius and Brian Magnus sometimes."
"Will you share it?" asked Treya.

Lord Gwydion handed her his harp. She began to play a somber rhythm in 4/4 time.

"It's no small wonder I have lived this long
 It has not been only to know right from wrong
 But with the dream of finding my own heart's song
 By the grace of the Gods have I lived this long."

The song was in a minor key. Sira Conn began adding a bass-line.

"Many's the night I've lain hurt and shaking
 Many are the times that I felt like breaking
 Many a cold dawn has seen my poor heart aching
 Yes, many's the night I've lain hurt and shaking"

She stopped singing and just played for a verse, listening. Then she continued.

"By the breath of the Gods I am more than clay
 'Tis the fire of their gaze that lights my way
 And though it seems that my life is just their play
 By the grace of the Gods I can face the day"

"By the breath of the Gods I am more than clay
 By the grace of the Gods I can face the day"

She stopped singing. The harps faded out. Everyone was still. They could hear
the creaking of the ship, and the cries of some distant birds.

The reverie passed, and the companions enthusiastically applauded.
"That was brilliant," said Lord Gwydion. "You wrote that when you were a
child?"
"That's right," she said.
"Oh Pippa," said Lowi. "Was your life really that sad?"

"No," she replied. "I wasn't sad at all."
"Happy people can write sad songs," said Lord Gwydion.
"It's harder the other way around," said Sira Conn.

Dina yawned hugely. Treya was feeling tired again too. The journey had been
exhilarating and exhausting.
Pippa handed the harp back to the King. "Thank you," she said. "It's a lovely
instrument."

He began to strum a familiar tune.
"O-ro, o-ro, we come and we go
 We welcome our friends to come back again
 O-ro, o-ro, o-ro"

They all sang it three times.
"Sira Conn," said Treya. "Did you already know this song?"
"He taught it to me," Gwydion said.
"We sang it together a lifetime ago," said Sira Conn. "And now we sing it once
more. It's true. We come and we go."

Chapter Fifteen - Dear Bertie

The Morhogh was anchored in the waters off of Dinas Dinlle. Lord Gwydion, Sira Conn, Marcus, Dina, and the An Dhew were getting ready to depart. They were taking the rowboats to shore. Pippa, Arghan, Lowi, Treya, Bruno and Brutus were going along for the ride. They wanted to see their friends off, and they also were going to scout the location and check out the trail that led up the hill to the road. This was the route that Pippa and Arghan would be taking in the fall.

The lens-key that had been Master Skell's was passed on to Sira Conn. Pippa suggested that Treya should keep Master Skell's bag, so she put her completed journal in there, next to the green bar, which she had wrapped in some linen.

The gear was stowed and the boats were lowered. The passengers put on their cork vests and climbed down into them. They cast off, and headed for the shore. The departing friends called their goodbyes to the crew. Piri and Piran were both on the lookout, waving. Santo stood at the rail and saluted them.

After the boats were secured on land, the travelers gathered their gear and headed for the narrow dirt trail. They climbed steadily up the steep ascent. After a while, it branched off to the left.
"This is the path we'll take on the way back," said Marcus. "It connects to the farm road below, not far from the entrance to Spiral Tower."

They continued along the main trail. It wound its way around some boulders and entered a field.

They all stopped and looked out. The trail ran across the field. On the other side, they could see the trees that lined the road to the Mill.

"There's the river road," said Marcus. "That didn't take long at all."
"That's not too much of a climb for a pregnant Pippa, is it?" Dina asked.
"No, it will be fine," she replied. "This is a nice short route."
"Then," said Dina, "we will meet you on the fall equinox, at the Mill."
"We'll have a comfortable wagon for you, Philippa," said Lord Gwydion.
"Thank you," said Pippa.

They turned around and followed the trail back down until it branched. Final goodbyes were said. They had gotten much of the hugging and crying over with on the ship, but it was still fairly emotional.

"Give our best to the Lady," said Bruno.
"See you in September," said Dina.

Then Lord Gwydion and his companions continued along the path to the tower. The rest of them turned around and went back down the hill. Lowi was sniffling. Bruno put his arm around her. Treya took Brutus's hand. He squeezed hers in return.

As she and Brutus rowed their boat back to the ship, Treya felt as if one great epic adventure was ending and another one just beginning.

The following afternoon, they were home. Back in Trevena, the fate of the Morhogh had been on everyone's mind. Now that the ship had returned sooner than most people had expected, much to everyone's surprise and relief, the tales of their adventures were being quickly told and retold. Rumors began to circulate before they had even fully disembarked.

The stories started off accurately reported, but then they quickly began to morph into apocrypha.
Treya and her companions didn't know about all the conflated rumors until they'd gone to greet the Royal Family, just a few hours after they had docked. After King Arthek had congratulated them on the success of their mission, Queen Elowen had said,

"Congratulations are also in order for our two newly married couples: Councilor Treya Meynack and Councilor Brutus Marianis, and Lady Borlowan and Councilor Bruno Marianis. I'm sorry that we all missed your wedding, but it's a wonderfully romantic story. A double ship-board marriage ceremony. We will sponsor a reception soon, so that everyone might celebrate your nuptials."

They think that we're already wed! Treya realized. *We can't possibly correct the Queen in front of everyone.*

Treya had looked at Brutus. He'd seemed very surprised. So had Bruno. Arghan and Pippa had exchanged confused glances. Lowi's eyebrows had been raised, but she managed to keep her composure.

"Thank you, your Highness," she'd said, "for your well-wishes, and the kind offer of a reception. We would be most grateful."

After the royal visit, the six friends had decided to go to the tavern. The men had brown ale, and the women had apple juice. Arghan stopped on the way in and spoke to the tavern keeper before rejoining the others.

"Unbelievable," he had said. "Everyone in Trevena knows that the Morhogh sailed further north than anyone ever has before, to Thule Litrík, a land of fire and ice. We found and rescued the King of the South. So far so good. Then we depart from reality. Apparently, while in Thule Litrík, we barely escaped from a foul monster that lived below the earth, thanks to a tribe of mountain dwarfs."

"Not exactly," said Pippa.

Arghan continued. "On the way back, they are saying, we encountered the legendary Krookie, and managed to scare it away with a magical stave that made shoals of fish appear in the distance to lure the monster away. The incident with the sea-monster was so unnerving that the two recently betrothed couples, Treya and Brutus and Lowi and Bruno, decided that, since life is so precarious, they wished to be wed, immediately. They were married by the ship's captain, and they all four danced the sword dance at their wedding while a rough tailed hawk sat on the ship's rail and watched."

"In Trevena, rumors fly faster than birds!" said Pippa.
"They fly faster than the truth, anyway," said Treya.
"Everyone thinks that we're already married," Brutus had said.
"What should we do?" Bruno asked.
"We should just act like we're married," Lowi had replied. "We can't tell them the truth. It would be way too awkward."

"Is that alright?" Brutus asked. "Don't you want to have a wedding?"
"I don't, really," Treya responded. "I was kind of dreading that part."
"Oh, me too," Brutus agreed.
"I don't blame you," Arghan said. "Weddings can be very stressful."
"Especially if the Royal wedding planners get involved," Pippa added.

"Then it might be in our favor that this rumor got started," Bruno had concluded. "What about it, Lowi? Do you have your heart set on a big wedding?"
"No," Lowi replied. "Big weddings are fun to attend. But like Arghan said, they're stressful for the participants. People tend to go slightly mad."

"We could still do some sort of ceremony," Brutus said, "if it matters."

"I feel like we did that already," Treya had replied. "The couples dance we did on the ship. That felt... ceremonial. I don't need anything else. I'm fully committed to making this work."
"Me too," Brutus agreed.
"And me," Lowi added.
"And me," Bruno said.

There had been a moment of silence.

"To the happy couples," Arghan had proclaimed, raising his glass.
"To the happy couples," they'd all repeated.

The reception had been a lot of fun. The entire Royal Family made an appearance. It was very informal. The King delivered a short speech congratulating the newlyweds. Then there had been entertainment: musicians, acrobats, dancers, games, and puppet shows. Del and Augustus performed a comedic routine about a hard-of-hearing doctor and his confused patient. There was a lot of food. Families came and put down picnic blankets. There were barrels of beer, ale and cider. Many cups were raised in honor of the happy couples.

"I don't know most of these people," said Lowi.
"I think they just needed an excuse to have a party," Treya had remarked.

After the reception, Pippa and Arghan had gone with them to the old quarters to view all the gifts that had been bestowed upon the two couples.
Treya had wandered up and down the boxes and parcels, looking at the cards.
"I don't recognize any of these names," said Treya.
"Do you know who they are?" Lowi asked Bruno.

"We know nearly everyone," Bruno had replied.
"It's part of our job," added Brutus.

He had picked up a card from the top of a squat cylindrical box that was wrapped in green silk with white ribbons.
"Dren of Portha Kernow. He's a wealthy grain merchant."

Bruno had been looking at the tag of a very large rectangular parcel. The box was dark blue with silver stars.

"Mona Zelda," said Bruno. "She and her family own a textile business in Tintagel. She was at the bridge-opening ceremony."

Brutus had gone over to a large flat cedar-wood box that was prominently set out on a fine round oaken table, which along with six cushioned and embroidered chairs, had been a gift from the King and Queen.

"Here's a fancy one. There's a metal plaque. Gemmo of Londinium. I don't know about him."
"He's a renowned Londinium silversmith," Pippa had explained. "Arghan has a pair of his candlesticks."
"Renowned in Londinium?" Brutus replied. "I thought that place had gone back to being a swamp."
"Parts of it did," said Arghan. "But much of Roman Londinium is still intact. And they've started a big restoration project."

"Restoring Londinium," said Brutus. "That might take a few years."

"That's a pretty box," Lowi said. "I wonder what's in there."
"It's silver flatware," Arghan replied.
"You can tell that by looking at it?" Treya asked.
"It's from us," Pippa said. "The card's inside."

"Let's see the loot!" Bruno had exclaimed. Brutus opened the box. It was full of simple but elegant silver spoons, forks and knives. Each piece had a subtle spiral design on the handle.
"Nice," the twins said together.
"Pretty!" said Lowi.
"What a thoughtful gift," said Treya. "Thank you."

"Let's open some more," Bruno suggested.
"Not until we're better prepared," Lowi replied.

"What do you mean?" Treya asked.

"Everything has to be written down," Lowi explained. "The nature of the gift, and who it's from. So you can use the information in your thank-you letters, which should include at least one personal detail about it: how much you like the gift, or how you are displaying it, or how delicious the tin of candied fruit was, especially the gingered pears. I had some of those when one of the Queen's attendants was wed, and I was helping to catalog her gifts."

"So," Bruno said, "there might be food in some of these packages?"
"We'd better get busy," Brutus had replied. "Treya, are you ready to scribe?"

They had spent the next few days opening gifts, and enjoying the bounty of the haul. There *was* candied fruit, including the gingered pears that Lowi was hoping for. There were chunks of honeycomb, cheese balls covered in ground hazelnuts, smoked fish spread, spelt-crisps and sweet-rolls. They had sipped elderberry wine and ginger-beer while they wrote thank-you cards.

Arghan and Pippa had helped to find good places for all the new items. The once rather spartan rooms were filled with fine furnishings and decorations.

It was a rainy April evening in Trevena. The sun was beginning to set, casting a golden hue onto the pale wet sky. Treya and Lowi were at home in the old quarters. Treya was in her own little room, the former study by the terrace. The two couples had learned to cohabitate with relative ease.

The rooms that had belonged to Cassius and Brian Magnus had been left unchanged. Treya had taken Master Skell's green bar and placed it on the shelf in the room of Brian Magnus, alongside the other mementoes. It was beginning to oxidize, and take on a bronze hue. There had been some concern about mice or bugs getting into it. Pippa had decided to take a tiny bite to try it. She had chewed for a brief moment, then she'd spit it out, declaring that no self-respecting mouse or insect would be interested in it.

Lowi had taken the room at the far end, and Bruno stayed in there with her most nights. Bruno's original room had been overwhelmed by Lowi's wardrobe. It was amazing, the clothing she was expected to wear, and the number of times she had to change her clothes during the day. Lowi had morning ensembles, luncheon outfits, afternoon frocks, and evening-wear. The others knew what the time was by when she came home to change.

Treya had her little room, with a bed just big enough for two. There was an opening onto the terrace. The room was bright and sunny when the weather was fine. When the cold came, it was shuttered in darkness. There was no fireplace, but hot air was piped into a space under the floor, and it was tolerably warm.

When it got too cold, she and Brutus would go sleep by the main fireplace on the soft, thick rugs that had been Mona Zelda's gift to the happy couples.

Brutus bunked with Treya most nights, but he still had his original room, and kept his gear in there. Treya kept her clothes in there too. It made space in her little room for a small drafting table and a shelf full of scribing materials and art supplies.

She had just gotten back from an afternoon at the Kovskrifva. Treya Meynack was now the Royal Archivist.

When she had returned from sea the previous year, Lugarn had been happy to greet her, although he was sad that Master Skell was not returning. While Treya was away, he had done a good job of running the place. The Lady Kaya's nephew Jon had helped, and Jon had managed to complete a few documents, before he'd gone back east. Lugarn had been relieved when Treya took the keys to the building.

Treya was entitled to sit in the Vault Alcove, but she preferred her own little desk. She still thought of the big desk as Master Skell's. It had been emotionally challenging for her to explain to people why he would not be returning, but nobody seemed too surprised that such an old man would want to retire.

She missed him every day. His presence still filled the space, even though there was no physical sign that he'd ever even been there. Only the silver apple pendant, which had become one of her most treasured possessions, along with her An Dhew horn and dagger, her lituus, her beautiful blue boots, and the Óttastafur plank that Brutus had carved for her.

Lady Borlowan was at home too, on that golden, rainy, spring evening. She was out on the terrace, sheltered from the rain under an awning. She was resting after spending the day at Court with Princess Merryn. Lowi was stretched out in a recliner. The terrace had new chairs. They were cushioned, with adjustable backs, so you could sit or lie down.

In the common room and dining area, there was comfortable new seating as well. The rooms had been sparsely furnished before. The ex-soldiers had tended to sit on the floor. Now when visitors called, there were nice places to receive them. And visitors did call. Del and Augustus came around regularly. So did Santo, Piri and Piran, and the Pol-Pri family. Even Princess Merryn, with Lord Auryn and little Princess Grassi. The new old quarters had become a warm and inviting space, as well as a historical archive of the time when Cassius Ambrosius and Brian Magnus dwelt in these rooms.

Bootchie had been reinstated in the old quarters, with new toys and a fluffy bed. Before he and Pippa had departed last fall, Arghan had built a wide carpeted shelf that went around the room a few feet from the ceiling. The cat loved to run around and around. His friends would scatter balls of yarn along the shelf, so he could play with them and knock them off at his leisure. He now had a special sort of plaintive 'mew' that he used when the shelf was empty. Then someone was expected to pick up the balls and scatter them around again.

The cat-shelf was deemed a success, and Arghan was congratulated on his ingenuity.

Pippa and Arghan had sailed away on the morning tide, the day before the equinox. Edern Pinbren himself had joined the crew of the Morhogh for the journey. After dropping off their passengers, the ship was going to continue to Caern Arfon bay to look for trade. Treya, Lowi, Brutus, and Bruno had stood on the pier and watched the ship sail out of the western bay.

Five days later, the Morhogh had returned. The four of them had gone down to meet the ship. The hold was filled with bushels of hazelnuts and bags of spelt, which were being unloaded.

Piri had come over to greet them.
"I went with Pippa and Arghan," she'd said, "up the path from the beach. I bade farewell to them at the top. Last I saw, they were walking across the field to the river road."

That was in September. They hadn't heard anything since then. So when Bruno and Brutus came home that spring evening with a message from Caer Hudol, the four of them were all excited, and a little nervous.

They gathered in the common room. Treya lit the lamps. Brutus unsealed the message and read it aloud.

To Bruno, Lowi, Brutus, and Treya in Trevena, by way of Dina and Marcus in Vindavia Nova.

Greetings all! First things first. Pippa had a boy. Born on the ides of February. He's a strong and wiry little fellow with brown hair and brown eyes. He has been a happy baby so far. We named him Phillip, after Pippa's father. Only everyone calls him Bertie. You know how Pippa likes hazel nuts. Because of the hazel nut being the filbert, we started to call him Phil-bert, which was eventually shortened to Bertie.

Filbert actually means 'full-beard', after the way the nut grows. Speaking of full-beards, Lord Dmitri, for that is how he is called here, has grown a long, full, silky beard with curly whiskers. I'm sorry Marcus, that's got to burn!

They all laughed. Brutus continued.

Lord Dmitri and Lady Gwynalli are both doing fine. The children take up much of their time and energy, as you would expect. Dmitri helps Lord Gwydion with his projects. Gwynalli makes clothing for all the little ones. Since they keep growing, she stays busy.

Pippa is doing well, but she is still recovering. She managed to walk up to the Argos Down yesterday for the first time since the baby came. It was a difficult birth. I'll spare you the details, but we were right to bring her here. I fear that she would not have survived this otherwise. Apparently, the problems she encountered had nothing to do with the dart piercing her side. It seems that she would have most likely had these issues anyway.
So, according to Pippa, getting hit with the dart is the thing that ultimately saved her life, since without the fear that going through birth would cause complications, we would have just stayed in Trevena. And following that trail of Pippa logic, Cassius Ambrosius is now responsible for saving her life, because she wouldn't have been pierced in the first place, except for him.

Everyone else is fine here. Lord Amatheon keeps busy, planting and landscaping. He seems happy, and his work is really beautiful. The Lagaloor are thriving. There are even some new babies. You should have heard Gwynalli and Pippa squeal when they first saw the little bug-eyed squeakers. They are adorable, I have to admit. Fishy has gotten fat and lazy, but I guess he's earned a retirement.
Pompi is as talkative as ever. He is still very much attached to Lord Gwydion, but he loves Sira Conn too. He hops from one to the other. When the Sire first showed up, Pompi flew to him and landed right on his head.

Sira Conn has mostly settled in. He did get to spend some time with Lady Arianrhod before coming back here. He seems a bit at loose ends sometimes. But he is greatly revered at Caer Hudol. Everyone rejoiced at his return.

Lord Gwydion asked him if he wanted the crown back, but he emphatically declined. I think he's trying to figure out how he fits in after all this time. He is quiet, and likes to spend time with the little ones, or up in the High Meadow with Amatheon and the animals.

Cassius and Nico are both learning to walk. They fall a lot. Tyronius and Mear's daughter Lani is their best friend. She's about the same age of course, but she is much more advanced and confident than they are. She's pretty, with golden-red hair and green eyes. She bosses the boys around mercilessly, and they obey her. She's actually the one who is inspiring them to walk. They see how easily she gets around and they are motivated to try.

I suppose that's all for now. We plan to return to Trevena in the fall, as long as everyone is up for traveling. We miss you, friends, but we are very grateful to be here.

with love,
Arghan Pen Avalen

Beneath that, Pippa had written,

"Hi all. Arghan pretty much covered it. Here's a picture of us. Love you!"

At the bottom of the page, there was a sketch of Pippa and Arghan. They were holding Bertie up between them. All three were smiling.

"Bertie," said Lowi. "What a sweet name. Little Bertie."
"I'm so relieved," said Treya. "But poor Pippa. What an ordeal."

"There's something else," said Brutus. He held up a small piece of parchment. "It's from Marcus." He read it aloud.

Friends,

Here is a short note to let you know, Rosa had a litter of seven pups! They are cute and squirmy fluff-balls. Azario and I have agreed to keep the runt, Beryl. Dina wants to keep them all, as does Parmaggio. They both are besotted with these little dogs. They've had to accept the fact that two of them are going to the shepherd elders, and one to Dmitri. That was the deal. Parmi and Dina want to keep the other three, and Beryl.

Right now, Azario is convinced that they will change their minds when these dogs get older. I'm not so sure about that. But I am fairly sure that we don't need all four pups right now, none of which can be sold, because Dina finds the idea of trading dogs for coin to be intolerable.
So much for Dmitri's and my dream of becoming wealthy dog breeders.

The puppies would have to go to our most special companions, in order for Dina and Parmi to let go. I am close to persuading them into giving two pups, not one, to Dmitri and our friends down in Caer H.

I am making the same offer to you, of two pups, but I understand that you live inside a castle, and then there's Bootchie to consider. He might not appreciate it. Cat's can be territorial. You don't want him spraying your new furniture.

Still, if you are interested, let us know.

M.C.

"Two Agassian hounds?" said Lowi. "They need room to run, don't they?"
"Yes," said Bruno. "A great deal of room."
"Some people keep dogs in the castle," said Treya.
"Only the best behaved dogs," said Brutus.
"Rosa is the smartest and most well-behaved dog you could ever want to meet," said Treya.

They were quiet for a moment.
Then Bruno asked, "How can we say no?"
"There's plenty of space on the lawns," said Lowi.
"And there's four of us," said Treya, "to share the burden."
"But then," said Lowi, "what about Bootchie?" They all looked up. The fluffy orange cat was asleep up on his shelf. The shelf was wide enough for him to stretch out in. Still, he lay on the very edge of it, with his legs sticking out and his tail hanging down.

"Bootchie gets on fine with the King's hounds," said Bruno.
"Yes," said Brutus, "but they don't live with us."
"What does Marcus mean by spraying?" asked Lowi.
"Cats sometimes express themselves by spraying items with urine," said Brutus. "They can be very territorial."
"Ugh!" said Lowi. "Bootchie doesn't do that, does he?"
"No," said Bruno, "but he's never really been put to the test. Still, he's so friendly. I think he might like some goofy puppies to play with. Besides, he might go back to live in the Angove suite, when Pippa and Arghan return with Bertie."

"Well?" said Lowi. "Bruno?"
He looked at his brother, then at the women, and said, "We want to do whatever you want to do."

"Aren't you sweet," said Lowi. "But we're not courting any more. You can say what you really think."

No one spoke.

"On the count of three," said Lowi, "everyone either say 'dogs' or 'no dogs'. One, two, three."
"Dogs," they all said.
They all raised the cups and said it again.
"Dogs!"

"Hear that, Bootch?" said Bruno. "You may be getting some new friends."
The cat's tail twitched.

"The courier said that the ship that brought the message will be here for two more days," said Brutus, "if you want to send something back."
"Of course," said Treya. "I'll write to them."

"I wish there was an easier way to get messages through to Caer Hudol," said Bruno. "I thought perhaps we could send them through the Root Road, but Lord Gwydion had that entrance by the Mill sealed back up for now, while they decide whether or not to cloak it."

"I understand that, taking security precautions," Brutus replied. "But it's such a convoluted route we use now. To have to send a letter by ship to one of the southern harbors, so that it might be carried to Vindavia Nova, where it's taken underground."

"And then," Treya added, "the messenger has to make that exhausting journey through the Red Sands to reach Caer Hudol."
"Too bad there's not a more direct private route," said Lowi.
"Maybe there is," said Brutus. "Perhaps we could try to find out. We could take our new hounds on an underground adventure."

"Speaking of adventures," said Treya, "tomorrow is market day. We're up at sunrise, Lady Borlowan."

Tintagel Saturday market day had become a major weekly event. The selection and variety of goods in the small remote village was surprising. It began very early in the morning, and was all but over by noon.

"I'm going to bed right after we eat," Lowi responded.

After a light meal, Lowi said goodnight and went to her room. Brutus and Bruno were both in the recliners out on the terrace, having a cup of wine. Treya was tired too, but she was thinking about the letter that she said she'd write.

She sat at her desk and lit the lamp. There was so much that she wanted to say to her faraway friends. She didn't know where to begin. She had always been better at copying than composing, although keeping a journal during their travels had sharpened her skills.

She thought about Pippa, and the close call it sounded as though she'd had. She thought of baby Bertie and smiled. Then she had an idea, and she began to write.

Dear Bertie,

Welcome to the world. Caer Hudol is a special place. You are blessed to have been born there.

I want to tell you about your parents, Philippa Agrippa and Arghan Pen Avalen. They are both brave, generous, creative people who inspire deep love and loyalty in others. I've no doubt that you will be like that too.
This Mighty Land has made them what they are. It has provided the resources, and the means of travel. It is a place where friends are well met. Throughout all their adventures, your parents have been sustained and nurtured by the elements, and by the community they found with others.

Treya paused, thinking of her faraway friends. Then she continued.

It's sad that we are all so distant from each other. But it also gives us a sense of connectedness, across this wide land. It's comforting to know that there are routes that we can take, ways to meet with each other. Even if it means a lot of hard work to get there.
Right now, our job is to keep these islands safe for future generations. One day it will be your job, little Bertie. Remember to look ahead. The world may not always be kind, but we can be. Each act of kindness and compassion is like a drop of water. They come together to create a sea of love.

Your mother and father brought us all together. There was no other place where that could have happened. Only in An Tir Gallósek. Only in The Mighty Land.

Your loving friend,
Treya Meynack

Treya read it back. It would do. She felt as though she might weep, but she didn't. Tomorrow she would get Lowi to help her compose another letter to send too, a more usual one. And she would write to Marcus, saying that they would love to have the dogs.

But she was happy with this. She had written from deep within her heart, mind and soul.

Treya cleaned her pen and put it away. Then she took out a sling bag, ready for the early morning. Grain cakes, dried grapes, water bottles, empty bags, shopping list, raincoat, and a bulging coin purse.

Market day in Tintagel. It was always an adventure.

Annotations, Map and Charts

Lyverva- Library
Pobel Môr- the Sea People, Phoenicians
Lady Kaya - 'Platform', Librarian at Trevena
King Gelvin of Trevena- a distant ancestor of King Arthek of Trevena
Kovskrifva- the Archive
Master Skell- 'Shell', Chief Archivist
Lugarn- 'Lantern', assistant to the Archivist
Seth-ros- 'arrow-wheel', a siege engine
Lady Borlowan- 'Morning Star', a lady of Trevena
Spiral Castle- a hidden tower in western Wales
Ornithomancy- Augury, divination by bird behavior
Kolon- the Heart
Lituus- the Augur's wand
Kombrogian Harchif- the Western Archive
Prince Benneth- son of King Arthek and Queen Elowen of Trevena.
Princess Grassi- daughter of Auryn Pen Avalen and Princess Merryn
Dinas Dinlle- 'The Lost City', the hill fort known as Bryngaer
The Fortress of Lugh- Another name for Bryngaer, after the Celtic
God of light
Twr Troellog- Spiral Tower
Cassius Anagnostopoulos Conn-Danu- the son of Dmitri and Gwynalli
Nico Anagnostopoulos Conn-Danu - the son of Dmitri and Gwynalli
Ffyrdd Gwraidd- the Root Roads
Tref Gwraidd- Root Town
Caer Liwelyd- Lugh's Castle, Roman Luguvalium, modern Carlisle
Afon Carog- Stony River
Afon Foryd- 'river ford', estuary
Morhogh- 'Porpoise', a ship of Trevena
Piri Glowbrenn- mariner, daughter of Piran
The Shoe- Ynys Esgid, Gwair's Island, Lundy Isle, off the coast of western
Wales
Gwydion Dewin- The Wizard Gwydion
Kanndir- kann-dew, double stone, Iceland spar
Morloi- grey seals
Kler lew- clear to the left side.
Portha kler- clear to the right
Gwaed y Cawr- Giant's Blood
Caern' Arfon- Carnarvon Bay, on the Menai straight in Wales
Lady Arianrhod- sister of Gwydion, Amatheon and Gofannan Conn-Danu

Tir Coll- The Lost Land.
Hedyn- 'Seed'- captain of the Tower Watch
Pen-Arth- Bear Head.
Hen-Un- Old One
Hir Fyw- Long Lived,
Hanner-Dynion- Half-Mortals.
Druids- spiritual leaders of the Celts
Ynys Pwynt- 'Point Isle', Anglesey, Wales
Castra Deva- modern day city of Chester
Verum- Latin for true/truth
Alítheia- Greek for true/truth
Melin- Mill
Crydd- Shoemaker
Amser Gwas- Time Servant
Awyr Porth- Rain-gate
Seren Porth- Star-gate
Glaw Porth- Sky-gate
Tegan- 'toy', helper in the Spiral Tower
Sira Conn- father of the Conn-Danu clan
Hornafirði- Horn-Harbor
Höfn- Port.
Vatnajǫkull- glacier pool
Hellisland- White-land, Iceland
Thule Litrík- Colorful Land of Sacred Winter Fire- Iceland
Nordvegr- the North-Way, Norway
Otturstafur- eight-fold protection symbol
Fros Tredan- electric current
Khan-y-Kumus- King's Men
Krookie- the Kraken

TREYA MENACK IN THE WESTERN AIR

HELLISLAND

THE PATH OF THE SHIP
MORHOGH

THULE LITRÍK

FAROES

An Tír Gallósck
The Mighty Land

Maria Kay Anthony

HEBRIDES

ISLE OF
MANANNAN

BRYNGAER

THE SHOE

TREVENA

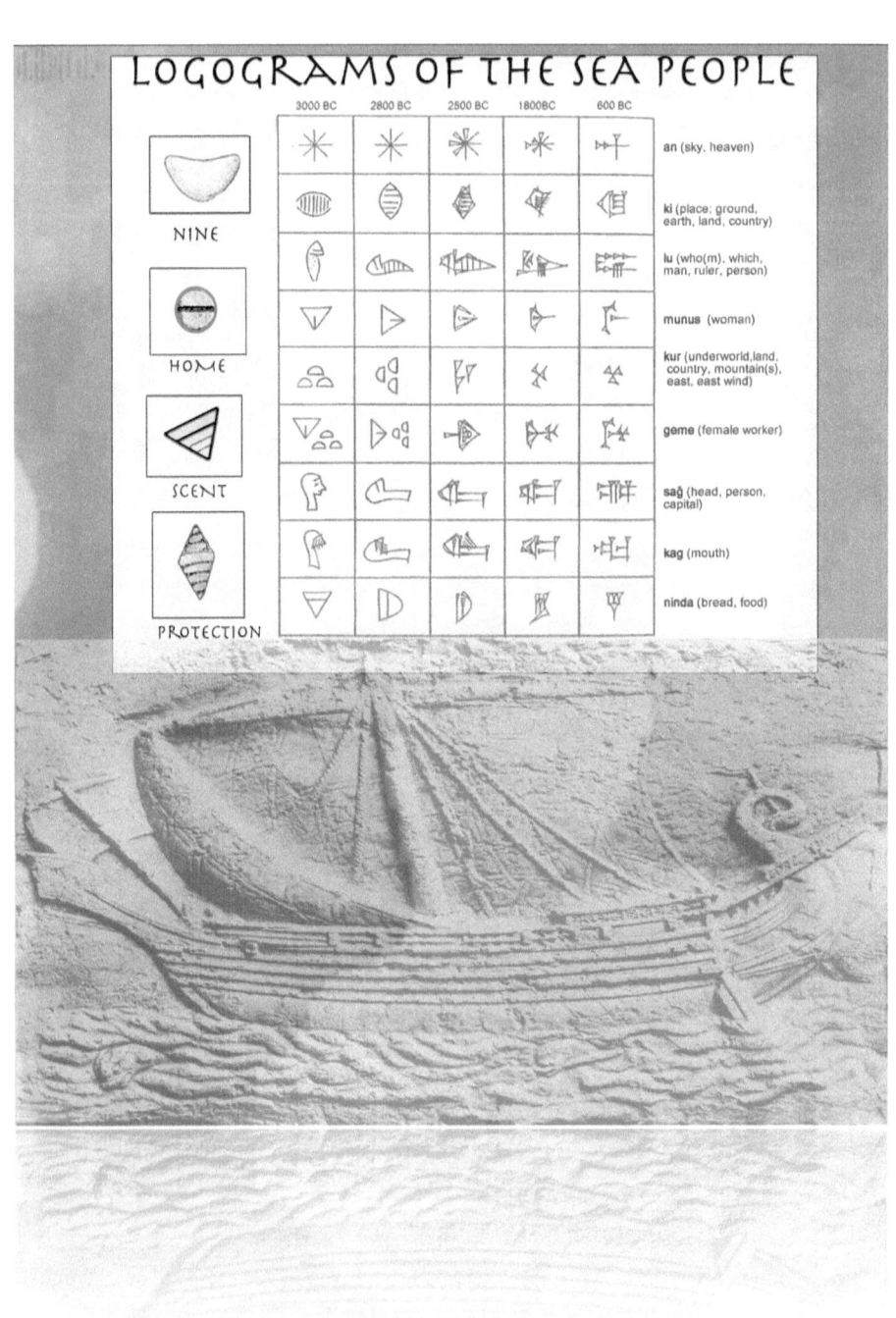

LOGOGRAMS OF THE SEA PEOPLE

	3000 BC	2800 BC	2500 BC	1800BC	600 BC	
NINE						an (sky, heaven)
						ki (place; ground, earth, land, country)
						lu (who(m), which, man, ruler, person)
HOME						munus (woman)
						kur (underworld, land, country, mountain(s), east, east wind)
SCENT						geme (female worker)
						saĝ (head, person, capital)
PROTECTION						kag (mouth)
						ninda (bread, food)

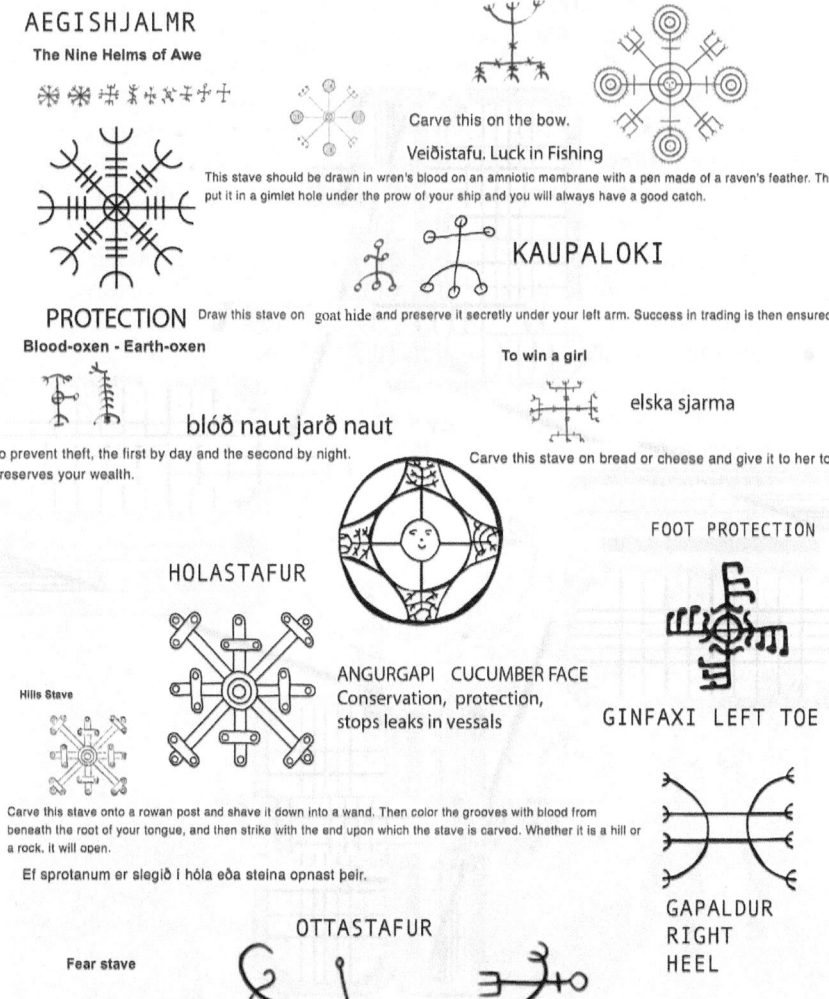

AEGISHJALMR

The Nine Helms of Awe

Carve this on the bow.

Veiðistafu. Luck in Fishing

This stave should be drawn in wren's blood on an amniotic membrane with a pen made of a raven's feather. Then put it in a gimlet hole under the prow of your ship and you will always have a good catch.

KAUPALOKI

PROTECTION

Draw this stave on goat hide and preserve it secretly under your left arm. Success in trading is then ensured.

Blood-oxen - Earth-oxen

blóð naut jarð naut

To prevent theft, the first by day and the second by night. preserves your wealth.

To win a girl

elska sjarma

Carve this stave on bread or cheese and give it to her to eat.

HOLASTAFUR

Hills Stave

ANGURGAPI CUCUMBER FACE
Conservation, protection, stops leaks in vessals

FOOT PROTECTION

GINFAXI LEFT TOE

Carve this stave onto a rowan post and shave it down into a wand. Then color the grooves with blood from beneath the root of your tongue, and then strike with the end upon which the stave is carved. Whether it is a hill or a rock, it will open.

Ef sprotanum er slegið í hóla eða steina opnast þeir.

GAPALDUR RIGHT HEEL

OTTASTAFUR

Fear stave

To scare your enemy, carve this stave on a piece of oak and throw it at the feet of your enemy.

Maria Kay Anthony is a musician with a lifelong love of history, myths, and legends, especially those originating from the British Isles. She has worked in a variety of professions. She has been a metalsmith, visual artist, touring musician, veterinary assistant, music teacher, science teacher, filmmaker, and farmer. She is also a US Army veteran, having served in her youth with the 26th Signal Corps Germany, where she built towers and installed microwave equipment. The Mighty Land series reflects her interest in these topics and others, such as astronomy, horticulture, boats, adventure, travel, technology, engineering, medicine, spirituality, philosophy, psychology, and languages. Maria currently lives in the green rolling hills of eastern Kansas with her husband Monty, but they hope to relocate ere long, with Cornwall being the preferred destination.